A Special Delivery

CLARE DOWLING

headline
review

First published in 2014 by HEADLINE REVIEW
An imprint of HEADLINE PUBLISHING GROUP

First published in paperback in 2014 by HEADLINE REVIEW
An imprint of HEADLINE PUBLISHING GROUP

1

Cataloguing in Publication Data is available from the British Library

ISBN 978 0 7553 9274 2

Typeset in Bembo by Palimpsest Book Production Limited,
Falkirk, Stirlingshire

Printed and bound in Great Britain by Clays Ltd, St Ives plc

Headline's policy is to use papers that are natural, renewable and recyclable
products and made from wood grown in sustainable forests. The logging and
manufacturing processes are expected to conform to the environmental
regulations of the country of origin.

HEADLINE PUBLISHING GROUP
An Hachette UK company
338 Euston Road
London NW1 3BH

www.headline.co.uk
www.hachette.co.uk

FOR ELLA

Acknowledgements

Thanks as always to my editor Clare Foss for her hard work, energy and enthusiasm, and for dreaming up the great title.

Thanks to the team at Headline for making this book possible, and to all at Hachette Ireland for rowing in behind me every year.

Thanks as always to my agent Darley Anderson, and to all at the agency.

Thanks to Stewart for the loan of his office when my deadline loomed.

A big thanks to Sean and Ella for being excited still at each new book.

And to my readers who have bought my books and supported me down through the years – thank you.

Chapter One

It was two days to Christmas and the Brady family was miserable. Not that anybody could admit to it, at least not out loud. It was like when somebody died and you were allowed a couple of weeks of grieving. But if you carried on for too much longer than that, well, it was just bad taste.

Besides, they were used to it.

That particular day their normal misery happened to be superseded by a fresh calamity: they had no electricity and it was just after turning dark.

'You fecking eejit,' said Aisling. This was directed at her husband Mossy. He ran a painting and decorating business and really should have known better.

'I don't know what's after happening.'

'The fuse box has blown. Even I know that. I have Zofia coming around tonight. I have mince pies to make, and a cake to ice, and God knows I'm bad enough with all the lights on . . .' She remembered something else and clutched his arm. 'Mossy. The fridge. The *turkey*.'

Great. Her entire family brought to its knees by E. coli on Christmas Day. Still, maybe next year they'd go somewhere else and she could be miserable in peace.

'It's okay. I'll fix it.' His brow was furrowed as he rooted about in his sturdy three-tiered toolbox. Everything about Mossy was sturdy and well built, from his broad brown face topped by a shock of red hair, down to his thighs, which threatened to burst out of his ripped jeans at any moment, along the lines of the Incredible Hulk. 'He's a big lad, isn't he?' her mother had hissed when she'd first brought him home twenty-odd years ago. 'There must be a fuse in here somewhere . . .' Well, there was everything else. Aisling had once found a tube of tomato purée in there. 'Did you see any hardware shops open while you were out?'

Aisling had a familiar moment of panic: where had she been? More importantly, where had she *said* she was going to be?

Then she remembered: it had been legitimate business. Phew. She'd spent the afternoon chasing a turkey from an organic outfit all the way out in County Meath. Not *actually* chasing it – they didn't expect you to kill your own – but trying to find the sign for Harriet's Farm. Harriet turned out to be a bloke called John-Joe with hairy forearms who had wordlessly led her into a dim, cold storage shed. There she was met with a terrible sight: row upon row of pale, headless turkeys hanging from stainless-steel meat hooks by their lifeless feet, over a blood-spattered floor. It was carnage. Then – *bam* – the shed door slammed shut behind them in the wind. When John-Joe stepped up behind her, so close that she could smell his garlic breath, she had a giddy thought: *I could be murdered right now and hung up there on a meat hook beside those other poor old birds, two days before Christmas.* What was worse was that the prospect didn't sound too bad.

'Here we go!' Mossy dug out a fuse and held it up triumphantly. 'Oh ye of little faith.' His delight quickly turned to doubt. 'Although I think it's the wrong one.'

'Mossy,' she said, in quiet desperation. 'You're going to have to stop this.'

He gave her a slightly defensive look. 'Stop what?'

'You know what.'

Mossy had gone mad on the Christmas lights. As in completely insane. It was probably his own little antidote to all the misery. But the whole house twinkled, flashed, pulsed and sparkled. And that was just the inside. The fluorescent reindeer he'd erected on the roof could probably be seen from Mars.

'They're all laughing at us, you know. The whole road.' Their son Anto had stumbled in from the living room in the dark. At eighteen he felt these things keenly. 'At school they break into "Little Drummer Boy" every time I walk past.' He searched about on the counter for the sliced pan and dived into it. If he didn't get food every two hours or so, things tended to deteriorate fairly quickly. 'Usually we just dig out the plastic wreath from the attic, with the wires sticking out of it. Do you remember the year I had to have a tetanus shot?' he reminisced fondly.

Mossy planted his paint-spattered hands on his hips and looked at the two of them. 'What, you want us to be like the Foleys next door, is that it? They're like Scrooge, that lot. They don't even bother with a plastic tree in that house.' He'd held a grudge against the Foleys ever since they'd refused to pay him for a wallpapering job ten years ago, pretending that they thought it was a neighbourly favour. 'They don't even put up a *card*. If you were walking past their gaff on Christmas Eve you'd have no idea if they were Buddhists, or Muslims, or . . .' He searched about for more religious groups to possibly malign.

3

'They're Mormons,' Anto supplied. He had half a slice of bread in his mouth. No, wait, the whole thing.

'Mormons!' Aisling looked at Mossy, suddenly unsure. Anto used to 'imagine' things. For several years he'd had an imaginary friend – nobody was allowed to mention it now or he went mad – called Bobo. They were inseparable. Mossy, who'd never believed in even the tooth fairy himself, eventually lost all patience with it; one evening that they all remembered still, he broke the news to Anto that Bobo had tragically died in a workplace accident. 'The next-door neighbours are *Mormons*?' she clarified.

That would certainly shake up the road. Give them something else to talk about for a change.

'No, no,' said Anto, the unexpected spiritual expert. 'Just Vinnie Foley. The one Aidan went to school with.'

It was out before he could stop it. The three of them froze. It was like the air had been sucked out of the room. Anto swivelled to look at his mother. His eyes said, *Sorry*.

For a minute Aisling's head was full of white noise and then she snapped back into normal mode. She had to; it was two days before Christmas, the show had to go on. 'I didn't know that, did you, Mossy?'

'No. Imagine that. And us living beside him all these years.' He nodded away as though it was the most fascinating thing he'd heard in his life. It was catching and Aisling started nodding too. She was quite worried that a hee-haw might break out of her at any moment. Maybe she should have gone on that short course of Valium after all, like Dr Iris had advised, to get her 'over the hump'. But she'd been worried that she would start sending the kids to school with turnip sandwiches or something, and so she'd reluctantly decided to tackle the hump without the help of strong medication.

A Special Delivery

The trouble was, it was taking so long. There wasn't a sign of her being over the hump. She wasn't even at its summit.

She was startled by a sudden violent flash outside, like lightning. For a brief moment several people in hooded, shroud-like garments were lit up on the lawn, staring in silently through the front window at them.

'Jesus Christ!' shouted Anto.

Actually it was Mary, Joseph and the three wise men, lit up by Mossy's malfunctioning outdoor Christmas lights. In another out-of-character act, he'd recreated the whole nativity scene on the front lawn. He'd found a baby's crib in some flea market and had bought figurines of the key personnel off the Internet. But – and this was false advertising, they all agreed – when Mary and Joseph had arrived in the UPC van, they'd turned out to be only three-quarters size, and the crib in comparison was massive. The local lads had gone to town altogether. 'It's like Christmas for the Smurfs!' Poor Anto had to climb over the back wall, because going through the front gate would be admitting that he actually lived there.

The crib thing left Mossy in a quandary over Baby Jesus. If he put in a life-sized baby, there was no way anybody would believe that Mary had given birth to it, at least not without considerable medical intervention. But a small baby would be even more of a laughing stock, lost in that massive crib. At this late stage, though, it seemed that an old Baby Bjorn would have to do the job.

'I think Mary and Joseph and the gang are being electrocuted by your lights, Da,' Anto commented.

'Everyone stay here,' Mossy commanded, whipping up his toolbox and tearing out. 'The whole garden could be live.'

He left them behind in the darkness. Aisling was immediately assailed by a moaning Anto.

'Make him *stop*, Ma. He's only bringing shame down upon us.'

Aisling shushed him sternly. 'Listen to me. Yes, the nativity scene is embarrassing. Yes, a tour bus stopped yesterday and everybody took photos. But he's trying his best to make this a—' She nearly said bearable. 'A nice Christmas for all of us, okay?'

Anto looked back at her out of cynical eyes. 'Better than last Christmas, you mean?'

There had been no organic turkey the previous year; just a frozen one bought in the supermarket at the last minute. But everything had been so fresh then; they weren't even two months into the misery.

'Yes,' she said. 'And it *will* be.'

It was only in the last few weeks that she had begun to realise that in fact it would be worse. Because last year she'd had hope; this year, as a second Christmas loomed, she had none.

Anto seemed to realise it too. He shrugged. 'If you say so.'

Christmas paper. Check. Diamond-pattern socks for Mossy. Check. A new phone for Anto, not top-of-the-range like he'd requested, but decent enough; five hundred mega-somethings to store such text gems as *Wat up?*, which was mostly what he seemed to send and receive. A mountaineering book for specialist climbers.

Aisling pulled the book on to her knee and shone her torch at it. The picture on the front cover was of a man hanging jauntily off the side of some ferocious-looking mountain. He was looking down at the camera like it was all a piece of cake, and it was his irreverence in the face of danger that had made her pick that one.

Her heart felt like it would burst in her chest with grief.

'Ma? Are you up there?'

At the voice, Aisling scrabbled to hide everything under the bed again. 'In here!'

A Special Delivery

Louise, their eleven-year-old, ventured in, hands outstretched in the dark. 'I was at Emma's when we saw the lights going out over here.'

Emma lived down the road. The two of them had decided in the last week that they were going to be hairdressers when they were older, and many hours were dedicated to practising on each other. Emma needed a good few hours more, judging by the state of Louise's plait.

'Emma's mother said there's never a dull moment in our house,' Louise reported. Her forehead crinkled. 'She made it sound like she was joking, but I don't think she was really.'

Emma's mother had her head permanently pressed up against her net curtains. Aisling had fantasies of someday marching down and slapping her across the face with a wet fish.

'Don't mind her,' she instructed Louise maturely instead.

Louise looked at her. 'What are you doing sitting on the floor?'

Aisling airily swung the torch around. 'Oh, just checking for dust.'

She was never normally bothered by the stuff. But Louise seemed to buy it.

'When are the lights going to come back on?'

'Your dad is working on them. Soon, hopefully.'

Louise stood there rocking back and forth a bit. Aisling braced herself. She could feel a bout of questioning coming on. She braced herself to deliver the usual slew of platitudes and half-truths.

But it was something else entirely. 'Emma says there's no such thing as Santa.'

'Oh, sweetheart.'

But Louise evaded Aisling's outstretched arms. 'Is she right?' She wanted a straight answer, Aisling could see that. And she'd be twelve this coming year . . .

7

But Mossy was right too. They had to start getting back to normal, and that included making this as nice a Christmas as they could.

'You know what they say, don't you?' she said sternly. 'If you don't believe in Santa, then he might not come.'

Louise's eyes grew wide. No pink sewing machine that she'd written on her list! No new set of foam curlers that you put in before bedtime and that gave you an awful headache but hair like one of those girls from *Riverdance* . . .

'That Emma one is daft.' Mossy loomed out of the darkness to back Aisling up. 'And you should tell her that too.'

'Yeah!' said Louise.

'Yeah!' Mossy echoed stoutly. 'Only no calling her names now, okay?'

Louise tittered – her da was always slagging her – and went off, giving a little squeak and swerving fast as he tried to tickle her in passing.

He peered at Aisling through the half-light. 'All right?'

She was suddenly filled with intense irritation. Did he really have to ask that?

'I don't want the kids to think we can't talk about things,' she said.

'What things?'

'Oh stop it, Mossy. Anto, earlier.'

Mossy's confusion, if it was genuine, cleared. 'I never said we couldn't talk about things,' he protested.

But that just irritated her more. Especially as it wasn't true; he mightn't have forbidden it out loud, but his body language was clear enough. 'But we don't, though, do we? Nobody ever says a bloody word.'

'Fine, then,' he said. 'Let's talk. Let's gather everybody together and we can get things off our chests.'

She didn't want to have some kind of family conference. She couldn't bear it. What was there left to say anyway? That these things happened and they had to move on?

She got to her feet and checked her watch. Half past five. 'I'd better start figuring out what we're going to eat,' she said, abruptly changing the subject. 'Seeing as we've no electricity.' That she *could* blame him for.

'The cooker is gas.' Mossy was trying to make amends now. 'We can throw on some pasta.'

'Fine.'

He stopped her as she went past to go downstairs, clasping her hand in one of his brown work-roughened ones.

'Aisling, I know this is hard. Especially at Christmas. But what else could we have done?'

She stared at him. *We.* But that had always been their strength as a couple, hadn't it? The fact that they'd stuck together, no matter what; through twenty-two long years of marriage. That was a lot of sticking together.

Which was why it was a bit disturbing, this feeling that it was coming undone.

'I'll see you downstairs,' she said.

Chapter Two

Aisling occasionally went up into the attic to shout. There was no other place to do it without the whole street hearing her; a big, animal bawl from the pit of her stomach. One time she'd caught sight of herself in the mirror; a woman slightly frayed around the edges and with straight blonde bobbed hair, face skywards as she howled at the moon. 'Ah, here,' she'd said in disgust, and marched downstairs to the kitchen and done an hour's worth of ironing to bring herself down to size.

'I shout too sometimes,' Zofia agreed. 'Sometimes I eat everything in the fridge. Even the mayonnaise.'

Aisling looked at Zofia in her all-skinny perfection, her shapely Polish legs encased in skin-tight fake leather, and said, 'You're just trying to make me feel better now.'

But that was Zofia all over: one of the nicest people you could ever meet. So was Olaf. They lived in the house directly opposite Aisling and Mossy, and they would do anything for you: child-minding, battery jump-starting, an emergency plate of *pierogi* (dumplings – Anto went mad for them). In return, Mossy had helped Olaf paint the house when they'd first moved to Ireland nearly two years ago, and given him a crash course in Irishisms.

'When people here say, "How's it going?" they don't actually mean it. It's just a way of saying hi.'

'Oh,' said Olaf, a little bitterly. It would explain why people walked away in the middle of his earnest description of his crocked knee or his trip home to Warsaw to his wonderful mother.

Olaf often worked with Mossy on painting jobs. He was a great man for detail, apparently. Mossy had gone looking for him one day after Olaf had been hours painting a child's bedroom, and found him feverishly finishing off a startling mural of a giant teddy bear. 'I got carried away,' he confessed shamefaced. 'I will paint it over immediately.' But the owners were thrilled, and paid extra, and now Olaf had billing as a mural specialist in Mossy's outfit.

Aisling and Zofia had had a slower start. Well, it was at the beginning of all the trouble, when Aisling was hiding away from prying eyes and trying to patch things up at home. She'd never been the type to blab out every single detail of her life anyway; when it came to her family, she was even more protective of privacy.

But Zofia was determined. 'Hello!' she'd shout across the road every time she saw Aisling, and wave like her arm was about to fall off.

'Eh, hello,' Aisling would say back, not giving any encouragement.

Undeterred, soon Zofia was shouting, 'Lovely day!' It would be lashing rain. 'For Ireland, I mean! Better than the gales we had yesterday!'

'Yes. The forecast is for more rain tomorrow,' Aisling would shout back, not wanting to be too rude.

'Great!'

Then one day there was Zofia, clattering out of her house in her high heels and a blingy jacket. And there was Aisling, still in her dressing gown at half past twelve – she was having a particularly bad day – sneaking out to take the bins in, her eyes swollen and red.

'What is wrong?' Zofia had bellowed across the road in alarm.

Aisling could see every net curtain on the road twitch. Emma's mother was practically fogging up the window. But she was so miserable she didn't care about them. She threw what decorum she had left to the winds and bawled back, 'Fucking everything!'

Zofia was across the road in a flash and took Aisling's elbow in a comforting grip. 'Tell me.'

And Aisling did. Zofia made strong tea, opened a packet of chocolate biscuits and put another on standby, and eased it out of her with a series of sympathetic clucks, sighs and pats on the shoulder.

'You feel better now?' she said at the end.

'Yes,' said Aisling, surprised. She looked at Zofia fearfully. 'Do you think I'm a terrible mother?'

'No! Of course not!' But the good was taken out of it somewhat when she said, 'I am used to Olaf's mother, who is a complete bitch.'

'But Olaf says she's lovely.' There was a photo of her up on their mantelpiece; an inoffensive-looking woman in a pink cardigan.

'Of course he does. She is his mother.'

The downside of this new friendship was that Aisling had been strong-armed into 'modelling' for Zofia once a week in her own kitchen. Zofia was a make-up artist in training. Her qualifications would eventually – fingers crossed – lead to her making beautiful film stars even more beautiful, but she also wanted to work with 'ordinary people like you, Aisling, to try to help you overcome your flaws and make the most of what you have'. Maybe it was the crispness of her accent as she delivered these statements, but they never sounded particularly flattering.

'Ready?' said Zofia.

Aisling braced herself as Zofia picked up a vast palette of eyeshadows and held it aloft. Judging by where her make-up brush was hovering, Aisling was in for either Atomic Babe or Tickle Me Pink.

'Are you sure you have enough light?' she said doubtfully.

Mossy was still wrestling with the fuse box. Meanwhile, the kitchen was lit by Louise's battery-operated disco ball, which merrily threw out revolving circles of pink and blue light.

'No, it is good,' Zofia insisted. 'It gives me inspiration. Tonight we will do club make-up!'

'Ah, no,' Aisling pleaded.

'You will be lovely.'

'Just don't go too heavy on the eyes this time. Please.'

Zofia had to produce a new look each time for her portfolio. Last week's session had been themed Smoky Eyes. Aisling had emerged looking like she'd done ten rounds with a heavyweight boxer.

'We start,' said Zofia, hunkering down. She discouraged talking during these sessions; it broke her concentration and didn't lend itself to clean lines, apparently.

'Would you like a cup of—' Aisling tried.

'Ssh!'

So she just sat there. The first few minutes of this always freaked her out, because it gave her a chance to remember all the things she'd forgotten. Such as – fuck! – the Christmas card she'd neglected to send to her friend Millie in Australia. Well, a bit late now. And a big foil tray for that blasted turkey; she stuck that down on her mental to-do list. That set her wondering what time Shannon would arrive on Christmas Day. She might have to delay the turkey, depending.

Shannon was their eldest child. Well, hardly a child. She was twenty-one, and in the second year of a social science degree, after which she would very likely go on to save the world. But pending that, she shared a flat near the campus with two other girls, and paid regular visits home 'just to say hi'. And to get her washing done for free and have a decent hot meal that wasn't baked beans or pasta. At least she was normal in that respect, Mossy often said.

But as Zofia's brushes went *swish*, *swish*, Aisling's breathing slowed and the to-do list faded mercifully into the background. She felt the tension of the day gradually leave her body and her mind start to drift. And that was the dangerous bit. It always wanted to go off in the same direction, and if it did, she'd have Zofia murmuring in her ear, 'You're tensing,' and she'd have to will herself into smoothing out her facial muscles again.

Swish, swish. Today was going okay so far. Very well, in fact. All the Christmas preparations must have knackered her, because she found herself being soothed into a semi-stupor, and it was only when she heard the cuckoo clock in the hall – Mossy's late mother's; they hadn't the heart to throw it out – chirp out seven o'clock that she came to with a violent start.

Seven. The day was nearly gone.

'Listen, Zofia.' She quickly checked over her shoulder that Mossy was still outside. 'I need to go.'

14

Zofia's eyebrows jumped up. She looked over her shoulder too and hissed, '*Tonight?* I thought you were going this morning?'

'Well I *was*, but I had to get the turkey and then the electricity went and I just ran out of time, okay?' She didn't want to cut Zofia's session short, but tomorrow was Christmas Eve and there would be no possibility of getting out at all then. 'Is there any chance we could finish up?'

'Okay, okay,' Zofia conceded. She reached into her make-up case and took out a selection of hairbrushes and straighteners.

'No hair,' Aisling pleaded.

'Only five minutes. I promise.' Zofia threw another look over her shoulder. 'If you really want to go, Olaf will drive you.'

'Will he?' Aisling was weak with relief. Her own car was hemmed in behind Mossy's van. It would only draw attention if she asked him to move it in order for her to reverse out.

Zofia was looking at Aisling's hair this way and that with lots of doubtful *um*s, clearly wondering how to work a club look into Aisling's straight locks, and then her eyes met Aisling's in the make-up mirror on the table. 'I think you should stop going. It is only upsetting you.'

Aisling looked at Zofia coldly. Except that she couldn't, of course, because Zofia was too nice, so the best she managed was a semi-chilly look. 'Have you a better suggestion? Maybe I should just close that chapter of my life altogether and cheerily move on?'

'Hardly.' Zofia's look was reproachful. 'I am just saying. Maybe there is something else you can do. Counselling or something . . .'

'I don't need counselling. Or Valium, or anything else,' Aisling said steadily. 'I just need . . .' She didn't know what she needed.

Zofia's eyes were full of compassion. 'You can't fix everything, Aisling.'

'Please,' she said. 'Can we just hurry up?'

Zofia gave up. 'Olaf won't be back until later anyway. He has to find a carp.'

True to Polish tradition, Olaf and Zofia were cooking the fish for Christmas dinner, which would be tomorrow, the twenty-fourth. After much deliberation, they'd chosen the biggest and best from an overcrowded temporary aquarium in a supermarket and taken it home. Or at least they'd thought they had. Zofia had actually put it down for a moment in the beauty section as she'd needed both hands to pour scorn on the supermarket's cheap and nasty selection of make-up, and had forgotten to pick it back up again. Aisling had seen Olaf's black face earlier as he set off belatedly to find another.

'Would you not just give the carp a miss?' Apparently they were having eleven other dishes too at the Christmas feast, so it wasn't as if anybody would be going hungry.

Zofia looked at her like she was missing a few marbles. 'I have two words for you. Olaf's mother.'

'Ah.' Apparently she was due in on a plane at some outrageously early hour in the morning for her first visit to Ireland. Zofia maintained that she had chosen the flight precisely so that Olaf would have to get up in the middle of the night to go and collect her, although Aisling thought that Olaf himself had booked the flight.

'She'll be expecting the carp?' she guessed.

'Oh yes. Olaf has told me many, many times about the wonderful Christmas feasts she used to prepare for them as children. The smells and the log fires and the way she used to sing Christmas songs in a jolly voice in the kitchen as she baked bread and all his favourite cakes.'

It sounded quite nice. But something about Zofia's face stopped Aisling from saying so.

'Still,' said Zofia brightly. 'It is only for three weeks. I will try my best for Olaf's sake.' She tapped Aisling lightly on the shoulder. 'Anyway, be ready at nine and he will take you.'

Nine o'clock, the day before Christmas Eve; God knows what excuse Aisling would have to come up with. But it didn't matter. She sat back in the chair, and her whole body was alive with longing.

Chapter Three

Across town, Nicola was having another bad day.

She walked along as fast as she could, her boots hitting the wet tarmac with a dull click. They were from Penneys. A year ago she'd have shopped in Office and River Island and Urban Outfitters. Fifty euro on a top she'd wear only once or twice? No problem. But she'd had money back then, from her part-time job. It was weekend work, nothing too taxing, just showing people to their tables with a smile and an 'Enjoy your pizza now!' She'd liked it. Okay, so she used to moan about going in sometimes, especially on a Saturday night, but the rest of them were good fun and the tips had been decent. Looking back now, she hadn't a clue how lucky she'd been.

'Mwum . . . mwah . . .' Darren started grumbling in his buggy.

'Shush. You're all right,' she said automatically.

Meanwhile, the monologue continued over her left shoulder. She could have recited it in her sleep.

'You're just going to have to get on with it, Nicola. Life doesn't always go the way you want it to . . .'

She'd let him get it out of his system, and then he'd give his usual sigh and offer (hopefully) to take the baby for an hour so that she could go meet her friends.

'Maybe if you tried to change your attitude . . .'

She wondered if she'd remembered to pack nappies. There were so many things to think of: wipes, baby food, soothers, nappy cream, bibs, spare vest, spare babygro, spare *everything*. And as for herself? She was lucky she'd managed to get dressed that morning. Some days she actually didn't. Seriously. If it had been a bad night, with him up teething or with a temperature, then somehow the hours all started to blur together until suddenly day had turned into night again, and she'd be there thinking, what the hell just happened? She'd still be in her vomity-smelling pyjamas from the night before, her back sore from carrying Darren around all day.

'Slow down, Nicola, there are cars, they're too high up to see the buggy—'

Suddenly she was whirling around in the middle of the pavement and shouting at him, 'I know! I can see the cars, all right? Do you think I'm fucking blind?'

He reared back. Good. Normally she didn't curse. Well, not in public anyway.

Finally he sighed – he loved sighing – and said in that quiet, even way of his, 'Nicola, you've got to stop blaming everybody except yourself for all this.'

She stuck a hand on her hip. 'And did I say I was blaming you? Well, did I? No! So you can relax, okay? You're off the hook.'

They were outside the shopping centre. She could see the late-night Christmas shoppers glancing across at them as they went in and out of the double doors. She knew how it looked: her, blonde and eighteen; him, craggy and forty-six, and Darren in the buggy between them.

Are those two . . .?
Dirty auld fella.
And he got her up the duff and all.
Disgusting!
Wait . . . I recognise him from somewhere . . .

Once, Nicola had loudly clarified the situation to two sniggering young ones. 'He's my dad, okay? Not my boyfriend. And this is his grandson. Happy now? So jog on, nothing to see here.'

Dad had kept this pained smile on his face – you knew he was mortified, but he wasn't going to let the side down any further – and nodded and smiled like it was all perfectly pleasant.

She'd like to see him lose his cool. Just once. She thought she'd driven him pretty close once or twice, but at the last minute, just when she'd actually got a bit afraid that he really might blow and do something you read about in the tabloids, like drive the car off the end of a pier with them all in it – she couldn't even swim – he'd pause and say, 'I think we should both take some time to cool off and we'll talk about this later, okay?'

He was doing his Mr Reasonable act as he followed her towards the shopping centre now. Something about her getting back into education. He loved education. He also enjoyed paperwork, routines and bulk-buys of nappies.

'Look,' she interrupted him, 'just take Darren, would you?'

She was meeting Mikaela and Becky outside Boots. She mightn't have much money – child benefit only went so far – but window-shopping was free. Anyway, mostly they just hung around laughing, and talking about Mikaela's new boyfriend, Murph. Mikaela had been going out with him for three weeks, and now there was this house party down in Wicklow for New Year's Eve and he'd asked her to go, which meant staying over . . . which meant . . .

A Special Delivery

U gonna ride him??
Shag off!!! Am not!
Send us a pic of his lunchbox!
Dirty cow!!!

The texts had been flying back and forth the whole week. But it was just for show, the slagging. Mikaela was actually very nervous. Murph had had a lot of previous girlfriends, including Sandra Hardiman, and she certainly knew a trick or two, if the word on the street was anything to go by, wink wink.

'What if he wants to do something really, like, way out, and I don't have a clue what he's on about?' Mikaela kept agonising.

'There's not much you don't know about,' slagged Becky.

'Shut up! You know I've only been with Mark. All he ever wanted was a blow job. If he could bend down that far himself he wouldn't bother with a girlfriend at all.'

They screamed with laughter.

'Anyway,' said Becky, 'you can always ask Nicola here. There was only one way she got up the spout with Darren.'

It was touch and go for a minute, then Nicola said, 'Shag off!' and they all roared laughing again.

'Seriously though,' said Becky, wiping her eyes. She watched Nicola. 'Was he any good? That fella you had Darren for?'

They waited. They'd been there that night too, but Nicola had got separated from the crowd. Well, she just hadn't rejoined them.

Nicola shrugged carelessly. 'He was all right.' She pulled a face. 'To be honest, I think he'd have preferred a blow job too, only I wasn't offering!'

'All the bloody same,' they agreed sagely.

Anyway, the plan was to get smoothies – they were all on diets – and talk Mikaela through her upcoming night of passion with Murph. Becky was threatening to bring along her girls-growing-up book, from when she was twelve, and draw Mikaela a little diagram, 'to show ya what goes where!' Then they were going to go and pick out some new sexy underwear for the planned seduction – that was going to be hysterical and Nicola was really looking forward to it. Even just to pretend that she was still one of them, though they all knew she wasn't.

'No,' said Dad.

Nicola blinked. She'd nearly forgotten he was there.

'I'm not taking Darren.' He lifted his chin. There was a little nick on it from shaving. For some reason the sight of it pierced her heart. But then he added, 'Not until you address your situation properly,' and she was annoyed all over again.

'Look, Dad.' She'd level with him. They were both adults here, even if he persisted in treating her like she was three. 'I need a break, that's all. It's nearly Christmas. I'm not going to see Becky or Mikaela for days.'

No harm, her dad's face said. He didn't like them. He never said it, but he thought they were a bit common. If it hadn't been for them leading Nicola astray, none of this would have happened.

'So can you help me out here at all?' She tried a flirty smile, but she had a suspicion that it came out as a snarl. She was very out of practice. 'Please?'

Still he said nothing. Just looked at her like she was feckless or something. As though she was making it up, how hard it was minding a baby. Had he not heard her last night, up at 2 a.m.? God knows she'd made enough noise, what with accidentally dropping the bottle on the kitchen floor. By the time she'd cleaned it up and made a new one, Darren was purple in the face with crying, and then he was too upset to feed properly and had brought the whole lot back up in a series of massive vomits. You'd think he'd had ten bottles, not one. At one point she'd nearly had to turn him upside down to see if there was anything left.

Not once had Dad got out of bed to offer to give her a hand. She needed to learn how to cope by herself, he'd said a few weeks back. It hurt him more than it hurt her, blah, blah. And she'd have to learn how to budget too. No more handouts.

'I know, my folks won't do anything for me either,' Becky had said sympathetically on the phone when Nicola rang to moan.

'Are you busy right now?' Nicola had asked. Maybe Becky would offer to come over for an hour and take Darren.

'Oh, I'm still in bed. I've a rotten head on me, we were out last night till three o'clock in the morning. You won't believe what Jason Gleeson did— Jesus Christ!' Becky's voice broke off. There was a muffled roar. 'I'm trying to sleep up here!' Then she was back. 'Can you believe my ma? Hoovering! She knows I was out last night.'

Nicola's eyes had prickled with sudden tears at the injustice of it all. Imagine lying in bed at noon with a hangover. She wouldn't give a damn if her mum woke her up hoovering. Not that that was likely to happen, seeing as her mum lived in Australia now, and ran an Irish bar called The Rotten Spud.

Stupid name.

She blinked furiously. Then, dry-eyed, she told her father evenly, 'I'm very sorry I've let you down so badly.'

Another sigh; a pained one this time. 'Nicola—'

'I fully realise I've made you the talk of the neighbourhood with my unplanned pregnancy, but the key word here is *unplanned*. As in, I didn't actually mean to ruin your life like this.'

Or her own.

He looked at her. Sometimes she got the impression he wanted to let himself go, hug her or something, but that would be sending out the wrong signals. 'You haven't embarrassed me.'

23

Sure. The average age on their road was about seventy-three. The entire time she'd been pregnant, they'd all pretended not to notice, even though her bump was so big it'd nearly take your eye out. And they'd only just recovered from Nicola's mother running off with the bloke who'd put down the patio and setting up shop with him in Sydney. The patio was a rubbish job, too.

'And I'm further sorry' – Nicola had been an A student before all this happened, with an eye on studying law – 'that I haven't "rolled with the punches" and "dusted myself off", and that I've moped around feeling sorry for myself instead of "looking upon all this as a challenge".'

She was quite pleased with herself. Three of his favourite sayings in one sentence. Even he had to appreciate that. He'd had a sense of humour once. She remembered playing Scrabble with him on wet Sunday afternoons and he insisting that *confuzzled* was a real word.

But no smiles today. He looked old, she noticed with a jolt.

She was sorry. Oh, when had it all got so difficult? They'd never spent so much time together as they did now, yet it felt like they barely knew each other any more.

The baby arched his back in the buggy. He had a right little temper on him when he got going. Wonder where he got *that* from, Dad was fond of saying. 'Mwum, mwum!'

He was probably tired. It was coming up to his bedtime.

'Sssh.' She reached down to stroke the top of his head. His hair was so soft. It slipped between her fingers like silk. Sometimes he seemed so fragile that she was afraid of him; petrified that she would somehow break him. A baby book that Dad had bought – one of many – assured her that any feelings of inadequacy would pass quickly. Maternal instinct would kick in and teach her all she needed to know.

A man must have written that book.

'Mwum, ummmm.' He started up a low cry now. It was like a trigger. She felt her stomach tense familiarly with worry, dread, fear, irritation.

'Now stop it, okay?' She sounded sharper than she felt. Poor little fecker. He didn't deserve this. He didn't deserve *her*. It was like they'd strayed into each other's lives by accident, neither of them actually belonging there.

'Nicola, I'm sorry. I can't mind him tonight.' Dad must have realised she was close to the edge. Why couldn't he give her a break, then?

'Please, Dad. I just need an hour to myself.'

It wasn't like her to be so conciliatory. But she felt perilously close to screaming. And if she started, she wouldn't stop. They'd have to come and take her away in a straitjacket.

'I said no, Nicola.' He was going to dig his heels in. Mum used to call him stubborn, and maybe she was right. But did he have to pick *today*? 'I have to go to work.'

Then she realised what it was for: the afternoon shave, the suit and tie she had barely noticed him putting on. He was on the night shift.

Right. Fine. Fuck it. Fuck everything.

She whirled around, dragged the buggy with her. It went over on two wheels and the baby cried again, but she marched away.

'Nicola! Where are you going?'

For a smoothie. But no. She couldn't. It wasn't that Becky and Mikaela didn't like Darren. They cooed over him – 'Hiya, gorgeous!' – and fought each other for the chance to cuddle him. But when he had to be fed or changed they got impatient that the conversation had to be interrupted. They'd stand outside the baby changing rooms chatting about Murph or Sandra

Hardiman – 'Did you hear she's going with Carl Ryan now? I know!' – and by the time Nicola got back out with Darren she'd have missed all the news, and it was nearly worse than not showing up in the first place.

'Nicola! Come back!' Dad was calling after her now.

But he wasn't running. He wasn't even walking. He just stood there, beside the doors of the shopping centre, arms hanging limply by his sides. Her outrage began to build: at her dad, her absent mum, Becky and Mikaela, randy Murph even though she'd never met him. And at Darren. Poor little Darren, whose fault none of this was.

'I'm sorry,' she told the top of his head.

He didn't know it yet, because he was only little, but he would grow and soon enough he'd realise it too: she was a bad mother. The worst. He'd be better off with her dad. He'd be better off with anybody except her.

It hit her then. The solution to all her problems.

At Boots. Where u?

The text was from Becky. She ignored it and pushed the buggy on harder, faster, away from them all.

Chapter Four

'What's that stuff on your cheeks?' Anto wanted to know.

'Oh, just some highlighter.' It was very expensive, Zofia had said, but worth every cent.

Mossy tipped his head to one side and peered at her too. 'It looks like Day-Glo.'

'Weird,' Anto agreed.

Aisling had thought she'd looked quite good up to now. 'Just get on with your essay,' she told Anto meanly.

'But it's so *stupid*.'

'It's not.'

'It is. Why do I need to know whether Macbeth showed more kingship than tyranny? I mean, what am I going to do, walk into a shop to buy a can of Coke and tell the assistant, oh, and by the way, did you know that Macbeth was a right nutjob?' Anto was mildly traumatised.

So was Aisling. Anto was doing his Leaving Certificate exam. Well, Aisling was doing it really, feverishly gathering up revision notes and poring over past exam papers for him. Anto occasionally looked over her shoulder, 'to keep you happy, Ma'.

'Only another six months to go,' Mossy told Anto sagely. 'You just have to knuckle down.'

He could talk. The last book he'd read had been a biography of an obscure brewer that he'd taken on holiday three years ago and had yet to finish. It still sat on the shelf over the bed, taunting them. And as for the idea of him actually rolling up his sleeves to give Anto a hand . . .

'But you're the brains of the operation,' he was always pleading, buttering Aisling up. 'I can only teach him how to cut a piece of plywood or change a plug. And to be honest, it's hard enough to get him to grasp that.'

The truth was, he'd stepped back a bit from Anto. There was distance there. Not as much from Louise maybe, but she was only eleven; she hadn't got to those difficult years yet. And in a way Aisling understood it, even if she resented the fact that it left a little gap for her to fill. But she filled it, with all her might. There was no way Anto was going to get short-changed by his parents.

'I shouldn't even have to study,' he was grumping now. 'It's the Christmas holidays. I should be having a rest.'

'A rest!' Mossy was highly amused.

'They told us at school. We're to come back fresh and ready to go,' Anto said earnestly.

'Well, the amount of sleep you're getting, you should come top of the class.'

'I'll finish the essay tomorrow.'

'You'll finish it now. You already spent an hour dozing on the couch while Zofia was here.'

Anto usually kept out of the way when Zofia was around. Her long legs and red lipstick unnerved him. Anto was what you would call inexperienced with girls, and looked set to remain that way well into the future, Mossy and Aisling often agreed with relief.

He had one last stab. 'But I said I'd play FIFA with Baz.'

Anto had told them that he'd once had a dream where he'd died and was buried with his PlayStation. He said it was great to be able to play in peace without someone coming along to kick him off because they wanted to watch *EastEnders*.

'How are you going to do that?' Mossy enquired. 'There's no electricity.'

'Oh man!' Anto buried his head in his hands, distraught. 'This day is SO bad!'

'Listen, son,' said Mossy. 'I have an idea.'

'What?' Anto looked up in hope; would Mossy pull a generator out of his back pocket and power the house up again? Okay, so blowing the fuse box was a bit of a cock-up, but usually his da fixed things rather than broke them. He'd even sorted out the water mains on the street one summer when the council took two days to come out. First he'd opened it up so that the water gushed out, geyser-style like you saw in American movies, and the kids ran in and out of it, shrieking in delight, and Anto had gone around with a puffed-up chest, saying, 'That's my da, you know.'

Mossy said, 'You could take your football out – you know, that round plastic thing in the hall that your ma is always tripping over? – and actually have a real game of football with Baz.'

Anto looked at him bitterly. 'Hilarious.'

'You won't find it so hilarious if you fail those exams.'

'Noooo. Not the if-you-fail-the-exams talk.'

'I'm just saying. Because if you're not careful, you're going to end up on the dole.'

'Ma, make him stop,' Anto begged. 'Otherwise the economy will be next.'

Too late. 'The economy's in meltdown, in case you haven't noticed.'

'And the job situation is awful.'

'No, the job situation is *terrible*.'

But Anto had a comeback this time. 'I don't need a job,' he said brightly, 'because I'm going to work with you, Da, painting and decorating. And I'll never have to pay rent or buy food because you two will need someone to look after you when you're old and feeble so I'm going to stay living at home.'

Aisling and Mossy exchanged looks.

'Very generous of you, Anto,' said Mossy. 'But you still need your exams.'

'Anyway, I don't think you working with your dad is such a good idea,' Aisling said.

'Thanks,' said Mossy, hurt. 'Thanks a bunch.'

'Well look what happened the last time.'

It was out before she could stop it.

Mossy shot her a betrayed look. She shot one back. It was true. *Beware: Insane Control Freak Inside* had been scrawled in the dirt on the back of Mossy's van the last time one of their offspring had worked with him.

'You needn't worry,' Mossy told her coolly. 'There's no question of Anto working with me. Because he's going to go to university, isn't that right, Anto?'

'Why are we all so obsessed with university in this house?' Anto howled.

'We just want you to do well,' Aisling soothed. 'Like Shannon.'

'That bloody Shannon. Raising the bar for us all.' Anto grabbed a random book off the table – Aisling suspected it was one of her cookery books – and stood, hitching up his jeans. They promptly fell down again, until the crotch rested somewhere between his knees, as was the fashion of the day. 'I'm going upstairs.' And off he marched in the dark, leaving a tense silence behind.

'We shouldn't put too much pressure on him,' Aisling said at last.

'*You're* the one standing over him all the time, bugging him about bloody Shakespeare.'

'At least I'm not banging on about the economy all the time, and how he's going to end up on the dole. *That's* encouraging, Mossy.'

'We want better for him, don't we? And I'm not ashamed to say it. Jesus, Aisling, we can't mess this up too.'

She felt hot. 'And this is the way to not mess up? By saying the same stuff, only louder?'

Mossy's mouth was pinched. 'I take it that's aimed at me.'

'You're dead right.'

The sound of Anto's bedroom door slamming upstairs brought the row to an abrupt halt.

They looked at each other. 'Let's not fight. Let's just get through Christmas as best we can, okay?' Mossy said.

Aisling's throat was suddenly tight. Bloody Christmas. If she had her way, she'd draw the curtains until 7 January, when the whole thing was over. It was hard enough getting through each week, each *day*, without having to slap a festive smile on your face on top of it all.

'Aisling,' said Mossy, seeing her expression.

But she didn't want his comfort. She used to. Lately, though, she found herself turning away from him. Lately she'd felt a tiny seed of something start to grow that she thought might be blame.

The back door burst open and Louise barrelled in. Aisling scrabbled about for her normal face. 'Hi, love! Listen, it's time to come in. It's pitch dark outside.'

It was practically pitch dark inside too; the candles were burning out.

Louise's face was fierce with excitement. 'You have to come and see something!'

Behind her was Emma from down the road. They were both wearing what seemed to be Emma's mother's shoes and some of her underwear. Marks & Spencer, 36D, and a pair of Spanx, Aisling saw. Finally she had something on that woman.

Anto stomped moodily back in from upstairs. 'I can't study with all this noise!' he declared, even though he could barely have opened the Mary Berry cookery book, and if he had, he wouldn't have been able to read it in the dark anyway.

'Shut up,' Louise told him dismissively. She grabbed Aisling's hand, pulling urgently. 'You really have to come. We're after finding something.'

'We think it's alive,' Emma chipped in. 'There was a noise out of it when we poked it with a stick.'

Anto threw his eyes to heaven. He got a box of cereal from the cupboard and sat down at the table. The enormous plate of pasta he'd had two hours ago had clearly worn off.

Louise and Emma galloped out the back door again. Aisling and Mossy exchanged sighs as they traipsed after them. 'If this is another hedgehog . . .'

It wasn't. It was an infant, asleep in Mossy's crib on the lawn, surrounded by malfunctioning Christmas lights.

'It's Baby Jesus,' said Louise, swooning.

Chapter Five

The baby was small. Maybe only seven or eight months old, Aisling surmised. Six, guessed Mossy. 'Two!' Louise chipped in, desperate not to be left out.

'Sssh!' said Aisling.

The baby stirred, gave a small, shuddering sigh and then settled down again into a sound sleep.

'Wow,' Louise breathed.

Wow indeed.

'I'm going to tell my mam!' said Emma, and rushed off into the darkness, M&S bra swinging, to alert the road to the fact that a baby had been beamed from outer space – maybe even heaven – into the Bradys' front garden.

Because that was how it seemed. There was no owner in evidence. Mossy looked up and down the street for a person or a car, but nothing. Nobody peered out of the bushes at them. No upset or unbalanced mother loitered in the shadows to see if someone would take her bundle in.

Or no father either; they'd better not be sexist about it. But

Aisling knew instinctively that it was a woman who'd carefully laid the baby there, covering it up meticulously against the cold.

'Now look here!' Mossy ended up calling into the darkness. 'Come on out, and, er, let's talk about this, eh? We'll have a cup of tea inside, and work something out!'

He waited expectantly, but nobody rushed forward to take him up on his kind invitation of weak tea and ham-fisted counselling. Well! If that was the way it was going to be . . .

'This isn't funny, you know! If this is some kind of trick or joke . . . You could get into serious trouble!' He waited, then hissed to Aisling, 'Should I threaten the police?'

'No!' She thought about it. She hadn't a clue about the protocol of these things. 'Not yet, anyway.'

Meanwhile the baby slept on soundly in the oversized crib, lit up by erratically flashing Christmas lights.

Except that the crib wasn't. Oversized, that was. 'Look,' Aisling urged, clutching Mossy's arm in wonder. 'It's a perfect fit for the baby. Your crib!'

He gave her a look. 'I think we have more important things to worry about now than the size of my crib.'

'Is it a boy or a girl?' she wondered.

They all looked at the baby again, hunting for giveaway signs of pink clips or Superman T-shirts. But the person who'd dressed this little mite either didn't have a whole pile of imagination or else was colour blind, because everything on the baby was tan, beige, cream, off-white or variations thereof. Stripped of personality.

'It's a boy,' Louise suddenly pronounced. 'Look.' And she unearthed a blue soother, tangled up with the beige coat. On cue the baby stirred again and this time grizzled.

'Will I . . .?' said Louise.

'Yes, yes.'

She tentatively held the soother to the baby's mouth. He turned his head and, vacuum style, gobbled it up and began sucking on it frantically, emitting loud smacking noises.

Louise turned wide, wondering eyes to her mother. 'But, like, who owns it?'

'Him,' Aisling corrected smartly.

Already she felt terribly protective of this small scrap of unwanted humanity.

'*Him*.'

'And of all the gardens in all the world, most of them less freaky-looking than this one,' Mossy said, 'why would anyone leave him in ours?'

They took the baby inside. It was four degrees in the open, with temperatures set to plummet as night drew in, and a possibility of ground frost later on with—

'Turn that shagging radio off,' said Mossy.

Anto looked up. 'My God,' he said, squinting through the gloom. 'What the hell is that?'

'A baby, Anto,' said Aisling.

'What's he doing with Da?'

'We found him outside. Now, make room.' Louise turned off the battery-run radio. Anto hurriedly moved his cereal bowl, and then the candles, for fear of setting the little critter on fire. Mossy gingerly took his place at the head of the table, the baby nestled in his paint-spattered arms.

'I'm a bit out of practice at this,' he said, looking rather foolish.

'You're doing great,' Aisling assured him. She couldn't take her eyes off the baby. 'Look, he hasn't moved even once. Bless.'

They all inched closer to look at him. He was incredibly still, his little eyelashes casting bluish shadows across his cheeks.

'He's not . . . he's still breathing, right?' Anto said suddenly.

Aisling was immediately petrified. It had been so cold out there. And God knows how long he'd been lying in that stupid, threadbare crib before they'd found him . . .

'He has to be!' said Louise. That would just be the worst luck. You find one and just as quickly you lose it again.

'Mossy?' gulped Aisling.

'Of course he is,' said Mossy, but uncertainly.

They were even more spooked now, and all surged forward to check. Anto and Louise clashed heads painfully.

'Ow!'

'It's your fault, you fat lump!'

'Shut *up*.'

The baby didn't move. Not a sound.

Then . . .

'I hear it! He's breathing!' Anto cried joyously, forgetting himself for a moment.

'I told you he was. All right, everybody, step back. Give him some space,' Mossy declared, acting like he knew it all now.

'I can hold him if you want,' Louise said eagerly.

'No, he's fine here.'

They were all dying to have a go now. 'You can't hog him, Da.'

'Back off,' said Mossy possessively. 'And wait your turn.'

Aisling found she was in a state of high excitement. A beautiful baby had just landed on their doorstep two days before Christmas. It was as if someone, somewhere, had wondered, 'Now, who's the most miserable family in Ireland this Christmas? Oh, the Bradys again. Sure, let's throw them a baby and see if it'll cheer the buggers up.'

And it had! *Thank you, God*, Aisling said to the ceiling. Or Santa, or whoever had rigged it for them.

'Right!' she called in a jovial voice that had them all looking around warily; what was with all the happiness? 'Louise, stick the gas fire on, both bars. We have to keep him warm. And we'd better put a saucepan of water on to boil in case he needs a drink.'

'I know it's been a long time,' Mossy ventured, 'but do babies drink boiling water?'

She searched that dusty part of her brain. Boiling water . . . oh, yes. 'We need it to sterilise bottles. The teats and stuff.' The baby looked well past the age when that might be necessary, but it was better to be safe than sorry. Nothing was going to happen to him on *her* watch.

Mind you, he didn't seem in need of much. He'd been looked after carefully, she could tell that straight away. There was a fresh, washed smell off him, and his fingernails were neatly clipped. And his hair! Strawberry blonde, and just a tuft really, at the front of his head, giving him such a cheeky look. For all his carer's suspicious love of beige, this little lad's personality still burst through. She had an urge to whip him out of Mossy's arms and warble at him, 'Who's a lovely boy? You are! You are!' but that would only give him the fright of his life. And Mossy too. He might think she was keen to have another. As if. The shop was definitely closed in *that* department.

And anyway, Mossy wasn't giving him up easily. She could tell that. Maybe he was quite enjoying having a child in the vicinity who wasn't answering him back. In the meantime Aisling would have to content herself with her mother hen routine.

'Anto,' she urged, 'run out to the shops and get a box of formula for me.'

'You what?'

'He's going to be hungry when he wakes up. Actually, you'll

have to get bottles too – we threw all ours out, didn't we, Mossy? Will they have them in the supermarket, do you think? Or does he need to go to a chemist?'

'Bottles!' said Anto.

'And nappies.'

'*Nappies!*' So far he'd regarded the baby as though it were some vaguely interesting creature you might spot in a zoo. Now he looked like he was wondering whether it shouldn't be behind glass.

Mossy intervened just as it seemed like the poor lad was going to faint. 'Hang on a second. What are we doing here?'

Aisling looked at him. This was surely her department. He fixed things around the house and she fed/washed/changed the kids; their marriage had always been a fairly traditional type of set-up in that regard. 'Trying to look after this baby, Mossy. Who will probably wake up at any moment, and need a feed, and probably do a poo.'

Anto took another step back from the baby.

'He's not ours, though, Ash.'

Aisling looked at him. 'Really, Mossy? You don't say.'

'What I mean is, instead of planning a trip to the supermarket, shouldn't we be doing something sensible like, I don't know, ringing social services?'

'Oh. Yes.' Her gung-ho attitude took a bit of a hit. She'd forgotten about them. But he was right, of course. Somebody in authority ought to know what had happened. They could be searching high and low for this baby right now, putting out the Irish equivalent of an APB. But she knew that the minute they made that phone call it would become all official, and they'd be bossed around and told what to do, and the little drama would be taken off them, along with this tiny fellow who looked like Tintin.

And they would be left even more deflated, in a house with no electricity. It wasn't fair.

'But I want to keep him!' Louise chimed in. Through all this she'd been silently stroking his little foot in its furry (beige) bootee. Aisling had already heard her whispering a list of possible names under her breath: Tyler, Preston, Blake, Ethan. They seemed to come straight off her favourite American TV channel.

'I know,' Mossy soothed, 'but his mother is probably looking for him right now, frantic.'

Really? So frantic that she was running up and down the road, tearing her hair out? No. There wasn't a blooming *sign* of her. Still, Aisling conceded, the baby might have been stolen, or kidnapped or something. Although that whole scenario was a little far-fetched. If you were going to go to the trouble of stealing a baby for a massive ransom, you'd hardly leave him in the middle of a cheap nativity scene in a suburban estate, would you? With lights that flashed on and off erratically like something from a horror movie?

'We could put off ringing the social people for a while,' Louise suggested, treacherously. In many ways she was her mother's daughter.

Aisling wasn't going to lie; it was tempting. She hadn't even had a cuddle of this infant intruder yet. All that creamy skin and the curled-up fingers and button nose . . . he was *gorgeous*. If she looked at him from a certain angle, he was exactly like all of hers when they'd been babies. There was no way she was giving him back until she got to hold him.

'Only until he wakes up,' she conceded.

Louise was crestfallen. 'I was thinking more a week or two.' Then she perked up again. 'I know! We could look after him over Christmas! It'd be great!'

Mossy moved swiftly to head all this loose talk off at the

pass. 'But then Santa wouldn't know where to bring his presents, would he?'

Louise gave him a wall-eyed stare. That was cheap, especially as Emma had apparently stoutly restated her position that Santa was just your ma and da who bought stuff from Argos and wrapped it up.

'Look,' Mossy reasoned, 'this isn't a dog we've found, you know. It's a baby. And what's happened is very serious. Here, Anto. Hand me the phone.'

'There's no electricity . . .'

'My mobile then, come on, use your head.'

That was exactly the sort of statement guaranteed to get Anto's back up, and it duly did. 'There's no need to take it out on me, just because someone dumped their kid on us,' he huffed.

'Can we stop using the word *dump*?' Aisling didn't want the baby to hear it. She knew it was stupid, but if he even subliminally thought that somebody didn't want him . . . Despite what all the evidence pointed to.

Anto found the phone and handed it over. Then, the appeal of their find clearly having worn off, he began edging towards the door, mumbling, '. . . Baz . . . Sean . . . telly . . . pizza . . . back in a while.' He gave the baby a look. Not wanting to seem rude, he said, 'Um, see you, little fella,' and then slouched out.

'Be back by half past ten!' Aisling called, belatedly.

'Right!' said Mossy, industriously picking up the phone. Then it seemed to occur to him that it was nearly nine o'clock. 'Who should we ring?'

Indeed. Social services would be long gone for the holidays, and it was unlikely they had a Missing Babies hotline.

'The guards will know.' Aisling reluctantly hunted for the phone book.

'I'll miss you so much,' Louise whispered to the sleeping baby.

'It would have been lovely to have had a baby brother. I'm the youngest, so I never got the chance to be a big sister. I was just the runt of the litter—'

'That's enough, Louise.'

With the help of a torch, Aisling found the number of the local Garda station. A horrible thought struck her. Would they remember the time they'd called them up before? Their number would probably come up automatically on some police database. *Here, Sam! It's that crowd from Sylvester Avenue! Right shower of troublemakers.*

But they must deal with loads of people called Brady, some of whom had surely done worse things than sell a bit of hash from their house, right? And that hadn't even been proven.

She eyed Mossy. He was thinking about the hash too. He'd been the one who'd made the call. She'd begged and pleaded with him not to, but of course Mossy wouldn't hear of it. 'We have drugs on the premises!' he'd shouted down the phone very excitedly, like he was in an episode of *Hawaii Five-0*. It had been a slight disappointment when the person on the other end hadn't shouted back, 'Copy!' but instead said, nasally, 'Okay, let's start with your name.'

But hang on.

The baby was waking up. Aisling waited, poised with the phone in her hand. She wanted to see the colour of his eyes before she rang. She hoped he wouldn't be frightened when he looked up and saw all these strangers. Would he hunt around for his mother? Would he cry?

'It's okay,' she whispered to him in anticipation.

It was strange, but she felt she knew him already. It was probably some hormonal thing. But there was something about this baby . . .

41

The back door opened again. Olaf peered into the darkness. 'Hello? Is there anybody there?'

'Would you be quiet, man!' Mossy roundly chastised him. 'There's a baby here!'

Olaf blinked uncertainly. Aisling knew he was wondering whether they were pulling his leg. It wouldn't be the first time. Last year, just after he'd started working with Mossy and Dave (his painting partner), they'd apparently sent him in to prep a lady's bedroom while she was actually in her en suite bathroom. Olaf only discovered this when she walked out to find him on his hands and knees outside the bathroom door. It was a mistake, Mossy protested vigorously, but Olaf had his suspicions and was alert now to any other wind-ups.

'I am here to collect Aisling,' he said stoutly, ignoring any red-herring talk of babies.

Aisling blanched. She'd forgotten all about it. She couldn't believe it; in all the excitement she'd actually forgotten. And why hadn't Zofia told Olaf to code things a bit in front of Mossy?

Summoning her calmest voice, she said, 'Oh, Olaf. Yes, I was going to ask you to run me over to Mum's; she said she had an extra cylinder of gas in case we ran out before the electricity's back up. But actually, I think we'll manage with what we have.'

Mossy was too busy with the waking baby to take much notice. She'd got away with it this time.

'Okay.' Then, to let her know that he was a bit miffed at this sudden change in plan – and not even a courtesy phone call – Olaf announced, 'I've been all over Dublin looking for a carp, you know.'

'I'm sorry, Olaf. Did you find one?'

'Yes thank you.' And he held up something that they all squinted to see in the darkened kitchen. Something round and plump. It didn't look much like a carp – or indeed any fish. 'I tripped over it in the garden. It was beside that crib thing.'

He handed it to Aisling and she shone her torch on it. She saw immediately that it was a baby bag. The baby's baby bag.

'Beige,' Louise sighed.

'I will go,' Olaf announced.

'And say hello to your mother for me.'

Olaf's face was suddenly wreathed in smiles. 'I will!' And he bounced out.

They examined the baby bag.

'We must have missed it in the dark and the excitement.' Aisling felt a rush of relief. The baby hadn't been kidnapped. What kidnappers would be so diligent as to leave a beautifully packed bag?

But just as quickly her heart dropped again, right down to her boots. Because now they had proof that this wasn't an accident, or a terrible mistake. It was on purpose. The baby had been left in their garden for a reason.

'Ma?' Louise was examining the bag. 'There's a note attached.'

A piece of paper was folded over neatly and wedged under the front flap. Aisling snatched it up.

'What does it say?' Mossy wanted to know.

Aisling didn't know yet. But she had a feeling they weren't going to like it.

Chapter Six

The *boom boom boom* worked its way up through the thin soles of Nicola's red heels, so loud that she could hardly hear herself think. Which was fine by her. The club was packed, sardine-like, with revellers cut loose from their desks for the Christmas holidays. Heaving, sweating bodies pushed up against her, and she let herself float along on the crowd, her body gyrating to the music, until she found herself back at the bar again.

That was handy. She was nearly out of drink.

'Excuse me!' She pushed back her shock of hair – she'd sprayed half a ton of product on it earlier – and waggled her plastic cup of alcopop for attention. 'Same again!'

Her hand was orange. The lights in Becky's bedroom weren't so great when it had come to the fake tan. Actually, it was worse than orange; it was more the colour of mud. But never mind. The rest of her looked great.

Feck. Her ankles were mud-coloured as well. And streaky. She crossed one over the other quickly to distract attention. Who'd be looking at her feet in here anyway?

She threw the last of her drink down her throat and handed the plastic cup to the barman. 'For the recycling. Want to do my bit for the environment,' she said with a wink.

The barman, hefty and unsmiling, took it and gave her a look. He must be new. But then again, she hadn't been here in a while. A year and a half actually. It was good to be back. She felt so giddy with freedom that it was like she was floating two feet off the ground.

'Hurry up then,' she told him smartly. 'I haven't got all day.'

His eyes dropped to her boobs, rudely, and then he turned and strolled off. She did a quick check; was anything popping out down there? No. But only just about. The dress was tight. It was Becky's. They used to be the same size – in fact Nicola used to be half a stone lighter. But *now* . . . Her legs and hips were still okay, but she had a little roll of baby fat around her middle, a permanent fixture, almost obscuring her neat Caesarean scar. She should probably do some sit-ups or something.

She would, she decided. She'd fix that too. She took a deep breath. This whole thing was going to be okay. She just had to hold on to her nerve, and the tiny seed of unnamed emotion throbbing under her breastbone. Panic, or terror, or something. Where was the barman with her drink to make it go away?

'How's it going?'

She looked to her left. It was some guy with dirty-blonde hair and a clingy shirt. He had strange, wet-looking lips.

'Sorry?' She pretended she couldn't hear him over the music. He so wasn't her type. But it was fun to play again.

He tried again, raising his voice to a shout. 'Do you want to dance?'

'Are you ancient or something?' she shouted back. 'Nobody asks anybody to dance any more.'

He laughed. It was a kind of a bray. 'I'm asking you. And I'm twenty-three.'

'I'm delighted for you. But I'm with my friends, okay?'

She turned back to watch the crowd. She thought she might see the old gang: Lenny, Denise, Sarah. But there was no sign of them, and secretly she was glad. What would she have to say to them anyway? She'd fallen out of touch with most of her old mates; she'd had great intentions, and so had they, but it was only Becky and Mikaela that she saw much of now.

Maybe she'd stuck with them because it was on a night out with the two of them that she'd made the most stupid mistake of her life . . .

No. She wasn't going to think about that now. Keep taking deep breaths, that was all she had to do.

'What's your name?'

Your man was still there. Bit slow on the uptake, was shiny shirt.

'Cassandra.' Well, why not? Tonight she could be anyone she liked. It was like she'd got a fresh start. She might even change her name for real. Although not to Cassandra, which, let's face it, was seriously gak.

They were playing Wham! now, 'Last Christmas'. The crowd was coming over all nostalgic, people hugging and swaying, couples wearing the faces off each other, eyes tight shut. Nicola closed her eyes too, half-cut now. This time last year she'd just found out she was pregnant, and it was the first Christmas without Mum in the house. It was *miserable* . . .

There she went again! She was supposed to be having a good time. There would be no wallowing tonight.

'Hey! Have you forgotten about my drink?' she shouted at the barman. He slapped it down on the counter and took her money.

Her phone vibrated in her orange hand. She didn't have to look at it to know who it was: Dad again, from work. He always checked in with her when he was working late. She hadn't replied to any of his earlier messages, and now he was getting worried. Quickly she texted back. *Going to bed. Wrecked. See u in the morning.* Anything else and she'd have to get into explanations. He'd find out soon enough.

'There you are!' Becky popped out of the heaving crowd, like a cork from a bottle. Her make-up was shiny from the heat. 'We thought you were in the jacks.'

'Sweet fuck!' Mikaela was behind Becky, tottering like a deer on enormous heels. She fanned her face furiously. 'I'm going to pass out in a minute! Oh, I see you got *yourself* a drink, thanks very much!'

'Sorry. I'm broke.' Nicola was down to her last twenty. And that was from a sub of fifty from Becky.

'You all right?' said Becky. She was looking at her. They both were. Concerned, like. They'd been exchanging little looks all evening behind Nicola's back.

'Maybe we should go home,' Mikaela said. She eyed Nicola's drink. 'We've probably had enough.'

'I'm not going anywhere.' Nicola threw back her hair, nonchalant. 'Your man at the bar tried to chat me up.'

'Who?' They immediately rubbernecked.

'The blondie guy.'

'Ew!'

And they all broke up laughing. Nicola felt a rush of warmth towards them. They were true mates. There hadn't been any inquisition when she'd failed to turn up outside Boots, instead pitching up unannounced at Becky's house with the empty buggy. They knew from experience that you didn't push Nicola; you waited until she was ready to tell you, if that ever happened at all. Instead Becky had made her a cup of tea, and had tried not to look too taken aback when Nicola had said, 'Here, let's go out tonight, will we?'

'Out?'

'Yeah. To a club.'

'But . . . what about Darren? I thought your da was working tonight.'

'He is.' Nicola could see that Becky was still worried. 'Look, Darren's being looked after, okay? Ah, come on. Please. It's ages since I've been out.' She knew she sounded a bit desperate. But she couldn't go home, could she? To an empty house? She was eighteen years old. She should be living life to the full.

Becky, fair play, finally said, 'Yeah, all right then, go on.' Then Mikaela came over, and Becky threw open her wardrobe and told Nicola she could borrow anything she wanted – 'Try the pink dress on, the colour suits you.' They'd had two vodka and Diet Cokes each because Becky's mum was out for the night with her new boyfriend, and then they'd slapped on the warpaint and the fake tan. 'I can't believe the three of us are hitting the town, just like old times,' Mikaela kept giggling. And she'd helped Nicola do her hair and there was no talk of Murph or school or Sandra Hardiman because they understood that tonight was about Nicola.

'I love you guys,' she bubbled now over the music.

'Ah, here,' said Becky, laughing. 'Leave it out.'

'I'm serious.'

For a minute she thought she was going to cry. Through all of this they'd stood by her, tried to help out when they could and not looked for anything in return. They hadn't even pressed her about who the father was. Not that there was a whole pile of information to give. But she was grateful that they'd been happy enough when she'd said he didn't want anything to do with the child.

Her dad hadn't been so easily pacified, but what was he going to do? Not telling him seemed like the only bit of control she had left in her life.

'Listen to you,' said Mikaela fondly. 'You're just pissed.'

'So are you.'

'I know!'

They broke up laughing again and, arms around each other, shoved their way back on to the dance floor.

'Look at the lezzers,' some guy shouted over.

'Look at the big spotty head on you,' Becky bellowed back, and that shut him up. And now they were playing boom-boom music again, and they passed Nicola's plastic cup of drink around between them, and when it was empty, Becky threw the cup into the crowd. Nicola lifted her hands over her head and began to dance, sinewy and hypnotic, pushing it all to the back of her mind, everything.

Even the awful thing that she'd just done.

'Wake up.'

Something landed on her face. Cold, wet.

'I said, wake up.'

Another cold splash. Some went up her nose. What the hell . . .? She coughed, and opened her eyes. The effort of it, and the bright light from the window, hurt so much that she felt close to death.

Becky was standing over her, holding an empty glass.

'Have you lost your mind?' Nicola shouted at her. But it came out as a broken croak. She realised that the pink dress she'd worn the previous night was missing and she was wearing only her knickers and bra.

'You have to get dressed,' Becky said. Her voice was hoarse too, and her eyes were ringed with last night's make-up.

Nicola hoicked herself painfully up on one shoulder. She scrabbled to pull the sheet out from under her leg to cover herself up. She was, she realised, in a makeshift bed on the floor of Becky's living room. There was her mum's overstuffed orange sofa, and photos of Becky on the wall in her communion dress, gap-toothed and ringleted.

'Quick,' said Becky.

But the effort of sitting up was too much for Nicola. The room began to spin and she leaned over and puked. Becky somehow produced a rubbish bin just in time and managed to catch it. Nicola ended up spewing over an old copy of the *Daily Mirror*.

'Oh Jesus,' Becky moaned, looking like she might be sick herself. 'You really had a skinful last night, didn't you?'

Nicola had a vague recollection of Becky and Mikaela trying to get her to leave. But she wouldn't.

'Sorry.' She lay back down. 'Sorry, Becky.'

She felt clammy and weak, and she couldn't keep her eyes open.

'No, no!' Becky was flapping around. 'You can't go back to sleep! Your da is here, looking for you!'

Nicola's heart nearly stopped. Her eyes fixed on Becky's in panic.

'You didn't tell him you were staying here.' Becky was accusing. 'He's been all over looking for you. He told my ma that he came home and you weren't there.'

Nicola could hear voices now, from the kitchen. Her dad's. And now Becky's mum, defensive.

'You should have texted him,' Becky insisted. 'I think you're in big trouble.'

And on cue, there was Dad, standing behind Becky. His face was a cold, hard mask.

'Um, I'll leave you two to it,' Becky mumbled. She shot Nicola a sympathetic look, and then fled.

'Get up,' said Dad, in a very quiet, even voice.

At least he wasn't roaring. Nicola's urge to vomit again was slowly passing, only to be replaced by horrible memories of the night before. Drink after drink. The crush of bodies on the dance floor. The fella at the bar with the blonde hair and the wet lips. Oh God. She'd gone back and talked to him. She'd *danced* with him. Disturbing images of him wrapped around her emerged from her swollen brain. His hands on her waist, sliding lower as he went in for the snog. But she'd surprised them both by starting to cry. Really cry; to bawl. 'Come on, love, cheer up,' he'd said, slightly taken aback. He'd pawed her bottom. But that just made her cry harder. Eventually he'd snapped, 'For fuck's sake,' and walked off and left her standing there in the middle of the dance floor, sobbing like a small child.

'I said get up,' her father said in that awful, strained voice. Nicola was frightened. Maybe this was it. Maybe he was finally going to bundle her into the car and drive it over the end of the pier. And she didn't want him to now. She wanted her warm, gentle dad back to make this whole mess right.

'Dad, I'm sorry—'

'I had the guards out looking for you. I got home and you weren't there and you didn't answer your phone. I was out of my mind with worry.'

What was left of her bravado crumbled and fell away. It was unconscionable, to have failed to come home. She knew from the bags under his eyes and the bluey-grey colour of his skin that he'd been up all night. But she'd wanted to punish him. If he hadn't been so . . . so *lacking*, then Mum wouldn't have run off with the patio guy, and left their home a fractured, awful place that Nicola had run out of every chance she'd got because she couldn't bear the scorched look on her dad's face.

'Where's the baby?' Dad demanded. 'Where's Darren?'

He was looking at her like she'd done something truly terrible. She hadn't, though. She had just made this whole situation a little better for them all. Not that he would see it like that. But give him time.

'He's okay.' She'd made sure of that. She'd climbed a tree on the road, like she used to do as a kid, and waited there where she could see the crib. She'd been hoping that it would be him who would come out of the house, just so she could see him again. But he didn't. The rest of them looked okay, though, when they finally discovered Darren. The stocky man with the shock of rusty hair seemed capable and strong when he stood under the tree shouting for her. But when they took Darren into the house, no lights went on; just some kind of flickering, like candles. If you put it together with all the religious stuff on the lawn, the Mary and Joseph figurines . . . hmm. Maybe not so okay after all. She was reminded of a programme she'd seen on TV once about a strange American cult where everybody inter-married and spent their weekends holding up placards against gay people.

She wished she was more certain about them now. 'He's just gone for a little while, okay?'

Dad's expression was one of controlled alarm. 'Where, Nicola?'

Her chin rose. 'To his father's.'

Chapter Seven

Darren was the baby's name, they'd been instructed in the note. He normally had four bottles a day and porridge for his breakfast (box provided in the baby bag), took size 4 nappies (six provided) and liked to wake up every two hours at night. The last bit they found out for themselves.

'Morning,' said Mossy, exhausted-looking. 'How are you?'

Aisling smiled at him. 'Get the hell away from me.'

She hadn't raised her voice in front of Darren yet, not even last night when there had been killing going on. Children were very receptive to the moods of those around them. Having brought up four of her own, she knew that much. So she kept smiling sunnily, and any threats or expressions of dislike were issued in a *Sesame Street* voice.

'Aisling, this is crazy.' Mossy was flinty-eyed and desperate. 'For God's sake. We have to sort things out.'

Sort things *out*? Aisling was reeling so hard from the note that she felt punch drunk. It was Christmas Eve. They were playing

Bing Crosby on the radio and everything felt surreal, horrible, shocking and amazing all at the same time.

The amazing bit was bright-eyed and banging a spoon off the table energetically. He showed no sign of having been up most of the night, shouting his head off. His round softness filled her lap, and she reached up again – it was a compulsion by now – to stroke his downy little head. There was a piece of her lost already to this strange child, who, it turned out, wasn't a stranger at all. It was just that his place in the family hadn't quite been nailed down yet.

Mossy watched him too. Only there was no oohing and aahing out of him this morning, no patriarchal possessiveness. He was looking at Darren like he was a nappy-wearing bomb. 'You really think he's mine?'

'Well he's not *mine*.'

It was the only thing she knew right now. That and the fact that there was a real baby sitting on her lap, and she was bouncing him up and down on her knee.

'Aisling. Please. Talk to me.'

She supposed she should shout or something. Take a frying pan to the back of Mossy's head. But she hadn't quite taken it in yet. Also, at the back of her mind one thought drummed away: it was all so . . . *unlikely*.

Mossy looked equally confused and wretched, and honestly, it was hard not to believe it was genuine. Or else he was a very good actor. And Aisling could strike that one straight away, because Mossy's great failing had always been his total inability not to call it like it was. Or how he *thought* it was, which was worse.

'Twenty-two years we've been married, Aisling,' he started up again. (She'd heard this last night, about fifteen times.) 'And you think I've been getting my leg over behind your back?'

Stranger things had happened, she told herself. There had been women turning up out of the blue on doorsteps for millennia carrying swaddled bundles and announcing, 'And this is your kid, you bastard,' whilst saying to the poor cuckolded wife, 'I don't know how you put up with that halitosis.'

Aisling wouldn't be the first and she certainly wouldn't be the last.

'That's what the note says,' she said.

'*No it does not.*'

The note, the awful note full of instructions for Darren's care, along with the damning little codicil, was in a kitchen drawer. They should have burned it, built some kind of funeral pyre out the back, and tossed Aisling and Mossy's marriage on to it while they were at it. Instead they'd put it away carefully, 'because we'll only forget what time to feed him in the morning'.

It was difficult to have a good old marital humdinger when you had to keep breaking off to change nappies and mash bananas into a gooey pulp.

She looked at Mossy now, his curly hair standing on end, his brown face drawn with outrage and grief.

'We've had a difficult couple of years,' she told him evenly. 'In a way, I wouldn't blame you.'

She bloody would. She'd lamp him and throw him out on his ear. But if she had to pretend understanding to draw him out, to get some kind of confession out of him, then she would.

Darren could be the kids' half-brother. That was all she could think of as she'd lain awake during the night, listening out for his whimper in the crib at the end of the bed (they'd brought it in from the garden and dusted it off. Mossy, naturally, had been banished to the couch.) He would be nothing at all to her, biologically. Zilch. She found she was both relieved and disappointed.

But Mossy wasn't falling for any trap. 'I don't cheat. Okay? And for you to think even for a minute that I would . . . For God's sake,' he said crossly, 'who'd even have me?'

Aisling did a quick appraisal. He was still a handsome man, if you went for the outdoorsy, slightly battered look. No pattern baldness yet, and all that physical work kept him muscular and strong.

'You've had plenty of opportunity,' she shot back.

'When?'

'I know that certain ladies ring up looking to get their living rooms repainted every six months—'

'Every six months,' Mossy scoffed. 'I should be so lucky.'

'They do. And all so they can watch your backside going up and down those ladders.'

'Says who?' Mossy was incredulous.

'Dave!'

'*Dave?* Tell you what. Why don't you ring Dave up and ask him whether I've been having an affair? Go on. Because you know what the answer will be, don't you?'

'The note, Mossy.'

'Fuck the note.'

Aisling clamped her hands over the baby's ears. 'Mossy!'

'No, are you seriously telling me you're taking the scribblings of some crazy woman over my word? A woman whose name I don't recognise? A woman who didn't even leave her phone number? I mean, come on. If you're going to dump your kid on strangers, at least have the decency to leave some contact details.'

'But we're not strangers. She was handing her baby over to his father. That's what the note said.'

A Special Delivery

'What father?' Mossy shouted, totally exasperated now. 'Who? Show him to me, because it certainly isn't me!'

Aisling calmly reached for the phone. The house phone this time, as Mossy had finally fixed the fuse box at midnight the previous night. But he hadn't switched on any of the Christmas lights. She didn't blame him. The mood was pretty much ruined.

'Ring them, then,' she said, holding it out. 'The guards.'

'What are you talking about?'

'If this baby is nothing to do with you, then we need to hand him over immediately to people who will find his *real* parents.'

Prove it, in other words.

'No problem,' said Mossy, and reached eagerly for the phone. Then, the clincher: 'I hope they don't remember that bloody episode with the hash.'

She knew then that he really would have rung them. Instead of handing over the phone, she put it down.

'Okay,' she said quietly. 'I believe you.'

Mossy said nothing for a while. He turned to look at Darren, now that he could do so again without incriminating himself. 'In a way I wouldn't have minded,' he admitted. Quickly, in case there were any misunderstandings, he clarified, 'He's a handsome lad.'

He was.

'We could never afford another one,' Aisling said. 'Anyway, we're too old.'

'Are you sure about that?' Mossy's eyebrows jumped up. They were almost cheerful, now that the crisis had been averted. 'Mid forties is too old?'

'*Way* too old. For me, anyway. You can go on and have a whole clatter more if you want.'

That sobered them up.

'Maybe if we'd done a better job with the ones we had,' Mossy said.

They looked at each other, the air thick with regret. And Aisling suddenly thought, maybe she should tell him where she went. And not have this awful secret hanging over her.

'Mwah!' Darren piped up, breaking the moment, and she was glad. Tell Mossy? What had she been thinking? He would never understand. Worse, he would go mad.

'Mmum!' Darren was enjoying the attention of two people. He beamed up at Mossy and banged his spoon again for Aisling's amusement. Then he broke wind.

'Nice,' Mossy told him.

Aisling felt she should apologise or something. 'Listen, about thinking you were the father. To be honest, I didn't really believe it for a second.'

'Thanks, Aisling.'

'You know what I mean!'

'Ah, I do.'

They were too sleep-deprived to do any more making-up, so they switched their attention to Darren. No matter how many times Aisling gently brushed his hair down, it sprang back up at the front.

'So what's going on?' she wondered eventually. 'Does she have, like, issues? The mother.'

At the surgery they saw it from time to time. Sometimes it was drugs or alcohol. Or a partner they were afraid of, and they tried to protect the child.

But they'd never come across something like this.

'Maybe,' said Mossy. 'Or else she's confused me with someone else.'

'How could she get the father of her own child mixed up with someone else?'

'I don't know, Aisling.'

It was baffling.

They were changing Darren yet again when there was the sound of the front door bursting opening and Shannon clattered in. She was like a female version of Mossy, except younger, taller and much, much prettier. A walking endorsement for the theory of evolution, in fact. If their children were that good-looking, Aisling often thought optimistically, then their grandchildren would probably be supermodels.

'So it's true,' she breathed, looking at Darren. 'I didn't believe Anto when he texted me that you'd found a baby. But you did.'

'I thought you weren't arriving till tomorrow?' Aisling said, delighted.

'I need a square meal,' Shannon confessed. She looked a bit rough around the edges.

'Too much drinking and student parties, I suppose?' Mossy said hopefully.

'No, I was on the streets last night to raise money for the homeless.'

Of course she was. She'd also asked for six hens for Christmas, for a family in Mongolia or Sudan or somewhere. 'At least you won't have to wrap them,' she'd said to Aisling.

They'd thought it was just a phase, her social conscience, much like Anto's thirty-six-hour stint as a vegetarian back when he'd been fifteen. Every teenager at some point woke up one morning and realised what a racist, sexist, ageist and generally appalling place the world was, right?

'But it usually doesn't last,' Mossy had pointed out.

So they waited for it to pass: her campaign against fur, her drive for a nuclear-free world, her love affair with the elderly, the homeless, the poor, the weak and the endangered whales of Japan. 'When is she going to take on the plight of teenagers who don't get enough pocket money?' Anto often wondered.

Every week Shannon found a new cause to embrace. The rest of the Bradys looked on in morbid fascination from their prone positions on the couch, although occasionally Aisling would help her with a placard for some protest or other. At least it kept her out of trouble, they decided sagely.

Then, as her teenage years progressed and there was no let-up in her mission to improve the world, Aisling began to fret. 'Should we not be encouraging her to get *into* trouble?'

But of course they didn't really know what trouble meant back then, bless them. They thought it was just stealing ancient bottles of Pernod from their drinks cabinet and getting caught in unseemly tussles with the local unsavoury youths before stealing a car or two. Harmless stuff like that.

To their credit, they tried. Mossy left the key to the drinks cabinet in plain view. But to their disappointment, nothing went missing. 'Do you want to, um, go out on the town and refuse to tell us what time you'll be back at?' Aisling had ventured, but Shannon had given her a kind look and said, 'Would you *like* me to, Mum?'

The rest of them went mad, of course. 'She just exists to make us look bad,' Anto fumed once. 'One day she's going to get a job as a stripper and then you'll see.'

'Anto!' Mossy thundered. 'Get up to your room.'

'I rest my case!'

But those outbursts were rare. Shannon might be the best human being any of them knew, but she wasn't stomach-turningly sweet. In fact she could be very sarcastic a lot of the time, and had an annoying habit of pointing out people's weaknesses. Plus, her room, when she used to live there, had always been reassuringly like a pigsty. Capping it all, she was a massive fan of *Top Gear*, which endeared her to Anto no end.

But Mossy and Aisling knew that they were spoiled with her as their firstborn. Cocooned, you might say. Aisling often wondered whether their standards were too high afterwards, and their tolerance lower.

'Do you want a cup of tea?' she offered now. 'Or do you still drink tea? You haven't moved on to organic nettle leaf infusion or anything like that?'

'In a minute,' Shannon murmured, her eyes on Darren.

He'd tensed at the new arrival. He wasn't used to all the people and noise, you could tell that. His big round eyes were alert and his face was all set to cry.

Shannon dropped fluidly to her knees in front of him. She didn't make any 'heLLOOOOO' noises into his face, or give him a merciless dig under the armpit with a bellow of 'Who's got tickles then!' She just ran her finger lightly down his cheek and crooned, 'Hiya, gorgeous.'

Like every other male she'd ever met, Darren fell into the palm of her hand. He gurgled, chuckled, squirmed and generally embarrassed himself under her attention.

'He's got your hair, Da,' Shannon said slyly.

Shannon did too; they all had. And looking at it in this light, it did seem more red than strawberry blonde. But then he turned his head and it looked blonde again.

Mossy shot Shannon a suspicious look. 'Look, I don't know what Anto's told you . . .'

'Just that you're a superstud and have been spreading it around.'

Another glare from Mossy. 'I have not been. The note is obviously some kind of misunderstanding.'

Aisling chimed in firmly, 'Your dad isn't Darren's father, okay?'

Shannon laughed merrily. 'Ah, come on, Mum. You didn't really think for a second that he was?'

She looked so amused that Aisling had a bit of a titter too. Mossy was left to look himself up and down in a defensive fashion and point out, 'I have some ladies ringing me up to get their living rooms repainted every six months, you know.'

'They must be desperate,' said Shannon.

'Where's Matt, then?' Mossy determinedly changed the subject. They hardly ever saw Shannon without her boyfriend Matt following closely behind.

'At his folks' place. Seeing as we're having Christmas dinner here tomorrow.'

Mossy gave Aisling a look. 'I didn't realise we'd invited him.'

Mossy didn't like Matt. He hadn't liked her previous boyfriends Ed and Andrew either. There was nothing wrong with them – decent, hard-working lads, all of them – but it was his duty to dislike them and he did it energetically and enthusiastically. And Matt had a whiff of desperation about him. He was so clearly in love with Shannon, but she'd rather do a two-hundred-mile bike ride for cancer research.

Shannon gave him a look. 'We can have dinner at his parents' instead, if you'd prefer. In fact, I'd quite like it. It's not exactly a laugh a minute around here any more.'

Mossy opened his mouth then closed it again. What could he say? He and Shannon hadn't seen eye to eye for some time now.

'No, have your dinner here. We want you to, don't we, Mossy?'

'Yes,' Mossy said quietly. 'Of course we do.'

A loud 'Waaahhhhh!' filled the kitchen. Darren had suddenly started crying. He looked as surprised by it as everybody else, especially as the fragrant Shannon was still in his proximity.

'I wonder if he's hungry?' Aisling guessed.

He was. The poor little devil was starving and nobody had noticed! They all stood around clucking as he drank a bottle in Shannon's arms. He looked up at her angel face, clearly thinking he'd truly arrived in heaven.

'Poor little fella,' Shannon said, rocking him gently. 'No father who can be identified, and a mother a few sausages short of a barbecue.'

Very well put. Mossy and Aisling nodded vigorously in agreement.

'Anything for breakfast?' Anto strolled in wearing a Chelsea shirt and a pair of striped pyjama bottoms. He acknowledged Shannon with a vague lift of his chin. 'Oh,' he said, taking in Darren in her arms. 'He's still here.'

'Where did you think he'd be? Out with the rubbish?' Aisling enquired.

'And just for the record,' said Mossy, 'I'm not his father, okay?'

'Oh,' said Anto, unperturbed. 'Okay.'

Aisling was a bit worried now about any of this filtering out. The neighbours would have a field day altogether. 'The note didn't name your dad, okay? Not specifically. So I don't want either of you mentioning it to anybody else. We're going to make some phone calls now and hand the baby in.'

'Louise is making him an outfit out of toilet paper,' Anto advised. 'She's going to be upset.' He set about seeing how many cornflakes he could fit into a bowl.

'I'll take her to the shops or something so that she's not here when they come to take him away,' Shannon offered.

'Great,' said Aisling. 'And I suppose we'd better put the note back into the bag. They'll want to read it, the foster carers or whoever he'll end up with.'

She took it out of the drawer.

Shannon came to look over her shoulder to have a read of it. 'She didn't give a second name?'

'No.' It was all a bit strange. 'She's just signed it Nicola.'

Behind them there was the sound of cornflakes spilling to the floor.

Chapter Eight

On a day off school, Anto would normally go back to bed and masturbate. He liked to do that a lot. He'd once made the mistake of telling Baz just how much, and Baz had told the rest of them and now they called him Whacker behind his back. They all seemed to have a constant stream of sexual encounters and casual girlfriends that they bragged about, and didn't seem to need to masturbate. Anto always felt very inadequate around them.

But that morning there was no comfort between the sheets. His willy was shrivelled up and petrified, pretty much like the rest of him. It was like someone had chucked a hand grenade and it had blown up in his face. *I'm trapped in my own personal video game hell!* he realised with horror.

He decided to ring Baz.

'Jesus, man, it's only half past ten,' Baz complained sleepily.

'There's trouble,' Anto blurted.

A silence. Baz sighed. 'What, did he come back?'

'What? No, nothing like that, don't be stupid.' He was sorry he'd phoned now. Baz had only gone and made him feel worse.

'Well you never know,' Baz was saying. 'What with it being Christmas and all. Your old man and lady might have had a change of heart—'

'It's not about that, okay? It's different.' His voice had gone a bit high-pitched and girlie with fright, like it used to do when it was breaking. It had taken three years for it to fully break, and the lads had ripped the piss out of him over it. They still took him off in falsetto voices sometimes. He fought to bring it down a notch. Besides, the last thing he needed was them hearing him downstairs. They were fussing with the . . . the *baby*. He could hardly bring himself to think the word. The whole thing was so crazy that he kept hoping it was just a dream and that Louise would barge in at any moment and yell, 'Ma says get dressed, you big lump.'

'Do you remember a bird called Nicola?' he said hoarsely to Baz.

'Nicola?'

'Yeah.'

'Nicola Ryan?'

Anto shook his head violently. 'No. The other one. With blondey hair.'

'Nicola McCarthy?'

'No!' Anto thought desperately. 'I don't know her second name. She was at that Halloween party last year, came with that Milo bloke.'

Nobody knew whose party it had been. There was just a free house down on the Beacon estate, and word had got round the whole place and about two hundred heads showed up, no kidding. Fucking place was thrashed and it had been a nice gaff too; big, loads of rooms, with separate little parties going on in each.

'Oh yeah, Milo, he's some head-the-ball,' Baz was musing admiringly.

Anto didn't like Milo. Milo had once said to him, 'How're you, Paul?' even though he *knew* his name was Anto.

'Never mind Milo. I'm talking about your one Nicola!'

'Relax, would you? No point taking the head off—' Baz drew in his breath sharply. 'The one you copped off with?'

'Yeah.' Anto felt sick as Baz confirmed his worst fears. He didn't know what he'd been hoping for. Maybe that Baz would declare that Anto had come away from yet another party empty-handed as usual.

'She was a right looker,' Baz breathed, half in disbelief.

In fact none of them had really believed it, not even Anto himself. Like, she'd been *gorgeous*. Loads of hair that kind of tumbled, like you saw in magazines, and she'd been wearing this vampire Halloween dress that was so short you could nearly see her knickers . . . Oh man. They'd spotted her trailing in after Milo; there were three or four girls, all locked and wearing those tiny dresses and with all the hair, but she was *really* locked and the best-looking of the lot. Like everybody else, Anto had looked, but then forgot about her, because girls like her didn't pay attention to lads like him, especially as he had a massive spot on his chin that he'd tried to squeeze earlier and now it had gone nuclear.

But he didn't give a shit. Because he was only there to get locked too. The stuff at home had wrecked his head. For months now it had been bad: some days you wouldn't know what you'd be walking into when you got home from school. But tonight the whole thing had gone mental. Anto was still shaking, his heart racing in his chest with adrenalin. He'd just wanted to leave, to get out. But his ma had stopped him, her face as white as his.

She'd begged him to look after things. She'd pressed some notes into his hand. 'And ask Emma's mother to look after Louise until I'm back.' And she'd been so distraught that Anto had just done it, no questions asked. Besides, his da frightened him, standing there so pale.

They'd knocked back a naggin of vodka at Baz's place, for medicinal purposes, and shared a couple of spliffs, and by the time they'd rolled up at the party, the room was already spinning on him.

The mad thing was, *Nicola* came on to *him*.

It was kind of weird, really. Like, she'd disappeared off with Milo and that gang right after she arrived, and he didn't see her again for hours, until he was coming out of the jacks, still wiping his hands on his jeans, and there she was.

'I've been looking for you,' she said, all husky.

It was nearly dark in the place, just candles everywhere for Halloween, so Anto looked over his shoulder – was she talking to *him*?

It was time for a witty retort. 'Uh, hi,' he'd said.

And then she'd coiled herself around him and just kissed him! No what's-your-name, or do-you-come-here-often. She'd snogged the face off him like she was trying to eat him up.

Anto was flummoxed. Then he gathered himself and kissed her back. All his fears about himself had been wrong all along, he understood in a wild moment of self-realisation. He was irresistible! She couldn't get enough of him, her hands wandering up and down his shirt, then around to cup his buttocks. Holy Mother of sweet divine. Something in his life was finally going right.

Baz, Sean and the lads sauntered by, clutching cans. Their eyes nearly popped out of their heads at the sight of Anto getting lucky.

'Tut-tut! Take it home!' Baz called.

'Fifteen Sylvester Avenue, love!' Sean leered at Nicola, always taking the joke too far.

'Get lost,' Anto retorted excitedly.

They did, reluctantly, still looking back over their shoulders in astonished envy. Anto found it as big a turn-on as the girl's breasts, which were mashed into his chest. He wished now that he'd changed his shirt.

'Sorry about that. What's your name?' he panted. Even though he'd miraculously turned into a superstud, for which he was eternally grateful, he wasn't going to lose his manners on the way.

She drew back, laughed like he was pulling her leg. 'You're funny,' she said.

Was he? Fuck, yeah, he was *hilarious*. So he laughed heartily too, even though he now suspected that he'd crossed the line from being well on into being really, really drunk. Damn anyway. On the one night he'd actually pulled. Even now he was kind of dribbling on her shoulder. Fuck, man. He tried to stand up straight, gather himself together. There was an angel in his arms; he couldn't blow this. He had to sober up.

'You're beautiful,' he cried, and lobbed the gob on her again with renewed gusto.

'Easy.' She put a hand on his chest, stalling him. She was swaying a bit, nearly falling off her huge shoes. She had this intense look about her, kind of dangerous and feral, and normally Anto would have been wary because that kind of girl meant trouble, but then she whispered, 'Come on. Let's find a room. I want us to be close.'

A room! *Thank you, God*, Anto said to the ceiling. The last virgin in the western hemisphere was no more.

He looked around unsteadily to see if the lads were taking in his new street cred. But it was so dark, and they'd disappeared somewhere. Anto decided he didn't care. This was the best night of his life.

If only his stomach would agree. Shite. He was going to be sick. He knew he had to sort that out fast. Imagine spewing up all over this vision in the middle of doing it.

'Gimme a minute,' he said urgently.

He left her there and staggered out the back door. At least he hoped he actually made it out. It was all very blurry at that point. He'd drunk about seven cans of cider on top of the vodka and the spliffs. He leaned urgently against a wall and brought a lot of it back up, convulsing helplessly as it streamed out of his mouth and nose.

'Ah, Jesus!' A couple of guys smoking stood back quickly to avoid getting splattered.

'Sorry. Sorry.' But he was feeling better already. He'd be able to do the business after all. Now, where was she gone? He fought his way back in through the crowd.

'Um . . . honey!'

Well, what else could he call her? Then he spotted Milo, smug git, surrounded by a load of playmates. Anto forgot his antipathy.

'Here, what's her name? The girl who just went past here? Blonde hair?'

'Can't remember,' said Milo, with a look that said, *WAY out of your league, mate*. He was arranging white powder in lines on the telephone table, Anto saw.

But one of the girls piped up, 'Nicola.'

'Thanks,' said Anto.

'Now fuck off,' said Milo, guarding his white powder, 'because you're not getting any.'

Anto pushed his way on through the crowd. He wasn't feeling too good again, but he tried to ignore it. All he wanted to do was sleep. He'd really overindulged. 'Nicola? Nicola!'

There she was! He saw the back of her head as she headed up the stairs through the throng, and he followed, heart swelling with love and trousers swelling with teenage lust.

'Nicola . . . wait for me . . .'

The next thing he remembered was Baz and Sean urgently shaking him awake. 'Come on. The cops are here.'

Anto came to life slowly and painfully to find that the party was emptying out fast. He was lying on the landing, half in and half out of a bedroom. He had no idea how he'd ended up there. One shoe was missing and his clothes were in some disarray. He'd never been this bad before; to have passed out like that. 'Where's Nicola?'

'Who?'

'The girl I was with.'

'Dunno. Let's get out of here, man.'

'Wait, I have to find her.' He peered into the bedroom he was semi-occupying, but there was no sign of her.

Baz shook him again. 'I'm not getting arrested, come *on*. You can text her.'

Except that she hadn't given Anto her number. The most beautiful angel he'd ever met had slipped away. He could still remember her perfume, the softness of her lips . . . Heartbroken, yet strangely triumphant, he staggered out into the night after the lads.

He never heard from her again.

'Once was enough for her, eh?' The group slagging started up almost immediately.

'Fuck off. She'll get in touch. I didn't give her my number either, so it's going to take a few days.'

Which turned into weeks, then months. Anto's new-found machismo took a nosedive. He must have been really crap in the sack. Not that he could remember much about it. Or anything

71

at all, really. His first night of passion and he ended up with serious blackout! It totally sucked. He wondered about those spliffs. They'd tasted a bit funny. What if they were responsible for him forgetting the whole thing?

He set about tracking her down, determined to make their second night together better. But that prick Milo wouldn't answer his calls, and he heard from someone else – a friend of a friend of one of the girls hanging out with Milo – that Nicola had dropped out of school – she was seventeen too, he learned – and that there had been all kinds of trouble at home, something about her ma running off to Australia.

Anto knew all about people leaving and not coming back, so he did her the respect of backing off fast. It had been a lovely interlude, but it was over now as far as she was concerned, clearly. And anyway, he had his own shit going on at home, as usual; the shouting and screaming had stopped, to be replaced by a chill misery. He thought he preferred the shouting and screaming.

He filed Nicola away in his head under Beautiful Memories (no way would he mention *that* to Baz) and returned to masturbation. At least it was reliable and would see him through to the exams, and then . . . well, he wasn't quite sure what would happen then. He'd get a job, maybe, or do an apprenticeship. He might even travel; go to Bali or somewhere and just kick back. The house felt lonely these days. He had no one to confide in any more; to talk shite with or to discuss Chelsea's position in the league. Well, there was his da, he supposed, but he'd gone a bit odd lately. Sometimes Anto would catch him looking at him, almost scared, like Anto was going to turn on him too.

Anto would never do that. But he didn't feel he could talk to him about football either. If he was left in a room with his da, he wasn't sure *what* he'd talk to him about.

And now this. Anto felt like his entire world had just imploded.

'She's after having a baby,' he blurted out to Baz on the phone. 'Nicola.'

'Wouldn't surprise me,' Baz said sagely. 'She'd obviously put out for anyone.'

'It's mine, you gobshite.'

Baz was silenced for once. For a tiny, savage moment, Anto was gratified.

'She dumped the kid on the doorstep with a note saying he's mine.'

Well the note had actually said the father lived in the house. He hadn't given her his name that night either. And she clearly hadn't bothered to find it out through Milo's network of contacts. Anto was still hurt over that, actually.

But back to the baby. Talk about a nightmare. He'd done stupid stuff, he'd acted like an eejit, but he was only seventeen. There shouldn't be *consequences*.

'She could have slept with someone else,' Baz tried.

'Baz,' Anto said heavily. 'The little fucker is the spit of me.'

It was true. There had been something spookily familiar about the child's face all along. He knew his ma had seen it as well. She'd look at him intently, her head cocked to one side, as though trying to work out who he reminded her of. *All* of them, it turned out: he was a Brady, Anto now realised with a dull thud.

And he barely remembered the child's creation. How bad was it that he'd blanked out the only good bit? He was done with weed, he vowed. And cider. Imagine having to confess to his son that he'd been so wasted that he couldn't even remember the act of conception. It was unbelievable. But true, it seemed.

'Bloody hell,' Baz breathed at last.

Anto had never heard Baz being flummoxed before, and it

spooked him even more. 'I don't know what to do, man! I'm barely eighteen! I can't be a . . .' he fought to get the word out – 'father!'

'No, no,' Baz soothed. Then, 'Is she still as good-looking?'

It was unmistakable. The grudging respect. Whacker Brady had only gone and got that Nicola bird up the duff.

'Jesus Christ!' Anto huffed. 'Is that all you can say!'

She was, though. Good-looking. He could have done worse for himself.

Then, fresh words of doom from Baz. 'We've got the exams in six months' time.'

Anto's stomach took a fresh dive. The exams. His ma was going to go pure mental. They were already acting like he was the next great white hope in the family. He was going to follow Shannon to college, blah, blah. They never bloody learned.

'She says in the note that she's looked after him for long enough,' he said to Baz heavily. 'And now it's my turn.'

He'd snuck it out of the drawer when his ma wasn't looking and read it word by word, hands shaking. It was written in purple glitter pen, and looked weirdly like a party invitation. But the words were stiff and cold. *I realise we barely know each other. But we made a baby and now you have to take responsibility too.*

'Have you told the rest of them?' Baz wanted to know.

Sean, Fitzer and Kian, he meant.

'No.' He hadn't even told his *parents* yet. Imagine their surprise. He could hear the baby through the ceiling, grizzling. Then his ma's voice, floating up. 'Sssh.' She sounded gentle. Happy, Anto realised, for the first time in ages.

Well that wouldn't last long.

With a heavy heart, he got off the bed and went down to claim his son.

Chapter Nine

There was a horrible sense of déjà vu about the whole thing. Most sentences started off with 'I can't BELIEVE you were so STUPID . . .'

The reply was, predictably, 'I KNEW you'd be like this, you NEVER listen to anybody else . . .'

Meanwhile, Aisling bopped the baby up and down on her knee in the living room and sang him 'Baa Baa Black Sheep'. When he raised no objections, she followed on with a lively rendition of 'Little Boy Blue'. She still remembered them after all these years, word for word. She drew the line at 'Rock-a-Bye-Baby', though – didn't it have a violent ending, with tumbling cradles and possibly fractured skulls? There was enough aggro in the house today as it was without going hardcore on the lullabies.

'. . . should have known better . . .' the shouting continued in the kitchen. '. . . unprotected SEX . . .'

Aisling got a bit of a jolt at that. Sex? What was that? Oh yes, that thing that people sometimes did, often after a glass or two of wine. There hadn't been any in her own life for a very long time now, unprotected or otherwise. She hadn't been exactly in the mood. Mossy neither. The one time he'd tried to initiate something, a month or two ago – 'before we grow cobwebs', he'd tried to feebly joke – she'd nearly bitten the hand off him.

Aisling felt bad even thinking about her own life, when her son was in desperate, deep trouble. It was depressing to find themselves here again. Christ, was it something she was *feeding* them?

'. . . how old is she, exactly?' Mossy was demanding.

Aisling would be quite interested in the answer herself.

It came swiftly.

'*Seventeen?*' Mossy shouted in astonishment. 'Jesus Christ, Anto!'

Aisling hugged Darren closer. Two parents, both practically children still, and neither of them possessing even the wit to use a condom. It wasn't the greatest start in life.

And to think that they'd thought Anto was so innocent! He used to run away from girls up to recently – literally. Cara Nugent used to come calling for him a year or so back and he'd hide upstairs and hiss, 'Tell her I'm studying.' (As though she was going to buy that.) And all this time he'd been drinking and partying and impregnating young girls behind their backs. Well, hopefully just the one.

Aisling wondered dully at what stage you stopped knowing your own children.

'What age did you think she was going to be?' Anto demanded. 'Thirty-five? You hardly think I go around sleeping with oul' ones!'

Fair point. 'Fair point,' Aisling shouted in.

Mossy poked his head round the door and glared. She wasn't supposed to be on Anto's side. She was supposed to be on *his* side. She knew the drill: if any of the kids suspected even a hint of weakness in the agreed position, then they'd drive a coach and horses through it, or at least a BMX bike. Once that happened, you might as well give up there and then, and hand them money for cheap drink and pole-dancing classes.

Today, she rebelled. Well, she'd been rebelling for quite a while now, but quietly and behind Mossy's back. 'Well, it *is*.'

Anto cautiously followed Mossy in, like a lost puppy in search of a kind word. His eyes avoided the baby. 'Anyway, she must be eighteen by now,' he said hopefully to Aisling. 'She was seventeen when I . . . uh . . .'

'Bonked her on top of a pile of coats?' Mossy thundered. He gave good thunder; Aisling would concede that much. Nobody did it quite as well as him. And he had the eyebrows for it and everything, all bunched up in quivering outrage. 'She'd better have been seventeen, otherwise you could be in real trouble here. Do you know what the age of legal consent is in this country, Anto?'

'Um, seventeen?'

'Don't you get smart with me!'

'I'm not! Jesus, you asked me a question!'

'You could have been up in court! You could have had a record!'

'Sometimes I think you actually *want* one of us to get a record,' Anto said coldly.

Mossy was incredulous. 'You think I enjoy standing here reminding my offspring that they might be breaking the law? I thought you were going to be different, Anto!'

'Yeah? Well it turns out that I'm not,' Anto shouted back.

'Stop. *Please*,' Aisling implored. 'No more fighting. Not in front of the baby, okay? What's done is done. We have to move on from this.'

Mossy gave her a look. So sanctimonious! At the very least they should be permitted a good period of haranguing the offender – in this situation Anto – and a decent post-mortem of his shocking deeds and misadventures. Then, and only then, when he properly understood what a selfish, irresponsible, disappointing and – there was one more; what was it? Aisling racked her brain. Oh yes – immature son he had been, could they move on.

Well, none of it had worked before, so there was no point in doing it again. 'So what are we going to do?' she enquired crisply.

Anto had an unfortunate habit of looking vacant when in fact he was deeply worried. He had that face on now.

'About the baby, Anto,' Mossy prompted heavily.

'I know!'

'Your son.'

There was a little silence at that; the officialdom of it, or something. Anto's Adam's apple gave a violent bob. Even Darren went a bit still in Aisling's lap, and his shoulders seemed to droop. Was that spotty youth in the grubby Chelsea shirt really his old man?

'That's if he *is* yours.'

'Mossy,' said Aisling ferociously. The poor little mite was sitting on her lap. And his supposed grandad was talking about him like he was so much baggage?

But Mossy was adamant. 'No. We have to be certain here before we go any further. The lad says he was drunk. He says he can barely remember any of it.' He looked at Anto now, and appealed to him quietly. 'Do we need to take a DNA test or something?'

They all turned to look at Darren; they couldn't not. Obligingly he lifted his little head and presented them with a perfect Brady profile. Then he gurgled with Anto's mouth, and slapped an

Anto-shaped hand to his wide Brady forehead and pushed back his hair, which seemed to have changed from strawberry blonde to auburn overnight.

'No,' said Anto miserably.

'No,' sighed Aisling and Mossy.

So. It was official. Baby Darren was the firstborn grandchild in the Brady family. As though sensing the weight of expectation upon him, he tried a little smile in Anto and Mossy's direction. He got nothing back.

'Jesus,' Mossy eventually muttered. 'I don't believe this. And on Christmas Eve.'

Anto said nothing. He was white-faced with shock, and fright. He looked very young himself. More like a big brother than a dad. And Mossy looked more like a bad-tempered stranger than a doting grandad.

It was up to Aisling to make things right. Now that they knew Darren's identity – that he truly was theirs – she felt something peculiar sprout inside her. Something fierce and alive, and that she hadn't felt in a long time. Hope, maybe.

'Listen to me,' she said, her voice even and surprisingly loud. 'So none of us expected this. But whatever Anto has done, or this Nicola girl—'

Mossy spluttered; *there* was another selfish, irresponsible, disappointing, etc. And no doubt he would look forward to telling her that too, when he got the chance.

Aisling cut his splutters short. 'Whatever has happened, none of this is Darren's fault. And from now on, everybody is to call him by his proper name. Not "the baby", or "him over there".'

Anto waited. He looked like he was expecting more. The hour-long lecture on how he'd brought shame to the family and ruin upon himself, perhaps (mind you, the bar was already set pretty high). His father was definitely the best at losing the head and having a good old rant, but it was Aisling's disappointment that they feared the most. She knew that the kids discussed 'The Look' – some kind of unblinking way she had of staring at them that made them feel like shit, apparently. She wasn't aware of it herself.

Anto didn't need The Look, she knew. He needed a cup of strong tea ASAP before he collapsed, and something hearty to eat.

First things first, though.

She stood up and hooked a finger at him. 'Come and watch. I think your son needs to be changed.'

'Oh my God, oh my God, oh my GOD.' Louise couldn't stop shrieking when she heard the news. 'So we get to keep him? For Christmas?'

'I suppose,' said Aisling.

'Seeing as the child hasn't got any better offers,' Mossy said sourly. At Aisling's look, he reluctantly corrected himself. 'Darren, I mean.'

'*Darren*, though? Seriously?' Louise looked at them. 'Can we not call him something else?'

'No!'

'Jared, maybe. Or Orlando. He looks just like an Orlando,' she pleaded.

'We're not calling him Orlando, okay?' Anto snapped. 'Ma, can you stop her pawing him like that? He doesn't like it, okay? And take that stupid hat off him. He's too young for a baseball cap.' Especially as it was pink.

Louise sulkily took the hat off Darren. 'I was just trying to look after him. Seeing as you're not going near him. You keep looking at him like he's going to bite you.'

It was true that Anto was standing in the farthest reaches of the kitchen. He'd watched the changing of Darren's nappy, and then he'd escaped upstairs as fast as he could to get dressed. It was going to take time, Aisling knew, for him to get his head around the situation. She hoped she had the blooming energy to teach him.

It was Shannon who saved the day. 'I'm an auntie! I can't believe it. So are you, Louise.'

'Am I?' Louise wasn't sure about this. It didn't sound as great as being a sister.

'Yes.' Shannon was definite. 'And it's our job to spoil this little guy rotten. We're allowed to take him shopping, dress him up in cute clothes and take him to McDonald's when he's old enough.'

'I suppose,' said Louise, no doubt thinking of the spin-off benefits for herself.

'This is really great, Anto,' Shannon enthused. 'I'm delighted for you. Obviously it'd have been better had you waited ten years, but hey, nothing's perfect. Darren is gorgeous and he'll make you very proud.'

Anto stood up a bit straighter. 'Yeah?'

Mossy was sighing heavily. 'Don't be encouraging him, for God's sake, in case he goes off and has another one.'

Shannon eyed him. 'And why not? It might bring a bit of happiness back into this house again. Unless you don't want that either?'

'Having unwanted kids when you're practically a kid yourself isn't the route to happiness, Shannon.'

'Do you ever hear yourself, Da? Really hear yourself?' Shannon marvelled.

'What do you want me to say, Shannon? Yeah, go on, get

smashed every weekend! Have loads of kids that you can't look after with people you barely know. Is that what you want me to say?'

'Imagine having Anto as a da!' Louise piped up. Then, 'How do you make babies anyway?'

Anto groaned in mortification. Because she was the youngest, they often forgot she was there, and she probably heard far more than she should, including arguments.

'You're too young to know,' Shannon told her gently.

'I'm not. Emma says that there's no such thing as the stork, that babies come from an egg that the daddy has to break open with something.'

Anto couldn't help himself. He tittered. It was nerves, Aisling knew. And in a way she didn't blame him. But it was the final straw for Mossy, who was already clearly feeling that nobody was giving the situation the gravity it deserved.

'Think it's funny, do you?' he roared. 'You, who's created this mess because you couldn't control yourself like a normal person? You're after throwing your whole life away, you bloody fool, do you realise that?'

'Mossy.' Aisling had to stop him. Anto had gone very still. And Louise was looking frightened.

'Don't do this again, Da,' said Shannon.

'Do what?' Mossy turned on Shannon now. 'Expect a bit of decent behaviour from my children? Well I do. And I'm not going to apologise to you or to anyone else for that.'

'Ma, say something to him. He can't go off on one every time someone in this family puts a foot wrong.' Shannon was outraged. And now Aisling was being judged too, for sitting there and saying nothing; for not leaping to the defence of her kids.

She was suddenly furious. Everything was so simple to Shannon:

if you loved people and afforded them enough tolerance and time, then it would all be fine.

Well sometimes it wasn't. Aisling had learned that. Besides, she *did* stand up for her kids, in ways that Shannon didn't know. Not even Mossy knew.

'Take Darren out for a walk, please, Shannon.' This time she actually did The Look. And it had the desired effect. 'And Louise too.' She took Louise's little face in her hands and plonked a reassuring kiss on her nose. She had to be protected in all this.

With a final disgusted look back at her parents, Shannon bore Louise and Darren out the door.

'Now,' said Aisling. Her heart was beating fast. She had to handle this right. 'We're going to sit down and discuss this like adults.'

'No we're not,' Anto shouted. 'All he wants to do is preach!'

'Why, because I have the nerve to point out your mistakes?' Mossy started up again. 'My God, Anto, have you learned nothing?'

'Have *you*?'

'Lads!' said Aisling. She brought her palms down on the table hard. The smack of them hitting the wood shut them up abruptly. 'Now,' she went on, more quietly. 'We need to think this thing through. You're eighteen years old, Anto. You have to think of your future.'

Mossy curled a look at Anto. 'Maybe you were right. What *is* the point in studying for your exams? Because you'll hardly need them now, will you?'

'Yes he will,' said Aisling.

'You really think he's going to go to university like his sister?'

'Oh not bloody Shannon again!' Anto howled.

'She's going to get a decent job. But you? You'll be stuck digging drains or carrying boxes around a warehouse because now you have a kid to support. Yes. And they're expensive. Every pair of shoes, every doctor's visit, you'll have to shell out for it. That girl Nicola, she'll make sure of that.'

Aisling could see that all this was freaking Anto out. Baby shoes? Doctor's visits? It was a far cry from FIFA with Baz. 'We don't know what's going to happen yet on that front.'

'I'm just saying. A baby is a massive commitment.' He fired another look at Anto, who wasn't doing himself any favours by chewing furiously on a hangnail. 'And don't think for a second that your mother and myself are going to support him for you.'

'I didn't,' Anto said dully. 'I know better than to count on you for anything.'

Aisling's heart felt pierced. 'You *can* count on us. You know that. Isn't that right, Mossy? It's just a lot for us to take in, that's all.'

Anto buried his head in his hands. A despairing 'shite' drifted out from the depths of his hoody.

Mossy took this as his cue to administer another dose of reality. 'One of the things about growing up, Anto,' he began, ignoring the groan that came from the hoody, 'is learning to take responsibility for yourself. This lad Darren here – he's your son. And you're going to have to face up to it.'

It was all too much for Anto, Aisling could see: Darren, them, disturbing talk of digging drains. And he hadn't had any breakfast either, not even those cornflakes, which were still scattered on the floor. His blood sugar levels must be critically low.

He stood up and gave his parents a scathing, blameful look. 'And what if I don't? Or let me guess. You'll throw me out too?'

He watched the devastation land on their faces. Then he turned and left.

Chapter Ten

I *heard something about a baby!* Zofia texted. *True or fake?*
      True. And it's true or false.

Thank u! Language tips always welcome! But the baby. Anto's?

Yes. 😞

He is so young. 😊

Then: *Sorry. Didn't mean* 😊. *On bus home and elbow jolted. Meant this.* 😞

Thank you, Zofia. Murder at home.

Then, in case Zofia called the cops: *Not literally. Mossy in terrible state.*

Like before?

Worse, maybe. Only time will tell.

I come over with bottle of wine? xxx

No. It's okay.

For me, I mean. Olaf's mother is already driving me 😔.

Sorry. But can't. I am going.

You are not! This evening?

Yes. Am nearly there.

Not a good idea. You will be too sad and confused, with so much trouble at home. Leave it till after Christmas. xx

Aisling simply texted back: *I need to.* Then she turned her phone off.

It was starting to turn dark. Dusk was best. It was easier to blend into shadows, to walk along unnoticed in the Christmas Eve crowd. She was in the centre of town. As always, she wore a big coat. She had no idea why. It just made her feel more invisible or something. But she caught sight of herself in a shop window and got a fright. How had she thought it was a good idea to attempt to go incognito in a voluminous green coat and a pink woolly hat? The hat belonged to Louise. Another attempt at disguise. She grabbed it off her head and stuffed it into her pocket. Maybe she was losing her touch.

She had a new address. There was such a lot of moving about, it seemed. She didn't know whether it was an attempt to shake her off. But she was dogged. Each time it happened, she managed to worm the address out of unsuspecting old housemates, and once from an envelope that had been sitting in the hall and that had a handwritten forwarding address. 'Cunning,' Zofia had breathed when she'd told her this. 'And manipulative. *Very* manipulative.' But what else could she do?

The new place was in a better area, marginally. More out of town, away from the narrow streets and run-down flats she'd had to hang around at first. She had on uncomfortable shoes, though, and her feet began to hurt. She hadn't wanted to stop to change them at home, in case Mossy wondered why. Anyway, she'd been desperate to get out of the house, away from him, away from Anto and beautiful Darren even. It was all too much. She was so fragile that when a stranger brushed against her shoulder as he passed by, it felt like a blow.

A Special Delivery

She walked for maybe fifteen minutes, checking the piece of paper off against street names. Eventually she found it. It was an older house, two-storey over basement, and not very well kept. But at least there were curtains on the windows this time. It was let in flats; there was a line of buzzers by the front door, numbered from one to six. Six flats, shoehorned into this building. They must be tiny. She looked up, already worried about fire regulations, and wondering which one it would be. There was a dim light upstairs; it looked like a hallway light.

At the sound of voices approaching she stepped back clumsily into the shadows by the bins. It wouldn't do to be seen.

It was a couple, carrying Tesco bags, and they were speaking in a language she didn't understand. Not Polish; she would recognise that. Chinese, she realised, as they walked in past her and up the stone steps to the house. Students, probably. The boy opened the door with his key and ushered the girl in before him. She said something and he laughed.

It was a lovely sound. It was also the loneliest sound in the world to Aisling tonight.

She waited for two hours in the dark by the bins but nobody else came or went. Eventually she walked up the stone steps and put down the gift bag that she'd brought with her. It probably wouldn't last five minutes in this area. But maybe any potential robber would look inside and decide that there was no resale value in a mountaineering book for experienced climbers. She'd put in a Christmas card too. She'd agonised for half an hour over what to write. In the end she'd just said, 'Happy Christmas'. Before sealing it she'd slipped in two hundred euros in ten-euro notes.

She gathered her enormous green coat around her for warmth, and turned for home.

Chapter Eleven

Nicola was lucky the guards weren't called in. It was a very serious thing to have done, VERY serious. No, they understood that perfectly. But the child was safe and sound, and all things considered it was probably best to keep it in the family, so to speak, if everybody was agreed . . .? She was just a bit tired, you see, what with having sole care of a baby so young, all that responsibility and pressure . . . No, nobody was blaming the Bradys, there was no question of that. They hadn't *known*. Nobody had. Nicola's father was only learning the parentage of the child today himself. She'd refused to say until now. It was a very unfortunate situation, both of them so young . . . (Dad's voice dropped here to a murmur on the phone) and as for little Darren . . . but the two families would just have to pull together . . .

Nicola, her hangover hammering at the base of her skull, strained to hear from her position on the stairs. He was probably discussing what a waste of space his daughter was, and that guy Anto. She must stop thinking of him as 'that guy Anto'. He was the father of her child. The only boy she'd ever been with,

88

properly. She'd thought it was wonderful. She'd thought she had met her soulmate that night. But he hadn't even sent her a lousy text afterwards.

Hadn't even sent her one *now*, after she'd left his child on his doorstep. It just went to show how wrong you could be about a person.

But then again, he hadn't known she was pregnant. She'd grudgingly give him that. But that was all.

Anto. She found it hard to get used to it.

'It's done.' Dad was standing before her, the phone in his hand, his whole body stiff with stress.

'Who did you speak to?' Nicola was fearful. She knew she'd done a terrible thing. She had given her baby away. It was just that she wasn't able to *feel* it yet. Everything was kind of numb.

A proper mother wouldn't behave like that. They'd be wailing and gnashing their teeth, and their nipples would be spouting breast milk, fountain-style, with all that separation anxiety. She'd read about it somewhere. Her own breasts were resolutely small and dry. She hadn't breastfed. Hadn't been remotely tempted to. The whole thing really, right from pregnancy to birth and beyond, was like it was happening to someone else; she felt that removed from it. And now here she was, sitting in her own living room, her baby miles away with a crowd of strangers, and she felt nothing except the dull pain that had moved from under her breastbone and settled in her stomach.

Which just went to prove it again: she wasn't like normal mothers.

'The father. I mean, the grandfather.' Dad looked at the phone, as though to ensure it was turned off. It was probably from his job. He wore a microphone on air and there wasn't a presenter on this earth who hadn't been caught out saying, 'Fucking crap interview, that!' while the mic was still live. Except for her dad, of course. His biggest sin had been murmuring aloud at the end of a piece, 'I think we can cut it there, Petey.' Talk about shocking the nation.

'His name is Mossy. He seemed like an okay sort. A bit excitable, but otherwise okay.' He looked at her. 'Given the circumstances.'

Nicola knew she should apologise. But she wasn't sorry. And that was the truth.

They sat in silence for a bit. Darren's stuff was all around the place. Dad leaned down to pick up a cuddly toy, a blue hippo, one of Darren's favourites. Nicola watched as he clutched it hard in his hands, as if for comfort, and it told her all she needed to know.

'You should have been straight with me before, Nicola,' he said at last. 'I already knew it was a one-night stand. So why didn't you give me his name until now? The Brady family' – he held up the phone for emphasis – 'they seem decent enough. They're not shirking their responsibilities, are they? And neither is this lad Anto. He got a right fright, mind you, a baby landed on him like that. All of it could have been avoided had you included everyone from the beginning.'

He looked bewildered by the events of the past two days. But it was the story of his life. Every time he turned round, another member of his family seemed to have disappeared. Nicola felt desperately sorry.

'What are they going to do?' she asked.

'With Darren, you mean?' Dad's look was chilly. It was worse than his anger. 'Well, what did you think they would do, Nicola? When you left him in their garden and walked off?'

She didn't really know. She hadn't thought too far into the future. She'd just acted in the moment. Darren would be handed over to the other side of the family and they would take care of him somehow.

But supposing they decided to do something mad, like have him fostered? That wasn't what she'd had in mind at all. She felt the stirrings of panic set in.

'They've agreed to keep him for Christmas,' Dad said, to her relief. 'They want to. They'd like to get to know him better.'

She felt the full weight of his judgement. They wanted him but she didn't.

'I just need a break, Dad.' It seemed so reasonable in her head, but it came out sounding self-centred and weak. But she had to make him understand. It wasn't just her flipping out. She truly, honestly felt that Darren shouldn't spend a moment longer with her. Nor her with him. It wouldn't be good for either of them at the moment.

'To go out drinking and picking up more lads?'

Fresh shame reddened her cheeks, as her hangover hurt more. 'I just went out with the girls. I didn't pick up anybody, okay? I don't do that kind of thing.'

'But you did once before,' he said flatly.

'Yes, but . . .' She wanted to say *That was different*, but it had turned out not to be after all.

'Will I go out for chips?' Becky offered anxiously.

'No, you're all right.'

'You had a right skinful last night. Go on, it'll be soakage, you'll feel better after it.'

'I can't, I'm a tub of lard as it is.'

The girls went into a flurry of reassurance. 'You are not! Stop that right now, Nicola O'Sullivan. You're just after having a . . .' Anxious looks flew between them. Best not mention the baby, in case it upset her. 'Your muscles are stretched. That's all.'

'You'll bounce back into shape in no time at all, you'll see,' Mikaela bolstered her.

Dad had reluctantly admitted them when they'd come round to 'see if you're all right, like'. It was bad enough she'd got pissed and snogged that horrible guy in the club, but when they'd heard what she'd done with Darren . . .! Dad had told them downstairs, apparently, and he hadn't put any gloss on it either, judging by the looks the girls were giving her and each other. It was one thing being tired and fed up and all that, but to leave your little fella in a garden like that . . . *They* wouldn't have done it, either of them.

But then again Nicola had been a bit off the rails since her mother had left. She knew that was the general consensus amongst the gang. Last year someone from school had sent around a list on email, with made-up yearbook entries, like they did in American high schools. Nicola had won two titles: 'Most Likely to Appear on Jerry Springer', and 'Most Likely to End Up on Welfare'. Becky had threatened to track down the writer and knock him or her into next week. Nicola had laughed it off. What else could she do? It was her only defence. And maybe it was a little bit true.

But it had made her more secretive and tight-lipped about her life. She hadn't even told Mikaela and Becky, her best friends, that she was pregnant. They'd found out in the shopping centre one Saturday afternoon, when they were trying on debs' dresses for the crack. Becky had poked her head into Nicola's cubicle, and her eyes had popped and she'd gone, 'Nicola . . . oh my God!' And Nicola had looked down at her rounded naked stomach too, as though seeing it for the first time, and she'd burst into hysterical tears. Mikaela had swiftly joined them from the cubicle across the way and bawled her head off too in solidarity.

'Oh my God, oh my God!' they'd all wept, huddled together in the cubicle, all of them bedecked to various degrees in pastel frilly frights.

'What are you going to do?' Becky had sobbed.

'I don't know, I don't know!' As if there was a damn thing she *could* do, at nearly five months pregnant.

'Have you been to the doctor?' Mikaela wanted to know.

Nicola shook her head. 'I haven't even told my dad yet.'

He hadn't noticed. Not even when he'd walked in on her when she was wearing only a tight vest. He looked at her all the time, but he never really saw her.

More sobbing. This was *terrible*.

Then, the inevitable question. 'Who's the father?'

They knew she didn't have a boyfriend, not since that thing she had going with Jamie Ross, and that had been over ages. And she definitely hadn't slept with him, even though he'd relentlessly bugged her to.

Nicola swallowed back tears. 'Just some bloke, okay?'

'When?' Becky's eyes were sharp.

So was Nicola's voice. 'It doesn't matter when.'

Becky broke the awkward silence with a renewed bout of 'Oh my God!' and in the end the shop assistant had to ask them to keep it down because they were disturbing the other customers.

She'd told Dad that night. He hadn't screamed or shouted, which actually would have been okay. He just looked even more tired and beaten than usual.

'Who's the father?'

'Just some guy,' she repeated.

'Some *guy*?'

'Yeah. I was seeing him briefly, okay?' One night, to be exact. But even so, she'd connected so fully with him, or so she'd believed, that it had felt like they'd known each other much longer. She couldn't admit to her dad that she'd so foolishly given away her heart like that, and ended up with nothing in return except for an unwanted pregnancy, and so she lied, disparagingly, 'He says he doesn't want anything to do with it.'

'He doesn't have any choice, Nicola. He's the father.'

'I'm not going there, okay?' Nicola said fiercely. 'He has nothing to do with this baby. And if you keep pushing me, I'll walk out that door and go and live with Becky. Her mum says I can.'

Becky's mum would have had a canary. But it did the trick because he was silenced.

He'd gone with her to the school to see the principal the following morning to discuss her options. It had been mortifying. Her sitting there bursting out of her uniform, and the three of them trying to ignore the last scandal that had enveloped the family, involving her mother and the patio guy.

'We'll support Nicola in every way we can,' the principal kept saying, without actually giving any specifics of what this support might involve.

'A couple of days off for the birth maybe,' Nicola said on the way home in the car. But Dad didn't see the funny side and they drove home the rest of the way in silence.

She tried getting on with school, she really did. And Becky and Mikaela were great, telling everybody who looked in her direction to fuck off. But in the end she couldn't hack it: the looks, the pointing fingers, the whispers of 'Who's she having it for anyway?'

She began answering them back. 'The patio guy,' she told one group solemnly. 'A balding judge,' she told another. Depending on what mood she was in, she was pregnant by a visiting celebrity, a homeless man or one of her dad's TV friends who was married with six kids. Dad had nearly had a kitten at that; did she want them both to end up getting sued?

Then one morning she just didn't go in. She stayed in bed the whole day, looking at the wall and listening to the silence in the house. The baby kicked and moved in her belly like some alien thing.

When Dad came home from work he sat down on the side of her bed for the longest time.

'Ah, Nicola,' he eventually said. 'What are we going to do at all?'

She knew he wasn't just talking about the baby, but also this sad little unit that they'd become, cast off and left behind.

There had been a chance that day, maybe. They could have said, 'You know something? Let's just move on. We have to. It's a bloody great mess, but we'll just have to manage.'

But neither of them did. Maybe everything was still too fresh. Maybe they were just too different. And after a while her father got up and said, 'At some point we're going to have to tell your mother.'

'No.'

'Nicola. You've dropped out of school and you're having a baby. We can't keep that from her.'

'If you tell her, she'll only think it's some way of trying to get her to come back.' She sat up in bed, fast despite her bulk, and said fiercely, 'And it's not, okay?'

Her mother had been gone six months by then. She'd phoned and written and emailed incessantly. Guilt, of course. Nicola had tried, mostly successfully, to avoid engaging. Her mother wanted her to go out for a visit. She bought a ticket and every-thing. *I miss you, Nicola*, she'd written in the accompanying note. Nicola had refused point-blank to go. What would she be doing out in Sydney in a pub called The Rotten Spud, with Mum and her fancy man?

Besides, Dad needed her at home.

He was still friends with her mother. Amazing, really. Or that was what it sounded like to Nicola; he was always on the phone to her, giving it loads of 'Oh, hello there, Eleanor, no, this isn't a bad time at all.' She didn't know how he stomached it. Why couldn't he say 'Get lost, you slag' down the phone, like any other self-respecting bamboozled husband? The patio guy. Come *on*.

Sunday morning was their routine. Dad put Darren on his knee and they Skyped Australia, and Nicola would hear her mum say, in an emotion-filled voice, 'Oh, he's got another tooth! Hello, pet! I can't *wait* to see you properly when I'm over in the summer.' Then: 'Where's Nicola, is she not going to say hello?'

When would she get it? Nicola never said hello.

It was time to square things with the girls, now that it was all going public. And they loved Darren too, in their own way. They deserved to know who he was with right now. 'Listen,' she said. 'The baby's father is Anto, okay?'

The name still sounded strange on her lips. The thing was, she'd been doing her trick that night of not giving her real name. Because it was Halloween, she'd told him that she was Morticia. 'Oh *really*,' he'd said, laughing. 'I guess that makes me Freddy Krueger.'

It was disappointing to discover that his real name was Anto, and not something a little sexier like Adam or Sebastian.

Puzzled looks from the girls. *Anto?* They were clearly thinking the same.

'From that party we went to with that bloke Milo that night?' Nicola coaxed them along. 'You were into him,' she reminded Becky.

'Oh yeah.' *Now* they remembered.

'Milo?' said Becky disparagingly. 'He's a total cokehead.'

But back to business. 'Anto? Was he that guy you were tight with in the kitchen?' said Mikaela. 'He was really good-looking.'

Yeah. Big, tall, tortured. That had been her first impression in that dark house that night. And beautiful. James Dean beautiful. They'd just looked at each other and, without being dramatic about it, it was like they had created their own force field. They were just the same, she knew in that instant. And she didn't even *believe* in any of that stuff. She was tough; she'd had to be. But she lost herself that night, and as they lay down on that bed together, her only thought had been *I'm not alone any more.*

But then she'd woken up and he was gone, and the cops were arresting people and everybody was legging it out of the place. She'd gone home with Becky and Mikaela and she'd waited to hear from him, because when he'd gone to the toilet after they'd slept together, she'd scrawled her number on a little piece of paper and stuck it into the pocket of his jeans, pushing it right down where he couldn't lose it.

She was embarrassed now. Angry at herself for being so taken in.

'He was only all right,' she said.

'He was *gorgeous*.' Becky was excited now. She was always looking for the glamour in any situation. 'Didn't you say afterwards that he was an artist?'

Piss artist, more like. 'No. I don't know what he did.' It sounded a bit daft, that she'd slept with someone without even knowing the basics. But they hadn't really got into the whole and-what-do-you-do stuff? They'd already known the important things about each other, if that didn't sound too icky.

Or so she'd thought.

Afterwards, when she didn't hear from him, she was upset. Then she was angry. Fifteen Sylvester Avenue, that was where he lived; she remembered his mate shouting that at her. But there was no way she was going around there like some pathetic groupie. In the end she banished him to the back of her mind, like she had her mother.

And then she discovered she was pregnant. She should have gone round and told him. Or written him a letter or something, if he was that anxious to avoid her. But then she thought, *Why?* After the way he'd treated her, she didn't owe him anything.

It was her little bit of revenge, in a way.

'Will you see him again?' Mikaela wondered.

'Well, yeah. If he's the father,' Becky interjected crossly. 'She'll be seeing him all the time from now on.'

Nicola hadn't reckoned on that. She wasn't sure she liked it. 'I don't know what's going to happen yet.'

'But it's Christmas Day tomorrow,' Becky chattered on. 'You'll be going over to see Darren, right? With all his Santa presents.'

The Santa presents. Shit.

'Oh, bring him this for me, will you? I got it in Mothercare for him, isn't it so cute?'

Pleased as punch, Mikaela produced a glove puppet in the form of a sheep, and put on her hand. She made it open and close its mouth. 'Baa, baa. Look at me, I'm sheepish! Baaaaa!' She looked at them and stopped. 'What?'

'You're a right fucking freak, aren't you?' Becky said.

And they creased up laughing. Nicola needed it. They all had a go with the sheep, making funny noises. Then Becky pretended the sheep was Murph, begging Mikaela to go to Wicklow with him – 'I can't wait to get my paws on your shapely bottom, mnom, mnom . . .' – and Nicola doubled up with mirth. Then Becky pretended to be Mikaela's ex, begging Mikaela for a blow job – 'Go on, I heard you were the best in the business' – until eventually Mikaela got into a huff.

'You're making me out to be a right slag, going around giving everybody BJs.'

'Ah, we're not. Come on. It was just a joke.'

'If anyone's a slag around here, it's Nicola. Getting off with that creep from the club last night after dumping her own kid in someone's garden! How sick is that?'

There was a flat silence.

'Jesus, I'm sorry, Nicola. I didn't mean that. I'm an eejit.'

'It's okay,' said Nicola.

After all, what she had said was only the truth.

Chapter Twelve

Amazingly, they got through Christmas Day.

Neighbours and family flooded round in the morning, as per tradition, for a Christmas drink and, this year, to admire Darren.

'Oh-oh-*oh*,' Zofia crooned ecstatically. '*Mala scwinka*,' she kept murmuring. 'You are such a *mala scwinka*!'

'That's Polish for little piggy,' Olaf explained. 'A pet name. I think her grandfather used to call her that.'

'Come here to me, *kotku*.'

'Kitty or kitten,' Olaf translated.

'You little *schnookums*! You *poopie-doopie*!'

'Those she just made up.'

Louise, who was on standby with a selection of rattles, brushes and bibs, was looking blacker and blacker. Darren was theirs; why did they have to invite all these people over to *share* him? Zofia was taking the biscuit altogether.

'Congratulations,' Olaf said, pumping Anto's hand vigorously. He handed over a small gift-wrapped present. 'It is just something small. Usually we give a gift for the baby's christening. We did not know if Darren had been christened yet or not . . .?'

'Neither do I, pal,' said Anto helplessly.

'Where's Magda?' Aisling looked around for Olaf's mother. They'd invited her over too.

Olaf's mouth turned down. 'She wasn't feeling too good. The carp I got maybe wasn't that fresh.'

Zofia smiled brightly. 'But nobody else got sick.'

'You know my mother has a weak stomach,' Olaf informed her.

Aisling's mother Jane was the next to arrive, with cries of 'Happy Christmas!' and a scattering of shop-wrapped glitzy presents. 'Yours is a book on birth control,' she told Anto, smartly.

'Leave him alone, Mum,' Aisling said.

'You do realise,' she said, 'that this makes me a great-grandmother?'

'I suppose it does.'

For years her mother had managed to hang on to a certain girlish youthfulness through ruthless dieting and dyeing her hair a startling blonde, like something from *The Golden Girls*, but now she declared, 'I might as well give up and let it all hang out.'

'Good woman.' Aisling handed her a glass. 'Let's start on the mulled wine.'

'Oh no, I couldn't, I have to go to Mass . . . All right, a small one then.' Another thought struck her. 'If I'm a great-grandmother, then you're a *grandmother*! At forty-four!'

Somehow that hadn't occurred to Aisling. Well, it had, but now it really hit home that Anto had only gone and aged her by about twenty years.

She shot Anto a glance: thanks a lot, buddy. He looked back, his chin up as he tried to remain defiant. But underneath it all he was soft. He was already sorry for his part in the row the previous evening. At some point he would approach Aisling and touch her lightly on her arm, which was his way of making up without losing face.

'Don't tell anybody,' her mother urged. 'Say the baby is yours when you're out and about. Nobody will question it; people are having babies into their fifties now, God help them. Donor egg thingies.' Her brow bunched worriedly. 'They're not thinking things *through*, though. All those broken nights. The blasted teething and the foul nappies and the tantrums. I don't mind telling you, I didn't enjoy it the first time round and I wouldn't be up for it again.'

'We won't be asking you to babysit Darren then?'

'No,' said her mother promptly. 'Where *is* he anyway? Are you absolutely certain he's Anto's?' She craned her neck to see past the crowd. 'Oh,' she said resignedly, upon spying Darren's sturdy little Brady face. 'Aisling,' she sighed, 'why do none of them ever look like you?'

It was true. They all had the stamp of Mossy on them; strong, with broad open faces and auburn hair. Aisling had got no look-in at all. But her mother always acted like this was Mossy's fault; much like the way he'd persuaded Aisling to marry him when she was only twenty-two. 'Twenty-two! Sure you barely know yourselves, never mind each other!' she had said.

'We know each other well enough.' Aisling had been untouched by her mother's concerns. From the moment she'd looked up and seen Mossy outside her bedroom window, a vision on a ladder in a tight torn T-shirt and brandishing a paintbrush, she'd known he was for her. (Her mother had never asked him to paint her house since.)

It hadn't helped that in the early years of their marriage Mossy had little to his name except a van and a disconcerting ability to impregnate Aisling on a regular basis. 'We can't afford a television, you see,' he was forever winding Jane up, 'so we just go to bed early instead, if you get my meaning.'

He must have known she was thinking about him. He turned and gave her a look across the Christmas crowd. *Sorry about losing the head last night.* But it wasn't a *sorry* sorry. It was more a *sorry-but-someone-had-to-say-it* sorry.

She looked back. *Take the mince pies out of the oven, idiot.*

Her mother was looking around the gathering again now, gossipy. 'And where's the new mother? I suppose I'd better meet her. Let her know that while I like babies, it's only for an hour at a time and *never* without prior appointment.' She gave a bit of a cackle.

'She's not here. Apparently she's had some kind of meltdown or something. Mossy spoke to the family. She needs a bit of a break.' Aisling tried to be sympathetic. But what kind of person went and left a baby out in the cold in December? Seriously? Already she felt a little grain of hardness towards this girl who would give up her own child like that, when other people would give anything, their own lives, even, to have theirs back.

'Anyway,' she said, 'we only have him for a few days until she sorts herself out.'

'Well that's great!'

'At least *try* and be diplomatic, Mum.'

'Look, love, I'm not against him. He seems like a lovely little lad. And very happy in himself. It's just . . .' Her face was full of concern. 'Don't you think you have enough going on in your life?'

Yes. She did. It was a rhetorical question.

Her mother leaned in. 'Did you go?' she hissed.

She nodded. 'Yesterday.'

'And?'

Aisling bit her lip hard, and gave her head a little shake. 'Nothing.'

Her mother's face fell. 'It's a busy time,' she tried. 'People are out. Socialising, Christmas parties. If you like, I could try going sometime.'

'No, no.' It was bad enough her going. If Mossy discovered that her mother was going too, well, it really would be a knife in the back.

'But I might have more luck.' She squeezed Aisling's arm. 'I might be able to get through.'

Aisling welled up. She couldn't help it. The tears were close to the surface today, what with it being Christmas. She'd already had a little cry up in the bathroom, and Darren had looked up at her from his place on the mat like he'd never seen anybody cry before. Maybe he hadn't, in that beige world he'd come from. And somehow that didn't sit right with her either, so she'd given him a good look at her swollen red eyes and her runny nose. Call it a life lesson. Then she'd smiled to let him know that she would survive it.

'I think we should leave it a while,' she said, having no intention of doing so.

'That's not a bad idea. Give everyone a decent cooling-off period.'

But that was what Aisling feared. It had been over a year now. Things had already gone stone cold; the more time that passed, the more hardened people's hearts became.

'Time to open the presents!' Louise announced loudly. She clearly saw a chance to dislodge Darren from Zofia's knee. Unsurprisingly, he had the biggest pile of stuff in front of him of anybody. Not only had the Bradys staged a last-minute raid on the local toy shop, but Nicola had left a big bag of presents on the front lawn amongst the remains of the nativity scene, which seemed to have become some kind of swap shop for her – a baby today, a pile of toys tomorrow.

Aisling had wondered whether they should leave something back out there for her – a bottle of perfume or some chocolates, just to say . . . what? Happy Christmas? Hope you feel better soon?

Except that she didn't really know how Nicola felt. She didn't even know what she looked like. The toys she'd left for Darren were a bit like Darren's clothes: anaemic and lacking in personality. She'd obviously tried hard – there was a lot of stuff, and none of it cheap – but you wouldn't know what kind of a child Darren was from those toys. Or Nicola either.

As though reading her thoughts, Darren turned to look at her. He was being bounced violently up and down on Zofia's lap, while Louise had hold of one of his hands and wasn't about to let go. Wide eyes stared beseechingly into Aisling's: *For God's sake, rescue me.* He flung out a chubby hand in her direction to underline the expression.

Aisling felt something close to panic. She could not get too attached to this baby. He was going home in a few days, and who knew when they would see him again? This Nicola girl was so volatile that anything could happen. Her poor old heart was bashed around enough as it was; she couldn't risk it taking another hit.

She turned away from him, and his little hand fell.

They held off dinner until Shannon arrived back at three o'clock, along with her boyfriend Matt. She wore a jaunty paper hat on her auburn curls and a badge in the shape of a sprig of holly that said *I'm Shannon!*.

'How did it go?' everybody clamoured to know. 'How many did you have?'

'About three hundred.'

'Three *hundred*!' They all nodded sagely, trying not to look at their own feast laid out on the table when Shannon had spent the morning in a centre in town feeding Dublin's homeless population. She did it every year. She was just great, they all agreed, even if she made everybody else feel like shit.

'Beer?' Mossy asked Matt, clearly still on his best behaviour.

'Please,' Matt said fervently. Aisling suspected that Matt's normal habitat on a Christmas morning would have been bed, probably nursing a hangover and a hot blonde, but he was madly, deeply in love with Shannon. In the six months he'd been going out with her he'd experienced puppy-walking, collecting for the deaf, and many, many mucky treks into the Wicklow Mountains (she didn't do that for charity, just for fun).

'Hiya, cutie,' Shannon said to Darren as she sat at the table, and he went purple with pleasure and emitted a kind of frantic 'Eeeeh!'

Matt, trying to impress her, reached over to chuck him under the chin, but ended up with a finger covered in dribble. 'Eh, hiya,' he said, rearing away hastily.

Shannon said to Darren, 'At least we don't have an empty space at the table with *you* here today, eh?'

It was like someone had broken wind. Glances flew back and forth across the table. Anto glared, knife and fork poised. As if there wasn't enough upset in the house already. She could at least have waited until they'd eaten.

Normally Aisling would rush to smooth things over; she could see that Mossy was waiting for her to trill, 'Pass down the gravy boat, then!'

The gravy boat and its saucer only made an appearance at Christmas dinner, and to get their money's worth out of it everybody usually spent the meal going, 'Stop hogging that fine-looking gravy boat, Anto,' or, 'Don't tell me that wonderful gravy boat is empty!'

Aisling said nothing. Mossy eyed the gravy boat. But he wasn't confident enough to take it on by himself.

Shannon, meanwhile, looked around at them all with her cool, defiant eyes. 'Sorry,' she said, 'did I upset anybody? I thought maybe the rules were relaxed on Christmas Day and that we might actually discuss things. But I can see not.'

Matt, the outsider, was looking at them all, beer halfway to his lips. He was clearly wishing he'd stayed and tucked in with the people he'd been serving earlier.

Shannon shrugged. 'Right, fine, have it your way,' she told Aisling and Mossy. 'But I hope I never get hit by a bus. Because I'm sure I'll be forgotten about in five minutes by you lot. It'll be like I never existed.'

Louise was looking around anxiously. 'Is Shannon going to get hit by a bus?'

'No, no,' Aisling said hastily. 'Of course not.'

'Did *anybody* get hit by a bus?'

'Nobody got hit by a bus,' Mossy said colourlessly. 'Everybody is safe and sound.'

'You know that for a fact, do you?' Shannon speared a piece of turkey on her fork and chewed it, watching Mossy, who seemed to have lost his appetite.

It was up to poor Matt to break the silence. 'Um, what did you get for Christmas, Anto?'

They couldn't help it; they all looked at Darren.

'Ai!' said Darren. He was delighted at this new sound, so much so that he said it again. 'Ai! Ai!'

'A phone,' Anto muttered, avoiding eye contact with his new son.

'Nice!' Matt soldiered on. 'Top-of-the-range, I bet,' he joked.

Just keep digging, you plonker, Aisling thought. In fairness, Matt was a nice lad. He just wasn't any match for this family.

'No,' Anto choked out. 'But it's fine.'

'*I* got a pink sewing machine from Santa,' Louise chipped in; thank God for her. 'Ma's going to teach me how to make a mermaid evening gown, aren't you, Ma?'

She'd already found a red-carpet picture in *Vogue* that she wanted Aisling to reproduce, 'Just a bit smaller.'

'Maybe we'll start with something simple,' Aisling tried.

'I have my hairstyle worked out and everything,' Louise assured her.

They all lapsed back into silence, eating mounds of ham and the organic turkey, Brussels sprouts with toasted almonds, delicious potatoes gratin, all smothered in the contents of the gravy boat. Aisling had been up since dawn creating this feast, trying to make sure that this Christmas was somewhat normal.

Who was she trying to kid?

She lifted her glass. 'I'd like to make a toast.'

All faces swivelled to her. Mossy was on red alert. She knew he was mentally calculating how much wine she'd had.

Not enough to upset things. 'To the newest member of the Brady family,' she said. She turned to Darren. He had a big lump of mashed potato on the side of his mouth, where Louise had missed with the spoon. 'To Baby Darren.'

Shannon was first to lift her glass. 'To Darren!'

Then they were all toasting him, one by one. Aisling was relieved when Mossy raised his beer and looked at the child. 'To Darren.'

Anto was the last. He lifted his glass of Coke. Aisling gave him an encouraging look. He was going to bond with this baby whether he liked it or not.

'To Darren,' he said tersely, and knocked his Coke back like it was a double whiskey.

'*And*,' said Aisling loudly, stalling everybody as they went to put their drinks back down. They all looked at her, waiting. 'And to those who can't be with us today,' she added quietly.

Shannon was right. They weren't going to pretend that people didn't exist.

Glances flew around the table. Tentative. Relieved. Approving, from Shannon.

'To those who can't be with us today,' everybody echoed in varying shades of loudness.

Mossy said nothing at all.

Across the table Darren locked eyes with Aisling. Somehow he kept gravitating towards her, even though she'd been keeping her distance, subconsciously, since she'd found out who he was.

'Ummm,' he said, and held out his hands to her again. Insistent.

She tried to resist. It lasted about six seconds.

'Oh, come here,' she said, and she picked him up and buried her head in his warmth.

Chapter Thirteen

'Aisling?'

Pause.

'I know you're awake.'

'I'm not.'

'Please. Talk to me.'

'Why should I?'

'Because it's Christmas night, and I'm lonely.'

'Well maybe I'm lonely too, Mossy.'

They lay in silence for a bit. She hoped he was feeling guilty.

She hadn't realised she'd spoken aloud until he hoisted himself up on to one elbow and looked down at her. 'And what have I to be guilty about?'

'Anto, for one.'

'Anto?'

'There you go again!'

'What?'

'Look at him, Mossy. He's miserable. He's confused. His whole world has just turned upside down. Can we not just cut him some slack?'

There was a silence. Then Mossy fell back on to his pillow with an *umpf* that she took to be concession. She let out a little breath. She could talk to him more easily when he was horizontal, and not so big and stocky and opinionated.

Minutes passed. But the silence was a little more companionable and she was glad for it.

'Where did we go wrong?' he said at last.

She sighed. They'd had this conversation many times over the last few years. Maybe even hundreds. 'I don't know.'

'You try so hard with them.' He sounded confused. Bewildered. Well, he could join the club.

'From the day they were born they got attention, didn't they? They got love. We were worn out reading them books, and taking them to basketball and football and karate and ballet, and what was that other one? Tae something, I've forgotten again.'

'Tae kwon do.'

'Tae kwon do! That was it! I wish we hadn't bothered with that one. Nothing but prancing about.'

Aisling smiled. Mossy always got exercised by the tae kwon do. Anto had taken it up with great enthusiasm, which waned abruptly the week after they shelled out for a year's tuition and the rig-out.

'We did it all, didn't we? We did the best we possibly could! We moved here when Shannon was three to get them into a better school. Couldn't afford to move, but we did it, and we're still crippled with the mortgage. Driving that van all over the country just to get the next job, to try to make sure that they had enough. And you working double shifts in that surgery—'

'Even when I was pregnant, yes, Mossy.' She could recite it word for word by now; the same old arguments.

He fell silent, rebuffed. Said nothing for ages. But then he couldn't help himself. 'You think I'm expecting too much, that they might try to thank us by not taking drugs and getting teenage girls pregnant?'

The hurt was coming off him in waves. The sense of having it all thrown back in his face.

But Mossy was Mossy. She tried to remind herself of that. Straight-talking, tell it like it is, no bullshit. And he was right, of course. The kids should know better. Had been *taught* better. But they couldn't control them. They made their own choices at the end of the day.

Mossy sensed criticism. 'If you can think of some better way to parent them, then please, let me know,' he invited.

'If I did, I'd say it.'

'So why all the looks, Aisling?'

'What looks?'

'I see them, you know. I turn in the kitchen and you're there, like all of this is my fault. The coolness; I get that too. I'm not stupid.'

'I don't blame you,' she lied. 'Look, I just don't want us to screw up with Anto as well, that's all. We can't drive him away, Mossy.'

'I'm not trying to.'

'So shut your mouth then.' She kept her tone light so he would know she was joking, kind of. 'Let the dust settle. He knows he's messed up. He doesn't need us pointing it out.'

Mossy gave another sigh. But he didn't disagree.

After a while he said, 'Do you want to hear something mad?'

'What?'

'I just heard Matt sneak up to Shannon's bedroom a minute ago.'

'*What?*'

A Special Delivery

They'd left him on the couch downstairs. He'd had too many beers to go home to his own parents. Shannon was staying back in her old bedroom, which was in the attic; right over their heads.

'It's okay,' Mossy reassured her. 'They're not having sex.'

'How do you know?'

That was all they needed: Shannon getting herself banged up as well. A family full of unmarried mothers and fathers. Mossy would fling himself off a cliff.

'Because I converted that attic with my bare hands,' he said with satisfaction. 'I remember every creak, every weak spot in those floorboards. If they were having sex, I'd know about it.'

A bubble of laughter escaped her. It was a great release after the long day.

'She wouldn't dream of getting it on over our heads anyway, would she?' she said.

'Not a chance. I'd say your man is going mad.' Mossy was chuckling too.

'I like him. He's a nice lad.'

'Matt? Soft,' Mossy declared.

'Mossy! He is not soft.' Just because Mossy had once stapled his thumb to a wall with a misaimed staple gun and barely made a squeak did not make other men soft.

'No man worth his salt would moon after a girl the way he does after Shannon.'

Then, the sound she'd been lying awake waiting for: 'Neh. Neeeehhh.'

They both looked to the middle of the bed. Darren was stirring between them.

'Sssh,' Aisling whispered.

'Aisling. Maybe it's not such a good idea to have him in the bed with us,' Mossy ventured.

'Where else do you want to put him? He's awake every two hours.'

'We should have left him in with Anto.'

Mossy had moved the crib into Anto's room. God knows what planet he'd been on. Anto, also on another planet, had walked in and said, appalled, 'What the hell is that thing doing in here? And where are my speakers gone?'

'I think he might have a touch of colic.' For the first time, Aisling felt a pang of sympathy for the child's mother. If this was going to be another night like last night, then they were in for it. No wonder the girl was exhausted.

'Neh-neh-neh NEEHHH.'

'Mossy, go find his soother, will you? I'll walk him for a bit.'

She picked Darren up, a little damp ball of misery, and put him up on her shoulder. He was heavy enough, and her arms already ached from carrying him around for hours after dinner. He wouldn't go to anyone else. For some reason she got great satisfaction out of that.

'Mossy. Move.' He was still lying there.

'I'm going, okay?'

He flung himself out of bed and opened the door. Anto's snores floated in from across the landing.

'Do you hear that?' said Mossy, incredulous.

To Aisling, Anto sounded fitful and distressed. But she didn't want to say it for fear of riling Mossy more. 'The soother, Mossy.'

He paused. Eyed her and Darren. He was naked on top and the six-inch scar on his side, just below his ribs, was livid and raised. That was probably what it would always look like, the doctors had said. 'Just don't get too attached to him,' he said softly. 'That's all.'

Chapter Fourteen

The lads came round to greet the new arrival.

'He's the spit of you,' Baz, the baby expert, declared.

'Yeah,' said Sean. 'He's got your mad red hair and all!' There was a little silence. The lads shifted from foot to foot uncomfortably. 'Um, congratulations, like.'

'Shut up, would you?' said Anto, and they had a nervous laugh at that.

They studied Darren a bit more. He was on the floor in the living room. Just sitting there, looking up at them all.

'Small, isn't he?' said Sean.

'Yeah,' Baz agreed. 'Pretty small.'

'So,' said Anto, when it looked like conversation was going to dry up again. 'What's up?

'Nothing much,' said Baz. It was a few days after Christmas. 'Just going to meet a few of them for a game of pool, if you fancy it?'

'I can't,' said Anto, nodding towards Darren.

'Can your ma not mind him?' In their minds, that was what

mothers were for. And for cooking dinners and washing dirty football kits and stuff.

'She's gone out. Anyway, my da says I have to start taking more responsibility for him.'

'Oh, right,' said the lads.

Anto knew what they were thinking: you didn't mess with his da. They thought he was a hard man. Like, in a good way. They showed him respect, not like their own das, who worked in offices or factories and had soft bellies that hung out over their jeans in the pub at weekends. They made fun of *them*. But Anto's da was fit and strong still, and they respected his van and the piercing way he might look at you if he thought you were taking the mick.

Try living with the picky fucker. They wouldn't think he was so great then.

On the floor Darren started to grizzle a bit. *Shut up, shut up*, Anto urged him in his head, panicky.

Baz and Sean looked at him, wary. 'What's wrong with him?'

'He has colic,' said Anto, trying to sound authoritative. At least he hoped that was all it was. If it was another dirty nappy . . . How could a kid that size produce so much crap? It was unbelievable. His ma had taught him how to change a nappy yesterday. As in, he did it all by himself. 'It's time, Anto,' she said. 'He's been here a week. You can't just keep watching.'

'Do you want to bet?' his da had said. Couldn't help himself, of course. But he said it low, because Ma always glared when she heard him making comments like that.

His ma had been great; so calm and cool, and she didn't even freak when Darren peed everywhere the minute the nappy was off him. All over the carpet and everything! She just laughed. Anto had been too appalled to laugh. He'd never had to touch someone else's willy before. Although when he finally plucked up the courage, nappy wipe in hand, it wasn't so bad. And Darren's was a grand big size too – you know, for a little fella. Anto felt quite chuffed. 'No one's ever going to call *you* Whacker,' he whispered to him when his ma went off to bin the dirty nappy.

The lads were discussing colic. 'I thought it was something horses got,' Sean said.

'Kids get it too. Like an upset stomach. Ma says he's a bit old to still have colic, but anyway we got drops in the chemist for him and he's calmed down a bit.'

The chemist had been another experience his ma had insisted he partake of. He'd been scarlet as this lady in a white coat had gone on at length about feeding technique, and proper winding afterwards. *Whilst looking at Anto.* Anto had wanted to disappear into the ground. He couldn't believe he'd found himself in the babycare section of the local chemist. Shouldn't he be loitering over by the counter, trying to inconspicuously buy fruit-flavoured condoms, like other lads his age?

'If you'd only actually *used* a condom . . .' That had been his da this morning. Again. He just couldn't let stuff go. He always had to bang on about fucking everything. You'd think he'd never done anything bad in his life. Ma said once it was because he'd had a hard childhood, what with his own da being a total tosser and an alco, although Ma said they weren't allowed to call him that, even though he'd been dead years now. Heart attack. Anyway, she said Da was a bit more of a perfectionist than other men because he'd had to grow up faster.

Sometimes she tied herself in knots, his ma. Trying to put a good slant on everything. It was like she was the only thing keeping the house on an even keel. Often Anto felt that if she let herself go – and sometimes she came close, he could see that – they would all literally fall apart.

It wasn't normal, his house. Shannon knew it, of course. Louise was probably too young. Louise was a pain in the neck, mostly because you could never get into the bathroom, and she was always calling him fat, but at the same time she was his sister and he wouldn't like to think that she was growing up in a house full of secrets and lies. And not being able to talk properly about people and things that had happened, even if they were bad. Anto was no psychologist, but he knew that wasn't healthy.

It had been Da's decision. He said he had to look out for the safety of the family. If things changed, and people came to their senses, then fine; but until then tough decisions had to stand.

But Anto had never felt not safe. Yeah, the rows had been bad, he wouldn't deny that; it was all bluster and temper though, there had been no real badness in it. And now he felt like a massive part of his life had been cut off. Everything had changed. He had Darren now, of course, but it was hardly the same.

'So,' said Baz. 'I suppose we'd better go. You know, into town.' His face was apologetic. 'Don't want to be late.'

'Oh,' said Anto. 'Right. Sure.'

But the lads clearly felt bad. 'Do you want to come with us?' said Sean.

They all looked at each other.

'And, like, bring Darren?'

'Yeah,' said Baz. The idea began to gain momentum. 'It's just a game of pool. Kids are allowed in.'

'Course they are!' Sean said. 'Come on, let's go.'

Anto thought about it. His ma had gone out somewhere, all secretive. His da was doing accounts downstairs. It would be a chance to show him that Anto was coping; taking Darren off into town on an outing. No sweat. No hassle. And he couldn't give up his old life altogether, could he?

'Great. Let's do it.'

It all went fine until Baz announced, 'Here's the bus.'

'What?'

'The bus is coming.'

Sean looked at the buggy. It was Louise's old one from the attic, dusted off for Darren. 'How are we going to get that on the bus?'

The three of them were plunged into panic.

'Fold it, fold it! No, not with the baby in it, you thick. Here, Baz. You hold him and I'll try and . . .'

'Um-um-ummm,' said Darren, gazing up at Anto. He looked a bit worried, and who could blame him?

Anto unstrapped him and thrust him into Baz's startled arms. 'Don't drop him, all right?'

'I won't! For fuck's sake.'

'And watch your language around him. Here, Sean. You grab one handle and I'll grab the other and we'll push at the same time. Sorry, mate,' he called in to the bus driver, who waited with the door open. Everybody on the bus was having a good gawk out the windows, of course. Half of them were probably reaching for their phones to ring social services.

They eventually got on the bus, all four of them. Anto fumbled to pay as Baz strode down the aisle with Darren held aloft.

'Now,' he said. 'Let's find a nice seat, will we?'

And he sat himself down comfortably in the mother and baby seat, next to a load of old ladies, and plopped Darren on to his lap. Normally they sat on the top deck and ogled girls out the window.

'Here,' said Anto tersely, sitting behind him. 'I'll take him.'

119

'Naw, you're all right,' said Baz magnanimously. He produced a set of keys and jiggled them for Darren. 'There you are, buddy.'

Darren grabbed at the keys. He let out a little squeal of delight.

One of the old ladies leaned in. 'He's gorgeous.'

'Thanks,' beamed Baz.

'He'll be next,' said Sean, gloomy.

'Yeah, well, I wouldn't recommend it,' Anto blustered.

They were nearly there when Darren started up crying.

'Colic again, is it?' said Sean, like he actually knew what he was talking about.

The old ladies weren't so adoring now, as Darren opened his mouth and really went for it. The noise would deafen you.

'Has he a dirty nappy?' Anto asked Baz.

'How would I know?' said Baz, spooked. 'Maybe he's hungry or something.'

Fuck. Anto had forgotten a bottle. He'd walked out of the house without a bottle. And it was exactly four hours since Darren's last feed. The little fecker was starving.

'Our stop is next,' Sean announced.

'Here you go,' said Baz, swiftly handing Darren over. There was no jangling of keys now.

'Thanks, lads,' said Anto bitterly. 'Thanks a bunch.'

'What?' said Baz. 'I'm just going to get the buggy, that's all.'

'Oh.' Anto deflated. He'd expected them to scarper.

'There's a Marks and Spencer on Grafton Street,' said Sean. 'They'll have something for babies to eat, won't they?'

Not nice warm bottles of formula. But they'd have yogurts and stuff, and it would keep Darren going until Anto could get him home.

'What about the game of pool?' Anto said. Typical. The one day he got out, and it was all ruined now.

'Another time,' Baz said. He braced himself. 'Right. Let's do this.'

The three of them stood cautiously, balancing baby and buggy.

'Here, do you want me to take him again?' Baz offered.

'Ah, no. You're all right.'

Darren clamped a plump little hand on Anto's shoulder as the bus suddenly swayed. Anto tightened his arm around him. 'I've got you, buddy.'

Chapter Fifteen

The O'Sullivan house was nice. Aisling didn't think it would be as nice as it was. A well-kept redbrick with a newish car parked out in the drive, even if the garden was a little overgrown. She was a bit ashamed of her preconceptions. It was much nicer than their own house, especially since the addition of the wonky nativity scene.

She was more taken aback when the door was answered by a man she recognised.

'Oh, hello,' she stammered. All the time her mind was racing . . . Where had she met this man before? Why did she feel she knew him? Was it just because he looked a little like Darren around the mouth?

He saw her confusion. He seemed used to it. 'I'm on the telly sometimes,' he explained patiently.

Of course! She felt daft now. She watched him at least a couple of times a month, at the end of the news, pointing at computer images and advising her sympathetically that a cold front was on the way.

'You're Hugo O'Sullivan,' she blurted. 'The meteorologist.'

She felt even more foolish; no doubt he already knew who he was.

Mossy had told her his name was Hugh. The big eejit. And so neither of them had realised that Darren was the grandson of a semi-celebrity.

Well, not exactly. But someone with a bit of a profile, anyway, at least amongst those of a certain age who liked to catch the forecast. Not that Mossy would be too impressed. He always said they got it wrong. 'Sunny spells, my arse. The last time they told us that, we had monsoon rains for three days.'

In fact, she already knew that Mossy would go out of his way to be *un*impressed: 'So he's Hugo O'Sullivan. Big deal! It doesn't make his daughter any better than Anto.'

Hugo, meanwhile, was courteously sparing her blushes. 'I am, for my sins,' he said. 'And thanks anyway, but I'm happy with my electricity service provider or whoever it is you're representing. Have a good evening.'

And with a final smile, he went to close the door in her face.

'Wait!' She put out a hand to stop him. 'I'm not . . . I'm Aisling.' At his blank look she added, 'Darren's . . . grandmother.'

He looked at her for a long moment.

'Then you'd better come in.'

The house was chilly. That was the first thing Aisling noticed. And it smelt a little of stale air. That made her feel better, because whenever anybody walked into *her* house, they were assailed by the stench of decomposing sports gear and paint stripper, so it was a relief that other people's houses didn't smell like spring meadows either.

Advancing into the hall, she saw a pair of pink pumps lying at the bottom of the stairs, and a purple jacket thrown on the banisters. So how come poor Darren always got stuffed into beige?

'It feels a bit odd, doesn't it? Being a grandparent,' Hugo was saying. 'As though we're too young for it. Well, *you* are anyway. I don't know about me.'

'Both of us are too young,' Aisling assured him with a smile.

He paused at the living-room door. 'You didn't bring Darren with you, then?' His disappointment was clear.

'I thought about it,' she said truthfully. 'But I wasn't sure . . .' She didn't want to take Nicola by surprise. And how would Darren react, suddenly being back in his home, and seeing his mother again, especially if she didn't want to see him? She didn't want to be responsible for years of psychiatric intervention. 'I decided it was best to come on my own.'

Hugo seemed to understand the complications too, because he just nodded.

'The house is very quiet without him,' he admitted. 'We're quiet kind of people, I suppose. He used to liven us up a bit.' And he smiled again to let her know that he wasn't taking himself too seriously, although she suspected he was quite a serious person really.

'Well, we're noisy kind of people,' she told him impulsively. 'Too noisy. I'm hoping he doesn't find it overwhelming at our place.'

Immediately she was sorry; she shouldn't have given the impression that Darren might be in any way stressed or unhappy. She'd wanted to give something back, that was all.

But he just said, 'Thanks for looking after him. And tell Mossy that too. You could have created a terrible fuss about the way he was . . . left in your garden.'

'Oh, we wouldn't have done that,' she rushed to reassure him.

'Maybe it would have been better if you had. It might have given her a wake-up call.'

Aisling looked past him to the pink pumps. 'Is she . . .?' Her stomach was bunching up a little at the thought of meeting Nicola. She didn't know what to expect. She didn't know the first thing about this girl. Neither did Anto, it seemed, despite the fact that he'd jumped into bed with her.

'She's out for the night.' Hugo sounded embarrassed.

'Well, I suppose she's only eighteen . . . it's Christmas time . . .' Aisling felt compelled to defend her. Not because she really believed what she was saying (*Out for the night!* All right for some). But she didn't want Hugo to feel awkward. 'Look,' she said, 'I didn't come here to catch you or Nicola off guard. I just wanted to meet you. And for you to meet us. Or, at least, one of us.'

She'd asked Mossy to come along. But he said he had to go out on a job. Maybe he had, but it felt a bit like an excuse.

'Thank you.' Hugo seemed even more embarrassed. 'But we're the ones who should have gone over to you. You've been treated very badly in all of this—'

'No, no.'

'You have. Having to learn about Darren like this. And Anto, especially, thrown in the deep end. Poor lad.'

Aisling was a bit taken aback by all this empathy. A lot of men in Hugo's position might have gone after Anto with a double-barrelled shotgun for getting their daughter in trouble, as Mossy kept pointing out. Mind you, Mossy would probably have helped him load it.

But she was grateful all the same. Anto needed any bit of sympathy he could get. He was looking a bit shaken these days.

'He'll adjust,' she said. Fingers crossed, anyway. 'We all will.'

'And you're okay to keep Darren for another few days? It's just . . . with Nicola, I'm not sure she's ready yet . . . we haven't sorted things out properly.'

'Yes, yes. Of course. Take as long as you need.'

Now he really *was* grateful. He gave a smile that reached his eyes this time. 'Please,' he said. 'Have a seat while I stick the kettle on.'

The living room was expensively furnished and a bit fussy. Now that she was alone – she had a quick check over her shoulder first to make sure she actually was – Aisling was able to have a poke around, to try to figure out who these people really were.

Hugo read a lot. That was the first thing that struck her. Books and more books; every shelf crammed. She dipped her head to one side to read some of the titles: *Ireland: The Story of Boom to Bust*, *A History of the Tudors*, *The Principles of Economics*, with the odd rugby biography thrown in for some light relief. She drew back, intimidated. She wouldn't tell Mossy about this. 'No social life,' he'd probably declare. He had little time for intellectuals, not being one himself.

The shelf underneath, though, was full of brightly jacketed books, many of them book club titles Aisling recognised, and some that she'd even read. Phew. Feeling marginally less ignorant, she wondered who they belonged to. Not Hugo, that was for sure.

Then she spotted them: photos! There was a whole row of them in shiny silver frames on the windowsill. Aisling loved photos. You could tell so much from somebody's tightly pursed lips, or the rabbit ears they gave their unsuspecting granny. She drifted over. One little peek . . . that wouldn't be *too* nosy.

She saw it immediately: the official wedding photo. It was massive, and an arty black and white – Hugo and the missus, on a windswept beach in their wedding clothes, trying to look as though they'd just happened to wander there by accident, and not been micromanaged by the photographer.

Hugo was good-looking. Well, he was still good-looking, but in the photo he was *really* good-looking. He looked very carefree. So did the wife; she was blonde and petite and laughing into the camera, as though she'd already knocked back a glass or two of bubbly. Great teeth, thought Aisling enviously.

'Tea or coffee?' Hugo asked, from behind her.

'Oh!' She jumped guiltily.

His eyes followed hers to the photo.

'Sorry, I was just . . .' Aisling mumbled. Having a good old snoop, actually.

'That's my wife, Eleanor. We've broken up. She lives in Australia now.' He said it matter-of-factly, but behind his eyes she could see he was devastated.

Aisling was mortified but strangely unsurprised; there had been no mention of Eleanor so far. In fairness, the two families barely knew each other; she doubted that Mossy had mentioned *her* in the phone call he'd had with Hugo. But already you could feel the absence of a wife and a mother in this house.

'I'm very sorry,' she told him.

Hugo dug his hands into his pockets. He looked at the wedding photo. 'I often feel none of this would have happened if she hadn't left. Not that I'm *blaming* her,' he hastily clarified. 'Takes two and all of that. But we're still trying to adjust, I suppose. Nicola's very angry. And I'm not sure I'm doing a very good job.' He stopped abruptly. He looked a bit taken aback at himself. 'I'm very sorry. I really shouldn't be offloading all this on to you.'

'No, no, it's fine.' She felt awful for having judged them so harshly.

'All the same.' He gave an embarrassed little laugh. 'It's probably the absence of adult company. Give me another few months and I'll be ringing the talking clock to confide in them.'

'I'm sure you're doing a very good job. We can only try, and hope things turn out for the best. Sometimes they don't. Sometimes life just slaps you in the face. And you have to live with that too.'

He was looking at her strangely. And she realised she sounded a bit fierce, or defensive, or something.

'Anyway,' she said, backing down. She looked at the photo again, and the smiling Eleanor, now in Australia. 'It's none of my business.'

'It is, though,' he said. 'We're family now, in a way. What with Darren.'

And she supposed they were.

Chapter Sixteen

Aisling had to ring the surgery to take another week off work. Mossy was worried. 'What if you lose your job?'

'I won't, I've used some of my holiday leave.'

'So you don't get any summer holiday?'

'Well what can we do, Mossy? Are *you* going to take care of Darren?'

As if. He was in the middle of a last-minute job with Dave on the Southside, painting a school before it reopened after the Christmas holidays on Monday. A baby would be surplus to requirements.

As for Anto, well, he was trying his best. But he wasn't quite there yet. Yesterday he went out with Darren in the buggy and arrived home with neither. 'Fuck!' he'd shouted in fright. 'I'm after leaving him . . . where did I leave him?'

'Jesus Christ!' Mossy had jumped up and grabbed the van keys, to dash to the rescue. 'Think! Think!'

'The park! No, wait. McDonald's! No, wait . . . I can't remember! This is terrible!'

Louise had ambled in then, pushing the buggy. 'You left him outside the front door,' she accused Anto.

'Oh. Yeah,' he said, sheepish. 'I had to look for my keys.'

Panic over. Phew. They were all so relieved to have Darren back safe and sound that they'd burst into a lively rendition of 'The Wheels on the Bus', which was his favourite, especially when Mossy made honking noises. Somebody broke open a two-litre bottle of Coke, and it turned into quite a sing-song. Aisling had looked around at one point and she'd suddenly thought, *Everybody looks so happy*.

But today Mossy was all grumpy again. 'What beats me is that it's been two weeks now – *two weeks* – and she hasn't even called round to see the little fecker.'

Nicola got a lot of bad press in the house. It didn't help that they hadn't met her yet or even spoken to her on the phone, which meant that everybody was able to heap their own prejudices and preconceptions upon her. 'She *is* coming back for him, isn't she?'

'Of course she is. Another few days, Hugo said.'

'Well, if *Hugo* said.' His tone was a little sardonic and it annoyed her. 'Sure he's been saying that for days now.'

'What am I supposed to do about it, Mossy?'

'We're going to have to do *something*. We can't keep him much longer. Anto starts back to school on Monday, so he's not going to be around. Not that he's much use anyway, but you know what I mean. And you can't take any more time off work.'

'I know that, okay?' She was tired. Looking after Darren wasn't like bringing up their own kids. Because they were only custodians, they were more paranoid; whipping nappies off him at the first sign of a whiff, that sort of thing. They couldn't be found *wanting*. Also, they were much, much older. When that *waaah* burst out of the darkness at 4 a.m. . . .

'I'm just saying. We've done more than enough.'

'They've had seven months of him,' she snapped. 'Maybe they're thinking the same.'

He was giving her that look again. 'Here we go.'

'Here we go what?'

'You've gone over to their side ever since that day you called around.'

'I have not!'

'You have. Always making excuses for them. Well, say what you want, but a baby should be with its mother.'

'Sexism now. Nice one, Mossy.'

'It's not. Look at him!' He pointed at Darren, who was propped up in his high chair seeing how much of his fist he could stuff into his mouth. Quite a lot, actually; he took after his father in that respect. 'Who do you think would rear him better? The girl who gave birth to him, or our Anto?'

'Anto never left him in the garden,' Aisling felt compelled to point out.

'He's left him everywhere bloody else.' Mossy sighed. 'Look, I'm not trying to pick an argument here, Aisling.'

'Are you sure about that?'

Her snarky tone drew a hurt look from him. 'I just don't want you taking on too much, that's all.'

'No, you're trying to railroad me, Mossy. Well guess what. You don't always get to decide who stays and who goes around here.'

The words were flung at him. They both kind of reared back from each other.

'I'm sorry, okay? I didn't mean that. I'm just . . . tired.'

Mossy wasn't going to be bought off that easily. He stood and pulled up his shirt roughly. As always, she had to look away from the bright red scar. 'I didn't do this to myself, you know.'

'I know you didn't.'

'I could have been killed.'

She wasn't going to stand for that. 'Oh for God's sake, stop it. You were never going to be killed. It's a surface wound. That's all. And you were partly to blame for it yourself.'

'Oh, *right*. It's all coming out now. So I brought it upon myself?'

'I didn't say that—'

'You might as well have,' he bit out.

Who knew what they might have said to each other next had the phone not rung. They both turned to look at it tensely. Eventually Aisling snatched it up and looked at the caller display.

'It's Hugo.'

'Again,' said Mossy tightly.

Hugo phoned every day, 'just to see if everything's going okay'. Aisling usually answered. Mossy was afraid he might say something bad about Nicola, and it would make the situation even more difficult. You know, like call her a dizzy bitch or something.

She turned away a bit from Mossy as she answered the phone. 'Hello?'

'Aisling? Hugo here. I hope it's not a bad time?' As usual, he sounded vaguely mortified by the situation.

But Aisling was glad to hear from someone who wasn't shouting at her. 'Not at all,' she assured him.

'Ask him if Nicola fancies seeing her son today,' Mossy hissed behind her.

Aisling coldly ignored him.

'I'm just ringing to see how things are going.'

'Everything's fine this end.' She always said that, even if the house was falling down around her ears. Often she'd have to run upstairs to take these calls because Darren would be bawling and sounding like he was being slowly tortured in the background.

'We saw you on the telly last night,' she couldn't help saying. It was the first time he'd been on since she'd called over. Every night they'd eagerly waited for the weather at the end of the news, but it was never him. Then, last night, when they'd just about given up, Anto had shouted, 'Look, look! It's him!' and they'd all stampeded in from the kitchen. He'd been wearing a nice suit and tie and looked 'ravishing', according to Mossy. Aisling had shushed him, straining to listen. She'd felt oddly shy or something, now that she knew him.

'Your future father-in-law,' Mossy had ribbed Anto, who looked rather cowed by Hugo. 'You'd better scrub up.'

'Oh,' Hugo said on the phone. 'Um, thank you.' A pause. 'Sorry the forecast wasn't better.'

'That's okay!' Aisling laughed, then stopped herself. She could feel Mossy looking at her. Was she coming across as some kind of groupie? She hurried on more soberly, 'Anyway, just to say that we think it isn't colic at all that's bothering Darren at night, but teething. He's having a bad time of it. He's using the bottle as comfort.'

'Is he? I wish we'd thought of that. We just assumed that he was going through some kind of growth spurt,' Hugo marvelled, and Aisling felt rather flattered at her detective skills.

'Well, he's certainly piling it on,' she said. 'In a good way, though,' she clarified hastily.

'I hope he's got your genes on that side of things. We've got a couple of porkers our end.'

Aisling's laugh was genuine this time. Mossy's eyebrows nearly disappeared into his hairline. She gave him a look: who said that weathermen couldn't be funny?

'Can I ring again in a day or two?' Hugo sounded hesitant. 'I don't want to bother you . . .'

'You're not bothering us at all,' she assured him.

'It's just, it seems ages since I've seen him.'

She could hear the longing in his voice, and she told him, 'Ring whenever you want.'

'You didn't ask him how much longer this is going to go on,' Mossy said, when Aisling hung up.

'No, Mossy. I didn't. I figured he would have said if she was ready.'

'So that's it? We all sit around here in some kind of limbo waiting for her to make up her mind?'

It did sound a bit unreasonable. But Aisling sensed that Hugo felt as helpless as they did. Pushing him wasn't going to help anything.

'You know his wife has left him. Nicola's mother.'

'Yes. You've mentioned it.'

'I'm just saying. It must be hard on them.' She willed him to understand. If anybody could sympathise with a broken family, surely it was them.

Mossy didn't argue it. He got up to go back to work. 'It's not fair on Darren,' he said, quiet and emphatic. 'The child must be confused.'

Darren perked up at the mention of his name. It was hard to know whether he missed his mother or not. Sometimes he got into a right strop and couldn't be comforted, not even by Aisling. He just curled in on himself, a little ball of hurt.

'Let's give them another day or two,' she said, feeling guilty even though none of this was her fault. 'Then we'll bring it up again.'

The January sales were hell. But not with a buggy. Aisling just sailed along calling out a cheery 'Excuse me! Coming through!' and if people didn't get out of the way fast enough then they got the ankles taken off them.

'Ba. Ba. Ba!' Darren craned his neck to look up at her. He liked to know where she was at all times. That morning, when she'd left him down on the floor mat to go and talk to some electrician who was looking for Mossy, he'd cried pitifully until she came back into the room.

'Got a good set of lungs on him, your young lad,' the electrician commented.

'He's not actually . . .' Then she stopped. Who had the time to explain? Her mother was right. Just pretend. 'He does,' she said cheerily.

Hugo was spot on, though: Darren was indeed having a growth spurt. That very morning he seemed to have burst out of every item of clothing she'd tried to button on him. They'd been making do with the clothes that had come in the baby bag. To go out and buy him stuff seemed . . . presumptuous or something.

But now she had no choice. They could hardly hand him back in clothes he'd outgrown. 'Too mean to buy him anything new!' Hugo might denounce scornfully.

She found she cared what Hugo thought. Maybe it was because he was so measured or something. You knew he was a thinker. You knew he would notice whether they'd bought Darren new clothes or not.

'Where will we hit first?' she asked the back of Darren's head. 'Mothercare or Next? Go on, you choose.'

Her own voice sounded a bit strange to her. It was chirpy and carefree and young.

Immediately she felt panicky. Darren was beautiful, but he was distracting, and she needed to remember that when he was gone, the misery would still be there, waiting for her.

But it was great to get a little break from it all the same.

'Oooh, my little baby-bugga-boo!' Zofia was in full flow, bouncing Darren around energetically on her knee. 'My doodie-maker!'

Smack, smack, as she planted two lipsticky kisses on his cheeks. 'Come here, chubby chops.'

'He isn't chubby,' Aisling protested, a bit defensive now. 'He's perfect for his weight and age.'

She'd had him at the surgery for his check-up a few days ago. He got a total MOT, by two doctors *and* the surgery nurse, all for free because Aisling worked there. 'Motoring along,' was Dr Iris's prognosis, and Aisling had felt unreasonably proud.

She reached for him. 'Here, I'll take him back now.'

She'd met Zofia for a coffee during a break in the shopping.

'No,' said Zofia stoutly. 'We all have to have a go. I've noticed you've gone very selfish with him these days. You are worse than Louise.'

Aisling was taken aback. 'I am not.'

'Yes you are. And look at your arms. They are sinewy from carrying him around.' Zofia tut-tutted. 'And not a scrap of make-up on! Your face is all shiny and tired, just like a real new mother.'

'Stop picking on me,' Aisling said sulkily. 'It's only for another few days. I have to enjoy him while I can.'

'You will get him at weekends, though?'

'I don't know. I suppose.' She hadn't thought about it really. But presumably there would be some kind of access arrangement. Imagine seeing Darren on a regular basis.

That would mean seeing Nicola too, of course. And Hugo, presumably.

'You have rights, you know,' Zofia said stoutly.

'I don't think there's going to be any issue about it, Zofia. It's clear that Darren's mother is . . .' She strove for diplomacy. She had to discard several other statements before she came up with '. . . open to getting a break from him.'

But she was doubtful now. What if Zofia was right? What if Nicola kicked up a fuss? She couldn't bear it, she realised: to never see Darren again, or only very sporadically, having just got to know him.

'And there's no possibility of her going to Australia, is there?' Zofia said.

Aisling's heart nearly stopped. 'What are you talking about?'

'Nicola. Isn't that where you said her mother is living now?'

'Well, yes . . .'

Zofia belatedly realised from Aisling's face that she might have stuck her foot in it big time. 'Forget I said anything.'

Australia. That was the other side of the world. It might as well be a different planet for all the chance Aisling had of visiting him over there. And what about Anto? To have his son grow up on some beach somewhere, while he spoke to him once a week on Skype? If that?

'I have upset you,' Zofia lamented. 'I have added to your misery, when you are already miserable enough.'

'Yes, you bloody have.'

But already she was making plans. She would talk to Hugo. Appeal to him. They would get some kind of access arrangement in place; nail the whole thing down before notions entered anybody's head about relocating.

'Can I do your make-up tonight?' Zofia asked.

'After what you just said, you can get lost.'

'Please.'

'What's the topic this time? Hooker Chic? Sultry Seductress? Because I'll bet it's not Glamorous Granny.'

'There is no topic. I just need to get out of the house for a couple of hours.'

Aisling sighed. 'What's Magda done now?'

The few times she'd met Olaf's mother she'd seemed like a pleasant enough woman, but you never knew what really went on behind closed doors.

'Oh,' said Zofia, 'I don't want to complain.'

'Good—'

'Bitch thinks I am putting on weight! Me! I don't eat. How could I be putting on weight?'

'You told me you ate the mayonnaise out of the fridge sometimes.'

Zofia flapped a hand irritably. 'Don't be stupid. I was only trying to make you feel better. She is an evil woman. She finds a person's weakest spot, and she goes in like this.' She made a motion of a knife being plunged and twisted. 'Every day it's something different. My dirty house, my bad cooking, how I don't fold the towels just right.'

'She complains about how you fold the towels?' That was a new low. And Magda looked like such a placid woman.

'She doesn't have to. She looks. Every day she just sits there and looks.'

'So she doesn't actually criticise you out loud?'

'That is the clever thing about her,' Zofia agreed darkly. 'That way, Olaf will never suspect a thing.'

Magda chose that moment to rejoin them from a nearby shop. She was wearing a nice lemon cardigan, and there was a spanking new one in the shopping bag she was carrying, if the size and shape of it was anything to go by.

As always, she gave Aisling a very friendly smile and a cheery 'Hello!' and made cooing noises for Darren, which pleased him greatly.

Zofia said to her, rather tersely, 'Have you finished, or do you want to go to any more shops?'

Magda looked at her, a little wary. 'Only if you want to.'

Zofia shot a look at Aisling, as though to say, *See what I mean?* Then she turned back to Magda, a forced smile on her face. 'Well let's go then!'

Chapter Seventeen

After the shopping centre, Aisling got into her car and drove. 'Mwah. Mwaaaah.' Darren was narky and tired.

'It's okay, sweetheart. Nearly there.'

'There' wasn't home, though. She was nearly in town. She wasn't even aware of having made the decision; it was like the car had a mind of its own. She should have turned round. It wasn't fair, not with the baby in the back. But it was because of Darren that she hadn't visited in two weeks, not since Christmas Eve, and she had a pain in her stomach like hunger.

She wouldn't even get out of the car. No, a quick peek and she'd be on her way. No harm done.

Please let him be there this time.

She knew the way now. There was no hesitation. Ten minutes later she was pulling up near the house. She didn't park right outside, because he would know the car. One time, in the early days, he'd seen it and he'd come out and shouted at her to go away, and she didn't think she could bear that again. And Darren would be frightened.

So she pulled in across the road and put on her sunglasses, even though it was January, and waited.

Come on, come on, she chanted under her breath. Then she prayed. *Hail Mary, full of Grace, just give me a fecking break down here, will you?*

Just a glimpse. That was all she needed. Although sometimes it only made her feel worse.

Then she remembered. It was Thursday. His dole day. Shite. She told herself not to be so judgemental. She'd be turning into Mossy if she wasn't careful. But there was a bitter taste in her mouth. She didn't cut the engine.

'All right, sweetheart?' she said, looking over her shoulder.

But Darren was fast asleep. His head was lolling to one side, and his little red pouty lips were slack as he snored away happily.

As she looked back, she saw it: a curtain falling into place on an upstairs window in the house. She wasn't quick enough to see the person standing behind it, but she knew it was him. He had seen her. She knew this with every fibre of her being.

Maybe this time would be different. She had to have hope, didn't she? So she turned off the engine, cracked open a window and waited. She never took her eyes off the house.

After half an hour she got out of the car and left the customary bag on the doorstep: just a newspaper this time – she tried to think of different things to bring, but always little – and an envelope with crisp twenty-euro notes in it that she'd just withdrawn from a cash machine. She would tell Mossy that she'd paid the dentist in cash. He wasn't to know that she hadn't gone to the dentist in well over a year.

When she got back to the car, Darren was awake. He sat there in his car seat, contentedly sucking his thumb. What a beautiful, easy child he was. And she suddenly felt sorry for Nicola, that she was missing out on this. Even the bad moments too, like the wrecked nights' sleep.

'Ba! Ba!' he shouted at her.

'Ba yourself. What are you, a sheep?' He laughed at this, even though he hadn't a clue what she was saying. 'Come on, little man. Let's go home.'

Somehow, driving away from the house was a tiny bit easier to bear that day.

Chapter Eighteen

They faced each other over the kitchen table.

'Her name is Mrs McAllister,' Dad broke it to her. 'She's going to come every day between the hours of eight a.m. and six p.m. to look after Darren in our own home.'

There was a picture of Mrs McAllister pinned to the CV the agency had emailed over. She looked painfully cheery, the kind of woman who entered every room with a bellowy 'Well now!' And her upper lip could do with a good waxing. Along with looking after Darren, she was going to do some light housework, to include ironing and cooking. Big hearty stews probably, and lumpy apple crumbles.

'Nicola? Are you listening to me?'

'Yeah.'

'She's very experienced. They sent references too . . .' He went hunting through the little pile of printouts on the table. 'All of them glowing.'

'Great.' She didn't know why she said that. Already Mrs McAllister was filling her with doom.

Dad put down the paperwork and looked at her wryly. He'd gone to a lot of trouble over this, as he did with everything. 'I think she might be just what we need.'

'What, kind of like a replacement mum for me and a wife for you, only she gets paid at the end of the week? And you don't get to have sex with her?'

Dad's face snapped closed. *Stupid cow*, Nicola told herself. She didn't know why she was doing this. It wasn't Dad's fault. Why did she keep taking it out on him?

'Look, I just think we should try the crèche first.' Spinelessly, she tried to make up for things by being enthusiastic. 'All the local kids go there. Darren would make friends. And I could drop him in on the way to school; it'd be dead handy.'

School was the other thing. She'd agreed to start back on Monday. She was going to have to repeat the entire year – drop down to the class below – which was going to be mortifying. And she'd have to study really, really hard to catch up; grinds after school and everything. Which was why Mrs McAllister was staying until six, so that Nicola could get her study and homework done before taking over the care of Darren for the evening.

Dad must have seen some of this on her face: the dread, the sheer terror at the weight of the task ahead. 'I know it's not going to be easy, Nicola. Schoolwork *and* childcare. But I'll help. And I'm sure the Bradys will take Darren some of the time too.' He looked at her warmly. 'The important thing is that you're getting your life back on track. You're doing great.'

Was she? She couldn't remember instigating any of this. But she must have had something to do with it. After a week in bed, just sleeping, she'd woken up one morning and felt semi-normal, or less detached from her own life or something, and she'd said to Dad, 'What am I going to do today?' because without Darren there was so much time. Oodles of time. What had she ever done with it before? Had she really just pissed about the shopping centre with Becky and Mikaela?

But Dad had looked at her like the sun had come out from behind the clouds, and he'd said, all emotional, 'It's so good to hear you saying that, Nicola!'

Was it? What had she said that was so great?

But it didn't matter, because suddenly it was all go: he began talking nannies and exams and plans. He was on the phone the whole time, booking appointments, sorting things out, arranging her whole life for her, and he looked so *thrilled*. He kept saying over and over, 'Maybe all you needed was a break, Nicola. To help you get back on your feet.'

And it had been so long since he'd smiled at her, since he'd approved of her, that she couldn't put up her hand and say, 'Just a minute! Yes, the break was great, yes, I feel better, but there's still something wrong inside.'

So she kept her mouth shut and went along with it.

'We'll have to make arrangements to collect Darren,' Dad was saying busily.

That was another fait accompli. Darren was coming home. And the thought of it made her feel really weird; she wanted to laugh, to sing, to fly into a panic of tidying, washing, cleaning.

Mostly she wanted to cry.

'I'll get to the supermarket this afternoon, stock up on stuff for him.' He was all excited.

Becky and Mikaela were too. They'd been over earlier. 'I'd say you're dying to have him back, are you?' said Becky.

'You don't want him to be away from you too long,' advised Mikaela, like she had a clue.

'No, of course not,' Nicola had agreed, because otherwise she would have looked like a monster.

Dad had been subtly preparing her for a few days now, Nicola realised: cleaning the house, changing the sheets on the cot, that kind of thing. And he was on the phone to Anto's mum Aisling. Normally he phoned her a *lot*; nearly every day, and he always came away in better humour. Nicola had heard him enquire about Darren's routine; and were there new foods they'd discovered that he liked or disliked?

Nicola was jealous of these easy, intimate conversations from which she was excluded. Aisling had had Darren a few weeks only; Nicola had known him his whole life, yet Dad persisted in treating her like she was a total amateur and Aisling knew everything.

But of course Nicola *was* an amateur.

Maybe it would be okay second time round. Maybe when she saw her baby again, all those natural, normal feelings would surge to the surface and this whole motherhood gig would click into place. And she'd realise she'd missed him dreadfully, instead of just having this dull ache in her tummy that she could ignore if she really wanted.

'Will you, um, ring Anto to arrange a pick-up time?' Dad asked. 'Or will I?'

Anto. The father of her child. The guy she'd had a drunken ride with on a pile of coats. She kept reminding herself of this in the baldest terms; she had to keep her expectations in check. They mightn't have seen each other since, but all the signs were that she'd blown their tryst that night out of all proportion.

Stupid teenage fumble. Look where it had got her.

'I will,' she said, making her voice hard.

Better to get it over with. She wasn't afraid of him. There was no way she'd make a fool of herself *this* time.

'Are you sure?' Dad asked. 'Because I could ring Aisling, get her to lay some groundwork if you like . . .' He was already reaching for his phone, eager to talk to Aisling, sure that she would sort it out.

'No. It's my job. I'll do it.'

And she could see that he was proud of her. No doubt he was thinking that she was maturing beyond all recognition.

Upstairs, she dialled the Bradys' number. She felt sick with nerves. Knowing her luck she would get Aisling, and it would all be awkward and horrible.

But a young, male voice answered. "Lo?"

He seemed to be eating something.

Nicola made her voice as cool as ice. 'Am I speaking to Anto?'

Chapter Nineteen

They had Darren dressed up in awful clothes. Sky-blue dungarees and matching blue socks, as though desperately announcing *Yes, he's a boy!* And someone had snipped the ends of his hair, around the fringe region. His beautiful soft hair . . . Nicola was surprised at how upset she was by it. And had they *dyed* it or something? Because it was looking very ginger.

'Come in, come in,' the Bradys urged, and she had to drag her eyes away from her son as Dad gently propelled her onwards.

The Bradys' kitchen smelled of laundry and chips and wet sports gear. Anto's mother Aisling was normal-looking enough in jeans and a top but had on these really strange fake eyelashes and glittery eyeshadow – wasn't she a bit old? – and her smile was trying too hard as she said, 'Tea?'

'I'd love a cup,' said Dad.

He smiled eagerly at her like they were old friends. Honestly.

Nicola just wanted to grab Darren and his stuff and go, but Dad was settling himself in at the kitchen table like he was there for the day. He turned to Darren in his high chair and began a game of pretending to steal his rattle.

'Nicola? Tea?'

'Um, no thanks, Mrs Brady.'

Cool blue eyes met hers. 'Call me Aisling.'

Nicola was afraid for a second that she might fall down under the weight of her judgement. And now that the initial blur had worn off, she saw that there were more of them too: Anto's dad had just come in the back door and was looking at her from under bushy eyebrows. He and Darren were the spit of each other; it was a bit unnerving, actually, this whole family resemblance thing they all had going on.

'Mossy,' he announced. 'Nice to meet you.' And he was shaking Dad's hand, and then hers, and his own was rough and dry and warm. 'And this is Louise,' he said.

Nicola had already spotted her; the little kid lurking behind him. She had her hair all crimped, like something from the eighties.

Nicola tried a smile. 'Hi.'

She got a scowl back.

'Anto will be home in a minute,' Aisling explained hurriedly. 'He got delayed at soccer training.'

Everybody murmured, 'Ah, soccer!' and there was a lot of nodding, and the Bradys tried not to look at Nicola, but they did anyway, and she knew what they were thinking. *Look at your one. The baby abandoner. The unnatural mother. Should be locked up. Fecking state of her in that pink T-shirt. And she hasn't even said hello to her own child yet!*

It was true. She hadn't. Darren had given a kind of involuntary leap the second she'd walked into the kitchen, and a thrilled 'Eeehh!' Their eyes had clung together for seconds. Then he'd reared back, suddenly suspicious. She could see the confusion in his eyes. *Where did you go to? Why did you leave me here with these strangers?*

And Nicola had had to drop her own eyes from his, because she couldn't bear the blame in them.

He hated her now. That much was clear. Indeed it was to Aisling that he held out those chubby little hands – Jesus Christ, what were they feeding him, non-stop pizza? – and he climbed up into her arms and sat there watching Nicola warily from afar.

'Well!' said Dad. He smiled at Darren, then at Aisling. 'It's great to see him again.'

He'd got all uncomfortable since Mossy had arrived in. You could see why. Mossy was the kind who wore his disapproval on his face for everyone to plainly see. But Aisling . . . she was good at hiding her feelings. Nicola had already guessed this, because she was good at it too.

Nicola knew more about these people than they thought, actually. Anto had told her things that night they were together; not much, but enough to know that they weren't as apple pie as they were trying to make out.

It gave her a bit of confidence. She wasn't the only parent in this room who had done a shit job.

So she lifted her head and said to the Bradys, 'Thanks for looking after Darren.'

Aisling looked a bit surprised. Did she think that Nicola didn't have a tongue in her head? 'That's okay,' she said. 'He was a pleasure.'

'He's looking well, anyway,' said Nicola. Despite the Village People dungarees.

'He's a great eater,' Aisling said proudly.

Hmm. The minute Nicola got him home, she'd be getting him weighed down at the health centre.

She wondered whether to ask to hold him. Not that she had

to *ask*. He was her baby; he belonged to her. But she was desperately afraid that he would refuse point blank to come to her. And that would be terrible. With all of them standing there to witness her shame. No, best to wait until they got him home.

'Ma!' Louise suddenly burst into tears, surprising them all. 'I don't want Seth to go!'

Aisling looked at Nicola. 'She, um, rechristened him. The rest of us call him Darren, of course.'

Louise continued sobbing noisily. Normally Nicola had no time for little kids like her. They were bolshie and annoying; she'd been that way herself. But there was something about Louise's heartbreak that was genuine, and Nicola felt sorry for her.

It was Dad who pitched in. 'I know you'll miss him. You're his auntie, after all, even though you're only eleven.' He winked at her.

Louise squirmed shyly at that. Who would have thought it? That Dad the fun guy would emerge again? Not that it was aimed at Nicola.

'But I hope you're going to see him all the time. Weekends, maybe, and some sleepovers.' He looked at Aisling now, as he had done throughout this visit, for guidance and support. 'That's if you want to, of course.'

Aisling's face was a picture of relief. Her shoulders visibly relaxed. Had she thought that Nicola was going to *refuse* them or something? 'Yes. Of course we do.' She turned to Nicola now, her smile tentative. 'If that's okay with you.'

Nicola knew she was being thrown a bit of a bone. Part of her wanted to tell them all to get lost. But this woman – Darren's grandmother, she kept reminding herself of that – was trying to meet her halfway. So she managed a bit of a smile back. 'Dad and I were saying in the car over that we'll have to work something out. Weekend visits and stuff. I want him to know his father.'

Bit late in the day for that. Nicola could read the words on Mossy's face.

'That's great,' Aisling gushed. 'Isn't it, Mossy?'

Nicola watched as his broody eyebrows lifted an inch or two, and those direct eyes settled on her. 'Yeah.' And then his face changed, softened a bit. 'Wherever he is. Knowing him, he probably missed the bus home.'

And they all laughed. It was a nervous thing. But it seemed to clear the air a bit.

Nicola relaxed a little. This was going better now. She wasn't so bad, Anto's mum. Or the dad either. Just a bit frosty at the beginning, which was only to be expected.

'Can I take him to say goodbye to Emma?' Louise said, lip quivering. 'I said I would.'

'All right. But just for a minute, okay?'

As they watched Louise carry Darren out, Nicola thought she saw Aisling's lip quiver too. 'Mossy,' she said, turning away to busy herself at the kettle. 'Go get Darren's things from upstairs, will you? I have them packed up. I'm sure Nicola and Hugo don't want to be hanging around here all day.'

Dad looked like he was quite happy to hang around. Maybe it was the bustle of the place; the people in and out, the noise, the life. Their own house used to be like that; well, not *hopping* – there were only three of them – but Mum had always had the radio on, and something in the oven, and the back doors would be thrown open to the garden.

'You can come round to see him whenever you want,' he was saying to Aisling. 'Not just on access days.'

'We'll see,' she said. 'We'll let everybody settle back in first.'

Nicola and the baby, she meant.

'You're right. But we'll stay in touch on the telephone. I'll let you know how it's going.'

'Only if it's not too much trouble.'

'It's no trouble at all,' Dad assured her, and Nicola wished he wasn't trying so hard.

'Hugo!' Mossy called in from the stairs. 'Open your boot there and I'll put this stuff in.'

'Sure, sure!' Dad went hurrying out to the car.

Then it was just Nicola and Aisling. Nicola couldn't think of a thing to say.

It was Aisling who eventually said, 'Oh, before I forget,' and she went to a drawer and took out an envelope. 'For Darren,' she said. 'Or you.' She gave an awkward smile. 'For you both.'

Nicola took the envelope, wondering.

'It's some child support. It's not a huge amount or anything. Just something to start you off.' Aisling seemed to be waiting for her gratitude. 'We'll pay ongoing maintenance, of course,' she added, in case that was the problem. 'Obviously we'll have to work something out. I can talk to your dad, maybe?'

And bypass Nicola altogether, in other words. Railroad her. Dad would like that – to sort things out with his new pal Aisling, who seemed to be running the whole show.

'I don't need child support,' Nicola said loudly. That was a lie; she did. Dad gave her some money but it never seemed to be enough. And her child benefit was swallowed up by nappies and formula in no time at all.

'No, I know, it's just . . .' Aisling looked a bit stung at it being thrown back in her face. 'Darren is Anto's responsibility also, not just yours, and we have to pay something towards his upkeep. That's all.'

Nicola wanted to turn and run out of the room. She was

overwhelmed at seeing her son again, and meeting all these people who'd witnessed her inability to cope. And now Aisling was talking money, and maintenance, and responsibilities, and Nicola felt completely and utterly out of her depth all over again.

Aisling seemed to see this. 'But it's not about the money, obviously. We're here to support you and Darren in any way we can. I've had kids myself. I'm not saying that makes me an expert or anything, but if there was ever anything you wanted to know . . . if you wanted the female take on things, you know?'

She meant now that Nicola's mother was gone. Nicola immediately realised that that was what she was getting at. And she was judging her. It was written all over her face. She saw it now: it had been a horrible mistake, leaving Darren with these people. She'd thought it would be something like respite care, and when it was over, she'd take him back and everything would go back to normal.

But instead she'd opened a door, and the Bradys – Aisling especially – weren't going to let it close again. Fool that she was, she'd invited them into her life, and even if she didn't want them any more, they weren't going to go quietly.

'I know what's best for him, okay?' Nicola tossed the envelope on to the table. 'He's my son. I got him this far without any help from you.'

But she had underestimated Aisling. She was suddenly before Nicola, face accusing.

'Oh really? Not even informing Anto of his own child's existence until three weeks ago, that's the best for Darren? And what about leaving him to the mercy of the weather on a December night? A seven-month-old baby! My God, he could have died!'

Nicola was shaking. She'd known all along that this would end up coming back at her. It was another terrible mistake; the worst she'd made in her life. She'd give anything to undo it. But she couldn't.

'I waited.' She knew how feeble it sounded. 'I saw you taking him in.'

'You didn't even know us! We could have been mass murderers for all you cared! But you were going to leave your baby with us?'

'I left him with his father! Not *you*.'

On cue, the back door burst open and a boy struggled in.

He looked at Nicola and she froze. Anto.

At least she assumed it was Anto. He was covered in mud, from the top of his auburn hair down to his large booted feet. Two thin white legs poked out of filthy shorts, and his lower lip was swollen, giving him a slight lisp as he gawped at her and said uncertainly, '*Nicola?*'

She knew from his face that he was thinking the same as her: that it was amazing how much better-looking people seemed when you were drunk. He was probably wondering to himself, *Where's the stunner I met that night? Who's your one in the leggings and looking a bit chunky round the middle?*

For Nicola, Anto was shorter than the version she'd bedded, and punier than she remembered. He was still good-looking, though, but in an angular, unformed kind of way. In the cold light of day, he was just a boy, she realised, not the passionate man she'd built herself up into believing she'd rolled about with on the pile of coats that night.

It was just as well she'd been keeping her feet on the ground about this great reunion. Because it was even more disappointing than she could have imagined.

'Anto,' she said crisply.

Aisling came rushing forward, flapping. 'Oh my God! What happened to your face?'

Anto waved her away. 'I was taken down by some fuck— I mean, some eejit. I'm grand. It's just a busted lip.'

He smiled shyly at Nicola, shifting from one muddy foot to the other. 'So! Um, nice to meet you again.'

The minute he said it, he knew he shouldn't have, because the three of them, his mother included, immediately pictured their buck-naked first encounter.

Nicola gave him a wall-eyed stare.

'What I mean is . . . Have you seen Darren yet?'

'Yes.'

She was aware of Aisling hovering. They weren't even going to be given any privacy. No chance to say to each other, *Well this is a right fuck-up, isn't it?* or *Thanks a bunch for never texting me afterwards, you loser!*

Everything was monitored, as it always would be, because Anto and Nicola were kids who didn't know what they doing, according to the adults. And it didn't matter if those adults had made a mess of things themselves; they were going to poke their noses in and screw it up for the *next* generation. For Darren.

She could hear him now, a distant *Waah!* that was getting louder. Some primitive alarm system went off in her, as it always did when he cried, and she turned anxiously to the door.

Here came Louise back in now, carrying a red-faced, bawling Darren. 'I think he wants you,' she said.

Nicola held out her arms automatically, but Louise walked past her without even seeing her and handed him straight to Aisling.

'It's all right, darling,' she said to him, cuddling him close. She jiggled him about expertly, but he didn't quieten. He looked from Aisling to Nicola and then to Anto, and you could see he was confused and unsettled, and they were all to blame.

'Sometimes he gets like this,' Aisling said. 'Shhh.'

Nicola's arms ached for him. She knew that she could settle him down. But that would only start the whole cycle again.

'He's probably hungry,' Anto tried. Nicola felt him look at her, as though hoping she'd be impressed by his parenting skills. He was as bad as her in that department. Darren had been landed with two disasters who could barely look after themselves, never mind him. And somehow it made what she was about to do less hard.

Mossy and her dad drifted back in now, back from loading up the car

'Hey. What's all the fuss about?' Mossy said to a crying Darren, playful.

Dad was looking at Anto and Nicola politely. Waiting for a formal introduction. But that would only delay things more. And Nicola had to do this while she was certain; while it was clear in her head that she was doing it for Darren.

'I want a word with Anto on my own,' she said, loud over the noise. She ignored them all, grabbed Anto's hand, and pushed him back out the door he'd just come through.

'Easy,' said Anto, taken aback.

They stood there in the side passage, which was littered with tins of paint and a ladder and bikes. Nicola was breathing hard. Her chest was so tight that she couldn't get enough air in. She searched Anto's face intently, looking for any trace of the connection they'd had that night; the sense that if you peeled back their skins, they were the same underneath.

But a pale, rather confused lad with a thick lip looked back at her.

'What's up?' he lisped.

And Nicola knew she'd have to do this on her own. 'I know you're going to be shocked. But when you think about it – *really* think about it – you'll realise I'm right.' She breathed out hard. 'I think we should put Darren up for adoption.'

Chapter Twenty

The only person who could reliably recount what had happened after that was Louise, mostly because she'd been standing on the sidelines. According to her recollection, Aisling had apparently said, 'Adoption? *Adop*tion? Adoption!' about twenty times, growing progressively louder and wilder with each utterance.

Hugo had kept interjecting, whilst throwing furious and stunned looks at Nicola, 'I don't know what's going on here, but we need to sit down and talk about—'

Mossy kept cutting him off with sarcastic cries of 'Great! This is just bloody great!'

Anto seemed to think that everybody was blaming *him*, because he protested loudly at regular intervals, 'This wasn't my idea! I had nothing to do with it! I thought Darren was going home today . . . Shite, my lip's bleeding again! Tissue, tissue!'

'Adoption!' Aisling again, aghast, holding Darren close.

'There won't be any adoption,' Hugo tried to assure her. 'This is clearly some knee-jerk thing—'

'Great!' shouted Mossy.

'It's not my fault!' bleated Anto, looking very upset.

'Waaah!' cried Darren, rattled at all the shouting.

Then it got really nasty.

'We'll settle him at home and call you later about this,' Hugo said, reaching for Darren.

But Aisling reared away. 'No. He's not going anywhere.'

Hugo, confused: 'But . . . you can't take this *seriously*. Look, I don't know what's going on here, but Nicola and I will be talking about it, I can assure you.'

'Talk, then. And come back for him.'

A beat.

'Nicola needs time with her baby right now, Aisling.' Hugo, a hint of steel.

'He's right,' said Mossy. 'Hand the lad over.'

'No.' Aisling clutched Darren like he was her own. 'How do we know she won't give him away again? She did once already.'

'Adoptions can't take place that quickly. Look, no decisions will be made about anything. I promise.' And Hugo held out his hands again for Darren.

'Get out,' said Aisling.

'Great!' shouted Mossy.

'This is not my fault,' Anto said softly and miserably.

'Waaah,' Darren cried harder.

'You want us to leave?' Hugo was stunned.

'Yes, I do. Darren is staying where I know he's safe. So you and Nicola . . .' Aisling flung her head in Nicola's direction; she couldn't bring herself to look at her directly. 'You can just go.'

'But . . .'

'*Go.*'

And after a moment, they did.

Mossy sighed quietly. 'Great.'

The only person who had said nothing was Nicola.

Chapter Twenty-one

S urprisingly, it was his da who talked the most sense.

'Let's just keep our heads, okay?' he advised. 'Let things calm down a bit. Then we can go and talk to her. Here, take those two out.'

Anto lifted two paint drums from the back of the van. They were in Ballyfermot, painting the outside of a house. A one-day job. Anto didn't normally go with his da. And it wasn't just because of Da's bad history of giving jobs to his kids either. Apparently Anto had butterfingers. He'd heard him say that in the kitchen after that time he spilled a whole can of primer all over the back of the van. You couldn't get in it for weeks without being over-whelmed by the fumes. Anto wasn't too put out at not going along any more, especially as his da never let him play any good stations on the battered old transistor radio they brought with them to pass the time. He always played country music – people with twangy voices wailing about lost women and cows dying in the field – and it did Anto's head in.

But today Anto was glad to get away. He got the impression

his da was too. Carefully he put the two paint drums down without spilling anything, and went back for the ladder.

'Hello, boys!' A lady with a startling blue rinse and a frilly apron came out of the house, like an apparition. 'You're here early!'

Anto suppressed a yawn and checked his watch. Eight o'clock on a Saturday morning! It was unnatural. In his old life, which seemed so long ago now, he'd only be turning over for his second sleep.

But it looked like he'd better get used to early starts, thanks to Nicola. Or the headcase, as he'd heard her called more than once at home.

'I've put on a nice fry for you,' the blue-haired lady was saying.

'Ah, you shouldn't have, Mrs Fagan,' said Mossy, brightening.

'And for this young lad here.' She twinkled at Anto. For a minute he worried that she was going to pinch his cheek. 'I'd say it's a hard job keeping you fed, is it? I'll put on extra sausages,' she promised him.

'No, don't, it's okay,' he said hurriedly, but she was gone back in.

Anto was completely off his food. And who could blame him? All the aggro was playing havoc with his whole system: he had exams coming up; he'd just recently discovered he was a father, and now, if Nicola had her way, that might be whipped away from him just as fast. He wouldn't see Darren again until he was eighteen! He'd end up being brought up by some nice but face-less couple in a small town in the midlands.

At least that was what he'd heard his ma say last night, when they were arguing in the kitchen.

It had started up again: all the rowing and bad moods. Just when he'd thought it was finally over. Only this time Anto was the one who'd brought it upon the family. His ma had looked wretched this morning. He'd felt terrible.

His da was looking at him. 'All right, son?'

'Yeah.' Troubled, he burst out, 'She can't do it, can she? Put him up for adoption?'

Every time he thought about it, he felt emotion rising up in him. It was like something from the sixties or seventies. Putting a kid up for adoption. *Darren*. His own flesh and blood.

'I'm talking, like, legally?'

Da looked troubled too. 'It won't come to anything like that.'

'Are you sure? Ma says that because we're not married or anything I don't have the same rights as Nicola.'

'You do have rights, okay? So don't be thinking like that.' He put his hand on Anto's shoulder. It was a bit awkward. Anto couldn't remember the last time his da had touched him. 'Look, I don't want you getting stressed about this, okay? Your ma and I, we're going to deal with it. There's nobody going to whip Darren away while your back is turned.'

Anto tried to take comfort from the words. But it was such a lot to take in. Even seeing her there in the kitchen the other evening was a shock.

Like, he'd known she was coming and all that. They'd arranged it on the phone. But then the bloody bus broke down, and he'd been hoping to make it home from soccer in time to shower and change . . .

He needn't have worried about making a good impression; the girl who met him was in a baggy jumper and with her hair in a big messy pile on top of her head. He honestly wasn't sure it was her at first. Her face was shiny and . . . well, a bit pimply. She'd crossed her arms over her chest rather hostilely, her jumper riding up to reveal a bit of a belly.

And he saw that she'd had it pierced. *Another* thing he didn't remember. But maybe she'd had it done only recently.

She didn't seem at all pleased to see him. She, who'd used him for sex that night and never tried to contact him afterwards! And she hadn't even changed her leggings before coming over to meet him. There was something spilled down the side of the ones she wore.

But he'd smiled. He'd been polite. Her mouth had only turned down further. There seemed to be no fond memories at all of their night of passion together.

And now the adoption. It was like she was trying to rid herself not only of Anto, but of Darren too. She wanted nothing more to do with either of them.

It was beyond depressing.

Da was easing the ladder out of the back of the van. Anto took the other end of it. 'Careful now,' said Da.

They extended the ladder and hoisted it up against the outside of the house. It bounced a bit on Anto's side as it hit the wall, and a piece of plaster fell down on him. He hoped his da wasn't going to give out to him. When he didn't, Anto plucked up his courage.

'Da?'

'What?'

'Ma says she's not letting Darren be adopted. That she doesn't care what she has to do, but there's no way it's going to happen.'

His da's mouth went a bit thin. 'I know what your ma is saying.'

'But supposing she's right? And he's not adopted? And he comes to live with us.' Anto was ashamed to say it, but he had to. 'What if I screw it up?'

His da looked puzzled. 'You won't. We'll help.'

'But I'll still have to do all the fatherly stuff and rear him properly and set him a good example. And that's only right. I just don't think I'm going to measure up, that's all.'

'You will, son.'

'Not to your standards.' He didn't want to hurt his da. He just wanted them both to be clear, that was all.

His da stared. 'Anto . . .'

'It's better that you know that now.' He turned away and walked back to the van.

'Look at the ball! Look at the ball!'

But Darren, depressingly, wouldn't. They were sitting on Anto's bedroom floor. Anto was trying to amuse him, which wasn't going very well. He was preparing to roll the ball again when there were thunderous steps outside and the door burst open to admit Shannon.

'I heard the news,' she announced with her usual candour, 'and I came straight over.'

'You could try knocking before you barge in,' Anto said ungratefully.

Darren, to add insult to injury, made a lunge for Shannon the minute he saw her. 'Eeh! Eeh!' He held up his arms frantically.

'Hiya, beautiful!' She looked to Anto. 'Can I . . .?'

'Take him, take him. He obviously can't get away from me fast enough.' It didn't bode well for the rest of their lives together.

Shannon made a fuss of Darren, cuddling him and kissing him – Darren laughed and cooed like billy-o, of course, just to twist the knife – and then she settled herself down on the other single bed with him on her knee. 'Look,' she said to Anto, 'have you talked to Nicola yet?'

'Why would I want to talk to her?' Anto said sulkily.

But Shannon had no time for self-pity. Usually she'd bore the culprit senseless with appalling statistics on those poor wretches who had a *right* to self-pity: 'Did you know that two-point-one billion people have inadequate water source and/or sanitation, with almost half of them living on less than two dollars a day?' Anto would often be left bamboozled.

She must have felt sorry for him today, though, because she confined herself to 'Why do you think, you plonker?'

'No,' Anto muttered. 'I haven't spoken to her, okay?'

He had Nicola's number now. Her cell phone *and* her home number. And her dad's too. One of the privileges of having fathered her child. A part of him felt he *should* contact her; even just to send a text if he hadn't the nerve to ring her outright. But each time he tried to compose one, he couldn't seem to get the tone right.

Hey there! So listen, about this adoption business . . .

Or, *Anto here. Darren's father. Yeah, the guy who has some rights too, you know!!!*

Everything felt wrong. So he'd sent nothing at all. But he was starting to regret it now. It looked like he didn't give a shit; couldn't even rouse himself to send a lousy text about the adoption of his own son.

Shannon watched all this play out on his face. She was like a fucking mind-reader. 'You can't just ignore this, Anto. You're going to have to take some kind of control.'

More pressure. Anto was fed up of it.

'Oh, just go on a three-day bender, Shannon, like other girls your age. Or give Matt a good seeing-to. God knows the poor eejit looks like he's dying for it.'

Shannon was immune to insult. 'We're talking about you here. Not me.'

'Well, seeing as you know so much, what do *you* suggest I do?

A Special Delivery

My life's a fucking mess! It's Friday night, my mates have all gone clubbing and I'm stuck at home trying to study while minding this fella!'

Who was looking at him right now with blatant dislike. Darren just didn't seem to take to Anto – his own father! – no matter what Anto did. He'd fed him his dinner, changed his nappy and read him 'The Three Little Pigs', even putting on funny voices, but Darren had stared like he was some kind of pond life.

Shannon took Anto's outburst in good stead. 'And to cap it all, he's just done a big poo,' she told him kindly. 'I can smell it.'

'Oh, man!'

'It's okay. I'll change him.'

Anto was partially mollified. That was why he always found it difficult to hate Shannon completely; she was usually pretty decent when it came down to it.

'How's school?' she asked.

'You're only humouring me now.'

'I'll stop if you want.'

But Anto quite fancied talking now. Nobody seemed to take much interest in him any more. It was all Darren this and Darren that. Not that Anto was jealous or anything. But he quite missed his ma bullying him into a chair and standing over his shoulder while he wrote some essay or other. 'School is shite!' he grumped.

He'd been back two weeks now since Christmas. Two long weeks of the lads slipping condoms in his bag for the laugh, and the girls saying, 'Oooh, Anto, impregnate me!' every time he walked past. Baz and Sean had been his wingmen, batting people off with 'Well at least he's not shooting blanks like *you*, Damo Murphy.'

He told Shannon all this. To cap it all, they were heading out to a new club tonight; it was going to be mental. Everyone knew why he wasn't going, of course.

'If they're all out clubbing, then there's bound to be some fresh gossip on Monday and they won't bother talking about you any more,' Shannon consoled him.

'Maybe.'

Anto felt a bit better now. Shannon could put a good spin on anything. But his mood plunged again when the door burst open once more. This time Louise barged in.

'Doesn't anybody knock around here!' he growled.

'Shut up,' Louise said efficiently. 'It's time for Darren's bath.'

She had a towel over her arm, and was clutching a collection of pink bubble baths and her new Pampering Pinkie nail set that she'd got for Christmas, God help him.

'Does Ma know you're giving him a bath?' Shannon said suspiciously.

'Of course she does.'

'Does she *really*?'

'Yes.'

'Look me in the eye when you say that.'

Louise buckled. 'OKAY! She doesn't. But I'm going to ask her when she gets off the phone to the solicitor.'

Shannon and Anto exchanged looks. What solicitor?

Louise was delighted at the position of power she suddenly found herself in. '*If* you want to have a say in what happens to Darren,' she informed Anto loftily, 'the solicitor told Ma you'll have to go to court and make an application for a garden chip.'

'I think you mean a guardianship,' Shannon said.

'That's what I *said*.' She held out her hands for Darren. 'Come on! Emma and the girls are coming around to visit and we need you looking your best.'

'You run the bath,' Shannon instructed sternly. 'Then I'll bring Darren and supervise, okay?'

'Okay.' Louise skipped off.

Anto looked at Shannon in fright. Solicitors. Court. *Guardianships*. He was just a simple lad from the wrong side of town; what had he ever done to deserve any of this?

'I know you feel a bit freaked out right now,' Shannon said. She looked slightly rattled herself. 'But you're going to have to make some decisions here, Anto, before the whole thing is taken out of your hands.' She gave him a meaningful look: their ma and da, in other words. 'Like, do you want to keep Darren? Bring him up yourself? Or do you want to try to convince Nicola to keep him, and you share him between you? Or maybe you think adoption is the best thing after all?'

'I don't know! I just don't know, okay?' Anto's head was boiled. He wanted to fling himself down on his bed in despair, but that wouldn't be a good example for Darren and so he kept his expression stoic.

'It would break Ma's heart if we were to lose him too,' he said.

'This isn't about Ma.'

They looked at each other. There was nobody there except them. They didn't have to censor themselves.

'But it is. It's about all of us. Since he's been here, people are talking again, laughing, chatting. He's done that. And if we were to lose him, well . . .' Anto trailed off. He didn't think the family would recover this time.

Shannon was shaking her head vehemently. 'He's not some kind of sticking plaster for the rest of us.'

Darren sat very quietly on her knee, his eyes tennis-balling between her and Anto. You would nearly think he understood what was going on.

'I know that.'

'Then stop thinking about everybody else. This is about Darren.'

Louise's voice floated in. 'I'm running the bath!'

Shannon stood up and hoisted Darren up. 'Right! Let's go find Louise, will we? Wave to Daddy!'

Darren wouldn't. Even when Shannon lifted his hand and waved it for him, it looked like he was shaking his fist at Anto.

'Wait.' Anto looked at the bed Shannon had vacated. 'Have you heard from him at all?' he blurted.

Shannon hesitated. 'No.'

'Me neither.'

It hung in the air for a minute, the hurt and the loss, then Shannon went off with Darren.

Anto was left looking at the empty bed. The stress of everything suddenly got on top of him; the tears came rushing out, and he bolted up and locked the door just in time. Nobody ever bloody knocked in this house.

Chapter Twenty-two

Mossy told Aisling they were going out for a meal.

'A *meal*?'

'Yes. As in something to eat.'

'I know, it's just we haven't been out for a meal together since . . .'

She fished around. Somewhere back in the Dark Ages, anyway. In the days when they used to have sex.

'Zofia and Olaf are going to babysit,' Mossy informed her crisply. 'I've already asked.'

'Right. Great.' Aisling was still baffled. Mossy didn't look that friendly. He certainly didn't look in the mood for a romantic meal.

But it became clear that romance was the last thing on his mind when he said tersely, 'We need to talk. And at least in a restaurant there's less chance of it descending into a screaming match.'

Things had been tense. Tenser than usual, that was. Probably more so since she'd engaged the services of a legal team 'without consulting any of us, not even Anto, Darren's actual father,' Mossy had stated coldly.

171

He was acting like she was in the wrong. There she was, doing her level best to wrestle her grandson's future from the claws of social workers and some nice but childless couple on a waiting list, and he couldn't even look the tiniest bit grateful?

Bring on tonight. She was ready.

Zofia and Olaf arrived at half past seven on the dot, and Aisling let them in.

'At least you'll get a bit of time to yourself, away from Olaf's mother,' she murmured to Zofia. According to Zofia, Magda had launched a particularly scurrilous and underhanded attack during the week on the way Zofia had been ironing one of Olaf's shirts. 'I've left a bottle of wine in the fridge, if you fancied a glass.'

'Thank you,' said Zofia, her face peculiarly tight. 'But that won't be necessary.'

She jerked her head violently backwards; Aisling looked past her to see Magda trundling in after Olaf. Olaf was all smiles as he helped Magda out of her coat and informed Mossy and Aisling, 'Lucky for you, my mother has offered to help us out tonight with Darren. She is *wonderful* with children. We had the best childhood ever, growing up in Warsaw with her.'

Magda blushed under all this praise. 'Stop that,' she chided him.

Zofia's eyes were a bit glittery. 'Yes. He will tell you about it sometime,' she said to Aisling and Mossy. 'In great detail.'

Olaf gave a bit of an uneasy laugh. Magda looked uncertain. 'Now, let's get you settled, Mama, eh?' Olaf said. 'Come on. The best seat in the house!'

He gave Zofia a look as he courteously ushered Magda past and deposited her in pole position in front of the telly.

'Maybe I will have that bottle of wine after all,' Zofia ground out to Aisling.

'We are not keeping Darren.' Mossy said the words quietly but forcefully.

'Let's order first, will we?'

'Did you hear me?'

'Because I'm starving.'

She was sounding all chirpy and normal, but inside she was quaking. With upset. With anger. He'd invited her out to dinner to casually reject their grandchild?

'Look,' he said, reaching for her hand. 'I know this is all very upsetting.'

She recoiled from him. 'For who? Not you, anyway.'

He kept on in that measured voice. 'I have to say it now, before it goes too far. You tearing in there with solicitors, and all this stuff about guardianship orders . . . This isn't your fight, Aisling.'

She didn't say anything for a moment. She couldn't; she was afraid she really would start that screaming match he was so worried about. Maybe that was okay, though. Maybe they *should* shout and scream. Better than this pretence, thin as gossamer now, that everything was okay between them; that they were united, singing from the same hymn sheet, whatever the hell you wanted to call it.

But she stayed calm. 'So, you want me to leave all this to Anto, is that it? And that loon of a girl who wants to give our grandchild away? We should back off and let them slug it out?'

'Yes.'

'An eighteen-year-old boy who doesn't yet know that nappy bins don't actually empty themselves? And a girl with a belly piercing in the shape of a butterfly?'

Actually, Aisling had been impressed by that. She'd always

wanted a belly piercing, but nobody had had them when she'd been in her teens, except very loose girls. Her hunger for one, or else a discreet tattoo, had only grown over the years, peaking around her fortieth birthday, but now it was too late to get one, because the only thing she could think of was the kids' faces if she came home one day and whipped up her T-shirt and went, 'Ta-da!'

'Yes, they're young. But they're not incapable. And Darren is their child.'

'I'm aware of that. But Anto is also our child. And we can't just dump this mess into his lap and assume he knows how to deal with it. He needs our guidance. Our help, Mossy.'

She couldn't believe he was being like this: capable of washing his hands of the whole problem, like it was nothing to do with them.

'What help is that exactly, Aisling? Darren's mother clearly feels unable to bring him up. She thinks he'd be better off in another family.' His eyes were a challenge. 'I'm presuming from your actions that you want that family to be ours?'

She lifted her chin in response. She wasn't afraid. 'And you want him adopted, is that it? Your own grandchild? Well come on, Mossy, spit it out. Seeing as we're being so honest here. I want him to be brought up with people who love him, in a family with his father and grandparents and aunts, and you'd prefer to let him go and live with people who have no biological connection to him whatsoever, and maybe never see him again?'

Let him say it. Let them both hear what he really thought.

Mossy's sigh was deep and beaten. 'We can't take on another child.'

'We can, Mossy. Anto's child.'

'Anto,' Mossy threw out. 'And before you think I'm dismissing him, he's got his exams. You only have to look at him to know he's finding things hard going as it is. Even if he agrees to this guardianship thing, he's young. He's got his whole life to live! Next year he'll be in college, or training, then after that it's a job, and who's left to bring up Darren? You and me.'

His face was set but his words had lit a fierce spark of hope in her. He'd thought it through. He'd fast-forwarded through the permutations. Which meant that he must be considering it at *some* level.

'I know it would be tough,' she said carefully.

'Tough! Jesus, Aisling, we're barely standing after bringing up our own.'

She couldn't let his happen now; for them to go down the awful twisted road of blame and failure. So she kept it light. 'You just don't want to do the night feeds all over again.'

He looked at her. 'Dead right I don't.'

'Or all the nappy-changing and the baby-proofing and the running around after a toddler.'

'No, no and no,' he agreed emphatically.

'You're sounding like my mother.'

'Your mother and I rarely agree on anything, but for once she talks sense.'

Aisling tried out a smile. She felt this was going okay. If they could just break it down into little bits, he would see that it was manageable.

'I'd do most of it,' she dangled.

'Aisling . . .'

'I would. I know we're older now, and it would be hard going while he was little. And I'd have to sort something out workwise. But we could do it, Mossy.' A pause. 'We *should* do it.'

They didn't really have a choice, as she saw it.

He said nothing for ages. Then: 'What if she changes her mind? Nicola. And wants him back? It's possible.'

'I know.'

'The thing is, we haven't even sat down and spoken to them yet about any of this.'

There had been no word from Hugo or Nicola in the days since. Not even the daily regulation phone call from Hugo. But then again, she'd more or less thrown them out of the house.

'When he gets his head around this properly, like the rest of us are trying to do, do you really believe Hugo's going to let his grandson be adopted?' Mossy wondered.

'Well, no . . .'

'No. And you can bet that right now he's doing his level best to get Nicola to change her mind.'

Aisling could just imagine it. The intense sessions between father and daughter. Him persuasive. Saying they could manage. That adoption would only haunt her and Darren for the rest of their lives.

'And if so, I hope he succeeds,' she said quietly. 'Truly. But if he doesn't, we need a contingency plan. That's all this is.'

Mossy's mouth twisted. 'For a contingency plan, you have it pretty well worked out.

'You're making it sound like I'm doing something wrong.'

'You're steaming ahead without asking what anybody else wants to do.'

'The O'Sullivans? Yes, Mossy, you're right. I'm not going to sit around while they threaten adoption. And Anto's too young to make this decision on his own.' She leaned in, appealing to him. 'Darren is part of our family and I'll do everything in my power to make sure he remains that way.'

Mossy said nothing. He was afraid. She knew this, because she was afraid too.

'Maybe this is a second chance for us,' she said.

His head jerked up. The look on his face was painful.

'We'd get it right for Darren.'

This boy would turn out okay. And maybe he might fix them too, Mossy and Aisling, and the holes that had appeared in their marriage.

'Hey, folks!' A waiter appeared at the table. He had sticky-uppy hair and was painfully happy. 'My name is Nigel and I'm your server for the evening! You ready to order?'

'No,' said Mossy flatly.

The waiter's smile faltered. 'Oh. Okay,' and he backed away.

Mossy rubbed his eyes. Ran a hand roughly through his hair. When he looked at her, it was hard to know which way it was going to go.

'Look, I want the best for Darren too. He's my grandson as well. But it's one thing accepting him, which of course we do, and another to make a commitment to raise him almost as our own.'

'Mossy.' Her mouth was dry.

'I'm sorry. But we can't introduce another child into the mess we've made.'

She scrabbled around for the words to make him change his mind, but instead ended up flinging at him, 'So let's just send him on his way, problem solved?'

'No.'

'Why not? It's what you did before.'

Mossy looked shocked. 'Me? It was our decision. Yours and mine.'

'No it wasn't. You made me choose between you and my child. And I've never regretted anything more in my life.'

She stood up and walked out.

Chapter Twenty-three

Aisling didn't go that night. She knew it would be dangerous in her present state of mind. Mostly she was worried that she wouldn't be able to stay in her car and just watch, like usual. She'd be compelled to ring his doorbell until he came out, and she'd end up pleading with him to allow some small contact – even just a weekly text to let them know that he was alive.

That would be a big mistake. It would be handing him back all the power again, apparently. He would look at her and say in that terribly cold voice, as he'd done before, 'Well, you asked for this. Now you've got it.'

She wasn't afraid of his rejection. She was well used to it. She was just afraid of it tonight. Because up to now she'd only got through this because she and Mossy were united. However awful it was, it was awful together.

But now it was like they were letting each other go too; floating off in different directions as they each tried to deal with what they'd done.

Lately, though, she'd been wondering whether this drifting

apart hadn't started much earlier – years before maybe, who knew? Maybe even when the children were first born, and they were flailing around the place trying to figure out what it meant to be a parent, and why on earth nobody had given them a manual as they were leaving the hospital.

From the outset there had been differences. The tree, for instance: the dreaded gnarly oak tree at the top of the road by the green that put the fear of God into the neighbourhood mothers, and out of which at least five children would fall every year, and duly break arms, elbows, wrists and, once, a leg in *five different places*. (This was probably an urban myth, but it was a good one.)

'That shagging tree,' mothers would curse as they bore yet another child off to A&E. 'Someone's going to get killed one of these days.'

Naturally Aisling took all this on board, especially as it seemed that she very nearly killed the children on a regular basis as it was, what with wonky stair gates, and leaving the tumble dryer door open, which Anto took as an invitation to see how much of Baby Louise he could fit into it.

'Do. Not. Go. Near. That. Tree. Go and pull the wings off defenceless bugs if you must, but stay away from that tree, do you hear me?' she would impress ferociously on the kids every summer morning before letting them out the front door. 'Someone should chop it down,' she was always saying to Mossy, half hoping that he'd whip out the chainsaw and do it himself. In case he didn't quite get it, she repeated the neighbourhood mantra: 'It's only a matter of time before someone gets killed, you know.'

Then one evening a crowd of children gathered round the tree ominously, looking up into its branches. Aisling raced towards it, her heart bursting with panic. Clearly something dreadful had happened this time: some mite had got impaled on a lethal branch, or was rendered helpless by altitude sickness, and the emergency services would have to be rounded up immediately.

Anto was up the tree. And Shannon.

'Hiya, Ma!'

They were very, very high up, higher than most kids dared to venture, and they were frightened, but also exhilarated.

'Oh my God,' Aisling whispered in terror. What were they doing? Anto was barely seven!

Then she heard it: Mossy's voice, from the other side of the tree. 'Higher!' he brazenly encouraged. 'Ah go on, sure you're barely halfway up!'

He said to Aisling afterwards that it was character-building. It'd toughen them up. He couldn't be swayed by the X-ray of the leg broken in five different places that was being touted about the estate to various *ooh*s and *aah*s.

'They're going to climb it anyway, so they might as well do it while I'm there,' he said calmly. (He didn't quite have the same attitude when it came to drugs and sex later on, but anyhow.)

'You overrode me,' she said, furious.

'They wanted to climb it, so I said I'd take them.'

For a second she almost thought he'd done it on purpose. To show her or something.

'We can't wrap them in cotton wool,' he said, as though he knew best.

In many ways they were hardly unusual. Ma was the worrier, like a lot of mothers. She was the soft touch. Da, on the other hand, was good for a dose of tough love, if you ever needed one, or a hammer and nail to put up that print of Eminem on your bedroom wall. A lot of couples were like them, and they got by quite nicely overall until they hit the wall, otherwise known as the teenage years.

'What are we going to do?' Aisling said, semi-scandalised, the first time they'd been told to fuck off. *To their faces.*

'Ground him. That's what.' Mossy was clear and resolute. If you did the crime, you did the time. Simples.

So he couldn't understand why, when he unveiled this punishment, he was succinctly told to fuck off again.

'Well if that's the way he wants to play it . . . We'll stop his allowance too,' he said excitedly. 'That'll sort him out.'

It didn't. In fact he got called some very colourful words that they thought they might have to ask Anto the meaning of.

'What the hell is wrong with him?' Mossy was flummoxed and upset.

Aisling weighed in with her own approach, which was to try to understand the situation. 'I think he's just going through a bad patch. They're at a funny stage. Hormones and all that.'

But Mossy had no time for hormones of any kind. 'No. No touchy-feely stuff. No rubbing his back and telling him it's okay.'

'I do not rub his back!' She was very offended at that.

'That boy has to learn, Aisling. Now, we need to stick together on this, okay? Otherwise he'll ride roughshod over us.'

He did anyway. No matter how much Mossy applied a hard line, things got worse.

After one particularly bruising confrontation, Mossy found Aisling making for the stairs with a plate of food. He had looked from the tray to her face.

'No,' he said. 'No food. He walked off a job with me today. And you're telling him that it's okay?'

'He walked off the job because he said you were constantly criticising him. Look, I know he can be lazy, Mossy—'

'Lazy?' He was incredulous. 'If he was in any other job, he'd have been fired after the first day and you know it.'

'Well . . .'

'He would have, Aisling.'

'All right!'

'So stop making excuses. Please. It's not helping him. In fact, it's doing the opposite.'

'In your opinion.'

Mossy had walked out, slamming the door hard.

Anto, Louise and Shannon came out from the living room.

'What's wrong? What's after happening now?' They were resigned.

'Nothing,' Aisling said brightly. 'Everything's absolutely fine.'

Chapter Twenty-four

Nicola had some kind of weird breakdown one day out of the blue.

They were just lying on her bed – her, Becky and Mikaela – talking about Murph. Mikaela had slept with him at the New Year's Eve party in Wicklow, and they were now officially an item.

'So, like, things are going well?' Becky probed.

'Yeah.' Mikaela was being unusually coy.

'And he's not after anything exotic in the sack after all?'

'I'm not talking about that! It's private!'

'It never was before.'

'Yeah, well this is different, okay? I really like Murph.'

'Are you sure he doesn't like to dress up in your suspenders or anything?'

'No!' Mikaela squealed. 'Anyway, I don't even have suspenders! Look, I'm not getting into details, but he's normal in that department, okay? He just likes to be on top.'

Becky winked at Nicola. 'That's probably only for starters so he doesn't freak you out. He might produce an inflatable doll one of these nights.'

They shrieked with laughter.

'He wouldn't know what to do with an inflatable doll.' Mikaela wiped her eyes. 'He's dead straight, Murph.' She looked happy.

'Makes a change from that last fella, eh? The one who wanted BJs all the time.'

'God, yeah. I mean, what was I getting out of that?'

'Well, presumably he returned the favour?'

'No way! He wouldn't ever go down there. Said it was dirty.'

Looks flew around. *That* wasn't right.

'And what about *his* bits?' Becky demanded. 'They smelt like roses, did they?'

'More like something that had been dead for a week.'

More hysterics. Nicola hadn't laughed so much in years. She felt giddy, light-headed. Like she was outside of herself or something. Then suddenly she was crying. It had happened the day before too, completely unexpectedly. She'd been in the supermarket, of all places, and she'd seen an old lady in a wheelchair. You could see her pink scalp through the wisps of her hair, and there was something about the vulnerability of it that had ripped Nicola's heart out. She'd stood there in the bread section, bawling, and she couldn't stop, and she was frightened.

'Nicola?' The girls sat up.

'S-sorry.' She couldn't stop now either. Tears and snot ran down her face.

'You're grand. It's fine.' They cuddled in around her on

the bed and they rubbed her back and stroked her hair. Motherly.

'That's it,' they soothed. 'Let it all out. You'll feel better.'

They tried to understand.

'It's this adoption thing, isn't it? Look at you, you're totally stressed out over it. Anybody would be. And when you think about it . . . giving your own kid away . . . you can't really be serious, can you?'

Nicola's face was swollen and hot but inside she felt okay again. For the moment, anyway. 'I'm not giving him away. I just want him to have a good life, that's all. With people who love him, and who'll look after him. It's *because* I love him that I'm doing it.'

They continued to look at her like she'd announced that she was handing him over to Scientology.

Becky cleared her throat, like she always did before she delivered a story. 'My auntie had a baby last year and she said she felt funny for ages after. And she'd been trying to have a baby for *years*. IVF and everything, ten rounds of it.'

'Ten!' breathed Mikaela.

'Maybe not ten, but loads of them anyway,' Becky conceded. 'And in the end she had a baby but instead of being delighted she said she felt all sad, like her old life was suddenly over and now she only existed to look after the baby. So you see,' she told Nicola, 'you're not weird at all.'

'I didn't say I was weird.'

There was a moment of embarrassment.

'Well no, of course not . . . I didn't mean . . .'

'What I'm saying is that I'm a bad mother.' It was a huge relief to finally tell others what she herself had known for months. She

185

felt a weight lift off her chest. The freedom of it. She wanted to shout it from the rooftops: I AM A CRAP MOTHER. If you admitted it, then you couldn't be blamed.

The others thought she was joking, kind of. 'Nicola!' they said, and took a slug of their Diet Cokes.

'No, listen to me,' she said, suddenly fierce. 'Because it might happen to you two some day. You'll probably have babies, and it doesn't matter how tired or bloated or fed up you feel, everybody will still expect you to be madly in love with this baby who's just ripped the insides out of you.'

Mikaela recoiled slightly at that, but Nicola didn't let up. They needed to know.

'And sometimes it doesn't happen that way, okay? All those mushy feelings, the way you're supposed to feel *completed* and all that. It didn't happen for me and that's all I'm saying.'

The girls were silent now, their round, young faces grappling about for the right words to say.

'And I just don't think that's fair on Darren. Why *shouldn't* he have a mother who's happy and cheerful and plays silly games with him? Someone who manages to get washed and dressed in the mornings, and put on a bit of make-up, like normal people?'

'You look grand . . .' the girls said, but in small voices. Nicola's hair looked like it hadn't seen a brush that whole week.

'Maybe even someone who . . .' She didn't want to say this. The couple of times it had happened had been terrifying. 'Doesn't worry about harming him.'

Dead silence now.

She lifted defensive eyes to their shocked faces. 'I bet your auntie never did that, did she?' she challenged Becky.

Becky's mortified silence was her answer.

'There you go,' Nicola said flatly.

It was official: she really was an aberration. Which was fine. She already knew this, from watching the other mothers in the park when she'd pushed Darren along in his buggy. The big happy heads on them, the exchanges of 'Oh wow, your little fella's got so TALL!' She would follow them round on leaden legs, like some alien who'd been beamed down, seeing how real people lived.

'You wouldn't . . . little Darren . . . He's so tiny . . .' Mikaela was wide-eyed.

Nicola was sorry she'd said anything. She knew they wouldn't understand. She didn't understand it herself; those sudden terrible images she'd had of dropping Darren on the floor deliberately, and then the panicky checks she'd make on his cot over and over again, to make sure that she actually hadn't.

'No. Of course not. I'm just saying, it's mad the thoughts you have when you're completely wrecked.' Better to just let them think she was being overly dramatic.

Their faces cleared a little. 'God, yeah,' said Becky, who'd probably had a lie-in that morning till noon again. 'And he was born early and everything, and so small to start off with. You've had your hands full.'

'Is school getting any better?' Mikaela wanted to know, in case that was part of the problem.

And now they were back on safer ground: teachers, classmates, who said what at break time. Things seventeen and eighteen-year-olds *should* be talking about. Nicola didn't blame Becky and Mikaela for not understanding. In a way she had brought all this on her own head; getting pregnant when she was still only a child herself. What did she expect? That it would turn out perfectly?

The girls were waiting expectantly for her response. They already knew school was pretty horrible, having to drop down a class, and in the middle of the year too. Stubbornly, Nicola wouldn't give them another sob story, and so she said, 'Yeah, it's good. Some of the girls are quite nice, actually. Anyway, I'm keeping my head down and studying. I just want to get my exams now, you know?'

She was saying all the right words, even though she hadn't opened a book all week.

Yesterday, she hadn't even gone in.

'So what have you done so far?' Dad enquired at dinner.

'Done?'

'The adoption, Nicola.'

The word sounded so strange and unfamiliar. She didn't think she'd ever even uttered it before now. Dad looked like he hadn't either.

'You think you can just throw it out as something you'd like to happen, and someone else will step in and organise it all for you?'

'Well, no . . .'

Neither of them had touched their dinner. It was chops. They had chops nearly every night, and peas. It was the easiest thing to pull together when there were only two of you.

'If it's what you want, then I'm afraid there's a lot of work to do. Having a child adopted is a very complicated business. We're talking about assessments. Evaluations. Counselling. It won't just change Darren's life forever. It's going to change yours too.'

And his. But he didn't need to say that. All week long she'd seen it in the rigid set of his jaw and the droop of his shoulders. There were no more long, chatty telephone calls with Aisling, although she'd seen him look at the telephone more than once.

And the silence. It had been quiet since Darren had gone, of course, but now there was the deathly quiet of two people effectively inhabiting different worlds.

'Well?' he said. 'Have you nothing to say at all?'

Eventually he sighed and turned back to pushing some peas round his plate in a lacklustre way. She'd looked down at his bent head, thinning slightly on top, and she wanted to say, *I don't know what I'm doing, Dad. I want Darren to be happy but I don't think he's going to be if he stays with me.*

But she said nothing. His hurt and sense of betrayal was so acute that the words died before they reached her lips.

'Your mother wants to Skype you tonight,' he said.

Her mother. Nicola felt her heart drop another inch or two.

'Naturally I've been filling her in on Darren, and about him spending time with his father. I told her about Anto, and the Bradys and who they were. Just so she's aware of things.'

He said it like her mother had every right to know; even after what she'd done.

'You'd better not have said anything about the adoption thing,' Nicola said fiercely.

That would have her mother on a plane in seconds. Nobody would be able to stop her. She'd barge in, like she was entitled. The last time she'd come back from Australia, just after Darren was born, Nicola had moved into Becky's for the week, even though she was barely out of hospital. Dad had ferried Darren back and forth between mother and grandmother. Nicola hadn't come home until she was gone.

Dad's eyes were dark. 'No, Nicola. I did not.'

'Good.'

She bolted to her feet. The smell of the lamb chop was making her feel sick.

'Where are you going? We need to talk about this.'

She couldn't. She wasn't up to another word of this conversation.

'Nicola!' he shouted after her, his anger bursting through. 'What the hell is wrong with you?

She was lying in bed that night, not able to sleep as usual, when a text came in. It was curt and to the point.

Darren was a bit off today. But we took him to the doctor this morning, where my ma works, and he's fine now. Just thought you should know.

It was signed *Anto*.

The pain in her stomach surged at the thought of Darren being sick. She had to press her fist into it, hard, to try to make it ease.

Just thought you should know.

She'd never get to sleep now.

Chapter Twenty-five

Work turned out to be fantastic about Darren.

'Bring him in! Bring him in! We'll all take turns looking after him. He'll brighten the place up, isn't that right, girls?' said Dr Iris Shanahan.

'Yes, indeed,' agreed her husband Tom, also Dr Shanahan. He was the only male in the building, and he enjoyed being one of the girls. They were in their fifties, a good-natured pair fond of woolly jumpers and both in need of serious haircuts. 'Anyway,' he said, 'we bring Nellie in, so it's nearly the same thing!'

Nellie was a gangling, mournful-looking dog of indeterminate breed who stayed in the back yard of the surgery while they were working. The atmosphere was all very casual, and the invitation to bring Darren along too – although presumably they didn't mean him to share the back yard with Nellie – seemed genuine.

'It'll just be for a week or two,' Aisling said apologetically, even though she had no idea really. 'Anto's at school, you see, and with his exams coming up he can't afford to miss anything. But I'll be sorting out some kind of permanent childcare.'

Mossy had quietly refused to have anything to do with the 'madness', as he kept calling it softly under his breath. Once Aisling realised just how impossible it would be to take on Darren full time, as well as hold down a job and do thrice-weekly super-markets runs and complete projects on Shakespeare, she'd soon come to her senses, seemed to be his unspoken stance. In the meantime he did his share of the childcare duties, lest he be accused of neglect. Sometimes she heard him laughing with Darren, but he killed it off quickly when she entered the room, just to punish her, she felt.

So it was with some sense of vindication that she crisply informed him, 'It's sorted. He's coming to the surgery for the morning.'

'Well that'll be stimulating for him,' Mossy said flatly. 'Watching you tap away on a computer all morning.'

'He'll be with me,' she said. 'That's the most important thing.'

He looked at her. 'You can put all the arrangements in place that you like, Aisling. But unless you have Anto and the O'Sullivans' agreement, then none of it matters.'

'I take it I don't have yours?'

'My opinion doesn't seem to count for much these days.'

Things were cold between them. Frigid, even. But at least Darren was still with them. And she wouldn't have to give up her job. She only worked mornings, in order to be at home when Louise came in from school. The surgery was always overrun with children anyway, half of whom she ended up looking after while their parents were in with either of the Dr Shanahans. The way she figured it, Darren would fit right in.

All the same, she checked with receptionists April and May ('We just need a June now!' Dr Tom was always quipping), and the other office administrator, Shirley, that they were okay with it too.

'I wouldn't want him distracting you or anything.'

'Christ, I hope he does,' was April's heartfelt response. 'Make the week go faster.'

May wasn't the maternal kind, she confessed honestly, but she didn't mind a bit of spit and poo so long as it didn't interfere with her. And as for Shirley, well, she was a saint anyway, having already covered for Aisling for nearly two weeks now, since the Christmas break was over. Aisling had bought her a massive box of chocolates as a thank-you, and Shirley fell upon them with cries of 'You demon, you demon.'

Aisling didn't go into detail about Darren. She just explained that he was her grandson, and that his father was Anto.

'Anto?' The girls could hardly conceal their surprise. He'd always seemed so awkward whenever he'd been in the surgery. Hands buried in his pockets and unable to sustain eye contact, that kind of thing. Aisling was forever taking him home free samples of acne medication and leaflets on *Growing Your Self-Confidence for Teens*. You wouldn't exactly think he was a Lothario. Which was great, they'd all agreed; Aisling and Mossy had had enough trouble from other quarters as it was. But now look: an unplanned baby. They hoped Anto wasn't going to take the wrong path too, Aisling had overheard them say in the office kitchen.

'And the mother . . .?' Dr Iris had enquired. She was forever dealing with teen pregnancies around here; a steady stream of young girls in Juicy Couture tracksuits and tiny babies in elaborate prams, and not a father in sight. She was warm and bossy with them, and she sent them back out after jabs and antenatal check-ups with a spring in their step and fresh confidence.

Dr Iris might be able to fathom Nicola out. Because she certainly continued to be a mystery to Aisling.

'Darren's going to stay with us for a little while longer,' Aisling said, non-committal. 'She's just having a bit of a rest.'

Well, who knew what Nicola was doing? There had been total silence from her end. Every time the phone rang Aisling half expected it to be her, with a rush of 'Listen, I must have been off my *head* with all that adoption stuff – pregnancy hormones and all that . . . Anyway, forget I said anything and I'll be around to collect him at teatime.'

Aisling could understand that. She'd been half crazed herself through lack of sleep and stress in those early days of mother-hood. Sometimes she'd wished for somebody – anybody – to take the baby away so she could get some sleep and go to the bathroom in peace.

But with Nicola, you just couldn't fathom her out. In the past week Aisling had got calls from her mother, the tax man, Zofia – 'Magda is driving me crazy, I might need you to steal me some antidepressants from the surgery' – but not a peep from Nicola.

'Has she been in contact with you?' she'd asked Anto. Casually, like.

Anto turned a pair of burning, bloodshot eyes on her – he was exhausted from getting up at nights with Darren, as well as mounds of history revision – and yelped, 'Like fuck she has! She's probably doing her nails while we slog it out with the little terror!'

'I'm sure she's not doing her nails.' Aisling felt compelled to defend Nicola against such slights. Especially as her nails had been bitten down to nubs. Whatever was going on with Nicola, Aisling knew it wasn't anything trivial. Carefully, without wanting to spook him, she said, 'Have you thought any more about what the solicitor said?'

Anto's face slumped further. 'Court and all that, you mean. Starting that whole garden chip thing.' The name had stuck.

'It would just put you more in control, Anto. You could even seek full custody if you wanted.'

'I don't know.' Anto chewed on his lip. The soccer injury wasn't getting a chance to heal, what with all the gnawing that was going on. 'It's not that I don't, um, love Darren. I mean, I *must* because I'm his da, right?' He turned troubled eyes on her. 'I just can't seem to get my head around taking him on full time, you know?'

This wasn't normal Anto moaning. He really did look on edge. At the same time, Darren was his son. Some day he would thank her for this. Well, he probably wouldn't. But he should be asserting his rights – for his own sake, and for Darren's.

Anyway, why *shouldn't* he do his share? In an unexpected teen pregnancy, why was it the mother who always ended up carrying the can? And getting the blame if she had the audacity to say she didn't want to do it any more?

She would give that much to Nicola.

'I'll do the night shift tonight, okay?' she promised. 'You get a proper sleep.'

Darren's first day at the surgery went great. He slept all morning in his buggy.

'Isn't he an angel?' the girls whispered, as they tiptoed around him. Aisling got loads of work done, whizzing through a whole week of accounts. When he woke up, she fed and changed him and he was happy to play on his mat on the floor for another hour, with her leaning over every now and again to activate his wind-up mobile. By the time lunchtime came, they were all singing lustily along: 'Three blind MICE, three blind MICE, see how they RUN.' After the tenth go, they had replaced mice with patients, hookers, airline pilots and slimming counsellors (Shirley was on a new diet).

'That was great craic, girls,' said April, hoisting up her bag. 'See you tomorrow.'

Aisling left shortly after that, telling Darren with relief, 'You're *such* a good little boy. An extra rusk for you tonight.' And Darren grinned back at her. He seemed to be back on form after the upset of seeing Nicola. For days after her visit he'd been grizzly and unsettled, pushing even Aisling away.

But today he babbled away in his buggy as she wheeled him to school to meet Louise, and played up shamelessly to the gaggle of little girls that rushed out of the school and surrounded him, kissing him and petting him and pronouncing him gorgeous.

The next day in the surgery he cried. All morning. Inconsolably.

'Sorry, everybody,' Aisling said in desperation. She dangled his set of plastic keys but they offended him. 'Three Blind Mice' outraged him altogether. 'Come on now, honey, let's stop this, eh?' she begged him.

The girls valiantly tried to cheer him up. 'Peek-a-boo!' Shirley called several times from her side of the office. When Aisling had to go deal with a medical rep, April bopped him up and down on her lap. 'Sorry, can you repeat that, please?' she kept having to say down the phone. 'You have competition here.'

Nothing would do him. Not Aisling, not April, not a piece of Shirley's cake that she carefully cut up into tiny pieces for him.

'I think he's teething again,' Aisling eventually deduced.

He had a high spot of colour on his left cheek and was drooling uncontrollably. May, who generally kept out of things, fingered a tissue in distress at the sight. Dr Tom eventually came in, clucking

196

sympathetically, and said, 'Now pipe down, young man! Here, will we give him a spoon of Calpol, Aisling?'

Calpol worked for half an hour. Then he was off again.

Aisling went in to see Dr Iris during a lull between patients.

'I don't think this is going to work out,' she said.

'Oh, but you haven't given it a proper chance.'

'I have. And it was daft to think that I could work and look after a baby at the same time. It's only going to get worse when he starts to crawl and walk.'

Dr Iris didn't try to talk her out of it. It had been a lovely idea all round, but impractical, they all realised now. 'What will you do?'

'I'm not really sure,' Aisling admitted. She felt a bit foolish, actually. She hadn't really thought anything through properly. And it looked like her job was going to be the first casualty of her and Nicola's actions.

'We'll get a temp,' Dr Iris promised her. 'Things are bound to settle down. You just let us know when you're ready to come back.'

Aisling put on Darren's coat and trudged off home.

Chapter Twenty-six

Magda told Zofia that she was very much looking forward to being a grandmother. Zofia sweetly informed her that she wouldn't dream of getting pregnant until her make-up course was finished, after which she would need at least two to three years' experience in the industry under her belt. 'But you will be the first to know!' she assured her chirpily, whilst making violent throat-slashing gestures to Olaf behind Magda's back.

'She actually said that? That you should have a child?'

'As good as. She was folding up some of Darren's clothes – remember I had to change him when I was looking after him last week? – and then she looked at me right here.' Zofia pointed at her midriff.

'But just to clarify,' Aisling probed delicately. 'She didn't actually *say* it. In words.'

'You don't believe me?'

'Zofia, it's not that . . .'

'You think I am making it up? All day long she sits in my house, just sits there, watching me, criticising with her eyes. I say to Olaf, how can you bear it, her calm, expressionless face, her sickly-sweet niceness, the cardigans? It is driving me mad.'

Clearly. 'And what does Olaf say?'

'*Olaf*. He is on her side, of course. He doesn't understand what I am complaining about. This morning he got angry, said that I was picking on his mother. Me! But this is exactly what she wants, of course. To have us fighting and falling out over her. And do you know what the worst thing is? She is staying an extra month. Her house – the house where Olaf spent many, many ecstatic years with her, baking and singing and dancing around the garden – it is leaky. The roof. Olaf has organised a whole team of workers to come in and replace it. Only the best.' She seemed a bit upset.

'Well, she is his mother, and she's on her own now, so I suppose he has to look after her . . .'

'Three years now I ask him to fix the shed door. He hasn't done it yet. But she needs a new roof? No problem! Sit still.'

Aisling was perched in her usual spot at the kitchen table, with Zofia's pots and potions spread out in front of her. Tonight's theme was A Night at the Opera. It was the full works: false eyelashes, thick panstick and a beauty spot painted on by Aisling's mouth that looked like Darren had spattered her in the face with chocolate ice cream.

Who the hell thinks these things up? she wondered. She was a bit nervous, given Zofia's black mood. Also, she was exhausted. She'd been home all week with Darren and it had been non-stop. Maybe she had rose-tinted glasses about raising her own brood, but how had she ever managed to load a washing machine with a wriggling, narky little bundle planted on her hip? How had she had a shower in comfort, or taken a telephone call without having to abandon it halfway through with an urgent 'I'll call you back'?

But she couldn't complain; not out loud, anyway. Mossy was there watching, waiting for her to admit that he was right; that taking on Darren full time was a massive commitment that she shouldn't have even considered.

She wouldn't give it him. She just wouldn't. 'Ouch!'

Zofia had accidentally poked her in the eye. 'Sorry. It is all this talking.'

'You're the one doing the talking. Anyway, I *like* talking. The only person I've spoken to all day is the checkout girl at Tesco.'

Since she'd given up her job, she was finding it quiet. Deathly quiet. The postman had begun throwing the post towards the front door and legging it, for fear of getting trapped in a protracted conversation about the weather.

'What is happening about the—' Zofia cut herself off. Darren was sitting on the floor watching them. '*Adoption*,' she whispered loudly.

'Very little. At least, we haven't heard anything. Maybe they're up to all kinds of things behind our backs.'

But she didn't really believe that. The more time that passed, the less Aisling believed Nicola had any intention of going through with it. In fact, nothing she did seemed to be the result of forward planning, right from the moment Darren was left in their garden. Everything seemed a bit panicked with her, and out of control; her actions were those of someone who wasn't really thinking straight, Aisling was beginning to realise.

'She is strange, strange girl,' Zofia announced.

'I don't know if I'd use the word strange.'

'Oh, you are defending her now?'

Was she? She tried to think of Nicola as one of her own children. How would she feel about her? The answer came: worried. 'Yes.'

'Well, there is *something* not right about her.'

Exactly, Aisling thought.

Zofia finished attaching the fake eyelashes. It was like two fat spiders had taken up residence on Aisling's face. 'We are done. Hey,' she said to Darren, 'do you want to see your glamorous granny?'

She unveiled Aisling by whipping off the sheet she'd had around her neck, and twirling her around to face Darren.

Darren looked, and froze. He opened his mouth wide and started to cry.

'Oh no, no.' Zofia was in a huff. 'Why are you crying? She is lovely!'

'The poor child probably doesn't recognise me.' Aisling reached for him. 'Come here to me, sweetheart.'

But Darren only cried harder, and tried to get away from her. In the melee Aisling managed to knock off one of her eyelashes, and Zofia went scurrying around the floor for it, lamenting, 'No! No! I have not taken the photo for my portfolio yet!' In the middle of it all the doorbell rang.

It was Hugo.

Zofia brokered the horrible awkwardness by asking Hugo for his autograph.

'My mother-in-law watches the news every night even though she doesn't understand a word of it. And she sees you talking about the weather, and she thinks you are gorgeous.'

Hugo looked mildly taken aback as he accepted a piece of paper and a pen from Zofia. 'I don't know about that, but of course . . .'

'If you could write "To Magda. Have a safe trip home to Poland. Soon."'

Hugo hesitated, but then dutifully scribbled away.

'It might put the idea in her head, you never know,' Zofia sighed to Aisling. Then she packed up all of her make-up stuff and set off home for another tense evening in front of the telly with Olaf and Magda.

'But the photo . . .' Aisling said.

'We try again tomorrow.'

'Can I . . .?'

'Please. Do.'

Hugo held out his hands to Darren, who needed no second invitation. He hopped up on Hugo's lap with speed, and told him, 'Ai.'

'We're still stuck on that, I'm afraid,' Aisling said.

Hugo just gazed down at Darren for a long time, his face a picture of emotion. Aisling felt awful. She'd effectively kept them apart these past few weeks.

'Look—' she began.

He cut in. 'I'm sorry for barging in on you like this. I should have phoned. But I didn't know if you'd want to speak to me.'

Talk about disarming her. There she'd been, all puffed up, ready for a fight.

'Of course we'd want to speak to you,' she said in a rush. 'And I'm sorry for throwing you and Nicola out that night. I acted in the heat of the moment, I'm afraid.'

'I think we all did.'

A small, friendly look from them both.

'How have you been?' she said, awkward.

'Oh. You know.' He shrugged. 'It's been difficult.'

Yes. Aisling could imagine. They'd been so fixated on their own feelings about Nicola's announcement, but Hugo's reaction had likely been the same.

'Look at him,' she said.

Darren's head was resting against Hugo's chest. He was industriously sucking his thumb. His eyelids were drooping closed.

'At least he hasn't forgotten me,' Hugo said. He saw her face. 'I didn't say that to make you feel worse!'

'You're not . . .'

'Everything I say these days seems to be wrong.' The poor man looked tortured. 'Would it be okay with you if we agree not to talk about Darren at all?'

'Oh. Um, sure.' A pause. 'What would we talk about instead?' she asked.

'I don't know. Work?'

'I don't work any more. I've had to give it up to look after Darren.'

'Have you? I didn't know. Sorry.'

He looked so woebegone that Aisling laughed. 'Relax, Hugo.'

And he did, a bit. He cuddled Darren in close, sitting there in companionable silence as Aisling made tea and took out the tin of biscuits. Except that it was empty, save for a mauled-looking fig roll languishing at the bottom.

'Anto,' she said apologetically.

'That's okay. I'm on a diet anyway. At least, the girls in work tell me I have to start looking after myself if I'm to find another woman.'

'No!' She was appalled.

'Ah, it's just a joke. At least they're not wheeling out their single friends and making me go on blind dates with them.'

He was very different when he smiled. When he didn't, loneliness came off him in waves. And Aisling was suddenly delighted he had those girls in work to take the edge off it.

'And you and your wife . . .?' She didn't want to say 'Eleanor'.

It was too familiar, and some part of her wanted to keep a little bit of distance from the O'Sullivans.

'We're done.' He was very definite. 'She's happy now, and I'm glad for her. Nicola can't understand it all. But what's the point in staying in a marriage if you're miserable? Things change, people change.'

'That's pragmatic of you.'

'There's not much point in being angry.' His eyes were on her face. 'And you and Mossy? You two must be clocking up the years.'

'Twenty-two now.' She tried for that jolly voice that people put on when they said these things, but it fell flat at the end.

Hugo didn't seem to notice. 'And three kids?'

She should have gone along with it. It wasn't anybody's business but theirs. But she wasn't going to sit there and deny Aidan, as though he was dead. Anyway, Hugo would find out eventually.

'Four, actually.'

'Four?' Cue his confusion.

'I have another son too. He doesn't live here any more.'

She tried to sound normal, but it was impossible to ever sound normal when she spoke about it.

'Anto's older brother. We don't see him, unfortunately. Not at the moment anyway.'

Hugo knew what she meant. He understood the language of separation.

'That must be very hard for you,' he said.

'It is.'

He didn't offer any platitudes. Instead he glanced down at a sleeping Darren and she was able to compose herself again.

Eventually he looked up. He watched her in companionable

silence for a bit and then said, reluctantly it seemed, 'I'd better go. I told Nicola I wouldn't be long.'

'Listen, Hugo.' She didn't want to bring this up, but at the same time she couldn't not. 'About Nicola.'

He was wary again. 'Please. Can we leave this? I just think she needs more time . . .'

'She doesn't, though.' That didn't come out right. 'What I mean is . . . Look, please, I'm not being judgemental here. If you knew even the first thing about my life, you'd know that I am the very last person qualified to give somebody else parental advice.'

'I doubt that. You're the best mother I've ever seen.'

'No. Really I'm not.' She couldn't be more emphatic. 'But I wonder if maybe Nicola could do with a bit more help?'

'I didn't follow up with Mrs McAllister – the housekeeper – because there didn't seem any point until we had Darren home . . .'

'Medical help, Hugo.'

He was astonished. But often when you lived in close proximity to someone, you just didn't see it. Aisling had learned that one first hand.

'She's fine,' he said.

'I'm not sure she is, Hugo.'

Chapter Twenty-seven

'Go on! Go-on, go-on, *go-on*!'

But Darren stopped, sat back on his plump nappied behind and smiled gummily up at Anto.

'Ai!' he shouted.

Anto was trying to teach him how to crawl. The problem was, he was only able to go backwards. 'Takes after you so,' his da had slagged. Darren was continually reversing into doors or chairs; Anto would pick him up and put him back down in the middle of the floor, and off he'd set backwards again. It was a right laugh watching him. But at the same time, Anto had taken on the task and it was a bit galling that Darren wasn't keeping his side of the bargain.

'You're a messer, do you know that?' he said to him.

'Ai!' It was Darren's favourite sound. Da said were they certain he didn't have Asian parentage in there somewhere as well?

Da talked to him a lot about Darren lately. He'd come stand in the doorway of Anto's room when he'd be dressing Darren or changing him. Or else he'd take the two of them out in the van.

A Special Delivery

He got a baby seat off his friend Dave, who didn't need it any more, and fixed it up in the middle of the van, and the three of them would head off, 'to give your ma a break'.

But Da needed the break too, from the house. Anto could see that. And he liked going out with his da now in the van, Darren sitting up between them. The Three Musketeers.

'Right,' he said to Darren. 'It's time to get tough here. If you keep crawling backwards, there's going to be no bedtime bottle, do you hear me?' Then, in case Darren took offence, he quickly assured him, 'Only having you on, buddy.'

'Ai!' said Darren.

Anto didn't want to muck things up now that they were getting on better. Or Darren seemed to be tolerating him at least, instead of frantically clinging on to his ma every time Anto came near. Yesterday Anto had taken him out to the playground and given him a bit of a go on the baby swings. He was mortified at first – he was the only male in the whole playground, amongst all the mothers – but then he forgot about everybody else and made faces at Darren when he was pushing him from the front, and Darren had starting laughing. Anto was dead chuffed.

'Okay,' he said. The crawling thing had taken his mind off stuff, but he was nervous now. 'We should probably get going.'

There was plenty of time yet, but Anto didn't want to be late. That wouldn't be cool. His nerves were jangling, but thankfully Darren stayed still for once as Anto put on his coat and hat and gloves. The gloves Darren would pull off in two seconds flat, but his ma insisted. She liked to lecture Anto. 'Helping' was how she put it. Mostly he was glad. But sometimes he'd like to do stuff on his own without her always looking over his shoulder.

'There,' he said. 'You're done.' Then he got a whiff. Oh no. Not *now*.

But it wasn't Darren. It was him. He was sweating. Fuck. And he'd only just had a shower, too.

'Don't move,' he instructed, and dashed back to the dressing table. Two blasts of Lynx under each armpit, a quick sniff, and he'd have to do.

'Not a word now, okay?' he cautioned Darren as he opened the bedroom door. He could hear the telly downstairs. The six o'clock news was just coming on. Nicola's da was doing the forecast that evening. Apparently he'd told his ma when he'd made his daily phone call to her earlier. Anto didn't know what they found to talk about, but Hugo kept his ma on the phone for a long time and sometimes she had to make an excuse to get away.

But nobody had mentioned the A word lately. Like, at *all*. It was all very confusing. One minute his ma was talking courts and applications, and now it was like she'd completely backed off. That morning Anto had heard them discussing it over breakfast, his ma and da, as he'd been coming down the stairs.

'We can't go on like this. No decisions being made. Them doing a U-turn every five minutes.' Da had sounded strained.

'Why? It's not affecting you, is it?' His ma, sharp. 'I'm the one looking after Darren.'

'It affects all of us and you know it. At least they could have the manners to meet up with Anto and ask his opinion on what should happen to his own son.'

They were wrong on that count. It turned out that they had.

Darren was great. He didn't make a single noise as Anto tiptoed downstairs and strapped him into his buggy in the hall.

'Is that you?' His ma's voice floated out from the kitchen.

'Just taking Darren for a walk!' he called back.

'What, now? Dinner's nearly ready!'

'Won't be long.'

He quickly pulled the door shut after him. This had nothing to do with them.

Nicola was where she said she'd be in her text: in a booth in McDonald's, sipping a milkshake. She was wearing a pink hoody and a pair of skinny jeans, and she looked up as Anto pushed open the double doors.

His heart was going *thu-dum thu-dum* at a ferocious rate. The Lynx was defeated in seconds as he pushed the buggy towards her.

'There's your ma,' he told Darren, but it came out all falsetto, through nerves. He fought to bring it down a notch. 'Over there. Look!'

He wanted Nicola to see what a good father he was being; that he was talking her up to Darren, not judging her at all. But after flashing a look at Darren, she went back to her milkshake. Self-conscious, he parked the buggy beside the table and slid on to the seat opposite.

'How's it going?' he said. He felt his knee clatter against hers under the table. 'Sorry.' He withdrew quickly, but not before a jolt of electricity ran through him. 'You're, um, looking well.'

She pitched forward viciously. 'Now you just stop it, all right?'

Anto reared back. 'What the . . .?'

'You know exactly what I'm talking about. Because I'm not going to put up with it, understand? I know what you're doing and you're not clever. Or your ma, if it's her who's behind all this. Right meddler, isn't she?'

Anto was stunned. He had no clue what was going on. 'You texted me. Said we needed to talk,' he began, confused.

'Stop acting the innocent.' She was really fuming now, and uncaring that the people at the next table were looking over with interest. 'You sent me this, correct?'

She hauled out a pink phone and thrust it in his face.

It was so close that Anto struggled to read the screen. 'I'm actually a little bit long-sighted,' he confessed.

More irritated, she flicked it back to herself. '*Darren had a high temperature today. We thought it might be meningitis but it came down after we gave him some paracetamol.*' She stopped reading and lowered the phone. 'Meningitis?'

In the buggy, Darren gurgled cautiously. He watched Nicola constantly, but in a guarded kind of way, and gnawed busily on his hand.

'Well, obviously it was a false alarm.'

'You don't say.'

Anto felt awful, but at the same time, Darren had spiked at thirty-nine degrees on the thermometer. What was he supposed to have done, just ignored it?

'I thought you'd have wanted to know,' he said stiffly.

'Oh, you mean like the message you sent me two days ago. What was it again . . .' She went hunting through the phone a second time. '*Darren had diarrhoea, which I was worried about because there's an awful stomach bug going around, but it turned out that puréed carrots definitely don't agree with him.*' She shot him daggers over the top of the phone again.

'There *is* a stomach bug going around.' Anto was beginning to feel foolish.

'On Monday you thought he might have had a dislocated hip!'

Okay, so Anto regretted that particular text. But Darren had been lying in the cot with his leg all bent up funny, and his ma and da had gone to bed and he wanted to share the worry with someone.

'I was just trying to keep you in the loop,' he defended himself. She snorted. She had a lovely nose, he noted through his distress. Neat and straight. 'No, what you're doing is laying a massive guilt trip on me. It's all part of your big plan, is it? "Oh, maybe she'll take him back if we keep poking and prodding her, reminding her how much her son needs her." Well I'm not that stupid, okay?'

Anto was actually a bit annoyed now. He'd walked all this way up to the shopping centre only to get attacked? 'So? He does need you. All kids need their mothers.'

Something flared at the back of her eyes. Anto was sorry now. He hadn't meant to make her feel bad. Somehow he knew that she didn't need any help from him in that department.

'But at the same time, he's doing okay without you. He's fine,' he tried to reassure her. 'Although sometimes I think he just puts up with me. You know, until a responsible adult comes along.'

'But I'm not a responsible adult,' she said.

'So? I'm not either.'

A beat, and then they smiled at each other. Not a massive everything's-hunky-dory-now smile. But it was a kind of truce.

'I won't text you any more,' Anto promised.

'It's fine . . .'

'No, it was stupid, making you worried like that. I just fired them off without thinking, I'm sorry.'

Now she was backtracking too. 'I don't mind getting the odd text.' She darted a look at him. 'It's actually kind of nice.'

'But not about meningitis,' Anto clarified.

'No.' She thought of something. 'But obviously if he really *has* meningitis, I'd want to know.'

'If it was that serious, I wouldn't text. I'd ring. Straight away,' Anto vowed.

'And I'd pick up. Straight away.'

Phew. At least something was sorted. Anto felt himself relax

211

just a little bit. He watched covertly as she wrapped her lips around the straw again and had another sip of milkshake. He remembered kissing those lips that night. He had to drag his eyes away from her before he said or did something stupid.

He cleared his throat officiously. 'I want you to know that I'm a modern man,' he announced.

Nicola looked at him askance. That hadn't come out the way he'd intended.

'What I'm saying is, I don't believe that it's only girls who should be left carrying the can when something like this happens. An unplanned pregnancy.'

Her eyes challenged him. 'So how come we usually do?'

'I don't know. It's just the way the world is,' Anto conceded honestly. 'But it's crap.'

'It is,' Nicola heartily agreed. 'Nobody thinks badly of the guys in all this. For you it's "oh poor Anto, getting lumbered with a kid at eighteen when all that's on his mind most of the time is food".'

Anto coloured. 'How did you know?'

Nicola looked confused. 'I don't. It's just that's what everybody presumes teenage boys think about the whole time. And sex.'

Anto dragged his eyes away from the Big Mac that had just passed him by on a tray and tried not to let them land on Nicola's breasts instead.

'But when it comes to girls, we're expected to get on with it. Raise the kid. Nobody says "poor you" to us. People just think we're slags and that it's a bit late to complain now.'

'Who's calling you a slag?' Anto demanded.

Nicola shrugged a bit tiredly. 'They don't say it to your face. But they think it, even if they won't admit it to themselves. Your mother, for instance. Even my own dad.'

'She doesn't.' Anto felt he had to defend his ma. 'If anything, she's delighted to have Darren. It makes up for all the other stuff.'

He stopped abruptly. He didn't want to get into that today.

Nicola was watching him. 'Does she think fatherhood will settle you down?'

'Maybe.' Although Anto didn't think he was particularly wild. He could be more motivated, there was no doubt about that. And he was a slacker when it came to studying. Darren wasn't doing much to improve that.

He caught Nicola sneaking another little look at Darren. Maybe she'd comment on how well cared for he looked; what a good job Anto was doing. But the little fecker was asleep. Anto was mortified. He'd dressed him up all nice and everything to impress her, and he'd gone and nodded off!

'Sorry about that. He's been crawling loads, you see. It gets him knackered. I can try and wake him up . . .'

'No, no. Let him sleep.' And actually she seemed more relaxed or something. She was looking at him openly now, from the tips of his toes right up past his new orange and blue gingham dungarees – his ma had bought them only yesterday – to linger on his face. 'He's grown even since I saw him at your place,' she said softly.

'Yeah. He's a massive appetite,' Anto confided. 'Eats all around him.' Something about her face alerted him. 'Like, I don't give him *junk* or anything. It's all good stuff. But he can really put it away.' He shot a shy look at her. 'I was the same. They used to call me the bottomless pit.'

But she didn't seem too riveted by Anto's past. Her eyes flickered back to Darren. 'And the sleep? I hear he's doing better at nights.'

'He has his moments,' Anto said grimly. 'But I suppose you know that.'

213

'Yeah,' she said.

Anto braced himself. It had to be said. 'So what are we going to do?'

'I don't know,' she admitted.

'Neither do I.' This was bad. Each of them as indecisive as the other. But he thought he might be sure of one thing. 'I don't want him given away, though.'

He wasn't sure how she'd take it. The truth was, he didn't really know Nicola at all. He might have slept with her, they might have a kid together, but she remained a mystery to him.

When she lifted those sad, tortured, *sexy* blue eyes to his, he felt his face explode into colour.

'Me neither.'

And Anto felt at least one part of his world shift and settle more comfortably.

But then she began to gather up her things — phone, some loose change — and stuff them into her pocket.

'Will you not have another milkshake?' Anto said quickly. 'I'm buying.'

'I can't. I'm meeting my da. I have an appointment.' That cagey, defensive look was back.

'Can I at least text you again?' he said. 'You know. About Darren.'

She gave Darren's sleeping face a long look before she turned to go.

'Yes.'

And suddenly Anto was on a high.

Chapter Twenty-eight

The date was getting nearer and nearer. Mossy was useless, though. Aisling watched him like a hawk but he gave no indication that 2 May was more important to him than any other day. On the calendar he'd scribbled up the usual stuff in his illegible scrawl – *Boyle's kitchen/living room*, which would be a day-and-a-half's work apparently, and *PJ/10 a.m./green!*, which could have meant anything.

He'd done the same last year: completely ignored it. He really could be an arse sometimes. But maybe – and this was giving him the benefit of the doubt – he just couldn't face it and was in denial. It was possible.

As for her . . . well, it was like she was on some kind of demented countdown. Every morning when she walked into the kitchen the fridge calendar hit her between the eyes. The eighteenth of April . . . the nineteenth . . . the twentieth.

Soon April would be over.

And still Mossy said nothing. Just continued to deface the calendar with his DIY ramblings, never once turning to her and saying, 'You know what's coming up again soon?'

'Arse,' she said that morning, actually aloud but still under her breath – she was too cowardly – and he stopped for a minute and looked at her suspiciously, and then he threw down his stubby pencil.

'I'm going out with Dave on a job.'

'Good.'

'I won't be back until late.'

'Great!'

It might give him time to think. It might make him realise that this could be a chance to build bridges. If they couldn't reach out on 2 May, then when *could* they? At least that was what she hoped. Hope was what got her through each day now. Foolish and misguided probably, but she hung on to it like a life raft.

'Ma? Do you know what day is coming up soon?'

Louise hadn't missed the significance of the date either. She had her own calendar in her bedroom, with pictures of elaborately coiffured cats on it, and she methodically counted off each day with a bright pink X: job done. At the beginning of each year she wrote in each person's birthday, and assigned them a sticker, and also Valentine's Day and Christmas Day and any other significant dates. She would make a fabulous CEO some day.

'I do,' said Aisling.

'The second of May.' Louise wasn't going to be outdone.

'I know.'

'That's Aidan's birthday.'

Aidan: meaning *little fire, ardent*. He'd come into the world mildly outraged, all seven pounds three ounces of him, and had pretty much remained that way.

'You're smiling.' Louise was cautiously pleased. 'Is that because we're going to see him this year?'

Aisling's hope seemed a bit empty now that Mossy had gone off in a mood. 'I don't know, love. I don't think so.'

216

'He's going to be twenty,' she said, in case Aisling had perhaps lost count.

'He is.'

As they were alone, Louise intuited that they could speak more freely than usual. 'We should bake him a cake.'

'Oh, I don't know . . .'

'A chocolate one. With frosted icing and loads of candles and we'll put jelly tots and blue M and Ms on top.'

Louise had remembered. It was the cake Aisling used to bake him every year, even into his teens. He hadn't cared about the embarrassment factor; he'd just stuffed big hunks into his mouth, making loud smacking noises of bliss.

'But he won't be here to eat it.' It would be wrong to let Louise think that a cake would make everything okay.

'You could ask him.'

'I don't think so, Louise.'

'But why not?' she persisted. 'We missed his birthday last year too. We can't keep missing all his birthdays.'

Aisling thought her heart would break.

'I know. But it's just the way things are at the moment.'

They had told Louise very little. How did you explain such things to a nine-year-old, as she'd been then? Of course, she'd heard the rows; it would have been difficult, if not impossible, to miss the conflict. She'd witnessed the near-daily dramas of drunken trips on the stairs, doors slammed so hard that they splintered; the litany of things, little and not so little, that had kept the whole family on edge.

But on the worst day, she'd been temporarily down the road at Emma's, for which Aisling was eternally grateful.

'Well, it's stupid,' she declared.

And Aisling saw that Louise wasn't going to be fobbed off.

Not by that Santa Claus guy – well, not next year, at any rate – and not by the stock parental defence of 'because I say so'.

'Look, Louise, I know you miss your brother . . .'

'You miss him too. And Anto. Anto used to share a room with him and now he just talks to himself. I hear him sometimes, it's weird.' Louise was a little accusing now. 'Why can't he come back?'

'He *can* come back. Once he agrees to certain . . . rules.'

'Like, what time bedtime's at?' That particular rule vexed Louise the most. Some of the girls in her class got to stay up till *eleven* at weekends, but oh no, she was marched off upstairs at half past nine.

'And a few others.'

And even then, who knew? Aidan wasn't the type to grovel and crawl, and Aisling suspected that for Mossy, nothing less would do.

Louise changed tack. 'He hasn't even met Darren yet.'

'Well, no . . .'

'He's his uncle. It's not fair that he hasn't met him yet. Why can't he come round and see him?'

Louise's questions were starting to feel like a magpie tap-tapping at Aisling's head. 'Because Darren's not here, okay?' she said, a little short.

Not at that precise moment, anyway. Anto had taken him off out somewhere with Shannon. He had quite a routine going now, did Anto. It had taken them all a little by surprise. 'I'm just taking Darren to the park,' he would announce breezily. Or, 'I'm going around to Baz's to watch a movie. Darren can sleep on the couch.'

Often Darren didn't sleep; Baz and Sean and the gang would all be down on the floor playing with him, the DVD forgotten, and Darren would arrive home tired and full of himself.

A Special Delivery

That morning the pair of them had ventured down to the local parent and toddler group in the community centre, although Anto had buckled at the last moment and cajoled Shannon into going with him. 'What they really mean is *mother* and toddler group, only they can't say that any more. If I pitch up there on my own, they'll all turn to look at me and stop talking about their crackled nipples or whatever,' Anto fretted.

'But that's a good thing, yes?' said Shannon.

'I just want to see what it's like, that's all. Darren should be getting to know the other kids around here.'

Darren was only just gone ten months old, and probably a little young to be concerned with social circles, but nobody wanted to dissuade Anto. After a rocky start, he seemed to have embraced this fatherhood thing more than anybody could have expected or hoped. In fact there were times when he even looked to be enjoying the whole experience.

'Who would have thought it?' Aisling said to Mossy that evening. True to his word, he'd come home late. The nine o'clock news was on in the background when he finally sat down to his dinner. 'And before you say it's early days, I know that, but Anto really seems to have stepped up.'

'I wasn't going to say it's early days,' Mossy said.

He was probably thinking it, though.

'I wasn't even thinking it. I happen to agree with you. He's doing a really great job with that young lad. In fact, we don't say it to him enough.'

Aisling's mouth must have fallen open slackly in surprise – Mossy, so effusive! – because he said, 'So you can climb down off your perch there, Miss High and Mighty.'

'I wasn't on my perch!'

'Oh yes you were. Very high up too. You've been up there for months, looking down at me, thinking, hmm, who *is* that arse me and my poor kids have to live with?'

Aisling was really shocked now. Mossy hadn't spoken so much in weeks, and certainly not so baldly. 'Not arse,' she managed.

'Deficient, then – is that what you were muttering under your breath? Controlling, maybe? Or just plain wrong?'

He threw her a look and she squirmed more.

'And maybe you're right.' He shrugged. 'Maybe I *am* wrong.'

'Mossy—' she began.

'But before you take that as an invitation, I know perfectly well that the second of May is coming up. And I know you're hoping for a big reconciliation or something, but right now I just can't see that happening.'

Again Aisling was left flailing by his forthrightness.

'Not a big reconciliation,' she began tentatively.

'What, then?'

She had to be careful here. They were actually talking. Really talking; maybe for the first time since all this had happened.

'It's been a year and a half now. Everybody's had a chance to take a step back. Think.' She chose every word deliberately. 'Maybe now is the time to reach out.'

Damn. She hoped the reaching out bit didn't turn him off. Mossy hated all that TV confessional speak.

'He hasn't reached out to us, though, has he?' There was a sardonic twinge there, all right.

'Well, no. But I suppose . . . Oh look, maybe he's nervous, Mossy, did you think of that? After the way we left things? Maybe he's afraid we wouldn't want to know.'

Mossy's eyes looked black in the shadows of the kitchen. 'And maybe we don't.'

He was just saying that. He didn't mean it.

'Nobody would blame you for feeling that way,' she said quietly. 'But we can't let this thing become permanent.'

Mossy took an age to reply. Then, just as she was about to give up all hope: 'We don't even know where he is.'

Aisling's Code Red swung into full alert. She was crap at all this lying stuff, but she'd just have to do her best.

'No,' she agreed in her most normal voice. 'But we could find out.'

'How?'

'Friends. I have numbers. I'm sure some of them are in touch with him still.'

'You think?' Mossy looked a bit cynical both about this and about the quality of Aidan's 'friends'. 'He could be in a different country for all we know. You know him and his notions.'

Dreams, other people might call them. Aidan had been going to work with endangered animals in a Kenyan reserve. Or to cut crops with one of those enormous machines in the middle of Kentucky. For one whole summer he'd talked of nothing but going walking in Snowdonia with friends, and after that it would be Everest base camp. He'd bought hiking boots and everything. He'd just somehow managed to get distracted along the way.

'I have a feeling he's in Ireland,' Aisling said cautiously. 'He wouldn't have the money to go abroad.'

He'd left the house with very little. Mossy had cut off all funding by then: if he wanted to be treated like a grown-up, then let him see what it cost to live like one, thunder, thunder, instead of sponging off them.

'I don't know for sure, but I think he'd want to stay near us,' she said carefully. 'Even if we don't see each other. He wouldn't emigrate or anything without letting us know.'

Even though she knew where he was, she truly believed this. If he'd really wanted to be shot of his family, why did he still live in the same city? Often within a distance of a couple of miles? Consciously or not, he didn't want this situation to go on permanently, no more than they did.

'We could do something small,' she tried. 'A letter maybe. We don't have to meet or anything.'

Again Mossy lapsed into silence. Aisling held her breath. This was the nearest she'd come to effecting some kind of reconciliation.

'And what would be in this letter?'

Good question. For some reason she'd thought just putting a piece of paper into an envelope would be enough of an indication of Mossy's intentions. Hers she'd already made clear enough.

But she continued to speak as though for both of them. 'I don't know . . . we'd have to work it out, but just even to say that we hope he's okay. And safe. And that we're sorry that things worked out the way they did—'

'Why should we be sorry?' Mossy cut across her.

Over Mossy's shoulder, Hugo appeared on the TV screen. He was wearing a navy suit and tie. He'd phoned yesterday and she'd never phoned him back. She'd just forgotten, what with her mind so consumed by Aidan.

'Because we have to start somewhere,' she told him, 'and I guess an apology would be—'

'Here you go again.' Mossy dumped down his knife and fork fast. 'Making excuses for him.'

'I'm not!' Aisling said. 'Nobody's saying we have to admit it's all our fault—'

'Good. Because it's not. My God, Aisling, he could do anything he likes, he could set fire to the house and murder us all in our beds, and you'd write him a letter, wouldn't you? Telling him how fucking sorry we were!'

'If you'd just let me *finish a sentence*.'

Hugo had the big coloured map of Ireland up on the telly. He looked concerned as he mentioned heavy rain and dipping temperatures and cold blasts from the west.

Aisling's fists were two balls of frustration and fear. 'We have to get over all this blame, Mossy.'

He was on his feet, eyes shining with injustice. 'Well that's where you're wrong, Aisling. Because this isn't about blame. You can only give people so many chances, and if they don't want to take them, then that's their lookout. We can't spend our lives running after him, telling him that it's okay, that he can do what he wants and it's fine. Because that's not doing him any favours. That's just enabling him.'

'So you've said before.' Her voice was colourless.

'And you agreed with me. Look. I know this is hard. You're not the only one who goes around like your heart's been ripped out. But this is the only way. For him; for our family.'

He didn't say 'for us'. But he might as well have.

'If he wants to come home, he knows where to find us.'

Chapter Twenty-nine

'I t's my brother's birthday today,' Anto announced shyly.

Nicola was taken aback. 'I didn't know you had a brother.'

Anto shrugged. 'We don't really talk about him.'

They were on their way to get Darren his first haircut. It had been an agonising decision. Having remained fine and silky until he'd been seven or eight months old, his hair suddenly realised one day that genetically it was Brady hair, and it had some catching up to do.

So it grew. And grew. Thick and luxuriously red, it tumbled down from his crown and fell over his face in a big pile of waves.

'Somebody thought he was a she today!' Anto rang Nicola one evening to report. The whole thing about texting only in emergencies had somehow given way, and now she was getting nightly phone calls from him. 'They went, "Aw, she's beautiful." *She!* I nearly fucking lamped them. 'Scuse my language.'

'Who cares what people think? He's fine.' Nicola didn't want to get sucked in. Decisions freaked her out. While Darren was with the Bradys, she didn't have to make any.

But Anto wasn't going to let it go. 'We should do it while he's young. That way he'll be used to getting it cut and he won't go mental every time.'

Then there was all the hassle of finding a suitable establishment. Anto's regular barber was a bit rough and ready, and not averse to lopping off the tops of your ears, apparently. Nicola didn't know any baby-friendly hairdressers and again tried to take a back seat, but Anto's research was wide-ranging and thorough, and the phone calls were coming thick and fast to discuss the possibilities. Nicola had eventually found this place at the top of the shopping centre where they cut the kids' hair while they sat in toy cars, and you got a photo of them to take home and a little box with their first hair clipping in it.

'Deadly,' Anto had said. Then: 'You *are* coming, aren't you?'

'Well, I . . .'

Last week he'd asked her to meet him in the park to mind Darren for an hour while he had a study group to prepare for his exams. What could she say?

And twice now he'd called around to the house, just on spec, to see if she wanted to come for a walk with him and Darren. One time she hadn't been there, but the second time she'd gone with him, and she'd pushed the buggy. It had felt strange yet familiar, and she hadn't slept at all that night, despite the new medication.

'Sure,' she'd said.

They walked on now, with Darren energetically greeting passers-by with a 'Meh! Meh!' He wasn't fazed by Nicola today. He wasn't overjoyed or anything, but he let her strap him into the buggy and spared her any guilt-inducing looks.

'Where is he?' Nicola asked Anto. 'Your brother?'

'Aidan? I don't know. He doesn't stay in touch.' Anto sounded very hurt and Nicola felt for him, despite the fact that he'd turned up in a shirt that had clearly just had its price tag cut off, and he stank of aftershave.

'You should text him or something,' she tried. 'To wish him a happy birthday.'

'I don't want to bother him,' Anto said, moody.

Nicola found she was curious. Maybe that was the medication too. In the last week or so she'd seemed more aware of things. Not that she'd admit it. She was just doing this to keep Da off her back. 'That night at the party . . .' she began.

Cue mortification. Whenever 'that night' came up, they both looked at their Converses, did an elaborate shuffle and went red. It had all so obviously been a mistake.

'Were you upset about him or something?'

Anto looked surprised. 'Yeah. That was kind of why I was off my face.'

'I was too,' she assured him, although she seemed to have slightly better recollection. Which was a bit of a curse, actually.

'So what happened?' she said.

'You don't want to know.'

'I do.'

He gave her a wary look; it wasn't like her to be so, well, chatty. 'Aidan and my parents – well, my da mostly – they were always kind of prickly with each other, you know? Aidan likes to lark about. He's a messer, but in a good way. Well, mostly. Used to build boats out in the back yard, that kind of stuff, just for the hell of it. They were really good, too. We took one of them down to the canal; it was just a raft really, but it floated and everything, he was that good.' Anto was smiling. 'He was always buying books, researching stuff. Mostly he never got around to half of it, but his ideas were class. My da never got it, though. Why was he building rafts instead of trying to find a job? They'd always end up having these big barneys.'

He shot her a tentative glance to make sure he wasn't boring her to death. Just in case, he shrugged and wound it up. 'You can guess the rest. The rows got worse. Aidan got involved with this crowd, started drinking and staying out. Da came down heavy, put down curfews, made Aidan go to work for him painting and decorating.' Anto's mouth twisted. 'Aidan couldn't handle it. Wasting his life redoing old ladies' kitchens, he said. Anyway,' he finished up flatly, 'he's gone now and we haven't seen him since.'

They walked on for another bit.

'Meh! Meh!' Darren shouted.

'Keep it down, you head-the-ball,' Anto told him.

There was no sign of Darren's first word yet. Anto kept waiting for it. He was convinced it was going to be 'Chelsea', as that was the word most often spoken in his house, he'd maintained to Nicola.

And suddenly Nicola heard herself say, 'You know my mum left too.'

She wasn't sure where it had come from. She, who never told anybody anything, was now dredging all this up again with this gawky half-boy, half-man. It was those bloody pills. She'd stop taking them, she vowed. If she was like this after a couple of weeks, what would she be like after a month? Going around taking her clothes off maybe, or something crazy like that.

'Yeah,' Anto said. 'She ran off with the patio guy.'

'Are you laughing?'

'What? No . . .'

'Maybe it wouldn't be so funny if she ran off with a doctor, or an IT consultant, is that it? But we can all have a snigger at the patio guy?'

'I wasn't sniggering! Jesus! I was just stating a fact!'

She searched his face suspiciously. She could see no traces of mirth there, only offence, and she backed down.

'Okay,' she said grudgingly.

Anto grumpily turned back to pushing Darren; it was clearly up to her if she wanted to expound. He would do no cajoling.

'It kind of *is* embarrassing,' she admitted. 'Going off with the hired help. That was one of the things that made me so mad. I had to face people after that.'

'Patio guys are okay,' said Anto. 'A bloke doesn't have to wear a suit, you know, to be attractive to women.'

She didn't know if he was having a pop at her dad, or feeling defensive about his own. Whatever, she was enjoying herself. Well, not exactly; she was enjoying the connection.

'What happened, anyway?' he said.

'You know what happened.'

'Well, yeah. I mean, she's in Australia, right? Running some bar called The Rotten Potato.'

'The Rotten Spud.'

A pause.

'Rotten name,' Anto said, and she suddenly laughed.

'She wasn't happy for a long time,' she said unexpectedly. She hadn't known she knew that until now. 'The patio guy, he must have lit a fire or something.' She said it sardonically, but she remembered the patio guy's big, jolly laugh and the way her mother used to turn towards the sound as though the sun had just popped out. Nicola herself used to turn; it was hard to ignore him. 'She said afterwards that she'd been going to wait until I'd started college, and had my own life, before she left Dad.' She wished she hadn't started this now; she didn't want to talk about it any more. 'But Dad found all these texts and stuff on her phone, so she got busted before her great plan came to pass.'

Poor Nicola. That was what Anto's face said. No doubt he was thinking that his own, messed-up family of delinquents and teen parents wasn't so bad after all.

'The night I met you,' she reminded him, 'she'd left.'

'The house?'

'The country.' She was a bit annoyed now; annoyed at his drunkenness that night, his immaturity.

She walked on coolly. She felt Anto watching her; he knew he'd offended her, but he didn't know how, the thick.

Anto caught up with her a moment later.

'Did she ever see Darren?' he asked tentatively. 'She's his granny too.'

Nicola looked down at the top of her baby's head. *His lovely hair!* was all she could think of.

'She came back after he was born. To help. Of course, he came way early, so she was caught short.'

'Did he?' Anto marvelled. But of course he didn't know any of this. And Nicola now wondered about her decision not to tell him she was pregnant.

'She saw Darren but I didn't see her.'

She felt Anto looking at her.

'What?' she said sharply. 'She ran out on us.'

'No, I know. It's just . . . that must be tough,' he said gently. 'Not seeing your ma. That's all.'

She wanted to cry suddenly. And she hadn't cried in three days. The medication again. She might only be seeing that doctor to keep Dad happy, but the pills were definitely helping with the crying.

Until now.

'Do you know something, Anthony Brady? You're a fecking eejit,' she said, and stormed ahead.

Chapter Thirty

An upstairs light had just gone on.

By a process of elimination and many hours of dedicated spying, Aisling believed she had identified the correct apartment. The Chinese couple lived on the ground floor – bell no. 1 – to the left of the front door, and a middle-aged single man who always wore a tired-looking overcoat lived to the right. Two groups of students were on the middle floor. Above them to the left was a haggard-faced couple who wouldn't be living there had they anywhere else to go. And the top floor on the right . . . She'd seen him come and go, and the light going on and off at corresponding times. He lived there. That was Aidan's flat, it had to be.

It looked like he lived alone. Which meant he must be renting. Which meant he had some class of income, however small. The relief she felt at this was profound. Up to now he'd been slumming it on friends' floors or, in the early days, a grim city-centre hostel. There had been one terrible month when he'd slept on the streets, and Aisling didn't think she would ever recover from seeing him trying to pull sheets of cardboard over his thin body.

'What do we do now?' Zofia wondered tersely.

'Nothing.'

She'd had to bring Zofia along for moral support. Zofia was delighted to oblige, as Olaf was spending the evening going over plans for the redecoration of Magda's newly roofed house with her. Magda had cooked up a batch of Olaf's favourite cabbage rolls – 'I've missed these so much!' he kept swooning, even though he rarely touched them nowadays – and the two of them had settled in at the kitchen table chatting and laughing at jokes that Zofia didn't understand. 'Join us, join us!' they had belatedly said, of course, but they didn't mean a word of it and Zofia had left in high dudgeon.

'Are you okay?' she asked Aisling.

'Yes.' She wasn't. 'I just want to see him for a minute and then we'll go.'

Zofia's eyes went to the dashboard. 'The card. Is that for him?'

'Yes.'

Maybe it looked a bit mean or something. All that way for a Hallmark greeting. But Zofia didn't know what Aisling used to do in the beginning. She'd load up the car, literally: clean clothes, a sleeping bag, home-made chicken stews in individual containers, first-aid kits, a new pair of runners when she noted that the soles were coming off the ones on his feet, a toothbrush and dental floss . . .

'Look what I brought you,' she used to say, in her innocence. 'You don't have to say anything. Just take it. Please. I'm not looking for anything in return.'

But he never did. He just used to give her this small, sad smile, as though she were pathetic.

It took her a while to learn. She gave up on the stews and began buying takeaway coffees and sandwiches, so it wouldn't seem like she was trying so hard.

'I picked these up if you fancied them. I'll just leave them down here.'

He would immediately give the sandwiches away to a passer-by, or else he'd pour the coffee down the gutter in front of her eyes in defiance.

Eventually she just brought money. Cold, hard cash, in small denominations, stuffed into an envelope. There was no longer any interaction or communication between them. She didn't even approach him any more. She'd give the envelope to a mutual acquaintance to pass on, or she'd post it through the door of whatever house he happened to be currently dossing down in.

She had no idea whether he ever got the money. Maybe he gave it away too. But it made her feel better. Sometimes at night in bed she drew comfort from imagining him buying himself phone credit with it, or feeding an electricity meter.

Equally he could have bought a supply of weed, but she never dwelled on that.

There was money in the birthday card she'd brought. Fifty euros. It was all she could spare, now that they'd lost her income.

'Maybe you shouldn't be here tonight.' Zofia was watching her with kind eyes.

'Where else should I be? No, please, tell me. It's my son's twentieth birthday. Maybe I should have gone bowling or something?'

Zofia was silent for a bit. 'What did you tell Mossy?'

Aisling felt her judgement. 'That you and I were going salsa dancing.'

'*Salsa* dancing?'

'It was all I could think of.'

It seemed that by now she'd used up every other believable excuse: a last-minute run to the shops for bread for lunches in the morning; meeting an old friend from work; a quick dash by her mother's. She might actually have to take up salsa dancing one of these days as a legitimate cover.

It was hard, all the lying. And she was growing tired. Darren's arrival had made the subterfuge more difficult. Her brain seemed to have a hundred more things to remember.

And for what? A glimpse of her son to dull the pain, like a little shot of morphine that would have worn off as soon as she got home?

Tonight she wouldn't even get that. Mossy's words had spoiled it now. He was turning it back on her; her concern for her son, her worry for him. He was twisting it into something malevolent. *Enabler.*

The word had followed her around since their row, souring her stomach and making her want to turn and scream at him, 'How can you sleep at night when you don't know where he is? How can you get through each day without wondering every second of it whether he's even still alive?'

She'd left him sitting in front of the television watching some comedy show with Anto and Louise. Shannon was coming over later too, to put on a wash, and no doubt Matt wouldn't be far behind. It was a bit of a strange evening; not only was it Aidan's birthday and no one was mentioning it, but Darren was gone too. Hugo had picked him up that afternoon and he was going to spend the evening with him and Nicola. It was great, of course; but it also felt like the beginning of the end of something else. Already there was talk of him going over at the weekend, possibly to sleep overnight.

No matter how hard she tried to keep her family cobbled together, Aisling seemed to be on a losing streak.

Mossy had sensed some of what was going on in her head because he'd patted the couch beside him. 'Sit down. Put off that salsa class until next week.'

She knew by his face that he was feeling the strain of the day too; that he had wanted them to be together, even if it was just physically.

But she couldn't. Not while Aidan was out there. Not when she hadn't seen him in weeks, and she needed to know that he was okay.

'I've promised Zofia,' she'd mumbled. 'Anyway, I have to pick up Darren later.'

And his face closed down a bit.

Zofia's phone beeped with a text, the third or fourth time now. She ignored it.

'Supposing it's something important?' Aisling wondered.

'It is only Olaf.'

'Look, he's probably worried about you.'

'Then why is he at home with his mother?'

Aisling tried a different tack. 'What is it about her that bothers you so much? Apart from her relentless silent criticism, of course, which would do anybody's head in.'

Zofia had the grace to look mildly embarrassed. 'I may have misread some of that.'

'Any time I've met her, and I hate to say this, she seems like a very nice woman.'

'She is okay,' Zofia conceded.

'So? Is she pinching you when we're not looking?'

Zofia sighed. 'This will sound very small. But all I know is that I can't stop thinking that she had twenty-four years with

A Special Delivery

him, and I have had only four. I thought I knew him well, but she knows *every single little thing* about him. She knows what his favourite TV programme was as a child, and how he has no wisdom teeth because they never grew.'

'Fascinating,' Aisling murmured.

'Maybe I feel inferior,' Zofia said miserably. 'She doesn't have to do anything, and I feel inferior. Like my place is worth less than hers.'

'But you're his wife. She's his mother. They're completely different things.'

'I know! And the worst thing is, it is coming between me and Olaf. All I want is for her to go home and for it just to be the two of us again.'

It would seem like the best thing all round.

'How much longer?'

'Who knows? The builders, they were optimistic.'

Yes. They usually were.

'You'll have to try to get on with her until then, Zofia. For everybody's sake.'

Aisling nearly jumped out of her seat at a rap at the window. She'd been so engrossed that she hadn't been paying attention to the house.

It was Aidan. He was right outside the car. Her heart leaped at the sight of his beloved, familiar face; thinner, paler, but otherwise the same.

'Aidan.' Her hands were slippery as she struggled to wind down the window . . . quick, quick, before he melted away on her again. 'How are you?' she said. 'It's so good to see you . . .'

His eyes went from her to Zofia, then back again. Guarded and expressionless.

'I thought you'd finally given up,' he said. It was half aggressive, half accusing, and she didn't really know whether he was pleased or angry to see her.

'It's been very busy at home.' She heard herself gushing forth with apology. The main thing was that he was still standing there, he hadn't walked off, and she had to keep talking. 'Lots of things have been happening, Aidan, I don't know if you've been in touch with Anto, or Shannon . . .?'

'No.' He looked away, but not before she saw a flash of guilt. He'd always been close to his siblings. It seemed that they'd become casualties of his behaviour too, though.

'But let's not talk about this on the street.' If she could just get him into the car, they could have a proper talk. Start fixing this thing. 'Maybe we could go somewhere . . . McDonald's or something?'

He smiled. And he looked just like the old Aidan, the one before all this. 'I'm not some kid, Ma, looking for a Happy Meal.'

'No, I know that.' Shite. What had she mentioned McDonald's for? 'Somewhere else then, you suggest somewhere.'

Zofia was diplomatically gathering her handbag, preparing to alight from the car and leave them to it.

But Aidan stopped her. 'I'm meeting some friends this evening,' he said.

'Oh. Right.' Aisling tried not to take it as a rejection. She'd pitched up here unannounced; she couldn't expect him to drop everything to go off with her. 'How are you?'

She shouldn't have asked. But she couldn't help it. He was so thin. And his clothes, though clean, were too big for him, like they belonged to someone else.

'I'm okay.' His eyes went scudding off to the side again, and she knew not to pursue this line of questioning; that he would walk away.

'I just wanted to wish you a happy birthday. That's all.'

'Right. Well, thanks. At least someone's remembered.' And he gave a short bark of laughter that pierced her to the core.

Before she knew what she was doing, she was reaching through the open window to touch him. Some primitive instinct. He took a step back to avoid her and her hand fell.

'Right, well, I'd better get going,' he said, shifting on his feet.

'Okay, sure.' She was euphoric; beaming like a lunatic out the window at him. It was going to be all right; her faith in keeping some small contact was paying off. He was coming back to them, slowly. Tonight might only have been a few words exchanged through a car window, but it was the best conversation she'd ever had in her life.

'Give me a call sometime, will you?' she said. Best to leave it casual. She started the car just to show him how unpushy she could be.

'Um, sure.' Still he loitered. There was a growing sense of unease in her stomach now, like something turning bad. And as he spoke, it came together in her head: his thaw, his pointed reference to her absence, his anxiety to hang around until she handed it over.

The envelope with the money.

'Is that my card?' he said, looking at the dashboard, eyes hungry.

He wanted the cash. It was nothing to do with her at all.

'Yes,' she whispered, and passed it to him.

She managed to drive herself and Zofia around the corner, out of his sight, before she wept.

Chapter Thirty-one

'Come in!' Hugo opened the door with a big beam. 'We've had a great evening. I hope you don't mind waiting a few minutes, Nicola's just getting him out of the bath . . .'

'Oh, I can't stay.' Aisling didn't think she was physically capable of small talk right now. She'd dropped Zofia outside her own house and then driven straight here, without stopping off at home. Zofia had given her some concealer and powder from her bag to put under her eyes, and thankfully Hugo didn't seem to notice a thing.

'You've time for a cup of tea.'

'Honestly, Hugo . . .' She was worried the smell of it might make her vomit.

'It's just that I have something to tell you.'

What could she say? She let herself be ushered into the kitchen, Hugo's hand warm on her elbow, before he turned to call upstairs, 'You able to manage by yourself for a few minutes?'

To which he got a shouted response. 'Like, *yeah*. I have done this before, you know! I'm not a complete eejit.'

'Just so you know. Aisling's here,' he called up in light warning.

'Oh,' came Nicola's guarded response.

Hugo chuckled and closed the kitchen door firmly. He seemed very pleased by the back-and-forth with Nicola. 'Just like her old self.'

He sat in close to Aisling at the kitchen table, so near that she could see the little flecks of dark brown in his hazel eyes.

'I just wanted to say thank you.'

Aisling floundered. 'For . . .?'

'You were right. About the doctor. Look, she doesn't want you to know this. Or Anto, or anybody. She's afraid people are going to judge. And I feel bad going behind her back like this, but I told her we can't go around acting like it's something to be ashamed of . . .'

Aisling was actually glad of the distraction of talking about somebody else's difficult child, even if she hadn't a clue what was going on.

'I should have seen that there was something wrong with her. Well, I *did* see – it'd be hard to ignore the moods and the apathy, the way she seemed so unhappy all the time. But I was that way myself for a long time. For months, really, after Eleanor left. So I suppose in a way it became normal. The two of us dragging ourselves through the day.'

Upstairs they could hear a few thumps and thuds, things hitting against the side of the bath. And Nicola's voice, quiet, alert. It was like she knew she was being discussed downstairs.

'But you were the one who saw that it was more than that. Eleanor would have seen it too. Not that I'm blaming her or anything.' His eyes ran over Aisling's face keenly. 'Mothers seem to know what's wrong with their children before anybody else does.'

At that, Aisling had to concentrate very, very hard on the sugar bowl on the table. Suddenly she didn't want to be here any more; she wanted to go home, to shut her eyes, to block everything out. 'Hugo, what's this about?'

'Sorry,' he said, humbled by her sudden impatience. 'Nicola has post-natal depression.'

The minute Aisling heard the words, she felt a flash of recognition: *Ah*.

'You knew, didn't you?'

The slightly evangelical way he was looking at her was unsettling. 'No, I didn't, Hugo. I'm not a doctor myself. But I suppose in the surgery we would come across it a fair bit.'

She didn't want to tell him that after Aidan had left, she'd fallen into a black hole herself. For years she'd run on adrenalin: mediating rows, coaxing reconciliations, doing her 'why don't we all sit down and talk about this!' act. When the aggravation suddenly stopped, leaving nothing but relentless worry and secret shouting sessions in the attic, she'd thought, *This is it. I'm officially going mad*.

It was Dr Iris who took one look at her in the surgery one morning – she was inputting the same data for a third time on her break because she was so anxious that she'd messed it up the first two times – and told her it was time to look after her mental health. And what had Aisling said, primly? 'It's my son I have to worry about, thank you anyway. Not myself.'

A flipping saint in the making. And where exactly had all that self-sacrifice got her? An empty purse and an emptier feeling in the pit of her stomach.

She'd take the pills, if it was now. She'd fucking take them, and look after herself, and then she'd worry about everybody else.

Oh, Aidan.

'I'm very glad that she's getting the help she needs,' she said, dragging herself back to the conversation. 'And I'm even sorrier that we were all so hard on her.'

'You didn't know what was behind it. Nicola's very good at keeping everything to herself. It's only in the last few days that she's even admitted there's something wrong.' He shot her a look. 'You must think I've been pretty wrapped up in myself not to have noticed that my own child was sick.'

'Trust me, Hugo. I'm the last person judging you right now.'

There was more thudding from upstairs. Footsteps walked across the landing. Darren must be out of the bath.

'You should go and give her a hand.' She got to her feet in the hope that he'd take the hint. 'And maybe tell Nicola that I'll explain things to Anto and Mossy if that would help.'

'Thank you.' Hugo was fervent in his praise as he stood too. 'You've been tremendous through all of this, Aisling.'

'Really, I haven't.'

'You have,' he insisted quietly. 'I don't know what we'd have done without you.'

'Like you say, we're family now,' she reminded him.

'Yes.' He was watching her closely, seeing beneath Zofia's concealer. 'Aisling. Is everything okay?'

'Fine, fine.' Then, because she couldn't put on a front any longer, 'Actually, you know something, Hugo? It's not. So if you wouldn't mind getting Darren for me, I'm going to head home.'

'But . . .' He was all consternation and concern. 'What's the matter? Tell me.'

'I can't.' It would look so sad and tawdry: her stalkerish behaviour and Aidan's using of her.

'You never know. I might be able to help.'

241

She thought again about the birthday card on the dashboard with the fifty-euros in it. A bout of nausea overtook her again.

'Hugo, I really can't tell you anything, except that my life is a bit of a mess right now and I need to go.'

Mossy would be wondering what was taking her so long. The thought of going home, of plastering on her usual calm front, was honestly enough to make her sink to her knees in Hugo's expensive kitchen.

Which would be just plain weird. Instead she walked towards the hall door. 'Is Darren's bag packed?'

Hugo was following. 'Look, let him stay here tonight. It's late anyway, and you're obviously upset.'

'I can't, Anto's expecting him back . . .'

'I'll ring him, explain.' Hugo was firm. 'I'm sure he can do with the night off. And I'll have Darren back at your house by eleven in the morning.'

'Thank you,' she said, and she really meant it.

They stood by the front door. Hugo's hand was on the latch. 'Will you be okay?'

'Yes.'

'I hate to see you go like this.'

'I'll be fine.'

'All the same.' As though giving in himself, he reached forward and gave her a hug. It was like a big security blanket wrapping itself around her. And she enjoyed it for a split second, before unease banished it and turned her body rigid.

'Hugo.'

But the word was swallowed up by his lips, which were suddenly on hers, warm and hungry as he kissed her. She was so shocked that she froze for a moment, and then she pushed on his chest, hard.

'*Hugo.*'

They both leaped back and stared at each other, wild-eyed. Breathing hard.

Then several things happened almost simultaneously, with a strong dollop of sod's law.

Nicola appeared at the top of the stairs, with Darren in her arms dressed in a fresh babygro and with a blanket wrapped around him.

'Sorry for taking so long.' Her eyes went from Hugo to Aisling, suddenly alert.

'Hi!' said Aisling, as casually as she could, and probably completely overdoing it on the friendly tone.

Darren went wild with excitement at the sight of Aisling. He also chose that moment to say his first word, pointing at her and declaring, 'Mama! Mama!'

Then Aisling's phone rang. She managed to haul it out of her coat pocket, hoping in a cowardly fashion that it would be her escape from this bloody awfulness.

And it was, but only to propel her into fresh awfulness.

'Aisling?' It was Mossy, terse. 'Where are you? Aidan's in the hospital.'

Chapter Thirty-two

It was an overdose. The fifty euros she'd given him in his card – the last cent he'd ever get out of her, she vowed – he'd gone right out and blown on dodgy drugs, and now he was having some kind of fatal episode. It had to be.

Mossy would never forgive her. This was it. It was all over. He'd look at her over Aidan's coffin and he'd go, 'Look what you've done. I told you, but you wouldn't listen, would you?

She'd no idea what Aidan might even have taken, but she imagined needles, tourniquets, pipes, powdery white lines stretching for miles. Also, for some reason, a massive bong – she might have seen it on a TV show once – spewing noxious dark fumes into the air like a toxic chimney, causing people to keel over like dominoes after one sniff. In other words, she hadn't a clue.

She was the one who'd found the hash in his bedroom that night Mossy had ended up calling the guards, and in all honesty she thought it was something Anto had brought in on the bottom of his soccer boots. The innocence of her. But in her day the wildest it had ever got was multiple bottles of Ritz, and watching other people at parties pass around damp, battered-looking roll-ups that you'd have more chance of getting a mouth ulcer from than any great high. Anything harder was strictly for celebrities, or else those poor, hollow-eyed people living in high-rise flats who would sell their firstborn for their next fix. They were like another species to Aisling and her friends.

Fast-forward twenty years and her knowledge of the current Irish drugs scene was just as vague. She kept it that way deliberately. Call it self-protection. She didn't actually want to know. Whenever she passed newspaper stands screaming out headlines like *Terry 'the Slab' O'Connor in €10 million drugs haul!* she always looked away. Aidan, she told herself, just dabbled in a bit here and there. Lots of young people did. It was probably harmless enough: a few smokes, maybe a pill or two at a party, or so she imagined.

She bitterly regretted her carefully cultivated ignorance now. She wouldn't have a clue when some young doctor turned round to her in the hospital and murmured, 'It was a lethal dose of methamphetamine combined with some stoppers and a few zeds, I'm afraid,' or whatever the current lingo was.

'Get out of the way,' she shouted at a hapless motorist as she drove at speed through the hospital car park. Then she saw it: Mossy's van, thrown into a parking space, and she threw her own car in beside it, grabbed her bag and ran.

Mossy was waiting for her in reception. He had a tight, shocked look about him. And no wonder. It was what they'd been dreading since Aidan had moved out: the phone call out of the blue, the knock on the front door in the dead of night. The awful words, 'Are you the parents of Aidan Brady?'

In a way Aisling was glad Mossy had been the one at home to take the call. She would have fallen on the floor with fright.

'There you are,' he said, and his relief at seeing her was so pathetically obvious that she tried not to think that she'd just been the recipient, albeit reluctant, of a snog from Hugo O'Sullivan.

Still, no time to think about that now. There was nothing like a hospital to reorganise priorities.

'I came as fast as I could . . . What happened? Where is he?'

She was prepared for intensive care. Mentally she'd factored in tubes and machines that beeped ominously.

'Still in A and E,' the porter said.'

A and E? Okay. Good. That wasn't too bad. If it was really serious, he wouldn't still be there, would he? They'd have admitted him in the thirty minutes since Mossy's call had come through.

'Have you seen him yet?'

'No. I've only just got here too.' Mossy wasn't himself. He was agitated; looking around, unsure. Mossy, who'd always been so certain of everything. 'They just said on the phone to come in. I don't know who I was talking to. She wasn't able to tell me what was wrong.' His face crumpled. 'Jesus, Aisling.'

'It's okay.'

And now they were clinging to each other, shaking with fright, both thinking the same thing. *If only we hadn't kicked him out. If only things had been different. If only he'll be okay, we'll sort everything else out. Please God, let him be okay.*

'Ma.' It was Anto, hurrying up to join them. He had a box of Roses in his hand. He seemed to realise how daft it was when he saw them staring at it. 'I, um, got them in the hospital shop. I didn't know what else to do.'

'Fecking food again!' Mossy rounded on him. 'He could have a tube stuck down his throat and you want to give him chocolate?'

'It's for when he's better, okay?' Anto huffed optimistically. He looked at Aisling. Awkwardly he touched her on the shoulder in comfort.

'He's going to be okay, Ma.'

'Well yes, of course he is.' Surely that was her job, to be reassuring him. But Anto had got so mature in the last few months. Serious.

He even looked different, she realised. Irrationally, given the gravity of the situation, she tried to figure out what it was. Then she saw. A *beard*. Her baby boy was growing a little beard!

Oh Anto, she thought fiercely. She missed him; the gawky, silly boy given to sudden grins and tantrums over homework. Fatherhood had taken him.

'Listen,' she told him. 'Darren's going to stay the night with the O'Sullivans.'

'I know,' Anto said. 'I was just chatting to Nic on the phone.'

Chatting? With *Nic*?

When the hell had that happened? This cosiness?

Then: had Nicola seen anything, when she'd come down the stairs? And if she had, would she believe that Aisling had had no part in it?

But again she pushed it from her mind. Her son was some-where down that corridor marked Accident and Emergency, and she was desperate to see him. 'Come on,' she said to Mossy. She was filled with dread. She had no idea what awaited her, but given that they were in a hospital, it wouldn't be good.

'Ma!' Louise came running up now. Her hair was pinned up into an enormous lopsided bun that threatened to destabilise her at any moment. 'Where were you? We were waiting for you to come home with Darren but you were *ages*.'

'I got . . . delayed.' She turned to Mossy crossly. 'You brought Louise too?'

'I had to, I couldn't leave her behind!'

'Ma?' Now Shannon came down the corridor, with Matt trailing in her wake carrying a fruit basket.

'Dear God,' Aisling groaned. She was surprised Mossy hadn't invited along the entire neighbourhood.

'Where's Aidan?' Shannon demanded, bringing everybody back to the matter at hand.

'In there somewhere.' Aisling pointed at the double doors. 'Look, they're not going to let us all in. So maybe the best thing is for you to go home and wait. We'll let you know as soon as we hear anything.'

Anto eyed Matt's enormous fruit basket. Matt looked at the little box of Roses. Anto's face said, *you fucking lick*.

Shannon had planted herself in the corridor to face her parents. 'We're not going home. He's our brother. We want to be here.'

'Yeah!' said Louise, with a wild toss of her bun.

Anto joined their ranks. He raised a fluff-covered chin. 'Whatever has happened, it doesn't matter now. We have to pull together. So we're staying.'

It was clear they were outnumbered. And then Aisling thought, he was right. It should never have got this far.

'Fine. But we're going in first.'

She took Mossy's arm. He resisted for a moment, but she braced herself, pushed open the double doors and marched them both in.

Oowww . . . OOooooWW . . . OOOOWWW . . . Nurse! It hurts so bad. Nurse? Does anybody know what time it is? Ah, you're lovely, do you know that? Lovely. You're like my mother, God rest her soul.

NURSE! Don't ignore me! It hurts so bad. Bloody kip. Bloody country is in the shits. Oh Danny Boy, the pipes, the pipes . . .

Saturday night in any capital-city A&E wasn't a pretty sight. Aisling kept in close to Mossy as they passed the usual plethora of drunk-and-disorderlies. There were two or three elderly people scattered about on chairs, looking lost and disorientated. Over there, a young man in rugby gear sat with his arm held carefully to his chest, his mouth in a thin line of pain. On another chair was a well-dressed middle-aged woman, not unlike Aisling, tending to a man in a jacket and tie who had a bloodied towel held to his nose.

'Bouncy castle,' she said tightly to anybody who looked their way.

There was nobody to ask where Aidan was, so they just started looking. Most of the cubicles had curtains drawn across. There were names handwritten on slates outside – Henderson R., Ryan P., Malik M. – but no Brady.

'Maybe he's not here. Maybe they've moved him.' Aisling's mind was stumbling ahead to operating theatres, bright lights, knives cutting slickly through flesh . . .

'Hey.'

It was Aidan. He was sitting up on a bed, fully dressed, having tea and toast. His eyes shifted from Aisling to settle warily on Mossy for a moment before looking away again.

'Aidan!'

They just gaped, the pair of them. Their expectations had been so grisly and graphic, and it was nearly worse to have them confounded like this by a calmly chewing Aidan. Not a bother on him! Except, now that Aisling looked, his shoe and sock were off his left foot and it was propped on top of the covers on the bed. It was swollen and already turning black and blue.

'They think it's a broken ankle.' He looked at it too. 'I'm going for an X-ray in a minute. The good news is that I'll only have to wear a cast for two weeks and then they put on this Velcro pad thing that you can take off when you have a shower and stuff, and I won't even need to use crutches all the time. The miracles of modern medicine, eh?'

He was talking so much because he was nervous. And Mossy and Aisling duly nodded back at all this information, as though they'd seen him only that morning, instead of a year and a half ago in Mossy's case.

At least he's alive, Aisling thought. Although he might have had the decency to look a little less so, given the shock and fright he'd caused.

The birthday card was forgotten in that instant. She wanted to fling herself on him. To stroke his hair and cuddle him and brush her fingers down his stubbly cheek. She wanted to bend over his foot and see for herself exactly what was wrong with it, and never mind about those doctors.

But Mossy was standing beside her. Flanking her, like a steel column. It would be a big mistake now to overtly choose sides.

For now all she could do was ask, full of concern, 'How did it happen?'

Drink? Drugs? Tripped over a pavement whilst off his head on her fifty euros?

'I dropped the fridge on it.'

'The *fridge*?' Even Mossy looked startled at that.

'It wasn't working properly, so I pulled it out to see what was wrong with it and it . . . fell. I twisted my ankle trying to get out of the way.'

He was half embarrassed, half defiant. He looked at Mossy again; his da would find that predictable, presumably, after all he'd tried and failed to teach him about the workings of the domestic home.

'But you said you were . . .' She stopped herself just in time. He'd told her earlier he was meeting friends tonight. And now this story about the fridge. A lie? Who knew, with Aidan? 'Are you in pain?' she asked instead.

'A little.' Which meant a lot. But he'd never admit it.

Mossy said nothing still. Not a word. Just looked from Aidan to his foot and back again. You would think he was made of stone. But Aisling could see a little nerve ticking around his mouth. Relief? Suppressed anger? Both?

She just hoped that nothing was going to kick off. Not here, amongst all the sick people, and with the rest of the kids outside.

'Sorry about that phone call,' Aidan offered. 'I had no credit left so I asked them to phone you. I should have realised that you'd get a bit of a shock.'

It was like a little olive branch. The fact that he'd had the hospital phone them at all wasn't lost on Aisling.

She flicked a glance at Mossy. *Please, meet him halfway.* 'The main thing is that you're okay.' She took a tiny step forward into the cubicle. 'Do you need anything? Water? Something from the vending machine?'

'Our health insurance number?' That was Mossy, his voice as dry as wood. 'I presume they're looking for that, are they? The hospital?'

Aidan reared back against the pillows. Aisling felt her throat close over.

'Mossy, please. I'm sure that's not why he—'

'Well, he's still on our policy, isn't he?' Mossy's eyes were on her now. 'We still pay for him. You insisted. A safety net, wasn't that what you called it?' He calmly took his wallet out of his jeans pocket and dug out a membership card. He tossed it down on the bed. 'There you go. That'll get you seen a bit quicker by the consultant. And maybe some physio afterwards, if you need it.'

Aisling felt like she was watching a car crash in slow motion. '*Mossy.*' She didn't believe that was why Aidan had phoned, despite the awfulness of the birthday money. Or at least it wasn't the only reason. She'd seen his expression when they'd arrived at the end of his bed. His face had been that of someone who wanted a way back but couldn't quite find one.

Aidan didn't move. Just stared straight ahead. With his good foot he flicked the card back at Mossy.

'You can keep that,' he evenly told a point above Mossy's head. 'I'll slum it with everybody else.'

Stalemate. Aisling didn't know what would have happened next had Anto, Shannon and Louise not gatecrashed the cubicle in a nervous little huddle.

'We couldn't wait any longer, we just wanted to—' Shannon began. Her eyes fell upon Aidan. '*Aidan.*'

She flung herself on her brother. As in she literally got up on the bed and wrapped her arms around him. 'It's so good to see you. Are you okay?'

Aidan was embarrassed. 'I'm fine, I'm grand.'

'Mind his foot,' Aisling cautioned.

They all looked.

'What happened?' Anto loved a good injury and immediately came forward to examine the black and blue swelling. 'Oh man, looks sore,' he breathed in delight.

'A fridge.'

'A *fridge*?' Anto was grinning at Aidan in disbelief. Aidan smiled back, getting over his mortification at all the attention being heaped upon him. 'You muppet.'

Aidan glanced at Louise now, standing shyly at the bottom of the bed. And no wonder; she'd been nine when she'd last seen him. 'Nice hair,' he said, with a wink.

Louise clapped a hand to the side of her head in consternation. The bun had slid down to her ear.

'Never mind, have a chocolate. Come on, Anto. Hand them over . . . Hey, who's the dude with the fruit?'

They turned; Matt had appeared by the curtain with the big basket.

'Pleased to meet you,' he said. 'I'm Shannon's boyfriend—'

'Oh, just wait in reception, will you?' Shannon waved him away impatiently. 'I'll be out in a minute, there's no room for you here.'

'You can leave the fruit,' said Aidan.

Matt was sent packing, and Aisling watched as chocolates and grapes were passed back and forth. Nobody could stop smiling, even though it was all a bit strained and weird, but ultimately great.

And even Mossy couldn't fail to see it, because when Anto held out the box of Roses to him, he took one.

'What's going to happen with your foot?' Shannon wanted to know.

'Are you going to be hobbling around the place on crutches?' Louise said enviously. Nothing that dramatic ever happened to her.

'Well, yeah, for a while . . .' It was clear Aidan wanted to shift the focus from himself; it was all too awkward. 'So, what's the news? What's been happening since I saw you last?' He made it out to be a joke, as though he'd just seen them the previous week.

And everybody swung to look at Anto expectantly. He was a little bashful, yet accepting of his place in the family as the head news generator.

'I don't know where to begin,' he said gravely.

'Oh, Anto,' everybody chorused. 'Just get on with it.'

'Okay, okay.' But he made a point of extracting a bit of caramel from his teeth before announcing his news. 'I've become a father.'

Aidan's surprise was almost comical. 'No. No *way*. You? You're kidding me, right?'

'I've got a little boy now.' Anto was proud. 'Darren is his name.'

'A boy.' Aidan kept shaking his head in wonder. 'Darren.' Half laughing, half in disbelief, he swung around to Aisling and said, with damning familiarity, 'How come you never told me that on one of your visits?'

Oh no.

It took a split second, then everybody turned to her.

Aisling was riveted by the look in Mossy's eyes. All bonhomie abruptly evaporated; any green shoots were swiftly crushed in that instant.

'You've been visiting him?' Shannon said faintly.

'Yes,' she said, because to try to cover up now would be a hundred times worse.

And everybody in the cubicle kind of bent forward into the brace position. This was going to be bad. Very, very bad.

Mossy finally broke the silence. 'I'll see you all at home.'

He didn't look at Aisling as he left.

Everybody else was frozen in position. Wondering what she was going to do now. And how she had managed to see Aidan without anybody guessing. Sneaky.

'Sorry, Ma.' Aidan was stricken. 'I didn't know you hadn't told him.'

'It's not your fault.'

And it wasn't. It was her own entirely.

Her mind was racing as she looked at him, surrounded by his

siblings, his face pale with pain and the undoubted emotion of the reunion. 'Let's just get you sorted out here first, okay?'

She glanced around for a doctor. When were they going to do this X-ray?

'You don't have to stay,' Aidan insisted. 'I could be here for hours.'

'That's okay. We'll wait.' There was nothing left to lose at this point, she figured. She might as well go the whole hog. 'Because you're coming home with us.'

Chapter Thirty-three

It was pure mental. All of it. Anto was starting his exams – his big, important, this-is-the-rest-of-your-life exams – in exactly a month's time, and he didn't even have a place to study. His bedroom, once a haven for sleeping and jerking off, was now the cramped home to him, his baby and his big brother. Well, until Aidan was off the crutches, anyway.

'You sure this is okay?' Aidan kept checking anxiously. He'd taken up residence on his bed, just like old times, where he would chew gum and expertly flick the wrappers into the bin – *bingo*. 'Like, I don't want to crowd you or anything.'

'No, no, it's cool.' Anto had thought that maybe Aidan might move into Shannon's old room, but he couldn't manage the attic stairs what with the crutches, and anyway, Shannon had practically moved back in herself, now that her college year was almost over and she had a few spare weeks before setting off for the summer to work in a tattoo parlour in New York. Well, that was just the family joke. She was actually going to volunteer in an orphanage in South Africa. Matt, naturally, was going with her. He'd probably have followed her to a tattoo parlour, too.

'Good,' said Aidan. 'Because it's kind of nice.' He put on his Marlene Dietrich accent and told Anto intensely, 'For us to be bek togever again.'

Anto laughed. It *was* nice. It was great. He'd missed the fun and the talking about stupid stuff until four in the morning. It was just a bit . . . busy, that was all.

'But seriously, it's only for a week or two,' Aidan reassured him. 'To keep Ma happy, you know? I'd be just as glad to be back in my own gaff. But you saw what she was like.'

Anto had. Aidan had done his best to resist, but when Ma got an idea into her head . . . 'You're not going back there on crutches. How would you manage? You wouldn't even get up those front steps, never mind make it to the shops. No, you'll come back home until the cast is off, where I can look after you.'

Da's face when Aidan hobbled in the door – you never saw anything like it. But everybody else wanted Aidan back, even for a little while. What could Da do? Anto felt a bit sorry for him all the same. Like, he could be a right pain, no doubt about that, but it must be hard for him, after everything that had happened. He'd been given no choice in the matter.

At least Aidan was tactful. Keeping out of his da's way and stuff. Mostly he stayed in their bedroom, talking on the phone, or accepting visitors.

Such as Baz and Sean descending upon them without warning. 'Hey, man! We heard you were back! Long time no see!'

They crowded into the bedroom and around Aidan like groupies. Aidan was a bit of a legend on the estate, what with being the resident bad boy, and getting the local cops all lathered up on a regular basis. Plus his penchant for a little GBH. Not that it had been. But that was the story going around.

'How's the foot?' The lads didn't really give a damn about Aidan's foot. What they wanted to know was what kind of a high life he was leading while they were stuck revising theorems for exams. Secretly they wanted to be like him, throwing two fingers up at the world, but they hadn't the nerve.

'Grand. My little brother here's been taking good care of me.' Aidan gave Anto a salute.

'I haven't done much,' said Anto.

'Don't mind him. Makes a great cup of tea, don't you, Anto? Here, if you're putting on that wash, I've got a couple of pairs of jocks that need to go in.'

It was just a joke, and Baz and Sean duly brayed. And Anto *was* collecting up a wash – an armful of Darren's babygros and vests from the floor, and millions of tiny socks.

'Wash your own jocks,' he threw back lightly. Just to make the point that he was older now and people didn't talk to him like that any more, not in front of his mates, anyway.

'He's gone very domesticated these days,' Baz slagged.

'Yeah,' said Sean, the eejit.

'Ah, fuck off, the lot of you,' said Anto with gusto, and threw the clothes back down on the ground. 'Shove up, you muppet.' He muscled his way in between the lads and took up a sprawled position on his own bed. The way they were going on, you'd think he was turning into a girl.

'Come here, what do you think of Darren?' Baz wanted to know from Aidan.

'Ah, he's a smasher.'

'Imagine. You're an uncle now.'

'I know, who'd have thought it? My little brother here, getting in there before me.'

Anto couldn't help preening a bit. And Aidan was mad about Darren; cooing at him and doing funny voices that reduced Darren to a heap of hysterical chuckles. Watching the two of them would have you rolling around laughing. But when it came to feeding Darren or changing him, Aidan was clueless. Well, so had Anto been before all of this, but Aidan was *really* clueless. He seemed to think that Darren took himself for walks, and mashed up his own dinner. He didn't really get it at all that Anto didn't have time any more to sit down with the blinds drawn and play on the PlayStation with Aidan for six hours straight.

'I thought babies slept a lot more than they actually do,' Aidan kept saying, marvelling at how much of Anto's time Darren took up.

Anto got the impression that Aidan sometimes thought he wasn't as much fun any more. But that wasn't either of their faults. It was just that so much had changed since Aidan had left.

Darren was at the O'Sullivans' for the day today. Anto would collect him after dinner and it would be all go again.

'So what's she like? Your mot?' Aidan wanted to know, opening a fresh packet of gum and sharing it around.

'She's not my mot.'

'*Sure* she's not,' chorused the lads.

'She's not!'

'What, so she's just some bird you had a kid with?' Aidan's eyebrows jumped up. 'Come on, Anto.'

'Yeah, we have a kid,' Anto blustered. 'But it was a one-night stand. We're not together, okay?' He wasn't keen on discussing her in front of Baz and Sean. In fact he wasn't even keen on discussing her with Aidan. Not in the way they usually talked about girls anyway. Nicola was different.

'They're definitely not together,' Baz confirmed to Aidan.

That annoyed Anto more. 'What do you know about anything? You haven't seen her in weeks!'

'I'm just saying . . . Jeez.' *Touchy*, Baz's look said. 'She's a stunner, though,' he told Aidan.

'Is she?'

'Absolutely gorgeous.' Sean sealed it.

'You don't all have to sound so surprised,' said Anto. 'You don't think I can pull a hot bird?'

'No,' said the lads, and they all burst out laughing.

'Ah, fuck off,' said Anto, hurt.

'Relax,' said Aidan, easily. 'We're just slagging. Darren's a seri-ously good-looking kid, so that just proves this girl is fit. And you're not bad yourself, what with that beardy thing you've got going. Plus, you've grown an inch or two since I saw you last; you must have been drinking your milk.'

'Leave it out,' said Anto, mortified yet pleased at the same time. He didn't know if Nicola liked his beard or not. She hadn't said. She hadn't given any indication that she'd even noticed it, although *he'd* noticed that her nails had started to grow, from those bitten down stubs. She must have got some of that special varnish.

'What's her name again?' said Aidan.

'Nicola. I must have told you a hundred times.'

It was like Aidan didn't listen half the time. He was enthusiastic and all that, but sometimes it was like he wasn't all that interested. Maybe it was because he'd been away for so long.

'Oh, yeah. Sorry.' Aidan watched Anto. 'So when am I going to meet her? I mean, she's practically my sister-in-law.'

Anto flushed violently. He was prone to it whenever her name came up.

'You'll meet her. It's just she hasn't been that well, okay?'

'What's wrong with her?'

'Nothing. Just stuff.' He was fiercely protective of Nicola, what with the whole post-natal depression thing going on. Anyway, she'd warned him that if he told anybody without her permission, she'd knock his teeth out. Not that he'd dream of it. He spent his time instead looking up the condition on the Internet; trying to find out how he could help. He'd even ordered some supplements for her that someone had recommended, but he hadn't the nerve to give them to her yet. 'She's got school too, you know,' he parried to Aidan. 'She's busy.'

'I still want to meet her.'

'And I'll ask her, okay?' It was a hard job getting Nicola onside when it came to his family. They hadn't exactly got off to the best start. And she was even tetchier since Darren had come out with 'Mama' to his ma. Talk about an insult! At least that was what Anto was putting it down to; the awkwardness that he'd observed between Nicola and his ma recently.

'What about yourself?' Baz said, clearly tiring of Anto's love life and hoping for tales of racier girls and maybe even super-models. 'Have you got a girlfriend?'

'I don't like to limit myself to just the one,' Aidan said gravely, and they all laughed. 'But right now I'm single.'

'I suppose there must be plenty. You know. In your scene.'

What scene? Anto wondered. Aidan hadn't a pot to piss in, as Anto had overhead his da saying. It was all very vague, what Aidan actually did nowadays, but it was becoming apparent that he had no job, he wasn't studying, and the origin of any cash flow seemed to be dubious and unable to be properly accounted for.

'You know,' said Baz. 'The music scene.'

The music scene? It was the first Anto had heard of it. Aidan couldn't even play the guitar, although Ma and Da had got him one for Christmas one year. He'd bought a book and a CD and everything – the usual – on how to teach yourself to play. The last time Anto had seen the guitar it had been abandoned in the garage, with its strings broken.

Aidan explained importantly, 'I'm not actually in a band. I just organise gigs. You know, put talent and venue in touch with each other, that kind of thing.'

'Since when?' Anto couldn't help saying.

'Just recently. But it's going well. Building up a lot of contacts, you know?'

'That's great, man.' Sean and Baz were well impressed.

Anto said nothing about the forty euros Aidan had asked to borrow yesterday. Anto had handed it over, only worrying about it afterwards. But Aidan didn't disappear off, or come back out of his head or anything. Although maybe his eyes had been a bit too bright, thinking back. Anyway, there would be no more loans, because Anto was broke.

'My God. The smell in here.' Shannon barged in. She looked around in disgust. 'How much Lynx have you lot put on?'

Baz and Sean got to their feet quickly. Shannon terrified them, mostly because she was so good-looking and she treated them like shit.

'Go,' she said, holding the door open wide for good measure. 'Get out. I want to talk to my brothers alone.'

And they ran.

'A lousy phone call wouldn't have hurt,' Shannon said. So far she'd held off on Aidan – 'to let you acclimatise' – but tonight her tone was blistering.

'Sorry,' said Aidan.

'Even a text to let us know you were still alive.'

'I changed numbers. I lost contact with a lot of people. I'm sorry, okay?' He gave her one of his rueful smiles. 'Anyway, Ma was keeping tabs on me. I figured she'd let you know I was all right.'

'How could she, when nobody knew she was visiting you?'

'I didn't encourage it. It was her own idea. I tried to get her to stay away, but she wouldn't listen.'

'Why? Why would you want her to stay away?'

'Why do you think? They threw me out, in case you've forgotten. She could have stopped it; could have stood up to that bully. But she didn't.' He had that intractable look on his face.

'Yeah, well, you've really dumped her in it now. Herself and Da aren't talking.'

'Aren't talking' was putting a very good spin on it. 'In terminal marital decline' might have been a more accurate description of the awful silences, the cutting looks, the air of hurt and betrayal that hung over the house like a nuclear cloud.

'It'll settle down,' Anto chipped in anxiously. He didn't know who he was trying to reassure, himself or the others. Every time he saw his da's back, stiff with hurt, or his ma's pale, defiant face, he felt his stomach drop. And the cause of it all was lying on the bed in front of him, flexing his toes in a cast. 'You know, once you go.'

'Thanks a fucking bunch.'

'Well that's the arrangement, isn't it? You're only back here until you're off the crutches.'

'It wasn't my decision.'

Anto sighed. 'We know, you don't have to keep saying it.'

'You think I want to be somewhere I'm not wanted? By Da, anyway? Let me tell you, the best thing that ever happened to me was getting thrown out of this house. Not having to listen to him in my ear the whole time. The rows, the nagging, the "get out of that bed and do something with yourself". I've my own life now, and as soon as I'm better, I'll be going back to it, okay? So you needn't worry, that I'm back for good,' Aidan finished up in a fit of hurt.

'I wasn't!'

'Oh shut up!' Shannon looked at the two of them, incredulous. 'Here we are, all fighting again. Sometimes I think it's the only thing this family is good at!'

Anto felt worse. Especially as he'd spent so many hours wishing that they could all be back together. Well now they were. It just wasn't quite how he'd imagined it was going to be: all tearful reunions and everybody hugging each and vowing that everything would change.

'Now apologise to each other,' Shannon ordered.

'Still the same old pain in the arse, eh?' Aidan muttered to Anto.

'Worse,' Anto muttered back.

'Apologise!'

'Terribly sorry,' Anto and Aidan told each other elaborately.

'Great,' said Shannon. She loved apologies. There wasn't a thing that couldn't be sorted on this earth with a good 'I'm so sorry!' even if you were just faking it. It was the thought that counted.

'And Da is next,' she told Aidan.

The smile died in his eyes. 'You want me to *apologise* to him?'

Even Shannon knew this would be difficult. 'Look, nobody's asking you to get down on your hands and knees—'

'I'm glad to hear that.'

'But you were in the wrong, Aidan.'

'So was he.'

'No. Not the same as you. And you know it.' Nobody else in the house would have the nerve to say it to his face like that.

'Thanks for the suggestion, Shannon, but I think I'll pass.'

Shannon pursed her lips and glanced across at Anto. He could see that she was finding this conciliator role harder than she'd thought.

'Just say you're fucking sorry, yeah? It wouldn't kill you,' Anto said impatiently. He hadn't time for this. Darren was going to be home soon, and it would be nice if his Granny and Granda Brady had affected some kind of reconciliation. All this aggro wasn't good for him. He was a very perceptive child.

'Hey. He called the cops on me. If anyone should apologise, it's him.'

'He just wanted to give you a fright, Aidan.'

'A fright? We all ended up looking like eejits! The cops swarming the house like it was some kind of major drugs bust, and all they found was a bit of hash in my sock drawer!'

It *had* been a little OTT. Even the cops had seemed disappointed. Da had kept insisting that there were all kinds of dodgy comings and goings – and there were – but nobody could prove that Aidan had actually been dealing. Although the hash *was* quite a large amount just for one person. Aidan had held his hands up and said, 'Okay, you've got me, I guess I need to cut down.'

They hadn't liked that. But that was Aidan. Not afraid of anyone.

'Are you looking for sympathy or something?' said Anto. 'Because it's kind of hard to muster any.'

Aidan looked at him flatly. 'You're starting to sound like Da.'

Anto felt terrible. Sounding like his da was possibly the worst sin he could ever commit, in Aidan's eyes.

But Shannon rowed in. 'He's right. You got thrown out for a reason. And we're all glad you're back, but not if you're going to keep trying to justify all this stuff.'

Aidan looked a little surprised. Maybe he'd been expecting them to stay quiet, like they'd done before. But a lot of time had passed. Things had changed.

'Sorry, okay?' he said. He looked at Anto. 'I didn't mean to imply . . . I know that things are different for you now, Anto. You've got a kid. And exams coming up, which you're obviously taking seriously.'

Now Anto was sounding like a nerdy swot. And he so wasn't. He just wanted to get by, that was all. 'Well, yeah, but—'

'Good for you, I say. Give yourself the best possible chance of getting out, of making a career for yourself. Because trust me, the last thing you want is to get stuck working in that van with the old man.'

'Like you say. Let's not bring that up again,' Shannon interjected quickly.

'Look,' Aidan said. 'I can say sorry if it makes everybody happier. But he's never going to forgive me, so what's the point?'

'It'd be a start.'

Aidan shrugged. 'Fine. If everybody thinks it'll help.'

Anto must have looked very surprised, because Aidan said, 'I know I did some bad stuff, okay? The drugs and all that. I realise I put everybody through hell, including both of you. And I'd like to say sorry for that now too.'

Anto felt a tightness in his chest; a fierce rush of emotion for his brother.

'But I've been trying to turn myself around. I've got my flat now, and I know the music stuff isn't paying much at the moment, but it's a start. And I don't do drugs any more or any of that shit.' He shot a sly look at Shannon. 'You love all this stuff, don't you? Music to your ears. Alleluia, another soul saved!'

'Hey!' Shannon said, but he was right: she *did* love it, and she couldn't resist giving him a massive, dazzling smile.

And Anto smiled too, trying to ignore Aidan's phone, and the text that had just come in, and all the other texts that arrived day and night from persons unknown.

Chapter Thirty-four

The house was bursting at the seams. Everywhere you went there were people: adults, teens-as-big-as-adults, pre-teens, little babies . . . For a year now it had only been the four of them – Aisling, Mossy, Anto and Louise – and it had been quite comfortable. But now that everybody had moved back in, unseemly queues had become to form once again outside the bathroom.

'What are you *doing* in there?'

'What do you think I'm doing?'

'Well can you do it faster?'

'If you don't like it, go back to your student digs.' This was Aidan to Shannon. 'You don't even live here any more.'

'Neither do you.'

The fridge was perpetually empty. Aisling would unpack a full week's shop into it on a Monday morning, and it'd all be gone by eight o'clock that night (except for the tub of Philadelphia with chives, which nobody liked). The washing machine deserved a medal for outstanding service, generating a constant hum in the background. Everywhere you went there were bodies splayed out on chairs, or coming in the door or going out; people shouting, 'Where's my keys?' and 'Who took my phone!' and, worryingly often, 'Mind the baby! You nearly walked on his head.'

It felt wonderful; the whole family back together again. All of her children, and her new grandchild, under one roof. It was like a fairy-tale ending in some book, with Aisling as the gracious queen, wafting around preparing massive shepherd's pies for the hordes, or matching three million pairs of socks with which to kit out her clan.

She was almost able to ignore the fact that she and Mossy were falling apart.

It was a kind of low-level awfulness. They were almost never alone any more, which helped and didn't help. Every time she tried to initiate some conversation, two or three people would walk into the room, demanding, 'Has anybody seen the remote control?' Their conversations were limited to shouted questions over people's heads: who was dropping Darren to the O'Sullivans' for the day? Would Mossy be home in time for dinner? Could he pick up milk on the way home? That kind of thing.

And Mossy was out working. A lot. The whole of Ireland needed repainting that particular month, it seemed. The van was gone early in the morning and often didn't come back until after Aisling was in bed.

She didn't know who he was avoiding, her or Aidan, who was upstairs in convalescence (Louise was reading a lot of Enid Blyton at the moment). Probably both.

Maybe she was avoiding him too. She knew she was in the wrong. But each day that Aidan was home, safe under her watchful eye, she felt less panicked, more in control of things. More able to apologise. To explain.

It was time to talk.

* * *

'Talk?' Mossy infused the word with cold irony. 'I thought you went and did things and then just informed me afterwards?'

'I was wrong.'

'Yes. You saw Aidan without telling me, you moved him back in here under our roof without telling me. Yes, you were bloody wrong.'

'He hasn't moved back in. It's just until he's better.'

He was incredulous. 'Is that what you're telling yourself this time?'

'Please, just listen to me.' His disillusionment was worrying. 'I did visit him. For eighteen months. I admit it. But it's not what you think. It's not because I was . . . enabling him.' How she hated that word. 'Look, I was afraid he was going to die, okay?'

'*Die?*' His eyes couldn't get any rounder.

She was suddenly furious that she was being written off as irrational. 'Yes. When he left this house, I was so afraid that he would kill himself with drink or drugs or something. I know you had the same fears too, I saw you at the hospital, so don't tell me I'm crazy. Don't you *dare* tell me I'm crazy.'

'And you thought you could keep him alive by running after him with, what, food, was it?'

He knew her too well.

'Yes,' she admitted.

'What else, Aisling?'

'Nothing. Some clothes, toiletries, that kind of thing.'

'And money? Did you give him that too?' He looked at her. 'The truth this time.'

For a moment they teetered on the edge of a precipice. She took a step back from it. 'Yes. Yes, I gave him money.'

Mossy exhaled heavily. 'You might as well have handed it straight to his dealer.'

She felt a bit sick. 'You don't know that.'

'Yes. Because we know that's what they do, people like Aidan.'

Suddenly she was tired of his heavy pronouncements of doom. 'Fine. I admit it. What I did was wrong on some level.'

'On a whole load of levels.'

'No, do not lecture me. I already know the party line. We're not responsible for him while he makes bad choices, he must be forced to face the consequences of his own behaviour, blah, blah. I don't need to hear it again.'

'Don't brush it off. We took advice, Aisling. We *agonised* over it. It wasn't some knee-jerk decision to throw him out, so don't act like it was.'

'Yes, but we didn't know how it was going to turn out, Mossy, did we? Our grand gesture of making him sort his life out. And he ended up on the streets. At nineteen. *My child.*'

Mossy looked bleak at this news. But then he said, 'What did you think was going to happen? That he was going to buy a semi-detached house and move in?'

She stared at him. 'It's like you wanted him to fail. Did you want to be able to say *I told you so*?'

'Stop it. He was my child too,' Mossy said roughly. 'Look, we knew it was going to be tough, Aisling. We knew he might have to hit rock bottom before things got better. But we said we had to stick it out for his sake. Not ours. His.'

'Then you must be a stronger person than me,' she said bitterly. 'Because I couldn't stand it. For the first time in his life I didn't know where he was, who he was hanging around with. I didn't know if he was still drinking, if he was smoking that weed, if he'd moved on to harder stuff. And if he was, where he was getting the money for it. What he had to do to get by.'

The thought of it even now was so distressing that she almost forgot herself and reached out a hand to Mossy. But she composed herself. 'I didn't know if he was cold, or sick, or whether he'd had anything to eat that day, or that week. Or if he'd spoken to another human being, even just to say hello.'

She always got into a state when she strayed into worst-scenario territory. Her imagination was too vivid, that was the problem. On a really good self-torture session she could conjure up dark gutters at the drop of a hat, and pouring, malevolent rain, and evil figures standing over a huddled Aidan screaming, 'Give us the money or we'll break your fucking legs! Oh, and we'll steal that stew your mammy made you.'

Deep breaths. That was better. She looked at Mossy levelly. 'Are you telling me that none of that crossed your mind at all?'

He wasn't that hard. In fact Mossy wasn't hard at all; it was just lately it seemed that way. But she knew there must have been nights when he'd imagined Aidan out there alone, as vulnerable and unpredictable as a carrier bag in the wind.

'Of course it did,' he admitted.

If it had been any of their other children – even Louise at eleven had a bewildering array of coping skills; in fact *especially* Louise – they wouldn't have worried so much. But *Aidan*. Upstairs now listening to music, looking at the ceiling, dreaming no doubt of the band he was going to discover some day. Any day now. U2 or one of those. Or even the Beatles. Yeah, bound to happen.

Maybe Mossy was thinking of his dreamy, volatile son too, because he said nothing for ages. Aisling hoped this meant that he was softening.

'I don't blame you,' she said in a rush of reconciliation. 'For being angry. If you'd done the same, I'd have been hopping mad.'

'You wouldn't have been, though.'

'I would.'

'No. Because you'd no intention of sticking to the plan at all, did you?'

'I did.'

'You agreed, Aisling. You stood in this kitchen and you said that yes, he was too destructive to stay in the house. That he was adversely affecting our other children. You nodded when I said we were done with financially supporting his drug use and that we would just have to stop. Nobody put a gun to your head.' His look was accusing. 'I'm always made out to be the baddie here, but you were behind this just as much as me.'

'I know, okay? I know.' She'd wanted Aidan to change; had been desperate for it. Mossy's short, sharp shock had seemed like the only way left. 'I just didn't think it would be as hard.'

'So you decided to ruin it all by going running after him.'

'Checking on him. That was all.' He made her sound so weak.

'Undoing everything we'd done.'

'With a few euros in an envelope? He was hardly going to party for a week on it.'

Mossy threw up a hand. 'It's not even the money. You basically told him that it was okay. That no matter what he did, no matter who he hurt' – her eyes went of their own accord to his belly, but it was covered – 'you'd still be there, telling him what a great lad he was.'

'I never told him that.' She wanted to curl in on herself, to protect herself and Aidan too. Yes, he'd wanted to see her in the end, for the money. He was selfish and thoughtless and a drug user. Fine. But she also knew that it was her job to still care about him, despite everything. Didn't it go to the very heart of being his mother?

Mossy would never understand that. Never.

'If I'd asked you if we could still support him in some way,

273

you'd have said no,' she told him. 'I'd have been given the whole lecture again in your big, thundery voice—'

'My *what*?'

'Your movie-trailer voice. You're so fucking intractable, Mossy. You just cut him off. You went about your daily business, and you waited for him to come home, cap in hand, lesson learned.'

'Hardly,' Mossy bit out.

'But wasn't that the object of your tough love? Aidan would realise how wrong he had been and we'd all live happily ever after.' Her lip curled. 'And how's that working out for you, eh?'

Mossy lifted his head to look her in the eye. 'Not very well, actually. He's still using. You know that, don't you?'

He tossed the words out one by one. Aisling flinched as they landed, even though they came as no great surprise.

'While we're down here, ripping ourselves apart over him – again – he's probably sticking his head out the bedroom window right now having a quick toke.'

If he thought he was going to shock her, he was wrong.

'Maybe,' she agreed calmly.

He stared at her. 'And that's okay with you?'

'What do you want me to do about it?'

'We said no drugs in the house. That was our unbreakable rule, remember? Yet he's back here, courtesy of you, being given the five-star treatment!'

'He's injured.'

'You'll always find some excuse, won't you?'

'It's not an excuse. It's a fact. But if you want to throw him out, be my guest.' She waved a hand at the door. 'Well, go on then. Take his stuff and chuck him out into the street for the second time.'

Mossy just shook his head vehemently. 'And have the whole

family hate me again? You'd like that, wouldn't you? That would get you off the hook nicely.'

Aisling looked at him coldly. 'You can't see it, can you? That Aidan being back might be some kind of opportunity.'

'Please,' said Mossy. 'Don't start all that stuff, because I'm not sure I can stomach it right now.'

'So you're just going to grit your teeth until he leaves?'

'As opposed to what? Getting some kind of family therapy?' His sneer let her know what he thought of that.

'Maybe, I don't know!'

'You know what he needs?'

'Yes, Mossy.'

'A good kick in the arse.'

Aisling threw her hands up. It had only been a matter of time. 'Of course he does! You're absolutely right. It'd solve all of his problems. In fact I don't know why more people don't cotton on to your way of dealing with things. Suffering from addiction issues? You just need a good kick in the arse. Feeling a bit depressed? Bend over and we'll sort you out. Maybe you should set up a sideline business. Fix everybody with one well-aimed kick.'

Their voices had risen now. Aidan might even be able to hear.

'Oh, because holding his hand has worked so well, hasn't it? All that love and support and understanding we lavished on him. All the chances we gave him. And where did any of it get us? Nowhere.'

He was on his feet now. Getting his coat.

'Mossy, please. We have to talk about this. We have to work something out.'

'You can't fix his life for him, Aisling. When are you going to realise that?'

Chapter Thirty-five

Hugo returned Darren one morning after a sleepover, and Aisling answered the door to him for the first time since the night he'd kissed her. Well, she couldn't put it off any longer, and it was unseemly to keep hiding in the utility room until he'd gone.

'Hi!'

'Hello!'

'Ah, there's Darren!'

'It is indeed!'

Darren got the full glare of their rather manic smiles.

'How are things?'

'Good, yeah. Not bad at all. And yourself?'

'Never better!'

'Great!'

'Great!'

Then they both ran out of steam, and it was all a bit embarrassing, and even more so when Darren looked at Aisling and swooned, 'Mama!'

'No, no . . .'

'*Grand*mama.' Hugo looked at Aisling uncertainly. 'Or Nana?'

'That's even worse. Just Aisling is best.'

'Aisling. ASH – LING,' Hugo tried, pointing dramatically to Aisling.

Darren looked at her and insisted, 'Mama.'

'We'll have to work on that one,' said Aisling. 'How is, um, Nicola?'

Thank Christ she hadn't come with him. Aisling was avoiding her like the plague too. The last thing she needed was to upset the poor girl more, and invite a shriek of 'Keep your hands OFF my dad!'

But maybe Hugo would have explained it to her. It was his fault, after all; at the very least he should have reassured her that Aisling wasn't some kind of female patio guy, ready to spirit her father off to another continent and open up a dodgy Irish pub.

'So!' said Hugo. A little shy. A little bashful. Then Aisling noted his fresh shirt, and she thought, *oh no.* She was raging with herself that she hadn't clarified things before now. He was vulnerable. Abandoned by his wife. And she'd given him days to think about things. To hope. Maybe even to fantasise . . .

Everything she did these days seemed to be wrong. And now she was going to end up hurting Hugo too.

'Down!' Darren demanded.

He was picking up more and more words. Aisling suspected that Aidan and Anto were teaching him swear words upstairs, but thankfully so far he hadn't regurgitated any of them.

'If you insist,' said Hugo, and he carefully placed Darren on his own two feet on the front step. Darren clutched the door jamb and balanced himself, a look of furious concentration on his face.

'Well done!' said Aisling.

'Good lad!' echoed Hugo.

They clapped him energetically. Darren gave them a gracious smile – hey, it was nothing – before dropping to his hands and knees and crawling off indoors like a little tornado. They watched as he found his favourite foam sword and settled back on his plump behind to contentedly bash the life out of an innocent piece of furniture.

Hugo looked at Aisling.

'Can I come in for a minute?'

Aisling braced herself. 'I think you'd better.'

It was just the two of them in the kitchen.

'I won't stay long,' Hugo assured her. 'I know you're busy these days, what with your son home again.'

'Yes.'

'Broken his ankle, Anto was telling Nicola?'

'That's right.'

Aidan had actually gone out for a walk, or a hobble, as he put it. Aisling had insisted. He needed a change from sitting upstairs on that bed, even if it was just the park around the corner. If he got tired, he was to ring and she'd go pick him up. 'The fresh air will do you good.'

It was all part of her stealthy rehabilitation programme. She'd already managed to persuade him to get up by ten, and to return to eating breakfast in the mornings. A proper breakfast, not just coffee and a cigarette. Aidan would sigh and call her a fusspot, but he'd eventually eat the porridge she put in front of him, and she'd have to turn away to stop him seeing her intense satisfaction.

He was steadily recovering, and – she hadn't said it out loud yet for fear of jinxing it – seemed better in himself. More settled or something. Despite Mossy's dire assertion that he was getting high out the window, there was no evidence so far of it; nothing concrete anyway. And as each day passed, Aisling was ever more hopeful that things – whisper it – had changed. If only a little bit.

'Tea? Coffee?' Today she even felt able to tackle this thing with Hugo. It was like a vital part of her was alive again.

'Oh. Well . . .'

She bustled to put the kettle on anyway. 'I saw you on the telly last night. Do you not think we deserve a bit of sun for a change?'

He stared at her for a second. Then he realised she was joking. 'Oh! Maybe next week.'

He was miserable, she saw. She abandoned the kettle and said, 'Look, do you want to sit down?'

'I actually don't think I do,' he said, in that serious way of his. 'I just want to apologise and go. I'm completely mortified, as no doubt you've guessed by now. I don't know what came over me. And I want you to be assured that you can come around to the house to drop or collect Darren at any time and I won't be lurking in the hallway, waiting to spring out at you.'

It was so unlikely, Hugo springing out at her lasciviously from dark corners, that she laughed out loud. She couldn't help it.

'Sorry,' she said.

Hugo took it in good part. 'I'm not sure whether you're laughing with me, or at me. The latter, I suspect.'

She laughed harder. His expression was so funny. He was like a grown-up Harry Potter or something.

'Some lucky woman is going to snap you up one of these days, Hugo O'Sullivan,' she told him impulsively.

He was smiling now too. 'But not you.' It was lightly thrown out; a statement, but also a tiny, tiny question.

She wondered whether she should let him down gently with the whole they-were-both-vulnerable scenario, with difficult/absent spouses, no action in the bedroom in aeons, et cetera. Especially as it was true. But a liaison, whilst enjoyable, even emotionally satisfying, would only create more problems than it would solve.

'No,' she ended up saying. Best to kill this one stone dead. 'Not me.'

He took it well. 'I guess it would have been a little too incestuous anyway. What with us both being Darren's grandparents.' His little joke felt rather flat, and he hurried on. 'Anyway. I'm sorry. I feel like I behaved very badly. And I didn't mean to. I just . . .'

He just liked her. A lot. Had come to rely on her and her no-nonsense support, that much was clear. She should have seen a bit sooner where all of this was leading.

'Maybe it's time,' she said to him lightly.

'Time . . .?'

'For you to put yourself back out there. Maybe the girls in your office are right.'

'Oh no, no.'

'Why not? You're clearly, um, ready.'

They both coloured a bit at that.

'I have Nicola to think about. I just want her to get better.'

'And she will, in time. Looking out for her doesn't mean you can't be happy too.'

'Well, we'll see.'

He was firmly ending the conversation. Distancing himself from her. And it was necessary, of course, seeing as how muddled things had become for him. But she felt a bit sad. She would miss their easy relationship, especially as her marriage was so tough these days. Maybe they would get it back some day.

She walked him to the door. 'How do you think they're getting on?' she asked. 'Anto and Nicola?'

She wanted him to know that they could, and should, still talk about their children.

'The lines of communication seem to be open anyway.'

'They do, don't they?'

They were always chattering away on the phone these days. It was great, in one way. Information and arrangements about Darren were made first-hand. There was no need for all those phone calls between Aisling and Hugo any more.

'Anyway!' He rocked a bit on his heels.

'I'll talk to you soon,' she said.

'Yes, absolutely.'

He ran out of the place.

Chapter Thirty-six

Aidan didn't come home from his walk. He wasn't in the park. Aisling went around it with Darren in the buggy, searching for him, and then she got in the car and drove around the whole estate twice. He was on crutches; he might well have decided to come a different way home, and had got tired and stopped to have a rest.

But he was nowhere to be seen. Worry settled familiarly in her like lead. She rang his phone. It went to voicemail. She texted. *Where are you?* She got no reply.

Damn him.

After an hour she had to give up and go to collect Louise from school.

'If he shows up I will ring straight away,' Zofia assured her when Aisling knocked at her door. Zofia had huge rollers in her hair and her legs had the reddish, shiny look of the freshly waxed. 'I have a hot date with my husband tonight,' she said loudly. 'We are going to the cinema, then for something to eat. We will be out until very, very late. Just the two of us.'

Magda passed quietly behind like a little ghost. Today her cardigan was grey, Aisling noted.

'That has put her in her place,' Zofia said triumphantly. 'It is my new plan. Now we will see who he loves best.'

It sounded like a terrible plan to Aisling, but she had other things on her mind right now. 'About Aidan . . .'

Zofia was immediately apologetic. 'Yes, of course, I will let you know.'

At the school, Louise was in a right mood. 'I want to bring in Darren for show and tell next Tuesday, but Mr Tavey says we're only allowed inanimate objects, but Nina brought in her hamster last week and *that* was allowed, so I want you to go in and complain, okay?'

'I will. Bitterly,' Aisling assured her.

She had to keep blinking back tears of rage and upset. At Aidan, yes; but mostly at herself. Making him fecking porridge. Thinking that because he was obediently resting on his bed upstairs, things had changed. Had she really believed that this time it would be different?

Stupid, *stupid*.

Instead he'd done another of his disappearing acts, leaving her to watch out the window and gnaw at her knuckles as she prayed for him to come home in one piece.

She could forgive the birthday card with the money. Everybody had to live. But *this*. The disregard for their worry, the casual dismissal of the normal civilities that family members extended to each other, as though none of it applied to him. He could do what he liked. He always had and he always would.

'Come on,' she said brightly to Louise and Darren. 'Let's go home.'

She carried on as usual that evening. She made dinner, and she helped Anto with a particularly difficult bit of revision.

'Bleeding poetry! Like it's ever going to help me find a job!' he kept grousing, but it was only for show now. He was taking these exams very seriously. Mossy never had to urge him to study any more. In fact once or twice they'd had to tell him to take a break.

Then she gave Darren a bath and made up a bottle, and kept Anto company in his room while he gave it to Darren, all the time trying not to look across at Aidan's empty bed.

The whole thing was depressingly familiar.

'He always comes back from the O'Sullivans' starving,' Anto commented disapprovingly.

It took Aisling a moment to cop that he was talking about Darren. Sure enough, he was guzzling back the bottle.

'Sometimes I wonder do they feed him over there at all.'

'I'm sure they do.'

Anto darted a look at her. 'I'm thinking of asking Nicola if we should take Darren to the beach some day. You know, when my exams are over. We could maybe head out on the train, the three of us. He'd never have seen the sea before.'

He was trying to be casual but she'd bet he'd already looked up the train timetable. And in a way she was glad; it was great for Darren's sake to see his parents getting on much better. But a part of her wanted to take Anto by the shoulders, the way she used to do when he was five, and say protectively, 'Now remember. Don't go off with any strangers.'

Not that Nicola was a stranger. But there was something about Anto's enthusiasm that made Aisling afraid for his heart.

'That's a nice idea, Anto.' What else could she say?

Belatedly he remembered his manners. 'I mean, you can come too if you want. And Hugo, I suppose.'

'No,' Aisling said hastily, imagining herself and Hugo traipsing after love's young dream on the beach. 'I think we'll leave you to it.'

Mossy came home at half past seven, just as Aisling was dishing up the dinner for Anto, Shannon and Louise. He did a sweep around the kitchen before looking at her warily.

'Where's Aidan?'

Usually they all managed a few minutes around the table together, though Mossy and Aidan rarely exchanged a word.

'I'm not sure. Out somewhere.' She didn't look at him.

'*Out?* On crutches?'

Shannon, quick as always to defend the underdog, even if he hogged the bathroom, said snippily, 'People do manage to get about with broken limbs, Da, you know.'

Mossy remained at the door, a big sceptical lump, and perversely Aisling announced, 'He wanted some fresh air, okay? I said for him to ring me if he got tired.'

Yeah – about six hours ago. But Mossy didn't know that. And even though her heart was like lead, she wouldn't give it to him. She would not admit that Aidan had stitched her up again.

'Anyway, he's going to be back soon,' Louise chattered on. 'We're watching *The Princess Bride*, aren't we, Shannon? We're making popcorn and everything.'

'Not again,' said Anto.

'Nobody invited you,' Louise told him loftily. 'Aidan wants to, he's never seen it.'

Anto glowered and went back to his dinner, clearly the second favourite brother now.

'That's nice,' said Aisling, knowing there wasn't a hope in hell of Aidan making it back for *The Princess Bride*.

But Shannon fired up the popcorn anyway, and gave directions to Louise on setting up the DVD, and Aisling looked at her amazed, thinking, she really doesn't realise he's going to stand them up. She'd genuinely forgotten how erratic Aidan could be. Or maybe, like Aisling, she'd subconsciously believed it was all better now.

'I'd better text him,' said Shannon, when another half-hour had passed.

'Shannon . . .' Aisling began, but then stopped. She'd find out soon enough.

Eventually they had to start the DVD, because it was getting late, and Shannon kept checking her phone for a response but got none.

'He's *missing* it,' Louise said, very peeved.

'Yes,' said Aisling. 'He is. But never mind. We're watching it, and we're going to enjoy it, okay?'

Louise looked sulky. Shannon said nothing at all. But her face was black.

'Room for one more?'

It was Mossy, and they all looked up at him suspiciously – he wasn't known for his love of princess movies – but they duly adjusted themselves on the couch, and he sank down between Aisling and threw his arm around Louise.

'*Da*,' said Louise. 'Stop it.' But she didn't move away.

'This better be good,' he said.

Aisling felt his eyes on her. But she kept her own trained on the television.

'You were right.'

'Sorry?' Mossy turned over in the dark. It was ten past four and they were both wide awake. Aidan wasn't home yet. That was if he ever decided to show up at the house again.

'I said, you were right.'

'It's not about being right.'

'Isn't it? I thought that was exactly what it was about. Which of us is the better parent. Who's handling the situation the best. Who gets to say *I told you so*.'

Mossy got up on one elbow suddenly in the bed. 'Don't let him do this again, Aisling. Pit us against each other.'

'He's not.'

He was fierce in the dark. 'He is. He's been doing it since he was five years old. Do you not remember? That was the first time he realised he could play us off against the other.'

'He is not some monster. He's a kid.'

'He's an *adult*. Why won't you accept that?'

She was jaded. Every bone in her body ached. 'He might be an adult to you. To me he'll always be my child.'

'And you've done your best for him. Nobody could have done better.'

She didn't answer. She didn't really believe it. She felt so naïve for thinking that being back home would be enough. That she, with her mother's love, would be enough to bring him back. It was sobering to realise that she couldn't help him any more.

There was a rustling of sheets and then Mossy's arm was around her, tentative, like he was afraid she would push him away. She didn't. She hadn't the energy.

'He'll be okay,' Mossy said into the dark. 'He always is.'

'But you don't know that,' she insisted.

'I suppose not.'

'You see, that's the problem. If I could just look into the future. If I could be sure that things would eventually be okay. Then I could live with it.'

Mossy sighed in agreement, his chest rumbling under her cheek. It felt a little forced, the two of them under the covers like that, after all the rows. Or maybe it was just because it had been so long.

At some point he fell asleep and rolled away from her. She lay there until the sun crept in under the blinds, and then she got up.

Chapter Thirty-seven

Darren was going to be one.

One!

No more 'Oh, he's five weeks and two days old' or 'He'll be six months next Monday – I know, I can hardly believe it myself', the way you did when they were very little. Now a whole year had passed since Nicola had gone into the hospital that night, Dad jogging beside her with the massive overnight bag – the things she'd packed . . . her hair dryer, for the love of God – and annoying the hell out of her with questions such as 'Can you feel the contractions, love?'

'No, Dad. I'm just making all this noise for the hell of it.'

And then straight into the delivery suite, because even though everybody had told her she would go way over because it was her first, Darren decided to come nearly six weeks early. Nicola had never seen so many people crowded into one small room. For a moment she thought it was because she was still only seventeen then, and that maybe they'd all come to have a gawk at her and go 'tut-tut' under their breath. Then she realised with a bit of a shock that all those doctors and midwives were there because things weren't going the way they should be.

'It's going to be okay. I'm right here,' said Dad, her reluctant birth partner.

They were both a bit reluctant. Who wanted their dad looking up their lady bits and going 'Push!'? It was supposed to have been Becky, but Becky was in Kerry visiting her granny, not expecting to be called upon for weeks and weeks yet. Mikaela was hopeless, fainting at the first sign of blood. And Nicola's mother was in Australia. She was due home in a couple of weeks' time, tickets booked and everything, all ready for the run-up to the birth.

Well, this had wiped her eye. Nicola got savage satisfaction from it even through the blinding pain. Her mother would miss out on her big moment, her chance to swoop back and be there for Nicola – she kept writing this in emails – as though it would make up for everything.

'Don't panic now,' Dad was telling her. 'But the baby's in a bit of distress.'

The baby. Of course. That was what was causing all of this. Nicola felt confused by the pain and the speed of things. Her baby books had said it would probably start slowly; that it would build over hours, and maybe even days. She mightn't even know she was in labour at first, she had been advised. None of them had said anything about suddenly being hit by a sledgehammer over and over again, leaving her slack-jawed with shock and pain.

It was like her body had turned on her; was chewing itself up in a desperate grim battle to rid itself of the intruder inside.

'Dad,' she whispered. He would do anything for her, she knew that. She wanted him to make this stop. Please. Just make it stop.

'You can do this,' he told her, his face almost as frightened as hers, but she couldn't. She just lay there, stunned, while people poked and prodded and monitors loudly beeped.

'Mum,' she thought she might have pleaded at one point. Sacrilege. But she was beyond caring. She just wanted to be in the back garden, sitting on a garden chair reading out daft bits from magazines while her mum did her gardening.

'Help! My excessive hair growth is ruining my life! Home waxing kits are no match for my rampant fuzz.'

Mum, brandishing garden shears. 'Send her over here, then.'

And they would rock with laughter.

Did they not have good fun, the two of them? Were they not close? Nicola had thought they were. Even if it wasn't working with Dad, why did Mum have to cast her off too? She would never choose a man over her child. Never in a million years.

She was in a corridor. She saw walls flashing by either side of her trolley, and passers-by looking down at her morbidly. Then she had to blink against the brilliant lights suddenly overhead, and a hard plastic mask was over her nose and mouth, and someone was smoothing back her hair.

'All right, Nicola?' said a man she'd never seen before. He wore a blue surgical hat and a blue gown. He was smiling. 'Let's get this baby out then, will we?'

'Dad.' The mask swallowed up the sound. Where was he?

Then she saw. He was the person stroking her hair. He was wearing a blue hat and a gown too. She was very confused. He was a meteorologist; what was he doing in doctor's clothes?

At some point she lifted out of herself a bit. She didn't float around the ceiling looking down at everybody, or anything mad like that. More like stepping outside and closing the door. She shut her eyes and felt tugs and pinpricks of pain, and she kept waiting for someone to announce, 'It's a girl!' like they did in the movies, but nobody did, and when she opened her eyes properly again, she was in a different place. A bed, with curtains drawn around it. Dad was there.

'Where did your blue hat go?' she said. Her voice sounded thick.

He whirled around, his face breaking into relief. He had a phone to his ear, she saw. 'She's okay,' he said into the phone. 'She's fine. She's waking up now.' He smiled at Nicola, and impulsively held out the phone. 'It's your mother.'

Nicola looked at him, floored. There was a searing pain starting up around her belly. She was all bandaged up, she realised; she couldn't move. A drip fed blood into a tube in her arm. She'd needed two transfusions, she found out afterwards.

Dad took a look at her face and hastily withdrew the phone. 'Maybe later, eh? When you feel a bit better.'

He said his goodbyes to her mother – Nicola could tell that it was difficult to get her off the phone; she wanted to be part of it all, even from Australia – and then he put the phone away.

'She's flying in Thursday. She's very worried about you.' Nicola said nothing. 'We all were. You gave us a bit of a fright.'

'Sorry. I didn't mean to.'

'No, of course not, don't be silly . . . Anyway, it's all fine now, thank God. You'll be very sore for a day or two, but you're young, and you'll be back on your feet in no time.'

He was smiling at her. Waiting.

And she was, too; for that door she'd closed to open again so that she could step back in.

But it didn't immediately, and she felt foggy and detached as she asked, 'The baby?'

Dad was ecstatic. 'You had a boy, Nicola.'

A boy. She turned this over in her head. For some reason she'd been sure she was having a girl. Absolutely certain. A *boy*. She wasn't disappointed; she was just blindsided again. None of it was turning out the way she'd thought it would.

'He's fine. He's in the ICU at the moment. What with coming so early, they'll need to monitor him for a little while, make sure his lungs mature properly and all that. You can see him tomorrow if everything goes well, they said. We'll take you up in a wheelchair.'

She didn't see Darren the next day because she developed an infection – they said it was unusual – and he was four days old before the nurse in the ICU carefully placed him into her arms.

'You've had quite a time of it, haven't you?' she said.

Nicola could only manage a nod.

'He's really beautiful. He's got your mouth.'

She was probably just being kind. Nicola searched his broad little face but couldn't see a scrap of herself there; nothing at all that might make her immediately connect with him. She felt exhausted and sore, and was overwhelmed at this little scrap of pink baby curled up on her lap. She held him for a minute or two under the nurse's professional gaze, and then she quickly handed him back.

'We should have a party for him,' she announced to Anto.

'Are you sure?'

'Why wouldn't I be?'

'Because . . . you haven't been, you know, well.'

'You can say it out loud, Anto. It's nothing to be ashamed of.'

'I know that.'

'Well don't keep tiptoeing around me then.'

Poor Anto. It was easier to have a go at him than to face her own lingering shame. Imagine her – so bolshie and bold, so quick to spot everybody else's weaknesses – being struck down by something so nebulous. When the doctor had said it, she'd looked at her, suspicious, and said, 'Are you making it up? I'm depressed because I had a baby?' She'd barely heard of the condition before; for some reason she thought it was something that happened to older women, women with five kids who sat in kitchens crying all day long, surrounded by dirty nappies.

'Okay,' said Anto. 'What's it like, then? Post-natal depression?' She hadn't expected him to be so *blunt* about it.

'I'm getting better,' she said, defensive. 'Like, I'm not as bad as I used to be.'

'You're not,' he said approvingly. 'You talk a lot more. You even smile sometimes.' He gave her an impish look.

'Shut up,' she said, but she was pleased. But then he had a serious face on again, and looked older or something.

'Go on,' he said.

'It's kind of hard to describe it. For a long time I thought I felt that way because I'd messed up my life by having a baby too young.'

Anto nodded, and gave a sigh that told her he totally related to that. He'd come to collect Darren from her straight after his Spanish exam, and he looked wrecked.

'I didn't tell anybody how bad things were because maybe I thought I deserved it. It was my punishment. And there was Dad telling me to buck up, expecting me to get on with things, because I had a baby now to think of. But a lot of the time he didn't even feel like mine.'

Was Anto shocked? She peeked at him. She'd become so good at keeping things to herself that it felt strange to be talking like this.

But Anto just said, 'Does he feel more like yours now?'

A Special Delivery

Darren was conked in the buggy. He'd worn himself out charging around the back garden on his hands and knees. He'd given up on trying to walk altogether, having figured out that he could get about much faster by crawling. He was too eager for life to be held back by the ludicrous act of trying to keep his balance.

Nicola looked at his sleeping face. She knew now not to expect that groundswell of maternal emotion. She was only starting her recovery and it would take time. For now it was great to be able to say to Anto, 'I miss him all the time when he's with you, so I guess that must mean he does.'

It would be coming up soon: the question of him going back to Nicola for keeps. But it was all softly-softly yet, nobody really wanting to rock the boat.

'It's funny in a way,' she found herself saying. 'Even though I didn't want to be pregnant, I was going to be such a good mother in my head. And in the end I turned out to be a worse mother than my own.'

'You did not.'

'At least she never left me in a garden at Christmas.' The thought of it still scalded her.

'You can stop that right now, okay?' said Anto, her greatest champion. 'You weren't well. You were doing what you thought was the right thing. If you hadn't, I might never have known he existed! I'm glad things have worked out the way they did. So no more of this blaming yourself, because nobody else does, okay? And as for your mother . . .'

'She's a selfish cow.'

But Anto spoiled the fun by not joining in. 'And you're not going to let her forget it, are you?'

Nicola's face felt hot. 'She went to Australia with the fucking patio guy.'

'Yeah. She did. But that doesn't mean she's refusing to be part of your life. Isn't she always ringing you up and trying to fly over and inviting you out to visit?'

'Well maybe I don't want to go.' She changed her mind about Anto. He was just a kid after all. He hadn't a clue about her family.

Anto shrugged. 'Fine. But you can't say she doesn't try. You're the one who's stopping her.'

She was furious at his judgemental tone. 'And what do you know? With that loser brother of yours back home again, and your ma and da rowing over him? I don't even know if I want Darren to be around the likes of him!'

'And what's that supposed to mean?'

'I know he smokes stuff. You told me. That he said he'd changed but he hasn't at all.'

'So what? He doesn't do it around Darren.'

'And how do I know that?'

'Because I wouldn't let him, okay?' Anto's eyes were dangerous. 'He's not there half the time anyway. Disappears off places, nobody knows where. He'll be back in his own gaff for good when he can walk properly again.'

'Good! Because someone like that, he's a bad influence.'

'He's a good bloke, okay?' Anto said fiercely. 'He just needs to give up the weed and get a proper job. But underneath it all he's all right.'

But somehow it lacked the conviction that Anto used to show when he first spoke to her about Aidan. There wasn't the same hero worship. There wasn't any at all, actually.

'You can invite him to the party if you want,' she said grudgingly. She mightn't like the sound of him, but she'd have to make an effort for Anto's sake.

'We're really going to have a party?'

'Course we are. It's not every day Darren's going to be one.'

'I suppose.'

'We'll do it in our place. Your family and mine, and Becky and Mikaela and Baz and Sean, and whoever else you want to be there. And I'm going to bake a cake, and we'll get some helium balloons and streamers, and maybe even a clown.'

Anto looked taken aback. 'A clown would frighten the life out of him.'

'Maybe not a clown then. A magician.'

'For a *one*-year-old?'

'He can look back on the pictures when he's older,' she said stubbornly. Couldn't Anto see? She had a lot to catch up on. From now on, Darren would have the best of everything. She mightn't have been herself, fully anyway, at the start of his life, but he wouldn't look back and think he wasn't loved.

'Okay, fine, whatever you want.' Anto caved in, like she'd known he would. Then he sighed. 'I'd better go. I've got to cram for economics tomorrow. Man, I can't wait until the exams are over.'

He remained sitting, though.

'How are they going?' Nicola had finished school the previous week; she would be doing these same exams next year. Already she was starting to panic about how she'd manage all the study and Darren too. But she couldn't say anything in case Dad whipped the dreaded Mrs McAllister off the back burner. Since Nicola's diagnosis, he was hovering all the time, watching her closely. It was nice, in a way, all this attention, but it was also starting to do her head in.

'All right, I suppose.' Anto examined a paper cut on his hand and then looked up at her intently. 'I'm hoping to get into college in September. Do accountancy. I know it's going to take a few years and all that, but I'll get a decent job at the end of it.'

'Good,' said Nicola neutrally.

'Because I want to be able to provide for Darren, you know?'

'And I do too. I'll be following you into college.' Hastily she corrected herself. 'Not *following* you, of course. What I mean is that it's great that we're both trying to get on with our lives. Even though we have a baby and all. We're not going to let parenthood hold us back!'

She was doing this a lot lately: steering the conversation into a kind of fake, happy-clappy place, because she didn't want things to get messy. And they were going to. She could tell by the look in his eyes.

'Anto,' she began.

Maybe it was time to clarify things. To have the conversation. She didn't want to hurt him. She liked him; in fact, if she had to choose someone to be the father of her child, he'd be right up there. But that all-important piece was missing. Call it attraction, connection, lust, the meeting of two souls. It just wasn't there, no matter how much she might want it to be.

Again Anto surprised her. 'Hey. Relax. You've had a lot to deal with. You're trying to get better. And right now that's exactly what you should concentrate on doing. There's no pressure from me. All I want is to be able to help you organise Darren's party.'

She felt tears spring up – she could still spout away at the drop of a hat – and she had to blink them back. He was decent, Anto. And good and kind. Darren was lucky to have him and so was she.

'I'd like that,' she said.

Chapter Thirty-eight

Aidan got the all-clear from the doctors and solemnly presented his crutches to Louise. 'All yours.'

'But . . . do you not have to give them back?' she said. She could hardly believe her luck. Every kid on the road had already hobbled up and down on them hundreds of times at speed, but to have them to *keep* . . . She'd really get one over on Emma this time.

'Nope,' said Aidan. 'Or at least they didn't ask for them.'

She snatched them up and ran off with them before he could change his mind. 'Thanks!' Belatedly she stopped at the door. 'Will you still be here when I get back?'

'Sure I will.'

'Okay.'

She'd come to accept now, like everybody else, that Aidan wasn't always where he was supposed to be. And he didn't always do the things he said he was going to do. He meant them at the time; it was his follow-through that let him down.

Still, that was probably just Aisling making excuses for him again. She still did it, despite everything. But she was learning.

'How does it feel?' she asked him.

Aiden flexed his foot cheerfully. 'I won't be kicking a football around just yet, but it's grand.'

It was hard to stay mad at him when he was like this: normal and chatty and full of wide smiles. And now, like a magician, he disappeared out into the hall for a moment and came back with an enormous bunch of flowers – lavender roses and lilies in cellophane and ribbons that must have cost a fortune – which he presented to her with a flourish.

'Just to say thanks for putting me up.'

'Oh, Aidan.'

'And before you ask, I didn't steal them.'

'As if I thought that for a second . . .' She had.

'Relax. I was only joking.' Kind of.

She buried her nose in the flowers – roses were her favourite and he'd remembered that – and said, 'Thank you. They're beautiful.'

He beamed. He loved giving people things. He was thoughtful like that. She hugged the flowers close and watched him. He looked so well. Despite his erratic comings and goings, the month at home had been good to him. He'd filled out and looked healthy and fit. He'd got his hair cut too – 'Clean yourself up, man,' Anto had exhorted – and the shadows under his eyes were gone.

He looked just like her beautiful boy again, and she couldn't bear it that he was leaving.

'Aw, Ma.' He waggled a finger at her. 'Remember what we said? No crying.'

She made her voice as light as his. 'I'm not going to start crying.'

'Anyway,' he said, 'it's going to be different this time. We're going to visit each other, right? And I'm not just saying that. You can come round whenever you want.' He laughed and said, 'Well, better give me a day or two's notice so I can get the flat cleaned up. And maybe I'll come over some Sunday for my dinner. That's if I'm lucky enough to get an invitation.'

Sunday dinner with Aidan. It was more than she could have hoped for.

'Would you really?'

'Course.' He looked at her, suddenly serious. 'Being back home, it was good, Ma. Seeing Shannon and Anto and Louise again. And you, of course.' He didn't mention Mossy. 'I don't want to lose touch like I did before. And now that young Darren's on the scene too . . . I can't be missing out on all that, can I?' He gave her another of his crooked grins.

Her throat felt tight with emotion. 'You know we'd love to have you.'

'Great. So dust off that gravy boat, yeah?'

'The gravy boat!' She laughed. 'Of course I will.'

And it was like they were caught up in a little bubble; that by talking and laughing and planning, it really was going to happen. Aidan would pitch up some Sunday and sit at the table and they would be like a normal family.

'When?' she said impulsively. 'Next Sunday?'

'Maybe,' said Aidan. 'I'll let you know.'

Slowly, slowly she deflated. 'Great,' she said, still smiling. 'You do that.'

They were interrupted by the clatter of feet on the stairs, and then a *thump-thump-thump*, like a dead body falling down them, and Shannon's admonishment of 'Jesus, be *careful*.'

She breezed into the kitchen followed by an enormous purple-flowered suitcase. After a moment, a panting Matt emerged from under it.

301

'Put it down there,' she instructed him.

'Mrs B,' Matt managed, 'can we borrow your scales? Want to make sure we don't run over our allowance. Nice flowers,' he added belatedly.

'What have you *got* in there?' Aidan looked at the massive suitcase.

'Bikinis,' said Shannon. 'What do you think I've got? Stuff for the orphanage. Crayons, learning aids, flash cards, pencils, solar calculators, that kind of thing.'

'Do those poor kids know you're coming?' Aidan asked gravely.

Matt tittered – in another life, he and Aidan would get on like a house on fire – but a look from Shannon killed that one dead. 'You should think about doing some volunteer work sometime with people worse off than yourself,' she told Aidan crisply. 'Do you the world of good.'

'Me? Naw. I'm not sure I have the disposition.'

Matt had to hide another smile by hoisting the suitcase up on its side in preparation for the weigh-in. Shannon was leaving nothing to chance.

Shannon remained unamused. 'Everything's a joke to you, isn't it?'

'Hey, lighten up. I'm leaving today to go back to my own place; you're flying out next week to save the world. We won't see each other for ages.'

'Knowing you, that's probably true.'

Aidan was taken aback by all the hostility. So was Aisling. It wasn't like Shannon to leave things on a sour note.

Shannon planted a hand on her hip and snapped, 'You were supposed to meet me in town this afternoon. Remember?' At Aidan's supremely blank look, she clarified, 'We were going shopping for Darren's birthday present.'

'Shit,' said Aidan.

'I stood outside that toy shop like an idiot waiting for you.'

'Shannon, I'm really sorry—'

'I rang you. You didn't pick up. I texted you. You didn't reply. Or maybe I just wasn't trying the right phone, seeing as you have about ten of them.'

Aisling knew she should intervene, as usual. But today she just didn't.

Aidan spread his hands in abject apology. 'I had the hospital this morning. I just completely forgot, Shannon. I'm really sorry.'

But Shannon was clearly made of sterner stuff than Aisling, because Aidan's charm offensive left her cold. 'It was your idea. You were the one who wanted to get Darren something special. I should have known you wouldn't show up.'

Aidan tried to appeal to Aisling for support. 'Tell her, Ma! Aw, come on, I'm here now, aren't I? So we can just head off and get the present now.'

'TOO LATE. I'm busy, in case you haven't noticed. You can explain to Anto tomorrow why you didn't get Darren anything.' A pause. 'That's if you're even going to turn up.'

The big party was kicking off at two in the afternoon. Everybody was invited; indeed, *expected*. Anto had already primed the camcorder, and from what they'd gleaned from the intense phone arrangements, there was going to be some kind of professional entertainment, a marquee and a ten-foot cake in the shape of the Orient Express. Or so Mossy was joking.

'Of course I'm going to be there,' Aidan said. When everybody looked at him with some scepticism, he snapped, wounded, 'I will! He's my nephew! I wouldn't miss it.'

He'd had no problem missing the dinner Aisling had invited Nicola and Hugo to last week. They'd had to mumble some excuse about him working late. It had been hard to keep a straight face at *that* one.

'Jesus,' he huffed. 'I'll go out and buy him a present myself this minute. Maybe that'll keep you all happy.'

Shannon gave him a cool look. 'You don't have to do anything for us, Aidan. Ma,' she said, 'the scales?'

It was a testament to Shannon's perfect figure that she truly had no idea where the scales might be.

'You could try the bathroom,' Aisling deadpanned.

'Thanks.' Shannon pointed at the suitcase. 'Take it back upstairs, will you, Matt?'

They had a kind of last supper that night.

'Sssh!' Darren insisted, sitting up in his high chair. He pointed at Aisling. 'Sssh! Sssh!'

It wasn't that Aisling was up on the table singing 'I Will Survive' or anything. It was Darren's version of her name, or as much as he could manage of it anyway. Maybe they should have stuck with Granny.

'Pipe down yourself,' Anto told him. 'And eat up your mashed carrots, yum yum.'

Anto was in terrific form. The exams were over at last, he'd spent the whole day with Nicola and Darren getting ready for the party tomorrow, and he was about to get his bedroom back to himself now that Aidan was leaving. 'No offence,' he kept telling Aidan cheerily, 'but your feet smell *baaaad*.'

Aisling had cooked shepherd's pie, Aidan's favourite, and about nine different vegetables, because God knows when he'd see a carrot again. She didn't realise she was dishing him up such a massive plateful until he began waving his hands frantically at her and calling, 'Whoa! Whoa!'

There was only a small bit left for Matt, but he took it in good part. 'I'll fill up on ketchup,' he assured her.

Shannon picked away at her dinner, and Louise busied herself hiding her peas in various pockets of mash.

'So,' Mossy said from his place at the head of the table.

Everybody lifted their heads. Followed his gaze. Froze. Was Da talking to *Aidan*?

He was.

You could have heard a pin drop. Or, in Darren's case, his plastic fork, which he dropped with a clatter on to the floor.

'Sssh!' he said to Aisling, pointing to it in expectation that she would pick it up. She did.

'So . . .?' Aidan said back to Mossy.

'You're heading back to your flat tonight then, are you?'

Aidan kept looking at him like it was a trick question. 'I guess,' he said slowly.

Mossy continued on in that same calm voice, even if he sounded a little awkward. 'And the ankle? Is it okay?'

More looks flew up and down the table. All this civility was unnerving, especially given that Aidan and Mossy had barely exchanged a word the whole time Aidan had been home.

'I got the all-clear anyway,' Aidan offered.

'Good, good.'

Things were turning positively chatty. Aisling tried to remember whether she'd put anything different in the shepherd's pie. A spoonful of hash, maybe.

'All the same,' said Mossy, 'you should probably take it easy for a bit.'

'I will,' said Aidan, trying not to sound surprised.

Aisling didn't really know what was going on. Mossy had made his feelings very clear. He would tolerate Aidan in the house but he would not facilitate him (his words). This meant not giving him money or lifts anywhere, doing stuff for him because he was on crutches, or even passing the time of day with him.

Mossy flicked a look across the table, and she suddenly saw that he wasn't making the effort for Aidan; he was doing it for *her*.

It was, she was beginning to realise, his way of moving a tiny bit closer to her from the outback in which he'd found himself. Of course to his mind *she* was the one in the outback. On the subject of Aidan, they hadn't been in agreement in a long time. That was no surprise to either of them. Since this whole thing started – and Mossy was right, it was years and years ago, back when Aidan had been young – they'd been pulling and tugging at each other, taking sides, forming alliances, creating just the kind of environment for mayhem to thrive.

And it had, on every front. Aidan had got more out of control, and they'd been left, well, like this. Trying to figure each other out across the kitchen table.

'Da! Da!' Darren shouted suddenly, looking at Anto.

It was the first time he'd said it, and it broke the tension beautifully.

'Aw! Did you hear that, Anto?' Shannon clapped. 'Well done, Darren!'

'About time,' Anto said, a grin splitting his face. 'I was starting to think he didn't know who I was.'

'Get him to say Louise,' Louise begged.

'He's too young. And eat your peas and stop trying to hide them; we can all see what you're doing,' said Anto.

'I HATE peas.'

'So does your brother,' said Mossy. He meant Aidan.

Louise was delighted at this. 'Do you?'

A Special Delivery

'They should be banned,' Aidan said gravely.

Aisling shot Mossy a look over their heads: *thank you*.

She thought she saw him give a little nod back.

Dinner took fourteen minutes, which was long by their usual standards – normally it took about six for everybody to stuff their faces and gallop off – and turned into quite a jolly affair, with Darren playing up to all the attention by reeling off every word he knew, including 'doggie', 'toe-toe' and, controversially, 'United', although it was only Aidan who insisted he heard that.

Then everybody drifted off. Anto went to take a phone call from Nicola, carting Darren away under his arm like he was a rugby ball. Shannon and Matt disappeared to earnestly discuss which educational item for the orphanage they'd have to leave behind, for weight reasons.

'You're getting stressed by this,' Matt insisted. 'I think I should rub your shoulders.'

'I'm not getting stressed.'

'You're definitely stressed. You need a good rub,' he said, deftly steering her upstairs.

'Leave the doors open,' Mossy called threateningly.

Louise went back out to taunt Emma with her crutches, and then it was just Mossy, Aisling and Aidan left, and a pile of dirty plates.

Aidan looked from one parent to the other, awkward. 'I guess I'd better hit the road.'

'Will you take some shepherd's pie with you?' Aisling asked, even though she'd vowed that she'd never go back to her dark days as a food pusher, the worst example of which had been her attempt to palm Aidan a cooked chicken in a squat he'd once lived in, rasping at him to 'Take it! Take it!'

'There isn't any left, Ma.'

'I made a smaller one. It's still in the oven, where Matt couldn't get at it.'

They all laughed. Aisling tried to tell herself it was with Matt, not at him.

'No, listen, you're grand,' said Aidan, and he began shifting and checking himself over, the way people did when they were about to leave.

'I can drive you if you want,' Mossy offered in another burst of reconciliation.

'Thanks anyway, but I'm going to get the bus.'

'With all that stuff?'

Actually, there wasn't that much. Just a rucksack, which he'd packed earlier with the clothes that Aisling had washed and ironed. He'd brought no spare shoes with him, no toiletries, books or music. Even the jacket he was putting on now was one of his old ones that he'd left behind in the wardrobe in his bedroom. He had very little really in the way of worldly possessions.

If it was anybody else, you might think they'd just chosen to live simply. But with Aidan you knew it was because he couldn't quite get his act together.

She watched now as he took his house key out and put it down rather ceremoniously on the kitchen table. And suddenly she couldn't bear it. Yet another wrench. It had been hard enough the first time around, but to find herself here *again* . . . And you would think this time she'd be okay, because nobody was shouting and roaring. Nobody was saying terrible, ugly things and assaulting each other.

But her heart felt like it was breaking into pieces. Despite the promises of Sunday dinner and visits and all of that, she had no idea when she'd see Aidan again.

'Well you take care of yourself,' she said, hoping to God she didn't burst into noisy bawling. That would be a total mood-killer.

Aidan looked at her face for a moment, and offered kindly, 'I don't have to go until the morning if you want.'

'Oh.' That would be lovely, but at the same time wouldn't it just make things harder? And everybody had made an effort to be around this evening to wave him off. 'No, it's fine. Go home and get settled in. And anyway, we'll see you at Darren's party tomorrow, won't we?'

'I'll be there,' he promised.

There was a beeping noise from his bag. One of his phones. They'd been going mad all afternoon. She got the impression the texts and calls weren't that welcome.

Mossy shifted. He wasn't one for prolonged farewells. 'Right then,' he said.

'In fact, you know something? I'd *like* to stay,' Aidan announced suddenly.

Aisling's eyes latched on to Mossy's. Something wasn't right. Her antennae, dulled over the course of an Aidan-free eighteen months, were suddenly on red alert. Mossy, she saw, felt the same.

But maybe she was being unfair.

'Why?' she enquired, tentative.

Aidan looked hurt. Did she really have to ask? 'Because this is my home. Or at least it was, until I got thrown out.' He didn't look at Mossy. 'I want to spend more time with my family, that's all. I'd thought you'd be glad to have me back. But, you know, if it's too much trouble, that's fine.'

'Aidan, stop.'

'No. I wouldn't dream of putting you out.' He was putting on a great show of being in a huff. 'You obviously can't wait to get rid of me again. Just tell the rest of them I said goodbye, will you? I don't want to take up any more of people's time—'

'You've lost your flat, haven't you?' Mossy chipped in baldly.

That was all it took. Aidan went wild. 'For fuck's sake! That's just typical of you, isn't it? Always suspicious, always thinking the worst. Christ. Nothing ever changes around here, does it?'

'Have you lost your flat?' Mossy persisted. 'Or is there someone you're afraid of out there? Because I know there's something going on.'

'What's it to you? I was gone for a year and a half and you couldn't have given a shit if I was dead or alive,' Aidan shouted at him. 'So don't pretend like you're suddenly interested now.'

'That's not true.'

'At least Ma cared. She was always there for me. If it hadn't been for her, I'd have been out of here years ago. We all would have. Anything to get away from you.'

'We're not talking about me,' Mossy insisted. He was trying his best to keep calm. 'We're talking about you, and the choices you keep making.'

'I'm not listening to you, okay?' Aidan flung at him. 'I don't have to any more.'

Aidan had physically moved away from Mossy to line himself up beside Aisling. She felt the weight of his neediness, and also his anxiety. Mossy was right. There was something going on in Aidan's world that he didn't want to face, and he was looking to hide from it. The flowers, the farewell dinner; he'd just been going through the motions until he worked up the nerve to ask to stay. Foolish, irresponsible Aidan.

'It'd just be for a few days, Ma,' he said. 'Until I sort a few things out. Then I'll be out of your hair for good.'

There wasn't even the pretence of asking Mossy's permission. If his ma agreed, then it would be okay. She would make it happen.

It was the hardest thing she'd ever done in her life. But there was no other way. And she didn't need Mossy to tell her that. 'No. I'm sorry, Aidan. I'm going to have to ask you to leave.'

He reared back like she'd slapped him.

And she felt she had, but worse; more like a terrible blow. Her, his rock through every bad decision he'd ever made.

The look he gave her was awful. 'So Da's done a job on you too,' he said, colourless.

'We have the rest of the kids to think of too,' she said haltingly. 'And ourselves. Whatever trouble you're in, you're not bringing it to our door any more.'

He curled his lip contemptuously. 'Even spouting the same lines. Thanks for nothing, Ma.'

He whipped up his rucksack and left without a backwards glance. The whole house rocked as he slammed the front door behind him.

'Aisling,' said Mossy.

But she couldn't talk. Not yet. First she sank down on to a kitchen chair and burst into tears.

Chapter Thirty-nine

Magic Marvin was having a rough afternoon.

'Who can tell me what's hiding in this top hat?' he asked in a forced, jolly voice.

He was answered by the burps, wails and screeches of ten toddlers. One of them kept crying every time Magic Marvin delivered his catchphrase of 'Magic it with Marvin!'

'I did not know that Darren had so many friends,' Zofia marvelled to Aisling. Anto had invited her and Olaf to the birthday party; they'd babysat him so often that they were practically family, he'd insisted flatteringly.

Oh, and could Zofia bring her make-up toolbox with her, and perhaps be in charge of the face painting?

'I am a serious artist,' she'd told Anto.

'Yeah, I know, but can you just do a few Batmans and maybe a princess or two?'

'Where is Olaf anyway?' Aisling wondered, looking around. 'And Magda?' She'd been invited too. Aisling was looking forward to a party cardigan, perhaps in bright red or pink, with little bows on.

'He will be here,' Zofia said, but she didn't sound too certain. 'We had a little fight.'

'Not another one.'

'It's not my fault. Our date nights have been going very well. Magda must have complained about being left alone or something, because this morning he accused me of being jealous.'

'Imagine that.'

'I know! Me, jealous of his *mother*. I said to him, sure, because I want to wear cardigans all the time and fiddle about with cabbages. Don't you criticise my mother, he said, she is a fine woman! If she is so great, I said, why don't you bloody go and sleep with *her*?'

'Oh Zofia. You didn't.'

'I did.' She suddenly looked stricken. 'What was worse, Magda heard me.'

'*Zofia.*'

'It just came out! Oh no, what am I going to do?'

'Apologise,' Aisling said firmly. 'When they arrive, just go straight over and say you're sorry.'

'Yes, yes.'

'And then for God's sake sit down with Magda and tell her how you feel. Like you should have done at the start.'

'You are right. I will.' Zofia cheered up immensely.

Magic Marvin, meanwhile, struggled on. 'Anyone want to guess what's going to pop up from this hat?' A look of semi-desperation. 'Anyone? Anyone?'

'A stripper!' Baz heckled from the back of the room, where he was lurking with Sean, nursing plastic cups of MiWadi Orange.

'Hey,' a friend of Nicola's called over. She looked a little ferocious. 'It's a kids' party. Keep it clean, okay?'

Aisling thought her name might be Becky. Anyway, she and

her friend were dressed like they were going to a club, in little pastel dresses and killer heels.

'Well *hello*,' said Baz.

'Don't even think about it,' Becky snapped, bored.

Baz seemed doubly sorry he'd drawn attention to himself when Shannon – on buffet duty – suddenly looked at him and said, 'I don't think you've sponsored me yet, have you?'

'For what?' Baz bleated.

'My trip to the orphanage. I'm leaving next week, but it's never too late for donations. And no small change please. Notes only. And your mate too.'

She stood over Baz and Sean while they were forced to empty their pockets, as Becky and her friend tittered.

'Here, Ma, take this, will you?' Anto hurried up and dumped a large gift-wrapped present in her arms. Aisling was in charge of the presents, with instructions to put them carefully away upstairs to be opened later.

As the host, Anto was taking things very seriously. Every guest was greeted at the door with a smiley name badge and had their photo taken with Darren, which would be transposed later on to a ceramic plate by Pottery Party Paula, who was setting up in the kitchen right now. The living room had been transformed into the party venue, with big cushions everywhere, and there were sucky cups for the kids, and tea or coffee – no alcohol – for the adults, along with a beautiful buffet of party food. Taking pride of place was an enormous banner which stretched across the fireplace shouting 'ONE TODAY!!!'

'It's going very well,' Aisling assured him.

'Yeah.' Anto couldn't have looked prouder. 'Where's Nicola?' His eyes had been following her around all afternoon.

'In the kitchen, I think.'

314

And actually here she came now, in a summer dress and balancing two plates of cocktail sausages like it was some kind of test.

'I'll just go and give her a hand,' Anto said eagerly. But the front doorbell rang again, signalling a new arrival, and he went reluctantly to let them in.

Aisling strained to see. Could it be . . .?

But it was just another latecomer, a crying one, and his dad, and she deflated again. A quick glance at her watch confirmed that they were nearly an hour into the party already. Soon Marvin would be wrapping things up and handing the guests over to Pottery Party Paula.

'I don't think he's going to come,' Zofia said gently.

'Why don't you tell me something I don't know?' snapped Aisling. Immediately she was sorry. 'Don't mind me. I had a terrible night's sleep last night.'

Zofia clucked. 'I am not surprised.'

She'd dreamed Aidan was dead. Nothing new there; it was a dream she'd had often before. But last night his face was being eaten by maggots, that had reduced him to a reddened lump of meat. She didn't even recognise him, her own son, and she'd awoken so upset that she had to go downstairs and put all the lights on and she was still there when Mossy got up hours later to go to work.

Zofia squeezed her arm. 'He will be okay. He always was before.'

'Sausage?'

Nicola appeared at Aisling's elbow, making her jump. She awkwardly held out the plate of cocktail sausages.

'Do you know, I actually don't know if I do or not,' Aisling admitted. Then, in case Nicola took offence, 'I'm hungry but I can't face a thing, you know that kind of feeling?'

Nicola surprised her by saying, 'Yes. I often feel like that myself. But I'll swing back by you in a minute and you might have made up your mind.'

'Thank you. Oh, and Nicola?'

Nicola turned, and Aisling was struck by how very pretty she was, with her hair pulled back off her face like that, and her eyes bright.

'Well done. It's a lovely party.' Damn. She hoped that didn't sound as patronising as it felt.

'Thanks. Although I think the magician might be a bit over their heads,' Nicola said, rather unnecessarily.

Aisling suddenly saw how nervous Nicola was. Petrified of being judged: as a children's party organiser, a hostess, a mother. Sometimes it was easy to forget what she'd been through. She covered it all up so well. And Aisling felt bad that she'd not done more for her; she'd been too caught up in her own dramas to extend the hand of friendship to this girl whose own mother was on the other side of the world.

'Not at all,' she said stoutly. 'I think he's great.'

On cue, Marvin pulled a white rabbit out of the hat with a flourish, crying, 'Magic it with Marvin!'

'Woo hoo!' Aisling felt obliged to call appreciatively, and gave him a rousing round of applause.

Baz and Sean looked at her like she was demented. Becky and her friend snickered.

The rabbit seemed to be the grand finale to the show. Marvin reared back as Darren and his friends boisterously surged forward to grab hold of the trembling animal. 'Mine! Mine!'

'Okay . . . just take it easy now . . .' he said. 'Everybody take a step back, please . . .'

'I think it's time for the face paint, Zofia,' Shannon called.

Zofia, who'd managed to procure a glass of wine from stashes unknown, grimly knocked the whole thing back and deposited the glass on the table. 'Sit down! Sit down!' she barked. The toddlers turned to look at her, startled. 'I am in charge now, okay? You will all be Batman, even the girls, so do not ask me for anything else.'

They all obediently sat down, even Marvin.

The smile on Aisling's face was ripped away when Nicola blurted out, 'I want Darren to come home.'

Aisling sighed inwardly. 'Yes. Of course you do.'

Nicola was wary; was this *agreement*? 'I thought maybe over the summer I could get him used to a new routine. And if Anto's hoping to go to college in September . . . well, it would be the best time to do it. If we are going to do it,' she offered, as a softener.

Aisling nodded. 'We'd still like to help. Mossy and I. If that's okay. With babysitting and the rest. Whatever you'd like us to do.'

It was hard in a way, handing the power back when they'd had Darren for so long now. But it was time.

'Okay.' Nicola was nodding slowly, still not entirely certain this whole conversation wasn't some elaborate trap. 'Sure.'

'And we won't even charge much.'

Nicola gawked at her. 'Oh. You're joking, right?'

'Yes, Nicola. I am,' she said a tad wearily.

Nicola smiled then, and Aisling was taken aback, mostly because she'd never actually seen her smiling before. And it was beautiful.

She smiled back.

Mossy showed up later on, still in his work clothes.

'Job ran over.' He studied her. 'Are you okay?'

'Fine.'

'You don't have to pretend with me. I know it's hard to show up here today and act like everything's fine.'

'Still, at least I did the right thing, eh?'

His head snapped up at the sarcasm in her voice. 'You did do the right thing.'

'Great. That's the most important thing.'

His face closed over, and she was sorry.

Zofia came over anxiously. 'I thought Olaf was with you?'

'No, I left him at your house ages ago—'

'It's okay, here he is.' Zofia arranged her face into a suitably humble expression as Olaf came through the door. Judging by his black look, Zofia's challenge to him to sleep with his mother hadn't gone down too well. 'Olaf,' she began, as he joined them, 'I am sorry for my bad behaviour recently. You are right. I am jealous and have treated your mother very badly.'

Olaf looked down at her, unmoved. Delicately she looked past him. 'And, um, where is Magda? I want to apologise to her too.'

'Then you will have to write to her,' Olaf ground out.

A pause. 'Well, if you think it will help, I would be happy to—'

'I mean she is gone.' With a shaking hand he held up a note. 'She says she doesn't want to come between husband and wife. She has flown back to Poland.'

He turned and walked out.

Her mouth in a mortified O, Zofia looked at Aisling and raced after him.

Aisling bumped into Hugo in the kitchen.

'Hiding?' she joked.

His face burst into colour. 'No!'

'Um, I meant from the kids.'

318

'Oh, right! No, I've actually been commandeered by the pottery person' – he lowered his voice and cast a look over his shoulder at the formidable Paula, resplendent in a hairnet and a checked apron and hat – 'to help with the ceramic plates, but I've broken two already so I'm not sure how much use I am.' Another embarrassed grin. 'Everything going okay out there?'

Aisling didn't want to rattle him with any tales of drama involving the official face-painter and her husband. 'Great!'

'All this for a baby.' He seemed slightly bewildered. 'But Nicola insisted. I kept telling her she was taking too much on.'

'They'll learn. They won't make so much effort with number two. Not that they'll . . . I didn't mean *together* . . .'

Hugo rescued her drily. 'Let's hope that number two is a long way off for both of them.'

'Yes. Years and years,' Aisling concurred fervently.

There was a little silence, but it was a friendly one. No unrequited lust hung in the air, thankfully – or worse, love.

'Anto was telling us earlier,' Hugo said. 'About Aidan leaving again.'

Aisling blinked. But of course Anto would have told the O'Sullivans. Hugo was practically his father-in-law. She felt herself curl in defensively all the same. It was hard not to feel like a total failure as a. parent when you had to face other people.

'He's not a bad lad. He just has some growing up to do.' It was mostly the truth, she felt. And she would never, ever bad-mouth him to strangers. 'He's going to drop by in a bit,' she heard herself saying. 'To say happy birthday to Darren. You'll meet him then.'

'Really?' said Hugo.

She realised that Anto hadn't even mentioned it to Hugo; that it was only Aisling who still harboured any hope when it came to Aidan.

Fine. So be it. She'd never give up on him, whatever anybody else thought. She lifted her chin and said defiantly, 'Yes. He'll be here any minute now.'

Louise barrelled in importantly. She'd been on lawn duty, supervising the mini bouncy castle. 'I was told to tell you that half the kids are falling asleep so we have to skip straight to the cake.'

'Oh. Right.'

'We need everybody in the living room to sing "Happy Birthday".'

It was a squash, but they all crowded in: young guests, grand-parents, parents, aunts, Baz and Sean, Becky and her friend, Marvin, Pottery Party Paula, and, of course, Darren.

'Ai!' he said. It was still his favourite word.

Everybody took a breath and launched into 'HAP-PY BIRTH-DAY to—'

'Wait!' said Anto. 'The cake.'

Oh yes. That would be handy.

Nicola went running off, and reappeared with an enormous chocolate cake upon which a single candle blazed triumphantly.

'Aahhh!' said everybody.

Mossy met Aisling's eyes: *Nice cake.*

She'd baked it that morning. She looked back at him: *Not my best. But it's okay, given the circumstances.*

Now stop that, his look said. *It's a fine cake; you're just fishing for compliments.*

She gave him a little smile. They hadn't lost all of their marital skills.

The candle was lit and they all sucked in their breath again. 'HAP-PY BIRTH-DAY TO YOU! HAP-PY BIRTH-DAY TO YOUUUU!'

Out of the corner of her eye Aisling saw the door open quietly and Aidan stepped in.

He'd come, just like he'd said he would. And he even had a present; it was still in its shop bag, mind, no fancy wrapping, but how thoughtful.

'Aidan!' She waved.

He chose not to look. Fine; well they'd talk later. He slipped in behind the singing crowd – 'HAPPY BIRTH-DAY' – nodded to Anto and joined in.

Mossy saw him then; he gave him a long look across the room. Aidan chose to ignore him too.

But he was here. He'd come for Anto and for Darren, and that was enough. And Nicola too. Of course, they hadn't met yet. Maybe Aisling could introduce them afterwards. It would be an ice-breaker.

'. . . DEAR DARREN . . .'

Nicola turned to look at Aidan, and the strangest expression came over her face. To Aisling it was as though she'd seen a ghost.

Aidan, sensing he was being watched, turned his head to Nicola. And did a double-take. He seemed very confused. He looked to Anto beside her, then back at her again, as though playing catch-up.

'HAPPY . . . BIRTHDAY . . . TO . . . YOU!' everybody finished up, clapping.

'Ai!' said Darren, delighted. Then, with impeccable timing, he looked at Nicola and said, for the first time, 'Mama!'

'Good lad!' said Anto.

But Aisling wasn't watching Nicola's reaction. She was watching Aidan's. He seemed blown away by Darren's pronouncement. He stared at the little family unit of three as a delighted Anto lifted Darren into his arms, then he blurted loudly, '*You're* Nicola?'

Nicola, who hadn't taken her eyes off Aidan, seemed enraged and bewildered in equal measure. She threw back, 'You shithead.'

And there was Anto, poor Anto, head whipping from one to the other, not knowing what was going on, but with a look of doom on his face.

Chapter Forty

Halloween night, twenty months ago: Aisling

'TRICK OR TREAT!'

Louise burst in from upstairs dressed as a very glamorous witch, complete with hair extensions. She posed, awaiting the family's admiration. 'Zofia did my make-up, but I don't think she put enough on.'

It was an accusation that had never been levelled at Zofia before, and Aisling felt she should defend her. 'You look fantastic.'

'I need someone to go around with me and Emma,' Louise said. She lifted up her trick-or-treat bag, which was, optimistically, a large black bin-liner. She must be expecting a bumper night on the junk front.

'I haven't had my dinner yet,' said Mossy. He was just in from fixing the garden shed and still had his big tool belt around his waist.

'Aidan?' pleaded Louise.

'No.' He was in a mood that day and had barely spoken to anybody.

'Just until Da is ready. If we don't go soon, all the good stuff will be gone and we'll only get apples and nuts.'

'I said no, okay? Anyway, I'm going out in a bit.'

Mossy looked at him with pursed lips but didn't say anything. 'Go get Emma,' he said to Louise. 'I'll eat when I get back.'

'Thanks, Da!' Louise sprinted off.

Then it was Aisling, Mossy and Aidan, and the inevitable confrontation. They'd agreed that Aisling would do most of the talking. With a *be calm* look at Mossy, she produced a sheaf of college application forms and laid them carefully on the table.

'Aidan, why didn't you fill these in?'

Aidan flicked a look at them. She could swear he'd never seen them before in his life, even though she'd printed them out for him weeks ago and left them on his bed.

A listless shrug. 'I forgot.'

That was the really worrying bit: he didn't seem to care any more. He hadn't cared when he'd flunked his first-year exams. He hadn't cared when he'd missed the repeats. His pals from college had all gone back to their courses the previous month, and he hadn't cared about that either.

'So what are you saying?' A part of her would like to shake him, hard, and shout, 'Cop on!' but she kept her voice steady and even. 'You're taking a year out? You'll apply next year? Or are you done with education altogether, is that it?'

Another infuriating shrug. 'I'm not sure. I'll have to wait and see.'

'What exactly are you waiting for?' Mossy couldn't help himself. He planted both hands on the kitchen table and bellowed, 'The fucking weather to change?'

'Get out of my face, will you?' Aidan lashed back at him.

He looked terrible: greyish, and the skin around his mouth had

324

broken out. He'd been out until all hours the previous night with some guy called Milo that Aisling had disliked on sight (his old friends, like Vinnie Foley from next door, had been ditched). And – she was afraid to tell Mossy this – there was a scrape on her car. A very big scrape this time. 'He's not even supposed to drive that car!' Mossy would roar. 'We banned him after the last time, remember? A hundred and sixty euros to get it out of the pound!'

It was her fault; she should have hidden the keys, like those people on the Internet had to do whose stories she would read.

My son is out of control. I have to keep my purse locked away because he steals money all the time to buy drink. He's broken every curfew we've set, and he talks to us like we're dirt . . .

She used to think, how had they ever let their child get so bad? Why had they not done something to stop him before now? She actually used to judge them.

And look at her now. She was one of them.

The shame of it made her voice harder than usual. 'Your dad is right. You have to have a plan.'

Aidan, bored: 'Why?'

'Why? Because . . . because you can't just drift along!' Sometimes it was like they spoke a different language to him. 'You have your whole life ahead of you, Aidan. But you're determined to throw it away, aren't you?'

'Oh for God's sake,' he groaned. 'By smoking a few *spliffs*?'

'We're not talking about spliffs—'

'Well that'd make a bloody change.'

'Hey. Calm down,' said Mossy.

'Or what? You'll ring the guards again? You might have to wait until they stop laughing.'

'You had drugs in the house,' Mossy bit out. 'Our house. With other kids around.'

'A bit of hash in my sock drawer. It was hardly *CSI: Miami*. But no. You had to go overreacting as usual. The neighbours all think you're crazy, by the way. Bringing the drugs squad into the estate for a few spliffs!'

Mossy was undaunted. 'You were lucky you got off with a caution.'

'And you were lucky you didn't get done for wasting police time. Big man Brady. Making a tit of himself.'

A vein in Mossy's forehead bulged worryingly. Aisling herself was semi-mortified at the gossip the whole thing had generated. Since the 'wake-up call', as Mossy dubbed it, tensions had been simmering away malevolently. There had never been what you'd call a meeting of minds when it came to Mossy and Aidan – they had more of a chalk-and-cheese vibe – but now they really couldn't seem to stand each other.

'About college,' Mossy began again doggedly.

'That's my decision.'

'No. Not while you're living in this house, eating our food, using our electricity.'

'Here we go.'

'Yes, here we go. And we'll go over it again and again until we come to an agreement. College, or else you'll have to get a job.'

'Fine. So I'll get a job.'

'Which means making an effort to find one, instead of sitting around the house on your backside.'

'Maybe I'm holding out for you to offer me one.'

Mossy's lips went even thinner. Aidan had last gone out in the van the previous week. It had ended in a huge row after he had disappeared off somewhere at lunchtime and not come back. 'You'll be waiting.'

'Are you sure? You don't fancy *Brady and Son* on the side of that van? I always thought it was your big dream.' He laced the words with contempt.

'Now listen,' Aisling hurried in, hating the high, pleading tone her voice had taken on lately. 'I don't want any shouting tonight, okay? From either of you.'

The neighbours were already exercised enough. Every time she set foot outside the door she had that prickly feeling on the back of her neck of being watched. Aidan and his antics were like a train wreck.

But Aidan was in a dangerous humour tonight. And now that Aisling looked at him, she wondered whether he had taken something today already. Normally, with just a hangover, he was tired but okay; he was still Aidan, funny and irreverent. But not mean, like this. Not vicious. Since he'd started hanging out with that new crowd, he'd changed.

'"An honest day's work for an honest day's pay." Isn't that your favourite saying?' he was taunting Mossy. 'Or what's that other old chestnut you're fond of . . . Here, Anto will know.'

Anto, arriving in on his usual pilgrimage to the fridge, stopped warily. 'Leave me out of it. I'm heading off in a minute.'

There was some Halloween party on an estate the other side of the park, apparently. Details had been typically vague.

'Anto, you'd want to be careful,' Aidan said. 'He'll start grooming you next to join the family empire.' And he laughed, slightly manic.

Anto smiled, but a little uncertainly. He adored Aidan; they'd grown up in that bedroom together. But lately even he had started complaining about his brother coming in at all hours, waking him up with loud singing, and doing stupid stuff. And there had been some falling-out over missing money, although Aidan swore it wasn't him.

'I said that's enough, Aidan,' Aisling snapped.

'No,' said Mossy. Icy calm. 'Let him say it. He thinks he's above the rest of us anyway, don't you, Aidan? With all your fancy ideas and notions. Painting a wall, that's beneath you, isn't it? You'd rather get off your head with your dosser mates and talk shite.'

Aidan kept smiling. 'I know. We're not real men, not like you, Da.'

'Real men don't lie around in bed until lunchtime and then get their mammies to make them toast.' He flicked a look at Aisling. *More fool you*, it said.

'Look, I'll see youse later,' said Anto hurriedly. He knew which way this was going to go.

'No,' said Aidan. 'You should stay for this. We're getting an important life lesson here from our father.' He managed to make that mocking too.

Something in Mossy seemed to snap. 'You want a lesson? Here's one. Get a job, a proper job, and stop being such a tosser.'

'Sorry to be such a disappointment to you, Da.'

'You want the truth, Aidan? You are. You were given every chance, and look at you. No ambition, no drive to do anything with yourself. Happy to scrounge off us and set a bad example to the rest of them.'

Aidan was standing too. 'Go on, have a good old rant, you'll feel better.'

'Don't you dare talk to me like that.'

'Oh, so it's okay for you to call me a loser, but nobody can criticise you?' Aidan's lip was curling. 'There was me thinking you were a tough guy, but it turns out you can dish it out but you can't take it. Now if you'll excuse me, you can all fuck off because I'm going out.'

'No you're not,' said Mossy.

Aidan looked surprised. This was new. 'Yes I am.'

'*No you're not.* This stops right here, this going out and smoking your brains out. Rolling in here in the middle of the night waking everybody up because you're so out of it you can't even walk straight, you pup.'

Mossy was at the end of his rope. They all were. But this was a bad idea, Aisling knew. They were all too angry and upset, saying things they wouldn't be able to take back later. 'Mossy, listen—'

'I'm done listening, Aisling. The only thing this smart alec here understands is action. If you go out tonight, you needn't come back.'

Anto, trying to calm things down, said, 'Da, leave it, he's not a kid any more, you can't stop him.'

Aidan walked forward deliberately. He said, 'Get out of my way.'

Mossy stood there like a wall. 'No.'

'I said get out of my WAY.'

'You going to make me, are you?' Mossy was dismissive.

'Mossy,' Aisling implored.

Suddenly Aidan lunged. Fuelled by anger and resentment, he delivered a blow to Mossy's midriff, surprising him. But Mossy's bulk withstood it easily, and with a deft twist he got Aidan in a degrading arm lock.

'Stop it!' Aisling implored. 'Mossy!'

Anto too was wincing at the display, the unevenness of the match. 'Da. Let him go, would you? For God's sake!'

'When he's learned his lesson,' Mossy panted, both of them breathing hard. Aidan was groaning in pain and humiliation. 'Well?' he shouted. 'Have you?'

'Get off me . . .' Aidan struggled like mad, twisting, trying to grab at Mossy.

'I said have you?' Mossy shook him like a rat.

Aidan roared, 'Fuck you!'

Mossy suddenly went slack and released his hold. He looked a bit shocked. Aidan did too. He had a screwdriver in his hand. The big one, from Mossy's work belt.

'Shit,' he said. 'I didn't mean to do that. *Shit*. I'm sorry, Da.'

As though wondering what he was talking about, Mossy looked down at himself.

There was blood.

'Mossy . . .' Aisling watched in horror as Mossy's shirt grew red at the side, an ominous spread. Mossy lifted it to reveal a six-inch gash, just under his ribs. 'Oh,' he said, in a bemused kind of voice.

'Jesus Christ!' Anto rounded on Aidan. 'You stabbed him, man! You fucking stabbed him!'

Aidan was really frightened now. His hand was covered in blood, Aisling saw. 'I didn't mean to. I'm sorry, Da. I'm sorry.'

He rushed to help, but Mossy threw up an arm to ward him off. He warded them all off, even Aisling. And she knew his pride had suffered almost as big a blow. He was like a wounded bear who didn't want anyone near him.

'It's just a surface wound, that's all.' And he gave Aidan a look as though to say, you couldn't even manage to do that properly, you loser.

Aisling's brain switched to autopilot. She needed to get Mossy to the hospital. As soon as she could. But first she needed to look after Aidan, who was in almost a worse state than Mossy.

'Anto,' she said. What would be best thing for Aidan right now? 'Get him out of here, will you?'

'Okay, but where . . .'

'Anywhere, it doesn't matter. Just until things calm down. And ask Emma's mother to look after Louise until I'm back.'

Anto nodded grimly. He pushed Aidan towards the door, careful to avoid his bloody hand.

At the door Aidan looked at Aisling, then Mossy. He looked terrible. 'I'm sorry.'

Mossy refused to look up. A moment later they heard the front door close. Only then did Mossy let his guard down. And Aisling knew that it was worse than he'd let on. He looked at her, eyes burning with fury and pain. 'He has to go, Aisling.'

'This isn't the time, okay?' She grabbed up her car keys.

'Don't tell me you're going to defend him.'

'No, of course not, this is a step too far . . .'

'Then we're in agreement. First thing in the morning, he's out of here.'

Aisling felt as though the walls were closing in on her. 'Okay.'

Chapter Forty-one

Halloween night, twenty months ago: Nicola

Nicola's mum had flown out that day.

'I'll ring the minute we land, okay? Just to say hello. And then we can Skype each other when we get to our hotel,' she said, along with a load of other promises and platitudes designed to make herself feel better. Or at least less shitty for walking out on her cuckolded husband and teenage daughter.

'Ring if you want,' Nicola told her blandly. 'But I probably won't be here.'

She would never give her the satisfaction of getting angry; of showing any emotion at all. From the moment her mother announced she was setting up a whole new life for herself in Sydney, Nicola had closed her down clinically and efficiently.

Looks flew between her mother and Patio Guy. *You try*, her mother's desperate face said.

He gamely did. 'You'll come and visit, won't you? We'll pay

for a ticket.' He had a loud, lively voice. 'Any time you want. We'd love to see you.'

'I have school.' This was directed to a point somewhere to the right of him. She never actually *looked* at him if she could help it. She wouldn't even walk on the patio stones he'd laid. She skirted round the edges, even though it felt a bit stupid.

'The Christmas holidays, then. You'll have two weeks off, won't you? Maybe you could come then. It'll be summer in Sydney!'

Nicola felt like everything was very surreal. There she was, being left behind with her father in a house that suddenly echoed, and this man, this mother-stealer, thought she'd quite like to go and sunbathe in his back garden in Sydney?

'Just fuck off and die, would you?' she said to him pleasantly.

'Nicola.' Her mother's voice, cutting across the room. 'I realise you're hurting, but there's no need for that.'

Did she really believe Nicola was merely 'hurting', like she'd scraped her knee? Nicola had thought that mothers always knew how their children really felt, no matter what kind of front they put on. You could never fool your mother, right?

But it turned out that you could. Nicola felt shredded inside. She could never begin to admit how awful this all was, though, because she was afraid that if she took the lid off, she'd never be able to put it back on again.

Besides, she had Dad to think of. They had to put a brave face on for each other.

'You'll miss your plane,' she said.

Her mother swooped to squeeze Nicola's shoulders in semi-desperation. 'I'll be back to visit. All the time, you know that, don't you? It's just, there's no work for Dave in this country any more, not in his line of business. And I suppose both of us want a fresh start.'

Indeed. The neighbourhood would dine out on this one for years. *He laid my patio too, but he didn't lay me!*

'Would you not change your mind?' The words came in a rush. 'Please. You know we'd love to have you come with us, wouldn't we, Dave?'

'Of course we would,' he enthused. He even sounded genuine.

'The lifestyle out there, it's fantastic, Nicola. Good schools, colleges. And the weather.' She smiled suddenly, and she looked like she used to, before the drawn face of recent weeks. 'We could go to Bondi Beach together at weekends and pretend we're in the movies.'

For a second Nicola actually entertained it: herself and her mum spread out on beach towels – the orange ones in the press upstairs – sipping cans of diet something and planning a whispered campaign against Speedos. They'd have such a laugh. The stories she'd have to tell Mikaela and Becky back home . . .

And then Dad passed by the kitchen window, a thin shadow, and it all came scudding to a halt. What was she thinking? Sydney, with her mother and *Dave*?

Her family was here, in Dublin. Her mother was the one breaking it up. Did she really think that Nicola would endorse her wrongdoing by going to live with her? And what about Dad? The *two* of them abandoning him?

She took a step back and her mother's hands fell away, leaving a little chill behind.

Her mother looked upset. 'These things happen, Nicola. People break up. It's not anybody's fault. It's just . . . one of those things. I'm hoping that one day you'll understand that.'

Please. Don't let her start crying again. Nicola couldn't bear that.

'I have to go,' she lied. There was no way she was hanging around for the big goodbye, the loading of the luggage into the boot, the look on her dad's face. 'I'm due at Becky's.'

Not till much later, but Becky wouldn't mind. They were going out tonight. Some bloke called Milo that Becky fancied had invited them along to a Halloween party. They were meeting up in Becky's place first to get ready and have a few drinks.

Nicola decided that she would start early. She needed it.

'Who's your Vampirella mate?' Milo asked Becky. 'You can bite my neck any time you like, darling,' he leered at Nicola.

Nicola was wearing a very short, very tight Halloween outfit, complete with fishnet tights and skyscraper heels. She didn't bother answering him. He was a creep.

'Hey,' Becky said to him, pissed off at being ignored. 'I thought you were getting me a beer?'

Milo barely looked at her. 'You know where the fridge is.' A group of girls dressed in naughty schoolgirl and sexy witch outfits caught his eye. 'Sarah! Karen! Long time no see.'

And he swaggered off into the crowd.

'Fuck him. There's no way I'm getting off with him now,' Becky said viciously.

'Yeah, let's just drink all his beer and go,' Mikaela backed her up. 'It's a crap party anyway.'

The place was so packed you could hardly move. Or see. The overhead lights had been knocked out; instead there were spooky Halloween tea lights dotted around the place, except that most of them had gone out, or had cigarettes stubbed out in them, and you could barely see your hand in front of your face.

Which suited Nicola fine. She didn't want to talk to anyone anyway. She just wanted to get drunk.

'We're supposed to be saving that till later,' Mikaela complained as Nicola took another swig from the bottle of Coke they'd brought along in her handbag, which was actually mostly Bacardi.

'Leave her.' Becky nudged Mikaela pointedly.

'Oh. Yeah. Sorry.' Mikaela looked sympathetically at Nicola. 'Are you all right?'

'I'm fine.'

'Are you sure?' Becky wanted to know. 'Because we can go somewhere else, just the three of us, if you want.'

'No, it's okay.' She gave them a watery smile. 'It's nice to get out.'

'Yeah. Take your mind off things.' Mikaela squeezed her arm. 'You keep the rest of that Bacardi.'

'Thanks.'

'Oh, and my ma said you're to come over for your dinner at the weekend, you and your da,' Becky said. 'You know, just until you get used to things.'

It was the third offer of dinner that they'd had already. Dad said people must think he was a total disaster in the kitchen. Nicola had been astonished: how could he joke at a time like this?

But after his initial burst of anger at discovering the affair, he'd seemed to move to acceptance of the situation pretty quickly. He was gutted, of course. Anyone could see that. But he didn't try to fight it. He didn't try to change her mother's mind. It made Nicola so mad, the way he just rolled over. Had he no self-respect?

'I know it's unfair, Nicola. But your mother's made her decision and we're just going to have to get on with it.'

Unbelievable. And worse, he seemed to expect her to be the same. It would all be nice and civilised, no screaming or bad-mouthing or any unpleasantness like that. Everything glossed over, no matter how she might feel.

Well tonight she felt . . . unanchored. Her mother was in the air right at that moment, flying further and further away from her, and her father was delivering the weather forecast to the nation, signing off with a 'Have a very good evening' while everything around him fell apart.

The Bacardi didn't last long, and nor did Milo's beer. Nicola had her hand in the fridge an hour later, rooting around for the last one, when another hand descended upon hers.

They straightened hurriedly: her and the tall guy with burnished hair, semi-lit by the golden light of the fridge. It was like he had a halo, she remembered thinking. Or maybe it was all the Bacardi.

There was a *zing* as their eyes collided. And she knew in that instant that he was in some way the same as her. It sounded stupid, but that was how she felt. The air hummed with connection; a strange energy that flew back and forth between them, pulling her in like a net. It was insane. But she'd never felt like this with any other person in her life.

'You can have it,' he said. His voice was soft, playful.

She realised that their hands were entwined around a bottle of Heineken. It was hardly the most auspicious start. And this *was* just the start of something. She was completely certain of that.

'I'll fight you for it,' she said back, light, free.

But somehow she'd made him sad. 'I've had enough aggro for one day.'

She wanted to stroke his cheek, to make whatever it was that was troubling him go away. Her! Not exactly known for her tenderness. All the usual rules had been blown away, though.

'Me too,' she said simply.

And that was it. It was like it was sealed or something. Them.

They found a corner that was even darker than the rest of the house. As they sank down together, close, the length of his leg pressed against hers, they managed to upend one of the last tea lights still gamely flickering, and it went out with a little hiss.

'I can barely see you now,' he complained.

'You'll just have to imagine me.' She already had a snapshot of him imprinted upon her brain: his tall, rangy body, the red of his hair, the lean, intense face, those eyes . . .

He opened the bottle of beer and they drank it, passing it back and forth.

'I want to know everything about you,' he demanded. He grinned. 'Actually, hang on. That'll take all night. Tell me the most important thing.'

He probably expected her to say she was a Scorpio, or that she was getting her nose pierced and no, she wouldn't regret it. (Mikaela was currently obsessed with getting something pierced.)

Instead she said, 'My mother left me and my father to go to Australia today with another man.'

Immediately she wished she could take it back. She was going to frighten him off, and she'd only just met him. Maybe she'd been imagining the weird connection. He was going to say, 'Ah go on, pull the other one,' or slowly back away.

But he just took her cold hands in both of his and kneaded them, warming them. 'That's rough. I'm sorry. You're going to miss her, aren't you?'

'No, I'm not,' she explained earnestly. 'It's her choice. She can do what she wants. But why should I uproot my whole life to go with her, just so she can still have her family? Because that's what she wants. But she's the one breaking it up. And that's fine; me and dad will survive.'

When she'd finished, there were tears running down her face and dripping from her chin on to her bare cleavage. She wasn't aware of crying; the tears were falling of their own accord, and she wasn't able to do a thing about them.

'Sorry,' she said.

Still he didn't run for the hills. He just had a brief but futile search in his jeans pocket for a tissue. Eventually, in the absence of anything else, he opened a few buttons on the end of his shirt and pulled up one flap of it to gently mop her face.

'You'll catch your death of cold in that dress,' he chided her, dabbing gingerly at her chest next.

And now she was laughing and crying at the same time. She sniffed hard, feeling better already because she'd shared her misery with him, and said, 'Your turn. Tell me the most important thing about you.'

He hesitated. 'I can't.'

'Yes you can.'

'I did something tonight I shouldn't have. And I can't tell you about it because you'll probably get up and walk away.'

'I wouldn't.' Couldn't he see? Didn't he know, like she did, that this was for keeps, no matter what either of them had done?

'I will sometime. I promise. Just not now, okay?'

They were sitting so close now that they were breathing the same little pocket of air. Nothing in Nicola's life had ever felt so natural and right. She wanted to stay here for ever, cocooned in this dark corner with this beautiful man.

Whose name she didn't know.

'What's your name?' he said, in another perfect meeting of minds. She wasn't even surprised any more. She wouldn't bat an eyelid if they discovered that they had the same small birthmark on their right hip.

Suddenly she was laughing with pure delight. The crappiest day of her life had turned into the best.

'Can't you guess?' she said, flicking her black dress, playful now. 'Morticia.'

'Oh *really*,' he said, laughing too. 'I guess that makes me Freddy Krueger.'

The only time he took his eyes off her was when that guy Milo passed, trailing the sexy witches.

Milo nodded affably in their direction. Then he lifted an eyebrow, murmured, 'Got something for me?' and went on.

'Sure, yeah.' He turned to Nicola. 'Hang on here a second, will you? I owe him a few quid. I might as well give it to him or he'll just keep bugging me.'

'He doesn't seem very nice.'

'Ah, he's okay. He's let me sleep on his couch a few times.' A little embarrassed, he explained, 'Family problems, you know?'

No one knew better than her.

'I don't get on with them so well.'

'Well you have me now,' she said.

Normally she'd have died rather than make such a cack statement as that. But that was before.

'I know,' he said, as serious as her.

She sat and waited for him. After ten minutes she decided to go and look. She wasn't panicked or anything; she knew he wouldn't have left without her. He probably just couldn't find her again in the dark.

'Excuse me . . . excuse me . . .'

The Bacardi had really kicked in now, and she was unsteady on her feet. Where was he? Suddenly she was desperate to see him; without him she felt like she was missing a limb.

He walked out of the toilet. Or was it . . .? Through the dark she made out the shock of red hair, the lean face, the broad, strong forehead. Yes.

She fought her way through the bodies. It was a crush. 'I've been looking for you.'

'Uh, hi,' he said.

She was so relieved to find him that she put her arms around his waist. It just seemed right. He was slightly shorter than she'd thought – at the fridge he had seemed to tower over her – but she was drunk, it was late, and the warmth of him pressing against her was so reassuring.

She knew that she didn't want to wait. This wasn't first-date stuff. They'd skipped all that. She saw absolutely no point in playing the whole relationship game. They already had a relationship. She wanted it to be complete, that was all.

So she kissed him. He seemed a little hesitant at first. Maybe *he* wanted to wait? But no. He began kissing her back; passionately, a little clumsy in his haste.

Some people passed by, lads with beers, and shouted something about getting a room. They seemed to know him.

'Tut-tut! Take it home!'

'Fifteen Sylvester Avenue, love!'

'Get lost,' he said back. He was panting a bit. 'What's your name?' he asked.

She thought he was teasing her, so she duly laughed. 'You're funny,' she said. Maybe he wanted to hear her say Morticia again.

He was laughing too, and he seemed a little out of it. Well, very out of it. But then so was she.

'You're beautiful,' he cried, and kissed her again.

He was really going for it now and eventually she had to push him away a little, just so she could draw breath. 'Easy,' she said.

They needed privacy, because this was important. 'Come on. Let's find a room,' she said intensely. 'I want us to be close.'

He didn't say anything. But his face was answer enough.

Then, abruptly, 'Gimme a minute.'

And off he went again, lurching into the crowd. Nicola was a little confused. Maybe he was going to get a condom off that Milo guy, or out of his coat pocket or something. That was what blokes did, right? Well, according to Mikaela; Nicola had never been with a guy before. After a minute of standing there feeling a little lost, she decided to leave him to it and went on upstairs to see if any of the bedrooms were free.

Several couples had had the same idea. There seemed to be a foursome going on in one room, judging by the sounds coming from the dark. She swiftly shut the door. The small room at the front of the house was empty. The single bed was covered in coats. She was throwing them on the floor when he found her again, groping his way along in the dark.

'I thought you'd left,' he said. He seemed anxious, like she'd given him a fright.

'Why would I leave?'

He looked at the bed, then at her. That electricity thing was going on between them again, and she had never felt more alive.

'Are you sure about this?' he said.

Her answer was to kiss him once more. And this time it felt different. It wasn't so messy and urgent. It was slow and intense and she felt completely lost.

She didn't remember falling asleep. They'd just been lying there, pressed chest to chest, no words needed.

She woke abruptly to people roughly pulling coats from under her. All the lights were on, and people were scattering like there was a fire.

He was gone. It was just her, with a coat pulled over her.

Someone was shouting about the cops, and she got up fast and found her vampy dress on the floor. One shoe was under the bed . . . where was the other one? Fuck . . .

She gave up and hobbled to the door. People were hurrying downstairs in various states of inebriation, guys helping girls. A shower curtain and its rail were draped over the banisters. Bottles and cans littered the ground. Her eyes searched each passing face but none of them was him.

'Go on. Get out and go home.'

She whirled around to find a guard there, in high-vis and helmet, like he was in the middle of a riot. He'd been going from room to room swinging a torch. He gave her a look, in her half-put-on dress and one shoe missing.

'Do you want to get yourself arrested?' he barked.

'No . . . sorry . . .'

'So go home.'

He wasn't downstairs either. There were guards everywhere. Blue lights flashed outside. Two guys were in handcuffs. One of them was Milo, she realised. They were searching his pockets. He looked bored. Nicola felt disorientated. She was still drunk.

'*There* you are. For fuck's sake, come on.' Becky grabbed her arm.

'Wait. There was a guy . . .'

Mikaela was fierce. 'I'm not getting arrested. My ma would go mental.'

Nicola let herself be pulled along. She'd find him tomorrow.

Chapter Forty-two

They had to call a halt to Darren's party early. Not that people needed much encouragement to go. They gathered up handbags and children swiftly, and made for the door with grim looks.

'Thanks for coming!' Louise chirped, on door duty with Darren. 'Don't forget your ceramic plate.'

'And sorry about the, um, language in front of the kids,' Hugo apologised, reverting to his natural state of mortification.

'What's going on?' Baz wanted to know, anxious not to be left out of anything. There was a sticky ring of MiWadi around his mouth.

'Go,' Anto said grimly.

'I thought Aidan didn't know your bird?'

'It looks like he does. Now *go*.'

Becky and her friend – Mikaela, Aisling had eventually found out – appeared to be having much the same conversation with a stony-faced Nicola, but eventually everybody left. The bouncy castle was unplugged and deflated with a sad hiss, and Louise took Darren upstairs for a sleep.

A Special Delivery

Now it was just them: Aisling and Mossy, Hugo, Shannon, Nicola, Aidan and Anto. Side by side, the two brothers were disconcertingly alike. They had Brady stamped all over them, except that Anto was a little shorter and thinner. You'd almost have them as twins, if it wasn't for Aidan radiating some kind of unnameable appeal. Of the two he was always the one you'd look at first. Anto managed to appear a bit ordinary in comparison.

Aisling spoke first. 'Would someone like to explain what the hell is going on?'

'Hear, hear,' echoed Shannon.

'You can start with her,' said Aidan roughly, pointing an accusing finger at Nicola.

'*Me?* And I have a name,' she came back with in a flash. 'It's Nicola. Which you'd have found out if you'd bothered to hang around that night, instead of sneaking off on me.'

'What night?' demanded Shannon.

'Keep out of this!' Anto retorted. 'It's nothing to do with you.'

'Hey, I'm on your side here.'

'Shannon, go up and check on Louise and Darren, will you?' said Aisling.

Shannon reluctantly went, giving Aidan a very black look. 'Sneaker-outer,' she threw in his direction.

'What night?' Mossy repeated quietly.

'Halloween,' said Nicola.

All the Bradys winced. Halloween had forever lost its appeal. Aidan shot a look at Mossy. Mossy gave it back and raised him one.

'That party,' she said. 'He was there.'

'So was I,' interjected Anto strongly, like he was still staking his claim.

'Then you both must have been there!' Nicola looked from

345

Anto to Aidan as though trying to work things out in her own head.

'We were!' said Anto.

'This is Aidan, by the way,' Aisling said hastily to Hugo. Nobody had actually introduced them yet.

'I guessed,' said Hugo shortly.

'Um, nice to meet you,' Aidan said.

Hugo's look said, *Yes, I've heard all about* you, *young lad.*

'Nicola,' he began, 'what are you saying here? Did you actually, um . . .' he searched about delicately for the word, 'meet this individual?'

But it was okay, because everybody knew what he meant.

Mossy turned to Aisling, boggle-eyed. This was too wild for him. What the hell had his kids been up to? Some kind of orgy?

Then all eyes were on Nicola again.

Her own were locked on to Aidan. 'Yes.'

Anto made some kind of strange noise in his throat. Then he turned on Aidan in a way that Aisling found frightening. 'I took you to that party, man. I tried to look after you. Jesus, you were a mess. But I calmed you down, brought you beers, washed the blood off you.'

Hugo was agog. '*Blood?*'

Aisling wanted to die. Hugo's face was a stark realisation of just how dysfunctional their family must look.

'We had an incident at home,' she said quietly.

Aidan put a hand on Anto's arm. 'Listen, Anto—'

'Get off me.'

Aidan still looked massively confused. To Aisling it appeared genuine. 'All I know is that I met Nicola at that party. I was with her all night—'

'You were not.' Anto's whole body was braced as though for a fight, while his ears tried to block out the truth. 'Okay? Because I met her too, I kissed her. Remember, Nicola?' He looked at her, willing her to confirm that they'd had a night of grand passion.

She didn't. She bowed her head and said nothing, which was worse.

'Anto,' Aidan tried again.

'No,' Anto shouted. 'You're not going to do this, okay? You're a selfish bastard, Aidan – you always were. Well you're not taking this. This is my life, and you're not fucking barging in.'

Aisling's heart was breaking for him, even though she still wasn't sure what the hell was going on.

One thing was clear, though: Nicola and Aidan had their own little gig going on, even amongst all these people. You could practically see the vibes flying back and forth. A lot of it was anger and hurt, that was true, but there were other things too, that made you want to look away in embarrassment.

'Nicola.' Anto turned to her desperately. 'Tell him to get out of here, that this is nothing to do with him.'

Mossy weighed in then, in his usual inimitable style. 'Look, which one of them did you sleep with? Or did you sleep with both of them?'

'*Mossy*.' Aisling was going to divorce him this time. She really was.

'What? I'm not judging. She can sleep with a whole football team if she wants, it's none of my business. Except when it comes to my grandchild.'

Hugo sprang to life. The mild-mannered weatherman was no more as he squared up to Mossy. His jaw jutted out impressively. 'Right. That's it. Get out of my house.'

'Dad,' Nicola sighed.

'No. They threw us out of their house once, and now it's our turn. They won't stand there and judge you. I won't let them.' He whirled back to Mossy. 'It's *you* who have some explaining to do, raising a scut like that. Not you,' he hurriedly added to Anto, whom he was very fond of. 'You're a great lad. It's that fellow there I mean.' And he looked at Aidan. 'Is what she says true? That you slept with her and snuck off?'

'I didn't!'

'You did,' Nicola countered ferociously. 'I woke up and you were gone.'

'All right, look, there were cops. I had to get out.'

It was Anto who informed Nicola viciously, 'In Aidan speak that means he probably had some class of drugs on him.'

Hugo was even more horrified. '*Drugs?*'

'Anto,' Aisling cut in. 'Stop it. I know you're upset, but this isn't helping.'

But Anto was in survival mode. He had to use whatever ammunition was at his disposal. 'Yeah. And he stabbed my da that night. He had to have thirty stitches. He's got a big scar, haven't you, Da? Go on, show Nicola.'

Nicola's eyes flew to Aidan, shocked. Aidan didn't try to defend himself; just stood there, his chin set at a defensive angle. There was no sign of his usual cocky self tonight. He looked a bit shell-shocked.

'That's enough,' Mossy said quietly.

'No it's not. She might as well know what she's dealing with. Come on, Da. If anybody can tell her, it's you. So do it.'

Aidan gave Mossy a look that was a challenge. *Go on, do your worst. Damn me completely in the eyes of everybody; you'll only be telling the truth anyway.*

But Mossy just looked at Anto sorrowfully. 'You're better than this, Anto. You always were.'

A Special Delivery

Anto didn't want to be the nice guy any more, though. He wanted to hurt Aidan. And Aisling could see that he was close to crying, too. She was close to it herself, at seeing her two sons torn apart like this.

'Anto,' she said. She wanted to comfort him, but he pushed her away roughly.

It was Nicola who walked over to put her hand on his arm. 'Let's go somewhere and talk,' she said.

Anto raised red-rimmed eyes to her. He didn't look at Aidan at all. 'I just need to know one thing.'

It was the question they all wanted the answer to.

'Darren. Whose is he?'

Even if they all knew the answer already.

Nicola hesitated. 'Aidan's.'

Anto gave a jerky nod before he turned and left.

Chapter Forty-three

'Anto?'

No answer. Aisling knocked again, a little harder. 'Anto, please let me in. I've brought you some lunch.' She waited. 'Anto?'

'Just leave it outside, okay?'

For a week now he'd hidden away in his bedroom, curtains pulled across and door locked tight. Occasionally he emerged to use the bathroom, and she'd race upstairs hoping to catch him but would just find the door shut in her face.

'Okay,' she said. 'But I need to change your sheets.'

It wasn't just an excuse to gain entry. The whole room must be rancid by now. Mossy said there was a swamp-like fog wafting out from under the door. It was his little attempt to lighten the mood in the house, but no one had smiled.

'My sheets are fine.' His voice was irritated and impatient; she was worried about *sheets* when his whole life had collapsed?

Aisling put the tray down on the carpet. She leaned against the door, resting her head against it. 'Anto, I know you must feel terrible. All this, it's so very unfair, especially when none of it's

350

your fault.' She didn't know if he was listening, but she went on anyway. 'It's a lot to come to terms with, when you thought you were a father and now suddenly you're not.' She faltered a bit. This was hard. She'd yet to come to terms with it herself; how did poor Anto feel? 'But Darren is still going to be around, you know. You're his uncle, nobody can take that from you.'

She thought she heard a noise from inside. It could have been a snort, a laugh, a sob.

'Listen to me, Anto. You and Darren, you have a bond. You worked hard for it; you got up nights, played with him, walked up and down with him when he was sick. And you shouldn't let that go, okay? You should fight for it. Fight for your place in his life. Do you hear me?'

She listened hard but there was no sound. No indication at all that he'd heard a word she'd said.

Mossy came out of their own room opposite. He looked at Anto's door, then at Aisling: *Well?*

She shook her head. Mossy's shoulders slumped. She picked up the untouched tray from breakfast time, and went back downstairs.

'You're to ring as soon as you get there, okay? Even if it's the middle of the night.'

Normally Shannon would roll her eyes and go, '*Yes*, Mother,' but today she knew that Aisling was too delicate for any kind of mockery.

'To be honest,' she said, 'I don't even know if I should be going at all. What with Anto.'

Matt, standing there with his Factor 50 on already, looked alarmed: all that steamy sex under the beautiful African sky in jeopardy?

'Maybe we could support him from Africa,' he ventured. 'Via email and all that . . .' He trailed off at Shannon's withering look.

But he got support from an unexpected source.

'Matt's right,' Mossy said. 'You two should keep to your plans. They'll be expecting you in the orphanage. You shouldn't let them down. Anyway,' he added heavily, 'there's nothing anybody can do for Anto. His head is just a bit wrecked, that's all.'

Mossy looked as though his own head was a bit wrecked. He'd been hanging around the house all week, having told Dave and Olaf that they'd have to get on with things themselves because he wasn't going in to work for a few days.

Mossy, not going into work? It hadn't happened since . . . well, since he'd got the stitches that time. They'd told him at the hospital to take at least three weeks off. He'd taken thirty-six hours.

But this whole thing over Aidan and Anto seemed to have really shaken him. And it worried Aisling. Mossy was always so strong and so sure, even when he'd been completely wrong. She'd relied upon that in a perverse way. He was her port in the storm. What if the pair of them went to pieces?

Louise sloped in, looking as cheesed off as everybody else.

'I thought you were going to play with Emma?' Aisling enquired.

'No,' said Louise gloomily, 'because I hate her guts now.'

'Really? That's a shame.'

'As if we did wife-swapping in this house!' she huffed.

Startled looks were exchanged. What with all the Anto drama, nobody seemed to have noticed the rampant wife-swapping going on under their noses.

'Emma said that's what the neighbours think we do on a Friday night, instead of watching the telly. You know, with Nicola. But I said to her that Anto and Aidan aren't even married to her, so she could piss off.'

'You didn't!' Aisling wilted.

'Good girl,' Mossy said fiercely. 'And I'll tell the rest of the neighbours the same.'

'Yay!' said Louise. They high-fived each other, and it perked Aisling up a bit, even if the road could add sewer language to the list of Brady transgressions.

Then it started. The music. They all looked towards the ceiling, and Anto's bedroom, in dread. Afternoons tended to be given over to awful, depressing-type music. Matt thought it might be The Cure, or worse, The Smiths. After a few minutes of it, everybody in the house started to have very black thoughts, and began saying things like 'I really hate myself' and looking about for anything to comfort-eat.

'I suppose we'd better think about going,' Shannon said hastily, all thoughts of sticking around for Anto rapidly disappearing. That fecking music would bring even her down. 'Ready, Da?'

Mossy was driving them. Their luggage was already stored in the back of the van, and hopefully would emerge at the other end without too many paint streaks.

'Let's go,' he said.

There was a last-minute flurry of passport-checking, hugs and kisses.

'Tell Anto I said goodbye, okay?' Shannon looked about expectantly, then stopped herself. Her face crumpled. 'I was going to give Darren a hug and a kiss, but sure he's not here any more.' And she burst into tears. Half of it was the emotion of leaving for the summer, but it was enough to set Louise off.

'I miss him!' she wailed. 'I had a new name for him, too.'

'What was it?' Shannon bawled.

'Dexter.'

'GAK.'

'Ah, girls!' Aisling wrapped them both in a big cuddle, her own voice a bit thick. 'He's not gone for ever. Isn't he only a few miles up the road?'

'With *her*.' Louise had reverted to disliking Nicola. In fairness, she'd never really warmed to her in the first place. And now that she'd taken Darren back permanently and broken Anto's heart . . . well, she needn't come looking for any favours off *Louise*.

'Yes, because she's his mother.' Aisling wasn't hearing a word against Nicola. They needed to keep whatever relationships remained. 'But you'll see him all the time.'

Shannon looked at her. 'Not all the time. Neither of his parents lives here any more.'

As if Aisling needed reminding of that.

'Mossy and I are still his grandparents, Shannon. I'm sure the O'Sullivans will take that into account. We just need to get round to making arrangements.'

Whenever they could stomach contact again, that was. Aisling was holding off for the moment. It wouldn't be fair on Anto.

'It won't be the same, though.' Louise was still whingeing. 'Why can't *you* have another baby, Ma?'

Aisling was firm. 'I can't, love. I'm too old.' Besides, raising another kid would probably finish her off altogether.

'Shannon, then.'

'Don't even think about it,' Mossy growled at Matt. But his eyes were a bit bright too. Darren had been such a presence in the house that it would take them all a long time to get used to the fact that he'd only be a visitor from now on. Hopefully, anyway. Once the dust settled.

'We're going to be late.' Matt was moving towards the door, anxious. Too much time with the Bradys tended to make him that way.

'Okay,' said Shannon. She released Aisling and looked around. 'I guess that's everybody.'

Except for Aidan.

They were back to not talking about him. Well, what was there to say? He'd left the O'Sullivans' house that day shortly after Anto, and nobody had seen or heard from him since.

It was all depressingly familiar. While Anto was up in his room, dealing with his emotions in the normal way by not eating and wallowing in appalling music, Aidan was probably off his head somewhere. And with a newly discovered son on his hands, and a scorned Nicola, he probably needed a double dose to do the trick.

It was such a shame, Mossy had said last night, that Aidan hadn't stayed away from Darren's party. Anto would have remained Darren's father – at least for the moment; there was bound to have been another party somewhere down the line – and everybody would have been better off: Anto, Nicola, Darren, even Aidan himself.

Especially Aidan, perhaps. Because he clearly wasn't up to it. And that wasn't Aisling making excuses for him; it was her admitting a sad fact. She was past making excuses.

'Don't worry about me, okay?' Shannon said at the door.

And Aisling suddenly smiled. 'Oh honey. You're the last person in this house I need to worry about, thank God.'

They piled into the front of the van, Matt looking slightly gorilla-like due to having to bend his head under the low roof.

'Mossy,' Aisling said, as he went to go round the driver's side. She wanted to buck him up a little. 'At least this one will be back.'

'Maybe she'd be better off staying away from us altogether,' Mossy said morosely.

Oh great. He was really gone off on one. Just when she needed him.

'Listen to me. So we might have made mistakes. Loads of them. But we didn't roll spliffs and put them in Aidan's hand. We didn't force him into an unprotected one-night stand.'

'Maybe we should have,' he declared.

'Rolled *spliffs*?'

'Well, it's not like coming down hard on him ever worked.'

Was that an *admission*? She was so surprised that she stuttered, 'Maybe not . . . but you can go too far the other way, and we did our best . . . Here, do you even know how to roll a spliff?'

'I'm sure I could learn in time for Louise. We haven't ruined her yet.'

'Now stop that . . .'

But Mossy cut her off with a pleading look. 'Can I be like Anto for a little while? Can I lie in bed and play terrible music and let it all sink in? Not literally, of course. Just in my head?'

'Oh Mossy. Of course you can.'

'Thank you.'

When the doorbell rang five minutes after they'd left for the airport, Louise and Aisling took bets on what Shannon had forgotten.

'Her purse!' Aisling guessed.

'Matt!' said Louise, with dread.

But it wasn't Shannon at all. Nicola stood on the doorstep with Darren in her arms. Hugo was parking the car behind her.

'Can we come in?'

Chapter Forty-four

'We thought you might like to see him,' Nicola said.

Crafty. Using the child to get at her. But then Aisling realised that they had nothing to gain really.

Anyway, she was dying to see him. She'd give her left arm for a cuddle. 'Yes! Thank you!'

'Go on then,' Hugo said. 'Go to your granny.'

Darren was handed over. For a horrible minute Aisling thought he'd forgotten her, after only a week (she'd read somewhere that small children and goldfish were worryingly similar in that department. Or had that just been Mossy, winding her up?).

It was fine. Darren gave her a friendly 'Sssh!' before plonking himself down on her lap, even though she suspected he had a dirty nappy.

'Hello, sweetheart.' She wanted to smother him in kisses, but was too embarrassed in front of the O'Sullivans. They were embarrassed too. In fact the whole atmosphere was toe-curlingly awful. It was probably best that Mossy wasn't there, because no doubt he'd have come out with some clanger that would have made things worse. 'You've got so big!' she told Darren. 'Even in a week.'

'I know. We can't seem to keep him filled up at all,' Nicola said, brow furrowing.

'He's trying to walk all the time now,' Hugo told her eagerly, seeming to forget that at one stage she was the one who used to dole out such information to him. 'Right little wriggler, aren't you?'

'Oh! Yes! I see what you mean.' She managed to catch him as he made a lunge to the left.

'He went the whole length of the hall yesterday, lurching from side to side like he was drunk. You should have seen him.' Nicola laughed. They all did. It went on a touch longer than necessary.

'We got it on video camera. I'm going to make you a copy,' Hugo promised, awkward yet anxious to make Aisling feel better.

He hadn't forgotten at all. He knew how hard this was on her, because he'd been there himself.

'Thanks. That'd be lovely.'

She was going to miss all those little milestones now. His first sentence, his first day at playschool. She might have missed them anyway; he'd been spending more and more time at the O'Sullivans' lately. But had Anto remained the father – why oh why had Aidan come to that blasted party last week? – then the law of averages said that some of those milestones would have been at the Bradys' house.

It was hard to swallow her disappointment. Aidan had spoilt it for her too.

Hugo cleared his throat. Here came the hard question. 'How is Anto?'

'Gutted, actually.' She gave it to them straight. She wouldn't deny him his hurt; he was entitled to it. 'He'd come to love Darren. He was building his future around him, as you know.'

And around Nicola. But of course it wouldn't be fair to say that. She'd never strung him along in that way, from what Aisling had seen. The opposite, in fact.

'Maybe I could talk to him,' Nicola began.

'I don't think that's a very good idea at the moment.'

Hugo looked at his hands, then raised his eyes to Aisling's. 'I'm very sorry about the way things have turned out.'

He too probably wished that Aidan hadn't turned up at the party. Just as everybody had got used to the curve ball that life had thrown at them, here came another one to upset them all again.

'We both are,' Hugo emphasised.

This was Nicola's cue to do a bit of breast-beating of her own. 'Yes. I, um, don't know how the confusion happened, really.'

Exactly the question Aisling and Mossy had been tossing about for days now, in whispered conversations in the dark. How *did* you mix up the father of your own child, or believe you'd slept with someone but hadn't? How drunk had they all been? Mossy admitted to having got fairly hammered a few times, but never so much that he couldn't remember doing the dirty deed; or at least the crucial bit of it anyway. Aisling came clean about snogging the face off some fella one night after six bottles of Ritz and then not recognising him five minutes later on the dance floor. Neither of them was proud.

But they weren't a patch on Anto, Aidan and Nicola. The three of them could have walked straight on to an episode of confessional TV with a Torn Between Two Brothers theme. Aisling and Mossy might also be dragged on stage to explain themselves and their appalling parenting.

'Well,' said Aisling, 'let's not dwell on it.' What was the point?

Hugo cleared his throat. 'No, let's not. The main thing now is to try to move on. Isn't that right, Nicola?'

Throughout all of this he'd sat protectively close to his daughter. There seemed to be no blame or anger directed towards her for what had happened. Which was good, Aisling assured herself, if slightly peeving.

'I don't suppose you have a photo of Aidan at all?' Nicola asked.

'A photo?'

'For Darren.'

Of course. It was probably all the poor lad would see of his da for a while, if ever.

'It'd help, you know?' said Nicola. 'To get him used to the idea.'

'Yes.' Aisling was mortified and ashamed by Aidan's behaviour, but there was no sense in them having false hope. She'd harboured it for a long time, and look where it had got her. 'I'm sorry,' she said, 'but it's very likely Aidan's gone on some kind of bender again. He tends to do that when he doesn't want to face things. Maybe when he's had a chance to think about it all . . . He was very fond of Darren when he was here, you know. So in time hopefully he might want to take some responsibility.'

Nicola and Hugo looked at each other. 'He has,' said Nicola.

Aisling went still. 'Aidan?'

'He's already been around to see Darren,' Hugo said.

'Right,' she managed. 'We didn't know.'

'Oh. So he hasn't been in touch with you?'

'Correct.'

'Um . . . sorry . . .' Hugo was in contortions trying to extract his foot from his mouth.

'Nicola,' Aisling said, because she could ignore it no longer, 'I think Darren's got a dirty nappy.' She handed him over, fiercely glad for the distraction. 'The changing mat is still in the living room. And nappies and everything.'

Aisling and Hugo sat in silence as they waited for Nicola to change Darren. There didn't seem to be a lot left to say.

Chapter Forty-five

Anto lay in bed until he heard them go. The clip-clop of Nicola's sandals on the driveway, the click as Hugo's car unlocked. Darren's shout of 'Doggie! Doggie!' which must mean the Foleys-next-door's mongrel was out. Then car doors opening and closing. The engine starting up. The car seemed to sit there, hesitating along with its occupants, and Anto could nearly feel them looking up at his bedroom window. He held his breath. Then they were gone, driving away, out of his life.

Baz rang. 'Oh, so you've decided to pick up!'

'What do you want?' His voice sounded thick and he swallowed quickly to clear it.

'Nothing. Just, do you fancy coming out for a game of pool?'

'What do you think?'

'Aw, come on, man. Becky's coming. And Mikaela.'

'Who?'

'You know them, they're mates of—' He cut himself off. 'Fuck. Sorry, Anto, I didn't even think.'

Anto found he didn't care. He was numb at the moment. It

was weird: every hour he felt something different. There was grief, rage, sadness, disappointment, despair and yesterday, for a perplexing few minutes, euphoria. He'd been laughing like a hyena, so much so that he'd heard them turn the telly down below him. But right now he was back to feeling like he'd been anaesthetised. Baz could have told him that the world was going to end horribly in two and a half minutes and Anto would feel . . . nothing.

'Are you into her? Becky?' he said, just for something to say really. Baz had been hitting on her like crazy at the party . . .

No. He wasn't going to go there.

'I am not! No way,' said Baz, clearly mindful of Anto's feelings. 'Sean invited her along,' he lied badly. 'I'm just going to make up numbers.'

'Decent of you.'

'Listen, if you're worried about what people are saying . . .'

'I'm not worried.' Although at some stage he'd probably revert to being Whacker Brady again amongst his mates. But that didn't seem as important now as it used to. What people thought of him. And he was pretty sure that was nothing to do with the numb feeling. 'They can think what they want.'

'Course they can! Anyway, Aidan's the one they think is a right shit. Getting Nicola up the duff the night he tried to top your da, and never contacting her after that.'

'He was thrown out of the house the next morning, remember?' Anto said shortly. He wasn't defending Aidan. In all honesty, he'd spit on him if he walked into the bedroom right now. But it seemed important that the facts were clear, having been muddied so terribly and at such an awful cost. 'No job, no money, nothing. So he probably had a few things on his mind. And for the record, he didn't try to top my da. It was . . . an accident.'

'Whatever,' said Baz, the drama dampened somewhat. 'But still.

What kind of a da is he going to make? A dropout. She'd have been better off with you than some bloke who's going to be smoking weed at the school gates.'

'Shut up, Baz, would you?'

'I'm just—'

'When he was back here after breaking his ankle, you were nearly crawling up his backside, yourself and Sean. Aidan this and Aidan that. It was sickening watching the pair of you.'

'Ah, fuck off!' said Baz. 'I was just trying to make you feel better, that's all.' He was in a right huff. 'I've been sticking up for you all week, while everyone's been wondering how Anto Brady could have convinced himself he'd actually slept with Nicola O'Sullivan!'

'Well when you find out the answer, will you let me know?' Anto said back.

A pause. Baz laughed.

So did Anto, after a bit. 'I suppose I just wanted to believe it,' he admitted.

'Who wouldn't? She's gorgeous. And she did snog you. We saw it, myself and Sean, I've been telling them all that.'

'Cheers,' said Anto drily. 'Anyway, I'm sure they all think I've got a great imagination.' This came out bitter. The numbness was wearing off now and he had visions of walking past the local shops, and Damo and that lot from school. No, not from school; school was finished now, and given that ambition amongst them was low, they'd be hanging around outside those shops for the next fifty years, making fun of him.

He groaned.

'Are you sure you won't come out for a game of—'

'No. Thanks anyway, Baz. Maybe next time.'

'All right, pal. Mind yourself.'

★　★　★

When Anto awoke next, there was no light coming in under the blinds, and the house was dead quiet. The alarm clock said 3.20 a.m., and this time he felt upset.

He looked to the middle of the room, where Darren's cot used to be. His da had dismantled it the night of the party. Just came in without a word and took the whole lot away as quickly and quietly as he could. And his ma, she took all the clothes and nappies and toys. And they hadn't said anything stupid to him like 'It'll all look better in the morning.' They had just let him be.

He was grateful for that.

He would give anything right now to have that cot back, and to hear the soft in and out of Darren's breath as he slept.

He knew people thought he'd been fooling himself about a future with Nicola. But in the beginning, he hadn't even liked her. He'd *fancied* her, yeah. You couldn't be an eighteen-year-old male and not. But she wasn't very nice. Snarky and cold and all bottled up. A good few times he'd wished he didn't have to set eyes on her again, and that was the truth.

But then he'd catch a glimpse of what lay underneath, before she pulled down the shutters again fast. And it was complicated. He liked that; found it intriguing. She was like a puzzle that you had to worry at, to spend time trying to work out, and each time they met he felt he understood her a little bit more.

She'd wreck your head in the process, though. And she could hurt you too, if she felt like it. But in a perverse way he liked that too. All the other girls he knew seemed lightweight in comparison. They were grand and all that, but he couldn't really be bothered with them.

And she'd started to like him too. He knew he wasn't fooling himself about that. It was nothing major; there was never any sense that the kiss of that Halloween night was going to be repeated any time soon. But she didn't look at him like he was an eejit any more. Maybe it was because he'd started to not be afraid of her.

If only he'd had more time. *You fucker, Aidan.*

He was so angry that he slammed his fist against the wall, hard, and a second later he heard footsteps running up the stairs.

'Anto?' His ma. 'Anto, are you okay?'

He didn't answer.

He was starting to smell. This was a problem. It was difficult to practise self-love when you reeked to high heaven. And his beard had grown too. He probably looked like a caveman, had he bothered to check in the mirror. But who was going to see him anyway?

'Anto?' It was Louise this time, outside the door. He hadn't seen her in a while. He wondered what way her hair was these days.

'I don't want to talk to you, okay?'

'I don't want to talk to you either. I just want to borrow your Celine Dion CD.'

'I haven't got a Celine Dion CD!'

'You have, I saw it on the shelf over your bed—'

'It was for a project, okay? On the *Titanic*. We were trying to recreate the movie.'

'Sure you were. Can I just borrow it? Me and Emma are making up a dance.'

'No!'

He should have made Baz keep that bleeding CD when the project was finished. He reached up, found the offending article on the shelf over his bed and aimed it at the bin.

Naturally, he missed. Aidan would have got it first time. Aidan hadn't missed the bin since he'd been eight years old.

Fuck him anyway. Fucker. Did absolutely nothing with his life and *still* got the girl. And a beautiful son, in the kind of spectacular two-for-one package that only Aidan could pull off. 'Fucking thieving, robbing druggie fucker!'

'I'm still here,' said Louise.

'GO AWAY,' Anto said ferociously.

There was a squeak from outside, then Louise's feet retreating down the stairs fast.

Anto felt drained. It took more effort than you might think to keep hating Aidan. Especially as it wasn't technically his fault. Nicola simply preferred him – you'd want to be blind to have missed the chemistry between them – and he was the biological father of her child. End of. There wasn't a thing Anto, or Aidan, could do about it.

Anto looked across the room balefully at his brother's empty bed. *That* was going for a start. This was his room now. There was no way Aidan was ever getting his foot back in here. Anto didn't care if he was broke, or sick, or desperately needed a place to crash for the night. He was a big boy now, whether he liked it or not, with a kid, and he'd better start facing up to it. The guy didn't even know how to change a nappy! He was in for some shock, was Aidan.

Anto allowed himself a grim smile.

He'd better treat Darren right, though. He'd better be a good father to him. Or else Anto really *would* hate him.

Anto was lying in bed one day, just looking at the ceiling, when a new feeling came over him. It was one he hadn't experienced since all this had happened, and he had to search about to identify it. It had him in a hollow grip, making him feel uneasy and a bit weak.

Finally it came to him, surprising him.

'Ma?' he shouted. 'Can I have something to eat?'

Chapter Forty-six

The first time Aidan came round was two days after Darren's party. He stood across the road under a tree and stared at the house, dragging nervously on his cigarette and generally looking hobo-ish. Five minutes passed, then ten. Eventually he turned and sloped away.

Dad sighed. They were watching from the kitchen window. 'I don't know whether to be disappointed or relieved.'

But Nicola knew he would be back.

'Uh, hi there.' Then, when Hugo failed to react, 'I'm Aidan.'

'I've hardly forgotten. I'm not senile, you know.' Dad reluctantly, very reluctantly, opened the door another five inches; no more, no less. 'Oh, and by the way, I don't allow smoking in this house. Of any description. Do you get my drift?' He snapped his eyebrows together in a way that said, *I have your measure, sonny, and if you think for a minute I'm happy about this, you're wrong.*

'I get your drift perfectly,' Aidan assured him.

Dad hesitated suspiciously: was this cowboy making fun of him? Just in case, he glared a bit more.

A Special Delivery

'Can I speak to Nicola, please?' Aidan asked politely.

'Not so fast. You wouldn't know this, because you haven't been around' – another scorching look – 'but Nicola's recovering from post-natal depression. So she doesn't need any more upset or drama. Police calling to the house, for example, or people too fond of sharp implements.'

He gave Aidan a moment to digest all of this: see? He knew stuff; he knew everything, in fact, so there was no point in Aidan pretending to be a nice lad when everybody knew perfectly well that he was a bit of a waster. To put it kindly.

'And Darren's barely a year old,' he went on. 'He doesn't need someone who's going to flit in and out whenever the mood takes him. A daddy who gets his hopes up and then disappoints him. Especially as he *had* a perfectly good daddy whom we all liked tremendously and who'd made a firm commitment to Darren.'

Not this inferior specimen standing in front of him right now with his hands in his pockets.

'So if I was you, I'd be doing some serious thinking. In fact I'd be considering whether my involvement in their lives is such a good idea.'

'Just let him in, Dad, would you?' Nicola sighed from behind him.

Aidan reacted at the sight of her; his whole body tensed. He remained standing there, though, his shabby trainers planted firmly apart.

Dad was defiant. 'I'm merely stating facts. He's not exactly father-of-the-year material.'

'That's true,' Aidan agreed.

'Finally!' said Dad. 'We're getting somewhere.'

'But I don't want to win any prizes. I just want to get to know my son.'

What about her? Nicola tried not to read anything into her exclusion.

'Shame you didn't want to do that a year and a half ago when you knocked her up,' Dad couldn't resist sniping.

'Dad. *Please*.' Nicola didn't know what had got into him tonight. Even Darren was watching his grandad, with his red face, with interest.

'I didn't know she was preg—' Aidan began to say.

'I'm not interested in your excuses! And I'm telling you right now, if you mess my family around, I'll . . . I'll come after you, do you hear me?' This sort of macho talk was completely alien to her father, but he was really going for it, waving his arms about as though explaining some giant weather map. 'Nicola's had a very hard couple of years, okay? Not many girls her age could cope with half of what she's gone through. But she's back at school now, and she's doing a wonderful job of bringing up that boy there on her own. And if you do one single thing to set her back, then by God you'll have me to answer to.'

And he really did look quite scary for a minute. With a last malevolent glare at Aidan, he went into the kitchen and slammed the door.

Dad had finally raised his voice. But it wasn't the volume that was important; it was the things he'd said about her.

Darren had no idea Aidan was his new da. He just launched himself at him in the living room and waited for him to do his Marlene Dietrich accent. Aidan duly obliged, gently roughing him up around the tummy region.

'Ve haff vays of making you laff.'

Well, the giggles out of Darren . . . It wasn't so much the accents as the silly expressions Aidan put on. His face seemed elastic and bendy, and there was an endearing lack of embarrassment about him as he threw all kinds of shapes for Darren's amusement.

Even Nicola wanted to laugh, but she didn't let herself. She could giggle some other time. Today they had serious things to discuss.

But oh, look at them! They were so alike. Darren had looked like Anto too, of course, and Mossy – those Brady bully-boy genes, leaving all maternal DNA in the shade – but he had Aidan's eyes: a beautiful blue, and kind of dreamy. You couldn't but know they were father and son.

Finally Aidan looked up at Nicola. 'We already know each other.'

For a moment she was confused: him and her?

'We shared a room at home, Darren and me. With Anto.'

'Oh. Yes.'

Well somebody had to bring his name up. Nicola felt regret flood through her. Of anybody in all this, Anto didn't deserve to be hurt.

Aidan didn't look too ecstatic either. 'Have you been in touch with him?'

'No. I tried, but . . .'

Aidan nodded. He rubbed his eyes. He seemed tired. But not hung-over tired. Emotionally tired. 'If I was him, I'd want to be left alone for a while.'

'It doesn't matter about me and him. Well, it does, but . . . You're his family. And I don't want this to ruin things between the two of you.'

'It might be a bit late for that. We'll just have to wait and see.'

Darren announced that it was time for a nap by giving a weary 'Ai, ai,' like he was an old man who'd finished working the rice fields after a long day. He climbed off Aidan's knee and trundled over to the corner, where his blankie lay waiting for him. He curled up on it, stuck his thumb into his mouth and closed his eyes with the minimum of fuss.

'You taught him to do that?' Aidan marvelled.

Nicola wanted to boast that yes, she had. That she was a marvel. But the truth was that Darren had grown from a fractious, insomniac baby into a laid-back toddler pretty much all by himself.

'He's a great boy. I know every parent says that, but Darren is really, really clever and strong and funny, and loads of other things that you'll see for yourself. I used to think my life would never be the same again, and you know something? It isn't, and it won't ever be, and I'm glad. Because he's my whole world now and he always will be.'

She probably sounded a bit fierce. And a little dramatic too. But he needed to understand. All that weak-kneed eyes-across-a-crowded-room stuff was great; no girl in her right mind would pass up a guy who beamed that he was The One with just one hot look. And they'd had that: a wonderful night of soulmatey sticky passion, and it was nice to think that Darren had been made on a night like that, as opposed to, say, a sixth wedding anniversary where both parties had put out because 'Well, we probably should.'

But it wasn't just her now. She was a package; she came complete with a small, demanding, frequently hungry person whose needs came way before hers. Or Aidan's.

Aidan seemed anxious to tackle the big questions too. 'You haven't been well,' he stated.

'No. But I'm better now. I didn't think I'd ever feel right again, but I do.'

She was surprised, actually. And she wished she'd told somebody just how badly she'd felt. She didn't know why; it just seemed like another failure or something, when it fact it was the cause of it all.

'I'm glad.'

'But my dad is right. I don't need any more upset, Aidan. I need to look after myself.'

'I know.' He shifted a bit. 'And about my grim and murky past.' A look. 'Most of it's true, unfortunately. I'm afraid I don't have much to offer you right now except honesty.'

Nicola digested this. 'That's . . . commendable.'

'But?'

'I was kind of hoping for something a little more practical right now.'

He seemed taken aback. 'Oh. I'm, um, kind of skint at the moment . . .'

'I'm talking about childcare. Obviously I can't ask Anto any more. So it would really help if we could work out some kind of timetable.'

She held her breath. Was he with her on this at all? Or did he think he could just come to admire Darren when it suited him?

He nodded cautiously. 'Okay.'

'And we have some pretty big decisions to make. Like, I start back to school in September and there's a new crèche opened up just round the corner. So I could pop in there at lunchtime and see Darren. Or else Dad can hire Mrs McAllister and keep him here at home, where I wouldn't see him at lunchtime but he'd have more one-on-one care.' She looked at him. 'It depends on what we want for Darren.'

'This Mrs McAllister. Is she as bad as her name?'

'I don't know. But in my head she makes a lot of stews.'

'The crèche, definitely. The food might be awful but he'll probably have more fun. And, you know, maybe some days I could collect him early? Take him off for the afternoon?'

This was going better than she had thought. He seemed to be capable and willing to pitch in.

But then reality came crashing in rudely, a rogue wave on an otherwise sunny beach.

'Aidan . . .'

'I know what you're going to say.'

'I'm going to say it anyway. You can't ever be under the influence when you have Darren.'

'I wouldn't be.'

'*Ever.*'

He looked at her steadily. 'I know that.'

'Promise me.'

'I don't do hard drugs, I never have. It's just a bit of weed . . .'

'I don't care. Promise me.'

'I promise.'

'And if you ever are . . .' She didn't need to finish. He knew what she was saying. He knew it was a deal-breaker.

'I get it, Nicola, okay?'

Now that some stuff had been ironed out – the important stuff; there would be plenty more, but that was enough for today – they both kind of gave a little sigh, and a shy smile.

'Well,' said Aidan.

'Well yourself,' she said back. Her heart was beating a little fast.

'I thought about you, you know. A lot.'

'Not that much. You never chased me down.' Her hurt broke through.

'No,' he said, regretful. 'I never did. I'm sorry. I did a lot of stupid stuff that caught up on me and I got sidelined a bit.' He looked over at Darren, conked on his blankie, snoring at the ceiling. 'I wish I'd known.'

'Would it have made a difference?'

'Yes.'

She believed him. Becky and Mikaela would throw their eyes to heaven, no doubt, and go, 'Yeah, right! He's just saying that to butter you up.' But she didn't think so. Well, time would tell, one way or the other, what Aidan meant and didn't mean. She'd be on her guard till then.

The door opened abruptly. Dad looked in, as though to make sure that Aidan hadn't made off with the family silver, then sniffed loudly and disappeared again.

'Your dad doesn't seem to like me.'

'Correction. He can't stand you.'

'I guess I'm going to have to change his mind. But I'll tell you now, I don't have a great track record with fathers in general.'

'Then you'd better try harder, hadn't you?'

'You're tough,' he said admiringly.

'You have no idea.'

She made him go then, even though he wanted to wait until Darren woke up so that he could say goodbye.

'You can see him again later in the week, if you want.'

'How about tomorrow?'

The look in his eyes let her know that it wasn't just Darren he wanted to see. And suddenly there it was: that rush of intensity between them that was like a physical shock. Wishing that she didn't feel like that, or at least not about someone with Aidan's reputation, didn't make a blind bit of difference. For a split second they swayed towards each other. Then some ingrained sense of self-preservation made Nicola jerk back.

She was part of a package. There was a long way to go yet before Aidan would be invited to become part of it too.

'Later in the week,' she said firmly.

Dad was out of the kitchen like a shot, of course, the minute he heard Aidan go. He'd want the lowdown. He'd even been talking feverishly during the week about random drug testing, as though you could just pop into your local health centre to get your coke levels checked.

But he had the phone in his hand. 'Your mother was wondering if you'd like a word.'

Already he was turning to go back in. Nicola never spoke to her mother on the phone, they all knew that. It was just a formality.

'Okay,' she said, her voice suddenly a bit jumpy.

And she took the phone.

Chapter Forty-seven

'W'ill you do my make-up for me?' Aisling asked Zofia.
     A startled pause. 'That is the first time you have ever asked me.'

'I know.'

'Normally I have to bully you, and you sit there under duress.' Zofia sounded almost emotional. 'But to *ask* me.'

'No funny business, though, okay? I don't want to look like a madam, or a show girl or a faded movie star. And definitely no neon fuchsia lips.'

'You rocked that look.'

'I don't want to rock anything. I just want to look like me, only better. Can you do that for me?'

'I will make you look beautiful,' Zofia vowed excitedly. 'What is the occasion?'

Clearly she expected nothing less than a wedding, or at least the annual night out at the local golf club, where Aisling occasionally – very occasionally – went to belt a few balls into the lake.

'We're just going out for something to eat.'

If Zofia was disappointed, she didn't let on. 'Good! Anto needs feeding up. I saw him in the park yesterday and you could tell it is a while since he has seen sunlight, what with his milky-white skin. A lot of women would give anything for skin like that.'

'Anto's not coming. It's just Mossy and me.'

'What, a *date*?'

'I don't know if I'd go that far. But it's just the two of us anyway.'

'I will make you look extra beautiful,' Zofia promised. 'To help things along. When?'

'Tonight?' Aisling confessed.

Emma's mother had invited Louise on a sleepover, probably thinking she was doing the little mite a service by giving her a few hours in a normal home, and Aisling had just seized the moment and booked a restaurant.

Zofia sucked in her breath. She looked at her watch. 'We will have to be quick.'

'I know.'

'Olaf has booked the taxi for five o'clock. It is so exciting.'

'It isn't, Zofia, so you can stop pretending.'

'I am getting into character, okay? If I have to spend two weeks in his mother's house in Warsaw, sucking up to her and acting like the perfect daughter-in-law, then I need to start practising now.'

Aisling had spent a long afternoon in the shopping centre with Zofia choosing a selection of new cardigans in various hues to try to 'right the terrible wrong done to my mother', as Olaf had said fifty million times in the weeks since Magda's swift exit from the country. Zofia's apologies had fallen on deaf ears. 'You have got what you wanted! She is gone!' Olaf insisted. Even Zofia's admission that yes, she was jealous, made little difference. It took the purchase of two tickets to Warsaw, so that she could apologise in person to Magda and retract any scurrilous insinuations of incest, to bring him round.

'I guess you'll just have to grit your teeth,' Aisling advised.

'I know. And admire her cooking, and ask her if she wouldn't mind sharing the story of when Olaf's first baby tooth came out when he ate an apple, and after that he wouldn't touch apples for years because he thought he would lose all his teeth.' Zofia laughed heartily.

'I know, it would bore the life out of you, but what can you do?' Aisling commiserated.

Then she realised that Zofia's laughter wasn't entirely put on. She really seemed okay. Had done for weeks now, actually. Even Olaf's ire hadn't really knocked a bother out of her.

'You're looking forward to this, aren't you?' she said suddenly.

'No. I wouldn't say that.' Zofia grimaced. 'But at the same time I am thankful to Magda for leaving like that.'

'Well, yes, in a way . . . but has it not caused a lot of trouble and bad feeling between you and Olaf?'

'Yes, terrible trouble,' Zofia agreed cheerily. 'And it will take a lot of time to win Olaf around again. But I do not mind. Because Magda was being very sweet.'

'Sweet?' This was a new one on Aisling.

'Do you not see what she did? She left *for* me, not because of me. She was saying that I am Olaf's main family now. Not her. And she did not want us to break up over her, so she left.'

'I suppose you could look at it that way . . .'

'That is what happened.' Zofia was certain. 'Mothers and daughters-in-law, it is not an easy relationship. Someone had to give in, and it was her. I admire her for it.'

'Or else she could be waiting for you at the airport with rotten cabbages.'

'I don't care. Because now I am Queen Bee! The competition is over.'

'You mightn't want to say that to Olaf. If you're trying to get back into his good books.'

'Don't worry. I will be nice as pie in Warsaw.' She gave Aisling a sly look. 'Besides, now it is my turn to sit at the kitchen table and watch her. We will see how she likes it.'

Nigel, the waiter with the sticky-uppy hair, was serving them again.

'Folks,' he said warily, clearly remembering them.

'It's okay,' Aisling assured him. 'This time we're going to eat. But to start off, we'd like a bottle of your house white.'

'House white,' Mossy murmured, when Nigel had gone. 'You're really spoiling me.'

'Well, you look so nice tonight.'

'Thank you.' He was wearing a shirt that he'd actually ironed himself, and a pair of jeans with no rips in them. 'You're looking nice too. That stuff on your eyes . . .'

'Plain old eyeliner.'

'You used to wear it,' he ventured.

'Yes, long ago, in a galaxy far, far away.'

'I like it,' he said stoutly. 'When I saw Zofia leaving the house with all her pots and brushes, to be honest I expected the worst.'

Now that they'd looked each other over and complimented each other sufficiently, there was a little silence. That was what happened when you got seriously out of practice.

'Just so you know,' she said, 'I didn't invite you out to talk about Anto, Aidan, Shannon or Louise.' She did a quick head count. Yes, that was all of them.

'Okay . . .' said Mossy.

'In fact, the first person who mentions any of the kids has to take off an item of clothing.'

'Steady on. This is a family restaurant.'

'Pay the bill then. And leave a hefty tip for Nigel.'

'Right,' said Mossy. 'You're on!'

Another pause.

'What will we talk about then?' he wondered.

'You and me.'

'Really? You think we'll get a whole meal out of that?'

'We might get to dessert. Then we can talk about our favourite TV programmes or something.'

'Sounds fair to me. You go first.'

'First?'

'Just to kick things off,' Mossy assured her.

'Okay.' What did she really want to know about Mossy right now? 'How's your head?'

'My *head*?'

'You said you wanted to go to bed for a while, but only in your head. Have you got out of bed yet?'

He thought about this. 'Almost. But at least I've stopped playing awful music.'

'Was it The Cure?'

'God, no. Abba.'

'You love Abba!'

'I just played the same song over and over again. It became a form of torture,' he assured her. He looked at her, gave a little sigh. 'Ah, I'm sorry, Aisling. And before you go rushing in to try to make me feel better about myself – because that's what you

381

do and you're very good at it and it's why we all love you so much – I do have things to be sorry about.'

Aisling let out a breath. She felt she'd been holding it in for years. 'I don't suppose there's a person in the world who doesn't wish there were some things they'd done differently.'

'That's for sure,' said Mossy quietly.

Nigel appeared at the table with the white wine. 'Now, would you like to taste—'

'Just leave the bottle and go, good lad,' Mossy instructed.

Nigel's fledgling smile died. He gave them a hunted look, did as he was told, and fled.

Mossy poured for them both, and took a long slug as though he needed it. Then he put the glass down and looked at her. 'They're going to leave, Aisling, whether we like it or not,' he said slowly. 'Our kids. Aidan's already gone—' He cut himself off, winced. 'I guess that's me picking up the bill and tipping that waiter eejit.'

'Yes,' Aisling said, but neither of them was smiling. This was too raw.

'Shannon's got another year of college and then she'll probably take on the fight to redistribute the world's wealth or something, and she'll go too. Anto's not got much keeping him here any more' – a painful look between them – 'so he won't be long after her. And Louise, well, we have a few years there yet, but some day she'll make her own life. And one morning we'll wake up, and it'll just be you and me, and I don't want to discover that all of this has made us strangers to each other.'

'No.' Her mouth felt dry.

'Because lately it feels a bit that way.'

'I know. Which is why I invited you out tonight.'

'I'm sorry I didn't invite *you*.'

'It's okay.'

'It's not. It can't be up to one of us. We have to meet halfway. On everything.'

Nigel was hovering in the distance with his order book, too afraid to advance further. Mossy gave him a look and he stepped back another yard and put the book back into his pocket.

'You never know,' Aisling said. 'Maybe we'll do better with the kids if *we're* better.'

'They did this to us,' Mossy complained.

'No. We let them do it.'

And she thought back over all the years of differences; the digging of trenches; the silent taking of sides. Like it was some kind of competition to see who could save the day.

She took another sip of wine and already she felt things loosen in her. Everything was still a mess, of course, but there wasn't a damned thing she could do about her children's choices. Her *adult* children's choices. Tonight she was only in charge of herself.

'Will we put that poor lad out of his misery and order?' she asked.

'I suppose.'

'And don't forget you owe him a big tip.'

'I was going to leave him a tip anyway.'

'You were not.'

'I was. He reminds me of Aidan.'

Nigel, with his boyish smile and nervous disposition, was the furthest thing possible from Aidan. But she knew it was Mossy's way of saying that it was okay to talk about him. That he was still their son.

Chapter Forty-eight

A nto had let his hair grow, and had trimmed his beard back to just-there stubble; combined with a certain air of tragedy about him, he had, in Shannon's words, turned into 'a bit of a ride'.

'Get lost,' he said, broodingly.

'You even sound like a ride!' she said, and she and Louise screeched with laughter.

'Leave him alone,' Aisling said, overprotective. She was allowed. Because today she was waving Anto off to his new life.

Mossy was shifting from one foot to the other. 'I suppose we should go . . .'

Aisling turned on him. 'What are you fussing for? His flight doesn't leave for hours yet.'

Mossy had been in the bad books for ages now. A few weeks after he had been banging on soulfully about how the kids would eventually leave home and move on with their own lives, blah, blah, didn't Anto get his exam results and they were BRILLIANT. And not just by Brady standards, either. The school principal himself had phoned up to congratulate him, barely able to conceal his surprise that such genius had suddenly issued forth from a student who up to now had been, well, mediocre.

It was great – they'd had a big party at home, with all the pizza Anto could eat – but even better news was to come in the form of an offer of a university place. Well, several offers, actually. One of which was in Manchester. Anto took it straight away, without consulting anybody – he had gone a bit like that, self-sufficient or something – and today he was leaving and Aisling's heart was in smithereens.

'Are you sure you've got everything?' she fretted. 'Do you want me to check your bag?'

Anto gave her a very mature look. 'Ma, I'm pretty sure I can pack my own bag.'

'You've got your hairbrush? Zit cream? Wash kit?'

'Fuck. My wash kit.' All maturity disappeared as he turned and thundered upstairs.

'Hey. Come on. He's going to have a fantastic time,' said Mossy, Mr Bad Karma himself, as he looked at Aisling's face.

'It's so far *away*, though.'

'It's Manchester, not Dubai. He'll be home at Christmas, if not before. Sure, we can't get rid of Shannon since she got back from Africa; she might as well move back in.'

'Thanks, Da,' said Shannon. She was actually moving in with Matt for her final year of college; things had gone that well in Africa. Apparently he'd taught the kids in the orphanage to play rugby, and they'd absolutely loved him.

'Still,' said Aisling, 'I don't know why he couldn't have accepted a place in Dublin.'

'Because he doesn't want to be running into Nicola at the shopping centre every two minutes, why do you think?' Shannon said succinctly.

'I'm sure he would handle himself very well if he did,' Mossy said firmly.

'All the same, you wouldn't blame him for wanting to leave all that stuff behind.'

Aisling didn't. And she suspected it was more than Anto just needing space and distance. In the past year he'd outgrown his old ideas of himself. He had ambition now. Drive. Of their children, he'd maybe been the one they'd had fewest expectations of. Not in a bad way; he was always just lacking that bit of confidence, always trying to keep up with the pack.

Not any more. Now he was hungry, and for the first time it was for something other than food.

In her head, Aisling gave Nicola a silent salute. And lovely Darren, of course.

She'd be seeing him later on. He was coming for his first sleepover since he'd left the house. They'd seen plenty of him over the summer, of course; they'd taken him out to the park and the playground and all that. But never at the house; not while Anto was still there. He hadn't vetoed it or anything; he would never do that. But he'd never brought up Darren's name either.

'Right,' said Anto, back with the offending wash kit, which he packed away. 'Sorted.'

He was anxious to go, she saw. He'd outgrown them too. But in a natural way. He was leaving home as a child should.

'Hurry up,' Shannon advised him, 'before Ma tries to slip a cooked chicken into your bag.'

'Wait!' Louise was in consternation. 'There's going to be nobody left now except me!'

'I'm not staying just to keep you company,' said Anto disparagingly.

'But I'll be lonely!'

'No you won't, because you'll be out in the van with me, helping me on jobs,' Mossy told her warmly.

There was a chorus of groans from everybody, and mutterings of 'No way,' and 'Funny guy, Da.' Mossy looked quite put out.

They were so busy having a laugh at his expense that they didn't hear the key in the door, and they looked up in surprise as Aidan walked into the kitchen, Darren in his arms.

Aidan was just as surprised. His eyes flicked to Anto, then to Aisling in confusion. 'Sorry. I thought I was to drop Darren over at three for the sleepover.'

Shannon looked at Aisling uneasily. Aisling shrugged; she had told Aidan four yesterday. She'd been quite clear about it.

'Sorry, my mistake,' said Mossy. 'I said three.' Aisling shot him a look. But Mossy looked back innocently, and she knew he had rigged this whole thing.

'Well, don't just stand there,' she said. 'Come on in.'

Anto was very still, his hand on his bag as though he would flee at any moment. He looked from Aidan to Darren, and even though he tried to keep looking aloof and angry, he couldn't help saying to Darren, 'Look at you, you little turncoat. You don't even remember me, do you!'

Darren had gone all shy, and he hid his face against Aidan's shirt, peeking at Anto from there.

'Not a word out of you today,' Anto went on more robustly. 'Where are all your *ai's* gone, eh?'

Darren giggled. So did Louise. She couldn't help it; it was the tension. She laughed harder and harder, until eventually her nose began to run. 'Sorry!'

'Jesus,' said Anto in disgust.

Aidan still didn't step inside fully. He hadn't been back home since Darren's birthday. They'd seen him a few times at the

O'Sullivans' house, and he'd come with Mossy and Aisling to the playground with Darren once. He hadn't said much about what he was doing, whether he'd got a job or was still living in that flat, and they hadn't asked. Mossy was bursting to, of course. His face had gone as red as his hair with the effort of holding a lecture back. But he'd managed it, even if he'd had to have a lie-down at home afterwards.

'Manchester, then?' said Aidan eventually, eyeing Anto's bag.

'Yeah.'

Aidan nodded. 'Ma told me they found a brain in there after all.'

A beat.

'Fuck you,' said Anto, smiling.

'Hey,' said Mossy. 'Language. There are kids in here, you know.'

Then just as quickly as he'd come, Aidan was gone, handing over Darren and the baby bag with very few instructions and a vague promise that Nicola would collect him in the morning. With a casual wave and a 'Good luck' to Anto, he sloped out, and when Aisling looked up and down the road a minute later, he was nowhere to be seen.

Ah well.

Mossy loaded Anto's stuff into the van, threatening under his breath to start charging, he was doing that many runs to the airport these days. Never to take a holiday himself, mind you. Not a chance of that.

'Shut up moaning, Da, will you?' Shannon sighed. 'We're trying to say goodbye to Anto.'

But Anto wasn't big on goodbyes and Aisling only managed a quick peck on his stubbly cheek before he got into the van and closed the door. But he gave her a quick wink through the window as they drove off, and she watched the van the whole way until it disappeared around the corner.

'Ma?' Louise tugged on her arm. 'What's for dinner?'
'Dinner's not for ages yet,' Shannon pointed out.
'We'll have to see what's in the fridge,' said Aisling.
And she put her arms around her girls and they went inside.

CLARE DOWLING

Can't Take My Eyes Off You

Clara's been away for too long. So, after ten years in London, and with her boyfriend Matthew in tow, she arrives home in Castlemoy, a town with nineteen pubs and a shiny new motorway to civilisation. Her family welcome them with open arms but Jason, her long-ago ex, seems to have old scores to settle and it's not long before Clara finds herself being watched, followed and manipulated from afar.

As her dreams of happily-ever-after begin to shatter, Clara decides it's time to wrestle her life back before it's too late . . .

Praise for Clare Dowling's previous bestsellers:

'Commercial fiction at its most entertaining' Marian Keyes

'Sharply written and engaging . . . an insightful and enjoyable read' *Irish Mail on Sunday*

'Very funny and original' Cathy Kelly

'Enjoyable . . . funny . . . captures the ups and downs of family life and love perfectly' *Closer*

978 0 7553 9270 4

headline
review

CLARE DOWLING

Would I Lie To You?

Would you lie to a friend if the truth was going to hurt?

When Hannah's partner unexpectedly walks out on her, she turns to best friends Ellen and Barbara in the hope of fixing her broken heart. At Ellen's farmhouse in France, where the organic carrots look like misshapen missiles, and the draught would cut the legs off you, Hannah finds her fighting spirit is coming back. Then something shocking happens that threatens to tear their friendship apart. Should Hannah come clean, or will she just bring more trouble upon herself?

Join Hannah on her rocky road to recovery, from love to despair and back again.

Praise for Clare Dowling's previous bestsellers:

'Commercial fiction at its most entertaining' Marian Keyes

'The intelligent detailing of relationship tribulations makes for an insightful and enjoyable read' Irish *Mail on Sunday*

'Very funny and original' Cathy Kelly

'Dowling's writing is sharp and observant' *Sunday Independent*

978 0 7553 5981 3

headline
review

CLARE DOWLING

Too Close For Comfort

There's nobody like your sister when things go wrong.

At least that's what Ali hopes as she flees America in the dead of night after sixteen years, leaving a bit of a mess behind. Emma will surely take her and the kids in, and it'll be just like old times, right?

But the last thing Emma needs now is her family tramping all over her cream-coloured carpet, and her well-ordered life. And how is she going to explain about fiancé Ryan, and why she suddenly had to boot him out?

Ali and Emma want more than anything to pick up where they left off – but not before it all comes out in the wash.

Don't miss Clare Dowling's previous bestsellers:

'A disarming light-hearted touch and a wry humour' *Irish Independent*

'Commercial fiction at its most entertaining' Marian Keyes

'Very funny and original' Cathy Kelly

'Warm and funny' *Mirror*

978 0 7553 5976 9

headline
review